D0547472

Paul Ware was born in 1900 in Bradley, Yorkshire, and lives today in the same West Yorkshire farmhouse where he grew up. He attended Rastrick Grammar School and Huddersfield Technical College and trained as an engineer before taking up work in the motor trade. His interests include fencing, weight training and motorcycling. His previous novel, *Flight of the Mariner*, is also available as a New English Library paperback.

Also by Paul Ware

Flight of the Mariner

Beyond Freedom

Paul Ware

NEW ENGLISH LIBRARY
Hodder and Stoughton

First published in Great Britain in 1998
by Hodder and Stoughton
A division of Hodder Headline PLC
First published in paperback in 1999
by Hodder and Stoughton

A New English Library Paperback

10 9 8 7 6 5 4 3 2 1

ISBN 0 340 68916 1

Typeset by Hewer Text Limited, Edinburgh
Printed and bound in Great Britain by
Mackays of Chatham PLC, Chatham, Kent

Hodder and Stoughton
A division of Hodder Headline PLC
338 Euston Road
London NW1 3BH

For
Mum, Dad, Heather and Jason
who were all there at the start
and Nigel and Julie
who made it in time for the big finish

CONTENTS

PROLOGUE

Fencing-club memberships tend to reflect an unlikely cross-section of the community, and ours was no exception. Alongside an eclectic bunch of university and college students we had machine-shop fitters and office workers; for every couch potato we had a marathon runner or a kick-boxer; we had an ex-army chap, all minimalism and focused aggression, and next to him a flamboyant pair who could have stepped straight out of *The Three Musketeers*. We also had one drop-dead gorgeous blonde, but that's a story for another day. And, of course, we had David Shaw.

I'd known Shaw years before, when he and I had attended the same sixth-form college. He had come up through the main school, which was an old established grammar school, but I had 'graduated' from the nearby comprehensive. I had been intimidated by Shaw even then, although he was in no sense a bully. In fact, he was never less than civil in all the time I knew him, and often quite genuinely friendly. No, the feeling of intimidation came from something that was inside Shaw, not from any outward manifestation of his personality. He was too old for his years, too strong in the way that only maturity and experience could make one strong. There was nothing about Shaw that could be called frivolous; and although he was as capable of enjoying life as any of us, even in that he displayed a peculiar intensity.

Seeing Shaw again, after an interval of perhaps four years, it was a moment or two before I was able to recognize him. His hair was much longer than I remembered, and fairer. Also, he wore it with three curious-looking braids, very narrow, down the left side, which gave him a somewhat exotic appearance, rather like an American Indian from the Old West. And, too, he had changed in other ways. Mostly I think it was his eyes. If the teenage Shaw had been intense, then this older version was possessed.

It was at my regular Tuesday-night fencing session that I saw him for the first time since college, and even after I had realized who he was I did not immediately approach him. Instead, I watched him as he fenced against the various members of the club. He fenced only the men, which I thought odd – newcomers, even ones as experienced as Shaw obviously was, tended to gravitate towards members of the opposite sex on their first night, for no reason that I've ever been able to explain. But not Shaw. And his manner throughout the two-hour session was singular and quite striking. During warm-ups and practice he was tentative, almost timid. He attacked, to be sure, but seldom with any conviction and rarely with any degree of success. He had a good style, and the athleticism to back it up, but he seemed disinclined to employ it. During the half-hour competition that rounded off the session, however, it was a different story. He won his first bout without his opponent scoring a single hit, either on- or off-target. He went on to win each successive bout in the same way. My own bout had been, I think, as closely fought as any, but I was never in any danger of upsetting his perfect score.

At the end of the session I approached him, uncertain if he would remember me. In fact, he not only remembered me but seemed genuinely pleased that I had approached him. I gathered he had been unwilling to initiate a conversation himself, and was somehow relieved that I had made the first move.

In the weeks and months that followed, Shaw and I became, to a degree, friends. The qualification is a necessary one because, despite the time Shaw and I spent together, I never truly felt that I knew him. He was withdrawn, often moody, somehow obsessed, though he never, in all that time, hinted at the nature of his personal demon. The more obvious perils of modern life, addiction in all its multifarious forms, I ruled out immediately. Shaw was a heavy drinker, though he avoided strong spirits and contented himself with beer and, occasionally, wine, but in no sense was he an alcoholic. He did not smoke, and although I am sure he deplored the fact that I did he never berated me for my weakness. Not surprisingly, he had the same paranoid aversion to drugs that many of my generation share. And if his problems were sexual in nature, they never manifested themselves in my presence.

The only clue I ever gained to the true nature of his trouble came during one late-night drinking session when we had both become extremely melancholy and had begun to reminisce about our schooldays. And I mentioned, casually, the matter of Mrs Catlin.

Mrs Catlin had been a young teacher at our school, fresh out of teacher training college and eager to make an impression. She made an impression on Shaw at their very first meeting, and became his nemesis forever after. Which made the fact that they spent so much of their free time together all the more perplexing. She was, allegedly, using Shaw as some kind of prodigy, apparently having seen in him a potential that was lacking in the rest of us. Why Shaw went along with this, given his feelings towards the woman, was a mystery that we, his classmates, were never able to fathom.

When Shaw disappeared immediately after the death of his father, and Catlin with him, a great many of the school's staff confessed to a long-standing suspicion that Catlin's interest in Shaw had not been entirely professional, and that her conduct had, for some time, been giving them cause for concern. We, the student body, never heard this at the time, but would have howled with derision if we had. Shaw? 'Involved' with Mrs Catlin? It was preposterous.

But their continued absence only added fuel to what was, essentially, little more than malicious speculation, and Catlin was eventually sacked *in absentia*, with a footnote on her file to the effect that should either she or Shaw ever reappear an official investigation into her conduct would have to be instigated.

I mentioned some of this to Shaw, curious to see his response. To say that his actual reaction startled me would be an understatement. In fact, it almost frightened me. And I realized, through the slightly drunken haze that hung over us both, that here, at last, was the root cause of Shaw's problem.

'Anyone,' he said thickly, spilling his drink, 'who would believe her capable of such behaviour did not know her.' He gazed down into his spilled beer, his eyes taking on a faraway look that was heartbreaking to see. 'I knew her,' he said, so softly that I could barely hear.

His response was totally unexpected. I had thought, if anything, that he would have found what I had said highly amusing, the notion of any kind of relationship between himself and Mrs Catlin too ridiculous for words. Instead, and despite the apparent sincerity of his words, his demeanour seemed actually to confirm the rumours.

Had we both been sober, I would probably have let the matter drop. But as it was, I pressed him further, unable to appreciate the true extent of the danger in which I was placing myself.

'Then you did run off together,' I said. 'I'd never have believed it!'

'We didn't "run off" together,' he snapped, 'not in the way that you mean. It was months before—'

He stopped dead, in mid-sentence, as though some kind of circuit-breaker had tripped inside his head. I could see it on his face; he had never spoken of this, and had come to take his own reticence for granted.

'Before—?' I prompted.

He looked at me. His face was composed, but there was murder in his eyes.

'Forget it,' he said.

I said nothing, but as he continued to look at me I think something of what I was thinking must have been evident on my face.

'All right,' he said, 'don't forget it. But let's not talk about it any more tonight.'

I nodded slowly, determined not to let Shaw forget that casual half-promise.

I think that for Shaw that night represented some kind of

turning point. In the months that followed it, I saw less and less of him, and when I did see him he seemed even less garrulous than before. It was as though his perennial intensity had suddenly found a focus, and somehow I had slipped into the background. He continued to be sociable when we met, but those occasions became infrequent as the months wore on, finally being limited to the weekly fencing sessions and one or two other pursuits that we shared.

The final contact that I had with Shaw came approximately a year after that drinking bout and was as mysterious as it was unexpected. I arrived home from work to find a message on my telephone-answering machine, and after rewinding the tape I was startled to hear Shaw's voice. As far as I knew, his house did not even have a telephone, and I could recall no previous occasion on which he had used this method to contact me.

'Hello,' he said, displaying the same lack of confidence when talking to a machine that I often heard when playing back these tapes. 'I, uh, I'm going away, and I don't know if I'll be back. Again. Ever. I, uh, just wanted to say goodbye. Uh. And thanks. You helped me get through a bad time, and I appreciate it. I'd like to ask a favour. There's some stuff at my house, papers that I'd like you to take a look at. I, uh, don't care what you do with them. Just do what you think you, uh, can get away with. This isn't making much sense. Sorry. You'll understand whe—*beep*.'

The tape ran out at that point, leaving me more than a little confused. I'd never been to Shaw's house; I wasn't even certain where it was. But I wasn't about to refuse his request, because I had a sudden premonition that now, at last, I was going to get the answer to that question I'd asked him a year before.

I won't go into detail about what I found at Shaw's house; that is recounted elsewhere. But suffice it to say that if you have read the account of his first visit to Shushuan then you will already know what the 'documents' were that Shaw had left for me.

As to what follows, and how it came to my attention, that is a story for another day.

CHAPTER ONE

The First Letter

———————◦◦◦◦◦———————

I awoke to the sound of hammering. It was a familiar sound these days, but one I did not expect to get used to. Behind it, more distant but no less intrusive, the *blatt-blatt-blatt* of a generator and the rumble of diesel engines added a basso harmony that hung forever on the edge of real melody. If nature truly has a song of its own, then the racket that had awoken me was its man-made technological antithesis.

I sat up. Aches and pains in a dozen places made themselves known, and I groaned through a brief disorientation as I tried to work out where I was.

Where I was was in my own kitchen. I had fallen asleep at the table, sometime in the early hours of the morning: a glance at the clock on the chimney breast told me it was a little after nine. At a guess, I'd had about five hours of not very restful sleep.

Stretching to take the kinks out of my back and shoulders I pushed myself away from the table and walked stiffly to the window at the far side of the room. I pulled back the curtains and surveyed the landscape beyond.

Once, not too long ago, the view from my kitchen window had been a pleasantly rural one. Back then, a modestly-sized garden that ended in a sweeping curve of drystone wall had given way to an expanse of green fields that ended, perhaps a quarter of a mile away, in a broken line of deciduous trees, themselves the beginings of a belt of woodland that went on for miles. The hand of man, in that landscape, was conspicuous by its absence, and for that I had been deeply grateful.

Three months ago, that had all changed. And the vista that now loomed beyond my garden wall was one of giant yellow construction vehicles, mountains of earth and sand, and the skeletal frameworks of what would become, in a year's time, the much sought after dwellings in the Thorp Hill Housing Development.

The sight of what was being done to the place that had been my home all through my childhood should, I suppose, have provoked an intense reaction from me, and the fact that it didn't no longer even troubled me. This place had ceased to be my home long before I had left it to journey, with Mrs Catlin, to the world of the Vinh, and all the good memories I had once had of it were now as dead as the father who had helped forge them.

I turned away from the window and looked instead at the cluttered interior of my two-hundred-year-old kitchen. It's a normal enough kitchen, though a bit bigger than you'd get in a more modern house. The open fire is a little anachronistic, especially given the presence of a microwave oven right alongside it, but on the whole the appointments aren't too outlandish. Until, that is, you get to the back wall, where the eight-place dining table stands. That whole quarter of the room is where I'd spent almost every free moment of the last year. I'd been writing an account of the time I'd spent with Mrs Catlin on Shushuan, and the wall was decorated with notes and charts and sketches – stuff I'd done to keep the continuity straight in my head – and the table was buried under all the rest of the manuscript. There were over a thousand pages, and not many of them were filed. I'd finished the account – or, at least, I'd brought it up to date – at four o'clock that morning. And in so doing had, inadvertently, put an end to the only thing in my life that had seemed until that moment to have had any sense of purpose, however contrived.

The last four years had not been easy for me. I had spent the first year as a bitter and lonely outcast, refusing to speak to my relatives and avoiding any form of social contact. I had exhausted what few savings my father had left until I was forced by the sheer necessity of providing for myself to seek some form of employment. Working with cars came naturally to me, and one of the local garages needed a mechanic who was prepared to work long hours for lousy pay: we might have been made for each other.

In the months that followed I settled into a routine of working from morning until night and then sleeping the sleep of the dead. It wasn't an edifying experience but it probably kept me sane.

Some time early in the third year I finally snapped out of my depression and resolved to do something with the time I had left on Earth. Never for a moment, not even when my mood was at its blackest, did I doubt that one day the Thirteen Gods of Shushuan, whatever those mysterious denizens of the Asmina Valley may truly have been, would summon me back to the world of the Vinh. Their parting words – that this exile was 'for a time' – were never far from my thoughts. And since my return to the land I now thought of as home was inevitable, it seemed foolish not to use the time until then in a productive manner.

(This rationalization could be sustained only so long as my mood remained optimistic; for every day that passed when I believed it, two would follow when the depression was almost unbearable.)

I joined a local fencing club to keep my skills from atrophying. I joined three fencing clubs in all, to maximize the variety of opponents I could face. I joined the gun club where my father had been a member, and practiced weekly with a selection of weapons. I went to a self-defence class – as an instructor – and sparred regularly with some martial arts enthusiasts. I renewed my membership at the local archery club, and learned how to make my own bows from yew and my own arrows from birch and elm.

I kept busy.

Because when I wasn't busy, when I had time to think, I wanted to scream.

I went back to the location of the Blind Spot, the gateway between the Earth dimension and that of Shushuan, weekly, sometimes daily. During that first hellish year I had camped out for weeks at a time in the small cave where Mrs Catlin and I had first passed between the two worlds, not daring to leave in case the worlds came back into phase during my absence and I missed my chance forever.

But reason had eventually won out over that fear. The Thirteen, whatever they were, did not work like that. When the rift opened, if they wished me to pass through it, I would be there. It was inevitable.

During the less unendurable times I had prepared for that moment. In the front room of my house were the results of my preparations. There was the biggest rucksack the local camping store had had in stock; in it were camping utensils, an axe, rope, torch, a compass (the value of which was problematic), a knife that Jim Bowie would have been proud of, matches, fishing line, a small tent, a first-aid kit, some basic provisions, and an IMI Desert Eagle semi-automatic pistol with a thousand rounds of ammunition. There was also a pile of durable walking/camping clothes, some stout boots, a pair of leather gloves, an army-surplus waterproof poncho, binoculars, a water canteen, a bedroll, a small tool kit, and a genuine, combat-worthy Japanese katana. I'd actually wanted a sabre, but the katana had proved easier to obtain – and cheaper.

My 'preparations' became a little over the top. But knowing that I was doing something that was genuinely useful made the waiting marginally easier to endure.

And yet even when my (for want of a better word) faith in the intentions of the Thirteen was at its highest, still there was a sense that what I was doing lacked focus, lacked any real purpose. Until, that is, a chance remark by a friend made me look at things with a different kind of clarity. From that moment, and for a whole year thereafter, I became fixated on one goal, one accomplishment. There was no logic in it, no pragmatism, but somehow I knew that it was what I must do. I would write down, in as much detail as I could, a complete account of what had happened to me on Shushuan, and of how Mrs Catlin and I had been transformed by that planet.

It was a daunting task, yet one from which I did not shrink. I recorded every detail of my adventures, drew sketches of places I had been – Benza, Asmina, the Ktikbat, Ragana-Se-Tor – and the things I had seen, in particular the ship that by Benzan law was mine, the *Mariner*. I redesigned her drive system a hundred times, so that upon my return I would be able to improve upon the work that the Ladden and I had done on her. I wrote whole passages in the High Tongue, so that my memory of it would not fade, and tried translating English newspaper and magazine articles simply for the practice. The manuscript grew and grew, and I made no attempt at editing or censoring. I wrote down everything I could remember, impressions, feelings, sensations, hopes and fears – it was, as I have elsewhere said, an exorcism. And now it was over.

I looked again at the clock on the wall. Today was a work day, and I was already an hour late. I tried to persuade myself that I didn't care, failed, and trudged wearily in the direction of the bathroom. There was an envelope in the letter basket behind the front door, face down; it was one of those off-white A5 things that just shouts *junk mail* at you, so I was more than a little tempted to ignore it. But it was a distraction, and right now a distraction – however slight – was what I needed. I fished it out, expecting the usual opportunity to win a car/holiday/Big Cash Prize and found instead a completely blank envelope. Puzzled, I turned it over in my hands, examining it. The paper felt strange; it was unusually thick, its surface coarse to the touch. It was more like . . . parchment. And the flap was glued down with something other than conventional gum.

I tore it open, and was irritated to discover that it was empty. I was on the point of throwing it away when I looked at it more closely; it was like an airmail envelope: the writing was on the inside. I opened it out and felt the world spin around me. I grasped the nearby doorpost for support, my senses reeling. After four years of waiting, this was not how I had ever expected to hear from Mrs Catlin again.

Shaking, I stared at the letter, unable for the moment to comprehend its contents. It was written in the Vinh language, the High Tongue, the single spoken and written language of the whole Thek continent, perhaps of the entire planet Shushuan. It began, 'My Darling Shaw—' and that was as far as I got. I found the nearest chair and collapsed into it, overcome with relief and joy and . . . fear. A letter was an ominous form of communication, especially given the circumstances.

After a moment I pulled myself together well enough to read on. The letter was brief, and startling. But it swept aside my fears once and for all.

It read:

> My Darling Shaw,
>   I am writing this on the day following your enforced exile back to Earth. I am writing it at the urging of Celebe, who promises me that it will be forwarded to you at the appropriate time. From her demeanour, I gather that this will not be soon.
>   Shaw, I do not know how long it has been since you last saw me, but know this: I will never stop loving you. And I will never stop waiting for you.
>   Forever Yours
>   C.

I stood up slowly, shaking, rereading the letter over and over. The words seemed to tear apart the tissue-paper fiction that my life had become, to expose the lie I had been living for the last four years, and to reveal a reality so intense, so tangible, that to deny it was to deny my own true self.

I folded the letter carefully and put it in my pocket. There was only one thing left to do now, and absolutely no reason in this world – or any other – not to do it.

CHAPTER TWO

Through the Blind Spot

The journey to the location of the Blind Spot took perhaps two and a half hours; on a fast bike it would have been quicker, but the amount of luggage I was carrying made a bike a bit of an impractical idea. I stretched the journey out even more by making two stops along the way; one at a telephone box, the other at a supermarket where I stocked up on a few perishable provisions. After that, it was non-stop on the road north.

It was a little after noon when I reached my destination. The sky was overcast and the clouds a uniform battleship-grey colour. A light drizzle was falling in sporadic gusts, but I didn't bother unpacking my waterproofs – ten minutes from now, I would be standing under Shushuan's blue-green sky, and once there I wouldn't care what the weather was doing.

I got out of the car and opened the boot. Not far away, I could see a party of walkers. I gauged the distance – they were meandering in my direction – and decided to quicken my pace.

I pulled the big rucksack from the boot of the car and struggled into it; with it in place I slid the Samurai sword into a sheath I had sewn into the side. I buckled the pistol to my right hip, using a military holster that I'd bought at the local gun shop. The gun itself was quite legal – I'd purchased it second-hand from a member of the gun club who was moving up to bigger things – but my wearing of it like this was definitely not.*

I left the car unlocked and the key in the ignition, a small gift to whoever might come across it; then I struck out across the field at the side of the road, the field that led to the knot of trees that concealed the entrance to the Blind Spot. The entrance itself was an irregularly shaped hole in the ground that gave access to a small cave. I'd long since made access to the cave easier than it had been for Mrs Catlin and me that first time. A rope, hidden under a tangle of thorns, led down into the darkness. I turned my back to the drop and lowered myself down.

It was only eight feet or so to the bottom of the sloping shaft, but once I had reached it the level of illumination had dropped considerably. I dug out my torch, flicked it on, and set off down the short stretch of tunnel that led to the rift.

Then I stopped abruptly.

Ahead of me, the cave had changed. Normally, it ended in a wall of rock in which was a narrow vertical fissure. When the rift was active, that fissure gave access to the valley in Ragana-Se-Tor where Mrs Catlin and I had first set foot on Shushuan. When the rift was not active, the fissure was just a crack in the wall of rock, with only more rock behind it.

The view ahead of me now, however, was entirely different to the one I remembered. Instead of a straight passage I beheld a narrow, twisted tunnel that vanished into the darkness ahead of me. I stared at it for several long seconds, too stunned to react. This was an eventuality I had never counted on. What did it mean?

Badly shaken, but realizing that there was nothing to do but go on, I took a step forward and

felt a flash of intense relief! The sensation, once felt never to be forgotten, of crossing the Blind Spot was right where I had expected it to be. That much, at least, was reassuringly familiar. Now there was just the oddity of this unrecognizable tunnel to deal with.

---

* Since the time of Shaw's writing, gun law in the UK has become rather more restrictive. Even so, I suspect he was breaking more laws than he realized on that day. PW.

I walked on, setting as brisk a pace as the uneven ground would allow. My relief of a moment ago proved short-lived, for as the tunnel stretched on and on ahead of me I found myself getting increasingly more concerned. I'd always assumed that the points of contact between the worlds were constant, that the same point on Earth always led to the same point on Shushuan. But what evidence did I have of that? Thinking about it, none.

After ten minutes, I was still walking. The tunnel was slowly rising, and was getting narrower. Negotiating it with the backpack on was becoming quite difficult. And then, ahead, I saw a sliver of light.

'Thank the gods,' I breathed softly; the remark, involuntary though it may have been, did not seem entirely inappropriate.

The passage was now too narrow to accommodate me with the pack in place. I struggled out of it and carried it along behind me, worming my way through rock walls that seemed oddly damp. From up ahead I smelled something that I couldn't at first identify, even though it seemed familiar. With each step I found my shoes slipping on the bare rock underfoot, and realized that I was now setting an incautiously brisk pace. Ignoring the potential dangers I pressed on.

I was within six feet of the splinter of light. It was a narrow crack in the rock face, but not so narrow that I couldn't squeeze through it. The angle of the passage meant that all I could see through the crack was sky. But it was a blue-green sky, a clean, clear sky, when I had left behind a leaden one over a rainswept Yorkshire moor.

'Shushuan,' I breathed. Adding, 'Home.'

I dragged myself on, the pack trailing along behind, and with a grunt of slight discomfort forced my way out into the open, to be confronted by the one thing I had never seen in all my earlier time on the world of the Vinh, and the obvious source of the smell that had pervaded the tunnel – and of the damp. I was standing on a wave-lashed cliff at the edge of a vast, grey ocean.

CHAPTER THREE

The Second Letter

The spray from the ocean was icy on my face and hands, but the air around me was warm, uncomfortably so given my current state of dress. The sun was halfway up the sky to my left, its golden disc set against a cloudless sky. The horizon was an unbroken line filling my field of view and the distant ocean, where it met the infinite sky, was a deep and vivid blue. Below me, perhaps a hundred metres below, jagged rocks tore the nearer ocean mercilessly, reducing it to a shattered mass of grey and white.

I turned carefully on the narrow ledge where I stood. Behind and above me, the cliff face rose irregularly to an unguessable height. It was an impressive chunk of rock, seamed throughout with multicoloured veins of quartz that caught the sunlight and split it into ever-changing rainbows in the spray from the sea.

The cliff wasn't particularly steep, but the rocks were treacherous and it was a long way down if I fell. There was a route to the top, however, and I began, slowly, to attempt it. Halfway up the cliff I was startled to find steps carved into the rock. They were crude and time-worn, but a pleasant surprise. There was evidence of a wooden rail of some kind having once flanked them, and in places ledges abutted the steps, as though people had often come here to sit and watch the ocean. It was a discovery whose prosaic implications were somehow comforting.

I climbed the steps to the top, by which time I was sweating. The salt spray from the ocean had dried on my skin, and I found that the gritty after-effect only served to intensify the discomfort afforded by the sun's heat. I paused at the top to take in my surroundings and to doff my outer garments.

Of the landscape around me I could see very little. I appeared to be at the top of a rocky promontory jutting out into ocean; but was it, as I was hoping, a promontory of the Thek continent or was it, perhaps, part of an island? For that matter, there was no guarantee that this place was even on Shushuan.

Up ahead, as the land continued to rise slightly, a rough avenue between two rows of trees led northwards, but as to what lay beyond it there was no telling. The trees could have been sard, but they could just as easily have been some distant cousin of redwood. The vegetation underfoot could have been the same yellowish grass I'd seen in Ragana-Se-Tor and in the Vohung Kingdoms. Or not. I was desperate for something that was undeniably Thekkish to leap out of the landscape, but I was too pragmatic – some might say obstinate – to take anything at face value.

I folded my coat, slung it over my rucksack, and headed up between the twisting ranks of trees.

Birds could be heard in the tangle of branches that formed a leafy ceiling far overhead, occasional brightly coloured bodies visible through the foliage. There was a fair amount of insect life as well, some of it quite intimidating-looking. My first-aid kit included Paludrine tablets for malaria, and various salves and sprays for disinfecting bites and stings, but how much good such things would be against alien infections I didn't know. And I didn't especially want to find out.

The wooded area wound steadily upwards, and for the better part of an hour I trudged through it, the sound of the crashing ocean receding until finally it could no longer be heard.

I emerged from among the trees and found myself looking down the gently sloping side of a river valley. The river ran from right to left, and on the far side of the valley, at an altitude a little lower than my present position and perhaps four or five miles away, I could make out the tops of what looked like buildings.

The valley itself showed signs of having once been divided into fields. Crumbled drystone walls and overgrown hedgerows were clear indications that at one time this land had been cultivated. There were depressions in the fields, barely visible now, that had perhaps once been tracks for farm vehicles or for animals being herded to pens or to market. But it had been many years since the hand of Man – or of Vinh – had shaped this landscape. It looked as though these fields had lain untended for generations.

I turned my gaze back to the buildings on the other side of the valley. The land beyond the next rise must have fallen away again quite quickly, because only the tops of the roofs could be seen. And something about the shape and layout of those roofs suggested to me that the buildings to which they belonged were not the huts of peasants.

I glanced briefly along the treeline to my right, but the view in that direction was obscured by the rise of the land along the valley side. To my left—

About a hundred yards away, standing away from the belt of woodland and surrounded only by an open field, was a grave. A simple pile of rocks with a stone slab at its head. A slab with writing on. And even from this distance, the writing was familiar.

I all but ran towards this unexpected find, my heart hammering in my chest from more than the exertion and the heat of the day. The writing was, I could now see, undeniably familiar, but it wasn't *yoti*, as the written form of the High Tongue is known: it was English. And it formed just two words. The words were *David Shaw*.

I stood and stared at the grave for what, to me, seemed a very long time. I was, frankly, lost for a response to it. Clearly it was not actually 'my' grave, but somehow I couldn't bring myself to believe that two 'David Shaws' has passed this way, and that the mortal remains of my namesake were interred in this simple cairn.

I looked more closely at the headstone. The name, I noted, had not been chiselled, but had been burned into the rock.

I came out of my stupor as the purpose of the 'grave' began to suggest itself to me: this was a message. But saying what? There seemed only one way to answer that question, and I was deeply reluctant to attempt it. Had there been an alternative . . . But there wasn't. I steeled myself and bent to the task, reflecting somewhat wryly that it wasn't every day of the week that you got to rob your own grave.

It was the work of only a few moments to disinter the contents of the cairn which, below the pile of rocks, was only a shallow trench cut into the topsoil of the field. These contents consisted of a man-sized bundle wrapped in a heavy blanket. With some trepidation, I unfolded the blanket to reveal the nature of the bundle. What I found turned my feeling of concern into one of relief. The bundle consisted mostly of a pile of garments: they were the casual dress of a Benzan Captain. With them was a small field kit, such as might be taken on a border patrol, and a weapons belt of unfamiliar design. There was no armour, but there were weapons: a pair of flintlock pistols, wide-bore and with relatively short barrels – I couldn't recall the exact formula for calculating their accuracy, but I doubted they'd be any more effective than a well-flung spear – a stout, double-edged knife, and a sword. I stared at it, dumbfounded. It was a sabre. My sabre, the bandit weapon that I had won in battle when I had been a slave of the nomadic Ladden. I had not seen the weapon since becoming a captive of the madman Droxus, when he had attempted to conquer the Kingdoms with his airship and his vast mercenary army.

I lifted the weapon from its resting place, sliding the blade from its sheath. The red leather hilt fitted my hand as though they had been made for one another. The blade, I noticed, had been recently oiled.

The only other item in the grave was a small, flat package, about a foot square, wrapped in waxed cloth. I picked it up and opened it. It contained a letter. It was written in *yoti*, and was from Celebe. It seemed to me that I shouldn't have been surprised. As a Knight of the Thirteen Gods, she was a natural choice to act as their intermediary. But equally, as their agent, she was not someone I felt an automatic need to trust.

The letter said:

> David,
>   I have prepared these items and left it to the Will of the Thirteen to see that you get them at the appropriate time.
>   Whatever you have brought with you from Earth you must leave here. Take the garments and weapons that have been provided. Continue heading north until you reach the city of Zatuchep. I will meet you there as soon as I can.
>   Celebe
>   For The Thirteen Gods

Underneath, in French, she had added:

> My Friend,
>   Remember why you were sent back to Earth. This is your second – and last – chance.

She had signed it 'Ailette'.

If I had no reason to trust Celebe, then Ailette Legendre, the young French girl who had given up everything, her humanity included, to honour the memory of the former Celebe, whom she had come to love, was a friend whose loyalty and faithfulness I would never doubt. And, if nothing else, her letter seemed to settle the one question that had been bothering me since finding the anomaly in the cave: this place was now almost certainly Shushuan. Whether it was a part of the Thek continent, however, was somewhat less certain.

I unslung the rucksack. Pausing only long enough to remove my perishable provisions – nothing canned, nothing that could not, at a pinch, pass for native produce – I cast the remainder into the grave. There were things in that rucksack that, if I gave them a moment's consideration, I would bitterly regret leaving behind. But Ailette's words had cut me to the heart, and had brought back the empty longing of those four years I had spent on Earth, separated from the land – and the woman – that I loved. I had no intention of losing either one again.

I unbuckled my gunbelt and threw the weapon after the rucksack. I would miss the Eagle: it was a fine pistol. Pushing the thought from my mind I quickly divested myself of my other garments, casting off every reminder of the life I was leaving behind. Only when this was done did I turn to the Vohung garments provided by Celebe and begin to pull them on. They felt good in a way that nothing on Earth ever had. I fastened the unusual-looking weapons belt around my waist, most intrigued by the pair of holsters that it carried. I picked up the brace of pistols that had been in the bundle and examined them. Their inclusion was puzzling: Vohungs in general, and Benzans in particular, disapprove of firearms. The use of such weapons is considered to be unmanly. It was not a prejudice I shared, but I would not openly have flouted Benzan tradition, especially not while wearing the uniform of a Captain.

The weapons were single-barrelled, smooth-bore, muzzle-loading flintlocks. They were less sophisticated than the muskets I had seen on my previous visit to Shushuan. This, in itself, was not surprising. Shushuan is an ancient planet, whose civilizations have risen and fallen countless times. The current struggle to rise again was occurring in fits and starts, and had been for millennia. Bits of the planet's chequered past frequently intruded into its present, seldom to the advantage of the majority of its inhabitants. I had heard the theory propounded, and did not know whether to believe it or not, that evolution had had enough of the Vinh race, and that in the fullness of time the species would pass into extinction. There was to be no new rise of civilization for Shushuan, just the slow and inexorable decline into barbarism and finally oblivion.

I slipped the weapons into the holsters on either side of the belt and picked up the ammunition pouch that accompanied them. There were perhaps fifty cumbersome cartridges and shaped priming charges, together with some raw materials for making more. I found a free buckle at the back of the belt and hung the pouch from it. I hung the double-edged knife from a second buckle, where I could reach it in a hurry if I had to.

I picked up the sabre. The feel if it in my hand, its familiar weight, was like the touch of an old friend. The scabbard had its own strap, which I opened out to its full length and then slung across my chest, the sabre at my left hip, Vohung style. I had occasionally worn the weapon over my left shoulder, in the manner of the bandits from whom I had won it, but today I felt like honouring my own city's customs.

I took a moment to restore the grave to its former condition, the pile of stones now covering the supplies and equipment I had brought from Earth. I rolled my perishable goods in the blanket that had come with my Vohung outfit and slung them over my shoulder. Then I turned towards the north and, without a backward glance, headed for the city that Celebe had called Zatuchep.

CHAPTER FOUR

Zatuchep

The walk across the valley was not particularly taxing, though the heat of the sun as it rose higher and higher in the cloudless sky was starting to get oppressive. When I reached the small river that had shaped the floor of the valley, I took a few minutes to cool my head in it. I sat on the grassy bank for a moment, filling the canteen from my field pack and trying to get a feel for the country in which I found myself. I saw movement out of the corner of my eye and watched as a lone animal, possibly a hap, one of Shushuan's rodents, hopped across the field behind me. I considered trying to bring it down with one of the pistols – hap meat is not entirely inedible – but decided against it. Apart from the fact that I didn't want to make that much noise while walking through unknown territory, I doubted that the pistols were sufficiently accurate for so small and agile a target. I watched the hap until it vanished from sight, and realized that I was prevaricating: it's safe to say, I think, that I was not looking forward to attempting the climb up the other side of the valley.

I took my time, yet even so I was getting out of breath when I finally crested the top of the hill. Walking was one of the few pastimes I had neglected over the past four years, an omission the irresponsibility of which only now occurred to me. Ahead of me, stretching down towards a distant shoreline, was the rest of what I could now plainly see to be an island. It was, perhaps, six or seven miles across, and a little longer than that along its

22

north-south axis. It was a picturesque landscape that lay before me, mostly open fields and meadow, with several stretches of woodland, mostly around the coastline. From this vantage point, I could see three settlements. The nearest – Zatuchep, I assumed – was a city. It sprawled along a sizeable stretch of rocky coastline, none of it navigable to shipping as far as I could tell, down the western side of the island. To the far north, on a rocky peninsula, stood a fortified encampment, smaller than Zatuchep and more martial in appearance. To the east, and dotting most of that side of the island, was a collection of small villages. Some of them were located on the coast, and might once have been fishing ports, while others lay on the intersections of the island's ancient roadways, amid the once-cultivated fields and meadows. In none of these places did I see evidence of recent habitation. I began to walk down the gentle slope leading to the city.

Zatuchep was not pleasant to look upon. It was not an ugly city by any means; in fact, from a purely architectural point of view, it was quite striking, but once you got past that first moment of admiration, you began to realize that all was not quite as it seemed. And the longer you looked, the worse it got.

The architecture was human, or at least humanoid, unlike the Y'nys constructions so favoured by the Ladden. It was sophisticated, though hinted at a low level of technology. The city sprawled in a random-seeming way, as though it had grown without ever being planned. Tall spires were everywhere, clustered around by domed one- and two-storey dwellings. The streets were cobbled with pinkish, age-smoothed, shell-shaped stones; there were no obvious pavements for pedestrians. In width they varied from shoulder-wide alleys to impressively broad boulevards, the latter usually bordered with stepped structures that might once have been hanging gardens or fountains of some kind, but which were now overgrown with yellow grass and creepers and a wild variety of weeds.

The building materials were not unlike those of the Y'nys. A white, marble-like substance, here formed into blocks and cemented together, interspersed with rocks of other, darker hues, formed the main part of most of the buildings that I could see, with the perished remains of wooden balconies, window shutters, doors and suchlike occasionally hanging from green hinges or lying in decaying heaps at the sides of the buildings they had once adorned.

What struck me most strongly about the place, however, was the unpleasant air of decadence that not even the passage of time had been able to erase. Every structure that I could see was adorned with decorative sculpture or engraving, most of it of an erotic or at the very least a hedonistic nature, and some of it quite disturbing in its subject matter. The labour involved in creating this 'art' must have been tremendous, but its content suggested to me that much of the actual work would have been carried out by slaves, with only the design conceived by their pleasure-loving masters. I decided, rightly or wrongly, that I was rather glad the owners of this city were no longer in residence. I didn't think my treatment at their hands would have been good for my health.

I glanced up at the sun. It was getting low on the horizon, the buildings around me creating a mass of shadows. I didn't relish the prospect of spending the night out of doors, and realized that if I was going to scout out a building in which to make camp I needed to do it while there was still some daylight left.

About half a block away was one of the tallest towers that I could see from my present position. A thought occurred to me, and I began to walk purposefully in the direction of the tower.

In many respects this structure was typical of the larger buildings in the city. It had a large open doorway fronted by a flight of steps fifteen deep. A shallow entablature was supported on six slender columns, three to either side of the open portal. The columns were decorated with relief work in the form of the intertwined bodies of naked men and women, the proportions of which were roughly human, but with what I considered an adolescent exageration of certain characteristics. As to what the figures were doing . . . well, I think the less said on that score the better.

I'd chosen this tower for several reasons, its considerable

height being not the least of them. As soon as I'd made camp I intended climbing to the top of the structure to try and get an overview of my surroundings and, I hoped, spot in the distance the coastline of the mainland – any mainland. Celebe had said she would meet me in the city, but I wasn't relying on her as my only means out of here. The plans of the Thirteen were entirely too elliptical for me to expect things to go that smoothly.

The first floor of the building, that immediately beyond its open doors, was a single chamber, perhaps an atrium. Its lofty ceiling was supported by more columns of the same design as those outside. The floor was a broken, weather-worn mosaic whose illustrations made the sculptures on the columns look decidedly tame. Not for the first time, I was seriously relieved that this city was deserted. If the rift had transported me in time rather than space, it would not have surprised me to learn that this place had once been called Sodom.

In the middle of the chamber were the remains of an indoor fountain; littered about it were bits of dead wood and dried grass that I assumed had blown in here over the years. The sight of them made me think of camp fires, and that made me think of food, and that brought home to me how hungry I was. I hadn't eaten in hours – not since, in fact, the previous day – but the nervous energy I'd been living off since getting Mrs Catlin's letter had driven all thoughts of food from my mind. Now, with the initial adrenalin rush fading, and the more prosaic aspects of daily life reasserting themselves, I began to appreciate just how empty my stomach was – and how glad I was that I had hung onto some of my hastily purchased supplies.

I gathered up enough of the litter to make a small fire, then used the tinderbox from my pack to get it started. The pack also contained a small billycan – everything in the pack fell under the heading 'small', being designed as it was for one man – and I hung this over my fire from a makeshift tripod. I half-filled the can with water from my flask and, while it heated, set to work on preparing my meal. Looking at the meagre collection of vegetables that now lay in front of me I began to wish I hadn't been quite so casual about letting that hap get away from me. Using the double-edged knife, I sliced the vegetables up small and threw them into the billy. Watching it as it began to steam while I threw fresh fuel onto the fire, I couldn't help but remember the last time I'd done this, the last time I'd spent a first night on Shushuan. I had been with Mrs Caltin on that occasion, and we had feasted on freshly caught fish, cooked over an open flame . . .

A sound in the doorway of the building brought my reverie to an abrupt end. I snatched up the knife, peering into the darkness beyond the light of my fire; there was moonlight coming through the open door and in it, silhouetted, a man-like figure. I didn't move, didn't speak; if an incautious word or gesture was going to be offered, it would not be by me.

The figure moved slowly into the room, and into the light of my fire. I stifled a gasp; my visitor, whoever it – he – was, he was clearly no member of any of the Vinh races. He stood about five feet tall, and although he walked with a slight stoop he was clearly humanoid. His skin was black. Not dusky, not brown, but anthracite-black; it was, actually, more like hide than skin. The creature was quite naked, its only hair being a shock of snowy white that sprang from its cranium like a crest. The contrast between hair and skin was striking; but actually, it was more than that, it was *too* striking. I had never seen such coloration in a humanoid creature before. It was almost . . . artificial.

The creature edged closer, and I was able to observe its features. In placement and probable function they were those of a human – or Vinh – but in actual appearance they were alien. The mouth and ears were the most human-looking, the nose a close second, but the eyes were like nothing I had ever seen. Twice the size of human eyes, they lacked whites or visible pupils. They were simply two ovals of brilliant amber, the edges flecked with gold. They were intensely disconcerting: it was impossible to know exactly where the creature was looking. Above the eyes there were no brows, and as I looked more closely I noticed that the forehead was oddly shaped, as though the bone beneath was ridged or furrowed. It was a minor effect, not easy to see except when a light source caught the profile and created odd shadows, but somehow I found it the most alien aspect of its whole face. I noticed other, subtle divergences from what, in a human, would have been the norm. The arms and legs were a little longer in proportion to the body than in a man, and the fingers were too long. The nails, which looked extremely sharp, were pale, almost white.

The creature squatted beside my fire, peering at the billycan and its contents. I wondered if the smell had attracted it. I relaxed a little as the creature offered no immediate threat of violence, but I kept the knife in my hand.

As I looked at the thing I became convinced that it was a child, or at least that it was not yet fully mature. Possibly it was something in its carriage that gave the impression, or a certain childlike inclination of its head – of course, if the thing was an animal, that too could explain its mannerisms.

A thought came to me.

'Tonoko da,' I said, which is the common greeting between two strangers on Shushuan.

The creature did not respond.

Refusing to be discouraged, I said, 'Kakanaaki no gozhinku gen hak Kaalinki et?'

The creature did not appear even to have heard. I decided to give up the attempt for the moment. Lifting the billycan from its tripod, I began to eat my rather unappetizing supper. The creature watched, but with a curiously disinterested air; if the smell of cooking was what had attracted it, the prospect of a free meal did not appear to concern it.

A new thought came to me: if this creature was a child, was I about to get a visit from its parents? Or from the rest of its tribe/herd? The thought did little to help my digestion.

I finished my meal quickly, one eye on the creature and the other on the open doorway. As soon as I was done I stood up and kicked out the remains of my fire. The creature scampered away from the flames, stopped, and watched me inscrutably. It seemed devoid of fear, beyond its natural caution, and that intrigued me. Had it never seen a human before, or did it believe it had nothing to fear from one? Those claws would make formidable weapons, but only up close.

I bundled up my belongings, slung them over my shoulder, and set off deeper into the building. If the architecture here was anything like that common to the rest of Shushuan, there would be stairs or, more likely, a ramp at the back of the structure, leading to the roof. And that, after all, was my main reason for being here.

CHAPTER FIVE

New Friends, New Enemies

———⟐———

I found what I was looking for at the rear of the large chamber: two ramps, one going up, the other down, led to the rest of the building. Their entrances were concealed by a pair of caryatids.

I looked up into Stygian darkness, wishing for the torch that I had buried several miles away. The creature, I noticed, was following me at a short distance. I began to ascend.

The second and third floors were almost identical to the first floor, though instead of an entrance they were each equipped with a large balcony. The balcony on the second floor had stone railings, weathered but sound. The one on the third floor had once had wooden railings, but they were gone.

On the fourth floor the ramps ceased, and I had to search about a bit until I found the means of access to the higher levels. Near the centre of the chamber there was a spiral staircase, narrow and open; I climbed it cautiously, clumsy on the shallow steps.

From the fifth floor upwards the nature of the levels changed. Each new floor was divided into rooms, radial corridors stretching out from an open hub through which the stairway ascended. From the placement of doors I guessed that the rooms, particularly those closest to the hub, would not be large. I did not stop to investigate.

A dozen floors later I was on the highest level, and once again the design had changed. This level was laid out in concentric circles, all corridors and no actual rooms. The corridors were littered with open archways, nor was there any indication that they had ever had doors, and the outer wall was completely open, only a ring of closely spaced columns holding up the roof. There was no obvious way to go higher.

I circled the outer corridor, looking out across the moonlit city. In every direction, to the limit of vision, was the flat line of the ocean.

'Damn,' I said, defeated. How far would I be able to see from here, even when the sun rose the next day: Fifteen miles? Twenty? Not far, geographically speaking, but it put me almost entirely at Celebe's mercy. Even if I could build a boat, where would I sail it to?

I was walking dejectedly around the roof of the tower when I chanced to notice something perculiar. Below me, perhaps ten blocks away, something had demolished a section of the city. It had demolished it in a clean, straight line, as though a giant bulldozer had ploughed a mile-long trench through the buildings. At the far end of the furrow, just too far away to make out, something was sticking up among the buildings, a grey something that was clearly out of place in these surroundings. I wondered what it might be, and it if had caused the destruction or had simply been unearthed by it. If I was still here in the morning I thought it might be worth taking a look.

I turned away from the stone balcony, intending to make my way back to the ground floor, when a sound brought me up short. It was coming from the street below, a strange, mournful howling, almost like the baying of wolves. I had started to look over the ledge when the boy-creature whom I had all but forgotten suddenly let out the same plaintive cry. It was almost deafening in the stone chamber, and not remotely human.

I turned to the creature in time to see him flee into the next corridor. It didn't take a genius to work out he was headed for the stairwell.

A new sound came from the street, muted by distance but unmistakable. It was gunfire. I leaned over the balcony, peering down into the moonlit streets. It took several seconds to get a bearing on the sound, and when I did there proved to be very little to see, and what there was gave only a tantalizing hint of what was going on.

About three blocks away, a running battle was taking place. On one side, and with weight of numbers very much in their favour, was a herd of creatures like the boy, but these seemed to be adults. On the other side, better armed but seriously outnumbered, was what looked like a group of about thirty Vinh. The distance was too great and the light too poor to make them out clearly, but the simple fact that they were carrying firearms suggested they belonged to no nation I was familiar with.

Without a second thought I turned and ran for the stairway. Whatever their nationality, they were Vinh.

I descended the stairs so fast I felt as though I should be going into free fall. On the fourth floor I hit the bottom of the stairwell and raced across the darkened chamber to the ramp at its rear.

Two figures, each over seven feet tall, loomed suddenly before me in the darkness. I knew instantly what they were: adult versions of the boy-creature. For an instant I hesitated, prepared to give them the benefit of the doubt as far as their intentions towards me were concerned. Then the nearer one gave out a snarl and leaped at me. A heartbeat later, his companion followed suit.

Their strategy was primitive, instinctive, and terribly effective. Against an unarmed foe, or one of their own kind, it would have resulted in a swift kill.

I drew the sabre and moved it in two rapid strokes; it took the nearest creature across the throat then flicked down into the shoulder of the other. It should have cleft his ribcage in two, but instead, to my very considerable surprise, it bounced off his collarbone, leaving him with a messy but singularly non-fatal wound. His companion, I was relieved to note, was already sinking to the floor, where most of his blood was pooling under him.

I recovered my composure in time to block the second creature's renewed attack, delivering several blows to his head and chest that should have felled him instantly. Somehow, his bones resisted the edge of the blade, and he was now on guard against any attacks on his unprotected vital organs. I had wounded him repeatedly, and he was clearly in considerable distress, but his now-berserker fury was keeping him going in spite of the blood he had lost.

He pressed me hard, using his bare hands to deflect my blade, and suddenly the room seemed to cartwheel, my equilibrium deserting me. I had stepped in the blood of his fallen comrade, and it offered no more purchase to my sandalled foot than a sheet of ice. I went down hard, barely retaining my grip on the sabre, and with a roar of victory the creature leaped at me. I was out of options, so I did the one thing I had been trained and trained *never* to do: I relinquished my hold on my weapon. I flung the sabre point first at the creature's belly; the blade vanished almost to the hilt in black flesh, and the creature let out a very different kind of roar now, a roar of pain and, I thought, fear.

I rolled out of the thing's path and scrambled to my feet, backing rapidly away. The being was mortally wounded, but a long way from being dead. It turned its blazing amber eyes in my direction, and I knew in that instant that when it died it intended taking me with it.

Belatedly, and cursing myself for my stupidity, I remembered the pistols. Neither was loaded, and I hadn't handled weapons like these in over four years. I drew the one on my right hip, reaching into the bag of cartridges with my other hand.

(The creature was on its knees, its lips bared back from bloodied teeth, a keening wail issuing from its throat. And it was beginning to rise to its feet.)

I tore the end off the cartridge with my teeth and emptied the powder down the barrel of the pistol, following it with the ball. I pulled the ramrod from under the barrel and pounded the ball home.

(The creature got one foot under itself and pushed itself upright. It lurched drunkenly toward me, trailing blood.)

I pulled back on the hammer, dragging it all the way to the full-cock position and . . . I'd forgotten something. What—?

(The creature snarled, spitting what sounded almost like curses, and charged.)

The primer! I flicked open the pan cover, fumbling in the

cartridge bag. The pistols employed shaped priming charges, which were more efficient than loose powder, and I'd *seen* them when I inspected the bag's contents earlier . . . There! I fumbled the charge into the pan, closed the cover, and looked up into the creature's face. The gun went off, only half by design, and the black face exploded in front of me, blasted to tatters by the three-quarter-inch ball.

I staggered backwards as the creature reeled under the damage I had done it. But, incredibly, it refused to die. And as I stared at it in horrified fascination, I realized that the wreckage that had once been its face was attached to a perfectly whole skull. The pistol ball had been no more able to penetrate the creature's skeleton than had the blade of my sabre.

Shaken, I reloaded the pistol and, taking a careful aim, shot the creature through the neck. It sank to the floor, shivered spasmodically for several long seconds, and lay still.

I bent over the body and, putting my foot against its ribs, withdrew the sabre. Then, getting a firm hold on my stomach, I rolled the creature onto its back and worked the point of the sabre into what remained of its neck, exposing the skeleton. Instead of the white of bone, what was revealed was a translucent, glassy substance, which began to turn grey even as I watched. I recognized it immediately, and understood now why the creature had proved so difficult to kill. Its skeleton was composed of Y'nys crystal. Which effectively proved one thing: whatever else the creature was, it was definitely artificial. Y'nys crystal and flesh did not occur together on any natural creature.

I turned away, sheathing the sabre, and hurried on. I loaded both pistols as I went, not intending to be caught like this a second time; though faced with a whole herd of these creatures I was going to have to shoot *very* straight – and reload faster than seemed possible at the moment.

I reached the street in seconds, and had no difficulty in locating the battle that had brought me here. In fact, the battle almost found me. I was running in the direction of the avenue where the conflict had been taking place when, rounding the corner of a building, I found myself facing a dozen or more of the creatures. They had not seen me, having arrived at the same junction from a different direction an instant before I did. I leaped back into the shadows afforded by the high stairway that fronted the building, holding my breath and freezing into total immobility. Hardly daring even to blink, I watched in silence as the creatures sped away, casting not even a single glance in my direction. I let out my breath very slowly; I was covered with a fine sheen of sweat, and beginning very seriously to question the wisdom of what I was doing.

Further down the alley, two streets closer than when I had first seen it, the battle was moving my way. The small group of Vinh, now somewhat depleted in number, was being herded towards me. In moments, they would be caught between two groups of the creatures. After that, the end would most likely be swift.

I adjusted the hang of the sword strap across my chest and checked that both pistols were cocked and ready. In the back of my mind, a quiet, rational voice asked me if I really knew what I was doing – and why. I told it to go away; rationality had little to do with this. And the reasons were all too subjective to be allowed out into the cold light of day.

The group of Vinh was surrounded by now, and seemingly very low on ammunition. Or perhaps they simply had not had the time to reload. There were less than two dozen of them still on their feet, most sporting cuts and bruises from the attack of the creatures, and all but two of them were fighting with drawn swords. They were clearly not from any of the lands I had visited four years earlier. They all wore drab, grey garments, and their pistols were very like the pair I was carrying. They fought proficiently, but without the flamboyance I usually associated with Vinh warriors. The two who were not engaged in the fighting were at the centre of the group, and a more disparate pair I had never seen. One was very obviously a warrior, despite his lacklustre accoutrements; his dark hair was cropped short, like that of his fellows, and in his pale blue eyes there burned a fire that spoke volumes about his unhappiness at hanging back from the fighting like this. The other was a tall, slender, somehow innocuous-looking individual whose status I was at a loss to fathom. He was dressed identically to those around him, but he bore no arms and his hair was shoulder-length, his face more that of a poet than a warrior. He seemed more annoyed than afraid at what was going on around him, as though the threat to his own existence constituted nothing more than a petty inconvenience. I wondered if his dead comrades had felt the same way.

I charged from my hiding place, yelling the war cry of Benza, and came upon the backs of the second wave of creatures like a raving madman. I emptied the first pistol into the neck of the nearest creature, switching hands and blasting the one beside him with the second weapon. Both creatures collapsed instantly, creating a gap into which I leaped. Even as I moved I shoved the pistols into their holsters and drew the sabre and knife, slashing to right and left as I ploughed through the startled bodies around me. Fists and claws lashed out at me, a few striking home but none doing any real damage, and then I was shoulder to shoulder with one of the Vinh. Between us we dispatched one creature that had been more determined than his fellows to bring me down, and then we were pressed fiercely by several of his colleagues.

The battle see-sawed back and forth for long minutes, the sheer surprise generated by my arrival seeming to lend fresh vigour to the sword arms of the defending Vinh, and for a moment it seemed almost that we might overwhelm the creatures through naked exuberance. Then, from somewhere beyond the buildings on our right, a great howling could be heard, and with a sinking sensation I knew that the creatures were about to receive reinforcements. Seconds later, a mighty herd of the white-crested devils, over a hundred at a guess, came pouring into the avenue ahead of us.

We were now so completely outnumbered that a standing fight wasn't even an option. We could kill four times our number and they'd still win. We could rush the group at our backs – there were obvious weak points in their circle – but to what end? They were so fast they'd overtake us in seconds, probably bringing us down before we could turn and fight. I didn't particularly want it to end like that.

I glanced at the two men at the centre of our own circle. The warrior's eyes told me that he had made the same evaluation of our position as I had. The other man still had that distracted, almost disinterested air about him. I had the feeling that if he spoke at this point it would be to say something like 'Haven't you sorted this out yet?' I wondered where it was he felt he needed to be, that its importance outweighed that of his own life.

I decided I was glad he chose not to say anything. Because, in one way, I shared his feelings. As bad as things obviously were, the strongest response I myself could summon up was one of disappointment. To have returned to Shushuan, to know that Mrs Catlin was separated from me now by mere geography, and then to die before finding her seemed to me the height of injustice.

And then, just as I was taking a fresh grip on the sabre, something new was added to the situation. Directly ahead of me, beyond the milling throng of creatures and across the broad avenue, in the narrow doorway of a squat, two-storey building, stood a woman. She was almost lost in shadow, only her outline visible. She appeared almost naked, yet a multitude of jewelled accoutrements caught the moonlight; billowy wisps of gossamer silk constituted her only visible garments. I could not see her face, but I could very clearly see the silhouette of her many-braceleted right arm, which was beckoning to me, calling me towards her.

I didn't think; even had there been time, there would have been no point; I just yelled 'Follow me!' and rushed the nearest creature. Whether my companions had also seen the woman, or just decided to go out fighting, they followed me in a screaming, fighting mass. My blade laid two creatures out in the first second, lightning-fast throat strikes that would have decapitated any other living thing, and then we were through the ring, racing across the avenue, the other creatures tearing at us and trying to impede our progress. Down the street, the herd of reinforcements howled maniacally and came charging after us.

We lost half our number in the rush, and the woman had disappeared when we reached the doorway. For an instant

I wondered if I had imagined her, but then, as we fought desperately to defend the narrow entrance, I saw her again, a shadow on a shadow at the back of the dimly lit hall in which we stood, beckoning yet again for us – for me – to follow.

I stepped back from the doorway, another warrior taking my place, and turned to the man whom I took to be the leader of the group. He had also seen the woman, and was sizing up the situation. He gestured for his unarmed companion to precede him to the back of the hall, then barked to his men, 'Hold this doorway!'

It was, under the circumstances, tantamount to a death sentence. The men fell to the task without hesitation, redoubling their efforts. In moments the narrow entrance was jammed with bodies, inside and out. The leader of the group backed away, and I read in his eyes as he did so just how much that last order had cost him. He smothered a grimace and turned to follow the girl. That she had some plan for spiriting us all to safety was something we both seemed to be taking for granted.

I grasped the shoulder of the nearest surviving Vinh and pulled him back from the door.

'Go,' I said. 'Back that way!'

He looked, but hesitated.

'Your leader is safe,' I said. 'Go!'

He went.

In the doorway, the creatures were wedged shoulder to shoulder, one of them dead and supported by the bodies of his fellows. The others had all sustained numerous injuries to their arms and hands. One creature had reached through the press of bodies and seized one of our men by the throat, and was resisting all efforts to release him. I thrust through the press of bodies and drove the sabre, point first, into the thing's deltoid, wrecking the nerves that served its arm.

I snatched the blade back and lashed out at every other creature that was within reach, doing a fair amount of damage to each. The man whose throat had been in the creature's grasp was now free, and I hastened all of the remaining Vinh to the back of the hall. Giving one last flash of the blade to the now indecisive creatures,

I turned and followed. Behind me, I heard a howl of anger and frustration and then the thunder of charging feet.

At the back of the hall I made out the silhouette of the girl, standing at the entrance to a ramp leading down to the building's basement. Of my companions there was no sign. I ran past her, hoping she had a plan, and heard the groan of a heavy wooden door closing behind me. Instantly, all was plunged into total darkness and a silence that was at once comforting and eerie.

I stopped in my tracks, not wanting to run into something that might be injurious to my health. In a moment, I felt a warm hand take mine — the girl's, I was certain — and I was being led further down the ramp. The girl seemed to have no difficulty in negotiating the passage, and I suspected it was a route she knew by heart. I was only half right, but I never could have guessed the whole truth.

We had descended what felt like about two levels when we stopped and the girl removed her hand from mine. After a moment there was a soft click and a warm, yellow light shone out from some kind of lantern that the girl held aloft in one hand.

We stood now in a long, narrow passage, the others in our group some yards ahead of us. At their first proper sight of the girl more than one of them let out a heartfelt curse. I myself stepped back from her, overcome by a brief but very real moment of horror.

The girl was a female version of the creatures.

She stood impassively while we glared at her, her manner not so much one of detachment as of resignation to the inevitability of our response.

As the brief flash of terror passed I found myself appraising the girl with a little more rationality. She had, after all, saved our lives.

Whilst there was no denying the resemblance she bore to the creatures we had been fighting a moment ago, there was about her a certain something that set her apart from them. In physical appearance she was clearly of the same race or species, yet whilst her male cousins had been little short of bestial, this woman was obviously intelligent, a rational being.

She turned her large, almost luminous eyes towards me. This, I observed, was the third time she had singled me out. I wondered why.

'Tonoko da,' she said. Her accent was strange, one I did not know. Yet beautiful.

'Da tono,' I replied. 'And thank you. You have saved our lives.'

'It seemed the least I could do,' she observed, 'under the circumstances.'

'Your . . . people attacked for no reason,' I said; I was assuming this to be the case, since I had not been present at the start of the battle.

'That would be consistent with their natures,' she said, 'but they are not "my people". We are of one species – the charlak – but I am not as they.'

'Why should we trust you?' demanded one of my new-found companions. 'For all we know, you are leading us into another ambush.'

'I am not,' the girl said simply.

The man who had spoken stepped forward and grasped her roughly by the arm. 'I do not believe you,' he said.

The girl's expression registered surprise, but not fear.

I took hold of the man's wrist and he released her, uttering a yelp of pain. 'I, on the other hand,' I said, '*do* believe her.'

The warrior whom I had taken for the leader of this group stepped between us, facing me, his hands clear of his weapons. He did not speak; he didn't have to.

From behind him, the man at whose side he had remained all throughout the previous battle spoke up.

'Luftetmek, have not enough died?' he said, and although his face retained that inscrutable, detached expression, I heard in his tone ample proof of the grief he felt at the lives that had been lost in his defence. 'Zamek, step back. Luftetmek, please introduce us to this warrior.'

The man I assumed to be Zamek, he whose wrist would ache for some hours yet, took a step backwards. The other man, the warrior I now took to be Luftetmek, gave me a brief nod of greeting.

'I am Luftetmek,' he said, 'Champion to Kanaat Yarissi. I greet you as a brother warrior.'

I recognized the formal phraseology. It was a veiled challenge. If I did not now identify myself without being asked it would be taken as a deliberate insult and an acceptance of the challenge.

'I am David Shaw,' I said, 'a Captain of the city of Benza.'

Luftetmek gave me the ghost of a smile. I gathered he had not wanted to fight me. Not for an instant did I believe that that was because he was afraid to fight me.

He indicated the tall, slender individual who I now realized was the true leader of this group.

'This is Yarissi,' he said, 'Kanaat of the people of Reshek.' He paused, then said, 'I thank you, Captain, for your efforts in defending the Kanaat. Will you yield now to his authority?'

I wondered if Luftetmek was testing me. 'Kanaat'? What was that? Some kind of title, obviously. And where was Reshek?

I decided it didn't matter. In the philosophy of the Vinh, there was only one possible response.

'I yield to no man save my Duke,' I said, smiling genially. 'Will you dispute with me?' I glanced at the man calling himself Yarissi. He seemed puzzled, then he caught some kind of signal from Luftetmek and smiled. He said, 'Not at this time, I think. But should you return to Reshek, I may have to allow my Champion to accept your challenge.'

'I have made no challenge,' I told him affably.

Luftetmek said, 'You dispute the authority of the Kanaat.'

'I cannot dispute what I do not recognize,' I replied.

'Will you engage in word games?' he asked. 'Or shall we speak plainly?'

'Plainly speaking,' I said, 'I do not know you, I do not know your House, and I do not know your country. I do not even know where we are. Until I know more, I will not commit myself to any course of action.' As an afterthought, and curious to see what response it would provoke, I added, 'My only business at present is with the

40

Thirteen. When that is concluded, perhaps you and I may speak again.'

Neither Yarissi nor Luftetmek reacted visibly, but I caught a few religious gestures from their followers. Worship of the Thirteen Gods is not uniform across Shushuan, but they are reverenced to one degree or another in all the lands of the Thek continent.

'Very well,' was all Luftetmek said.

He looked at the girl, who had not moved or spoken throughout the exchange. She did not meet his gaze, but looked steadily at me.

'Her loyalties,' Yarissi observed, 'seem in no doubt. Is she known to you, Captain?'

'I have never seen her before,' I told him.

'Interesting,' he said. He turned to the girl – what had she called herself? A charlak? I had never heard the word before today – and said, his manner open and friendly, 'What is your name?'

She said, 'I am called Zalmetta.' To me she said, 'If you will come with me, I can take you to a place of safety.' She paused, then added, 'All of you.'

I nodded. I looked at Yarissi, weighing up options.

'I intend going with Zalmetta,' I told him. 'How will you lead your people?'

I was doing my best to be diplomatic with the man – for all I knew, 'Kanaat' might be a title analogous to King in the Vohung lands, placing him as far above me socially as I was above the lowliest field-slave – but at the same time I wanted him to be in no doubt: he had no authority over me (legally) and I intended ceding him none.

Yarissi seemed amused by something I had said.

Luftetmek said, 'Captain, Kanaat Yarissi is our leader, but I am his Champion, and I command here. And I, too, will follow this female. For now.'

I nodded, now completely baffled by the organization of Yarissi's company. In Vohung, a leader was a leader. The most senior man – or, occasionally, woman – in a group led that group.

I wondered how far I actually was from the Vohung Kingdoms now, and how much a friendly alliance with them would mean to Yarissi or Luftetmek and the country of Reshek. If it meant anything at all, they would be unlikely to treat one of Benza's Captains – and hence one of her nobility – unnecessarily badly. If, on the other hand, it meant nothing, then I was an unwelcome tourist at best, and an illegal alien at worst.

We all moved off after the girl, Luftetmek and I side by side, Yarissi behind us, and the others following. The surviving warriors now numbered a meagre seven, and one of them, I noted, was keeping a very close watch on me. I decided that the best way to deal with that was simply to ignore it – until that was no longer possible. But whatever happened, I was determined not to be the instigator of any unfriendly act.

'Yarissi-jin,' I said, speaking over my shoulder, 'I have never heard your title before. What is the meaning of "Kanaat"?'

I had taken a bit of a gamble with the '– jin' suffix. It was a polite honorific, but a little informal in the present circumstances. Missing it off entirely, of course, would have been taken as a deliberate insult. The High Tongue is a perilous language for the uninitiated, and riddled with nuances and subtleties.

Yarissi seemed to take no offence.

'It is derived from an ancient Thekkish word meaning "people",' he said. 'It is by the will of the people that I lead.'

I was startled. Democracy? The concept was not even remotely a Vinh one.

'In my country,' he went on, '– Reshek – the people have risen against the oppression of the Empire and overthrown the tyrannical rule of the Bagalamak, the Imperial House, to establish a new order. I am Kanaat, First among the Many, but never will I take the title Emperor. I will lead, but only because the people would have it so.'

Revolutionaries, I thought. Revolution and democracy – on Shushuan! It hardly seemed possible. I wondered what kind of oppression these people had had to live under to provoke something that would have been unthinkable to the average Vinh. I also wondered just how far Yarissi's real authority extended. Was this revolution just beginning, or was it over? Did the Bagalamak family still rule over Reshek, possibly totally unaware of this man's existence, or were they even now chained in their own dungeons?

A thought occurred to me, an uncomfortable thought.

'Kanaat,' I said, 'where are we now?'

I caught Luftetmek's eye, and it was he who replied.

'We are beneath the ancient city of Zatuchep,' he said, 'on what was once one of the lesser islands in the Empire of Kai.'

That rang a bell with me. And as soon as I had placed the name so too did Reshek. I almost let out a cheer; I knew where I was! It was totally irrational, of course, because the knowledge did me little good. But just to *know*, after all the doubt, was a wonderful feeling.

Kai, I knew, had been an island empire, spread out across an archipelago of upwards of twenty islands of various sizes and degrees of habitability. The Kai empire had gone the way of the Thek in ancient times, their entire race migrating north to the main Thek continent, to a land they christened Reshek. And Reshek was on the southern border of Ragana-Se-Tor! The rift had moved due south – about a thousand miles due south.

I forced my thoughts back to the subject of revolution. The Vinh were, by nature and by social indoctrination, not much given to innovation. And Yarissi's people all bore firearms. The musket, I knew, had been reinvented on Shushuan a number of times, most recently within the last two centuries. Its use was far from widespread; in the Kingdoms it was banned as a dishonourable instrument. And even in the lands where it was used, its development and evolution had been painfully slow. The flintlock had replaced the matchlock over a century earlier, yet was still regarded as being in its infancy. I had never, until today, seen pistols among the Vinh.

These thoughts were all drifting through my mind in a disassociated way when I found myself muttering, 'I wonder where we're going.'

I glanced at Zalmetta. It did appear, on reflection, that I was placing rather a lot of trust in her, and for no obvious or intelligent reason. Perhaps it was the way she had so consistently singled me out from Yarissi and his followers, investing my presence with an importance I neither understood nor knew how to handle. Or perhaps it was just that I felt a degree of shame at my initial reaction upon seeing her clearly for the first time, and was trying now, in some way that was unclear even to myself, to make amends for that unwarranted judgement.

Yarissi said, 'Did you speak, Captain?'

'I was just wondering where we are being taken,' I told him.

Luftetmek grunted at my side. 'You are not alone in that,' he observed, displaying a dry humour that rather surprised me.

'What do you know of this city?' I asked him.

He glanced briefly at Yarissi, and once again I found myself not understanding the silent message that passed between them. He wasn't so much deferring to the authority of the Kanaat as making a polite gesture. Yarissi responded in kind, indicating that his Champion should reply as he saw fit. I really couldn't work it out, and it bothered me greatly.

'All we know for certain,' Luftetmek told me, '– other than that it should have been deserted and is not – is that somewhere within it there is a Mugaraht.' He gave me a cautious glance. 'You have business with the Thirteen,' he said, 'so I had presumed you also sought the Library.'

'Had I known it was here,' I assured him, 'I would have. How is it you know of it?'

'There are things of which I may not speak,' Luftetmek said, 'having to do with the Kanaat and our war against the Bagalamak. But this much is common knowledge: in recent weeks, the Thirteen have taken an interest in the affairs of Reshek, sending one of their Knights to visit us. She spoke freely and at some length with both the Bagalamak and the followers of the Kanaat, vouchsafing little and hearing much. Since the Thirteen are omniscient, and know all that transpires in the world of Men, none would dare to lie to their Knight. This questioning, then, could not be for knowledge of the revolution, nor of the reasons behind it, which must surely be known already, but instead was a test, a proving of those involved, to judge who was the most worthy of gaining the favour of the Thirteen, and perhaps even their aid. We do not know what passed between the Knight and the family Bagalamak, but following her talks with the Kanaat she issued a single directive, and no more: the secret of success for our battle against the tyrants was stored within the Libraries of the ancient Y'nys. And that only here, in the long-dead edifice once called Zatuchep, would that knowledge reach us in a manner that could be understood and put to use.'

'So here we have come,' Yarissi interjected, 'all that could be spared for the task. I have told you I am Kanaat of the people, but I am not their sole leader. In Reshek, continuing the battle in my absence, my comrade and partner, Kanaat Kandirak, leads our forces in the never-ending struggle. Should I not return, others will follow me, until the message of the Gods is finally read and understood.'

CHAPTER SIX

Tal Daqar

The discovery that Zatuchep contained a Library should not have come as a surprise. The fact that it did seemed to demonstrate how poorly my reasoning faculties had been working of late. Celebe's note to me, telling me that she would meet me here, was a blatant clue to the Library's existence; Celebe, because of her Y'nys armour, would be able to access the Library's travel facility, allowing her to join me here from the other side of the world if necessary.

I wondered how long I would wait for Celebe once I had actually located the Library. I am not normally an impatient person, but being this close to Mrs Catlin after so long apart was making for an intense frustration. If Celebe did not turn up fairly quickly, I suspected that I would attempt to gain access to the Library myself. This would necessitate locating a sympathetic Librarian, always assuming that such a creature existed where I was concerned.

If Celebe did arrive soon, then I would have her take me to the little-used Library at Gaahak in the Lost Kingdoms that lay to the south of the Vohung lands. From there it was only a few weeks' ride to Benza, and Mrs Catlin. With anyone other than Celebe this would not be practical – the Library at Gaahak is surrounded by a swamp, to which Celebe had the only 'map' – but whoever I contacted, they should at least be able to get me across the Plains of Ktikbat, the fearsome interior of the Thek continent that no sane man would attempt alone, and to a place from where safe passage could be obtained to the Vohung Kingdoms.

My speculations were interrupted by our arrival at what appeared to be a dead end in the maze of passageways. The girl stood motionless at a seemingly solid wall of stone, the lantern held high over her head. I noticed how steady was the golden light that fell from the device, and found myself wondering at its source. I knew from numerous past experiences that technology on Shushuan was a hit-and-miss affair, and that often the most sophisticated of devices could be found in the hands of primitive peoples. The lantern, I supposed, was one such device.

After a moment, as though at some unseen signal, the blank wall began to move. It rotated slowly about an unseen vertical axis, as silently and effortlessly as though it had been made of paper, yet the profile it displayed as it turned was over a foot thick. Having turned through ninety degrees it stopped. Beyond it, there was a lessening of the darkness that had pervaded the corridors we had so far traversed.

'We are now entering my master's dwelling,' Zalmetta said. 'Once through this door we will be safe, and may speak more freely of things that I am sure have been on your minds.'

She led us through the portal, which closed silently behind the last man. The darkness beyond was short-lived, a switchback in the corridor leading to a spacious and well lit chamber. It appeared to be a hall of some sort, with room for upwards of a hundred people to stand and not feel crowded. The walls and lofty ceiling were bare stone, their illumination coming from panels set at regular intervals high in the walls. I guessed that they were similar in design to the lantern that the girl carried. The floor of the hall was flagged, with patches worn smooth by the footsteps of ages. The room was a stark contrast to the others I'd seen in Zatuchep, all of which had appeared to have been built by the hedonistic Kai. This hall, size notwithstanding, would have seemed more at home in the Kingdoms.

Yarissi said to Zalmetta, 'You say this is your master's house? Are you then a slave?'

'I am my master's,' she said, 'to do with as he will. If it pleases you to call me his slave, then his slave I am.'

'Who is your master?' Yarissi asked.

'His name is Tal Daqar,' Zalmetta said.

I glanced at Yarissi; the name seemed to mean no more to him that it did to me. It was not a Resheki name, and although it had a ring of the Kingdoms about it I did not think it was a Vohung name.

'Of what city?' Luftetmek demanded, using a tone of voice I had heard others of the Vinh use when addressing slaves. It irritated me as much when Luftetmek used it as it always had previously. He sounded like Hareg of the Ladden. (I reminded myself that Hareg had eventually become my friend, but it did little to dispel my feelings.)

'Of this city,' Zalmetta replied.

'Of what House, then?' Luftetmek demanded, recognizing a dead end when he heard one.

'Of no House,' she replied. 'My master is above such trivia.'

Luftetmek bridled visibly. House allegiance is one of the fundamental cornerstones of all Vinh life. Having no marriage as we understand it (though there are some countries where it is known) the House is, for the Vinh, the ultimate family tie. In some cities, House loyalty is held to outweigh all other allegiances, even those due to the Crown. That no House has, to my knowledge, ever led a revolt against its sovereign is a testimony to the seriousness with which the Houses themselves regard this loyalty, and the responsibility it confers on them. I wondered how Yarissi's revolt had started.

'Your name intrigues me,' I said to Zalmetta, trying to change the subject before it led to violence. 'It means "harmony", doesn't it?'

'You know the old tongue?' she asked, slightly surprised.

'Only superficially,' I said, adding, 'I once belonged to a Librarian.'

'You were a slave?' Yarissi asked. His tone was . . . odd. It seemed as though this was the most unexpected revelation he had ever thought to hear.

'I was,' I replied.

'Legally?' Luftetmek asked. I saw *that* look pass between the two men again.

I knew what he was driving at: to be a legal slave was to be the lowest of the low in Vinh culture; to be an illegal slave was to be the victim of a crime, something the Vinh regard as monstrous – crime, as we know it, is almost unheard of on Shushuan.

'Legally,' I said.

'And yet now you are free?' Yarissi said, a hint of suspicion in his tone. The illegal freeing of slaves – or being a runaway slave oneself – is even more frowned upon than the unlawful enslavement of a free person. Slavery is one of the underpinnings of the Vinh social structure, and as such they take it, and its administration, very seriously.

'I was legally freed by my first master following the death of the Librarian,' I said, which was true up to a point. The events that led to my legal freedom were none of their business.

'I did not realize,' he said thoughtfully, 'that there were any cultures on Shushuan that still honoured the old ways as we of Reshek do. This is food for thought.'

I didn't quite understand what he meant – Vinh culture is millennia old, and has remained largely unchanged for countless centuries. Why should he believe his own people were any more faithful to that culture than the rest of the world? I found it inconceivable that the Resheki people could remember an even older social set-up than that of the rest of their race.

I wanted to learn more of this, and the dozens of other new things I was experiencing today, but any discussion was cut short as we arrived at our destination. (And in the back of my mind a part of me was laughing uproariously at my behaviour; on our first visit, I had frequently criticized Mrs Catlin for being too cerebral, for not living the experience as it happened. In her absence, I found myself playing her role for her. The irony was as inescapable as it was familiar.)

Zalmetta led us to a pair of huge doors, their arched tops stretching overhead to a height of three storeys or more. They were sard wood, dark and immensely strong, and were bound with steel. Their design and construction did not fit the rest of the city, nor did they mirror the design of the hall we had just traversed. Also, they looked new. They looked, too, as though they had been built to keep out an army.

Zalmetta touched the right-hand door – it had no handle that I could see – and a section of it swung open along a previously invisible seam, a rectangle that had the proportions of a normal human door. As it opened I noticed, to my surprise, that the massive doors were barely a quarter of an inch thick. Even sard wood, at that thinness, would yield to the lightest of battering rams. The doors, then, were a sham, a bluff. Or so it seemed.

We followed Zalmetta through into a huge, well lit chamber, and all of us stood for some minutes with our collective jaws hanging open.

The chamber occupied a space that could have accommodated its predecessor twice over. Yet it was not its size that created so powerful an impression, but its appointments. The ceiling, a triple-vaulted structure supported by six massive marble pillars, was a dazzling, luminescent mural, depicting, it seemed to me, one of Shushuan's creation myths. The Thirteen Gods and their predecessors were all in evidence, as were the First Men, the originators of the Vinh race, and the Mother of All, embodiment of Shushuan's most ancient matriarchal faith. Fabulous beasts, some bearing more than a passing resemblance to dinosaurs, were shown in scenes ranging from the hunt to primitive sacrificial rites and finally to domestication. The whole of Vinh evolution was encapsulated in a single sweeping, slightly grandiloquent tableau.

The illustration did not end with the natural boundaries of the ceiling. It continued on down the six marble pillars and the upper parts of the walls, until the actual shape of the room was distorted and, it seemed, redefined by the thing it depicted. It was a disorientating effect, yet one that it was difficult to look away from.

The lower part of the room did its best to be equal to the challenge set by its ceiling. Sumptuous tapestries lined the walls, interspersed with paintings and framed mosaics. Statues were ranged down the length of the chamber's longer walls, carved from a variety of substances and depicting a varied cross-section of Vinh life and culture. None of them, I guessed, was newer than several hundred years old.

The polished stone floor, whose visible portions were set with precious jewels and rare metals, was partially covered by deep pile rugs of elaborate design and a multitude of shapes and sizes. Strategically located around the floor, designed to blend in unobtrusively with the older artefacts, were a score of brazier-like wands, which were actually more of the light-emitting devices we had already seen. This room, like its predecessor, contained no windows. Its only openings were two very dissimilar doors, by one of which we had just entered, set at opposite sides of the room.

The only furniture in evidence was located at the far side of the chamber. It comprised a dining table that could have seated fifty in spacious comfort, with chairs to accompany it, including one of throne-like proportions that was placed with its back to us, and more chairs lining the nearest adjacent wall. The table was laid for a banquet, and the sight of it set my stomach to grumbling.

'Please,' said Zalmetta, breaking through our astonishment, 'my master awaits.'

I glanced down to the far end of the hall. By the impressively appointed dining table a man stood. Obviously he had been sitting with his back to us in the throne-like chair I had noticed earlier. I observed him closely.

He looked to be in his middle years, perhaps the same age that Sonder the Librarian had been when first we met, with shoulder-length, jet-black hair that was streaked with an occasional hint of silver. His skin was light, and his eyes were blue. He was clean-shaven, and his only visible garment was a heavily embroidered robe that looked as though it would have fetched a king's ransom in the Vohung lands: there were more gems set into its gold and silver stitching than I'd ever seen assembled on one garment.

He smiled warmly as we approached, seemingly genuinely pleased to see us. There was an open honesty to his face that was strangely at odds with the fortress-like nature of his abode.

'Gentlemen,' he greeted us, arms outstretched. 'I am so pleased you arrived safely. And,' his face becoming serious, 'so sorry for those you lost in the city. Had I known sooner of your presence I would have dispatched Zalmetta to meet you before you encountered the charlaki.'

I glanced sidelong at Yarissi. Did he know this man? He seemed not to.

'I am Tal Daqar,' the man introduced himself, 'master of this house. Please, won't you be seated? You must be hungry after your ordeal.'

I myself was famished, and suspected that the others would be too. Yarissi made no move to approach the feast, and I saw Luftetmek glance at him, hesitating. That the warrior would balk at accepting the hospitality of a potential enemy was natural, and his apparent willingness to defer to Yarissi's judgement was the most telling evidence of their true relationship that I had yet seen. I had no desire to force Yarissi's hand, but he and I were here on entirely different missions and were not necessarily destined to be allies. I stepped forward and took my place at Daqar's table. Yarissi gave Luftetmek an expressionless nod and the warrior waved his remaining followers forward. They fell upon the feast with a will.

Daqar smiled happily and resumed his seat.

'Eat, gentlemen,' he said expansively – and a little redundantly. 'My larder is well stocked.'

The feast that lay before us was astounding. It rivalled even the illusory repast that I'd been offered in the house of the Thirteen at Asmina. There were dishes here that must have taken hours – and an army of cooks – to prepare. I glanced up as unfamiliar hands moved to fill the glass that stood by my plate. Unnoticed, a dozen slaves had entered the hall and were now moving about the table, performing whatever duties may have been necessary.

I heard Luftetmek making perfunctory introductions to our host, giving away as little as possible – as a warrior, I was growing to respect him. His devotion to Yarissi, whatever their respective roles, and his conscientious execution of his duties, however self-imposed, bespoke a man who could be depended upon. And, if he thought me a threat, depended upon to lop my head off.

I was too busy studying Tal Daqar's slaves to pay much attention, however. They were an even mix of male and female, all with pale skins and shaven heads. Their garments were unisex, sleeveless tunics, their race indeterminate. They wore no collars or other badges of servitude. But their status was unmistakable. I glanced around, wondering where Zalmetta had disappeared to. Her presence here, and her origins, troubled me, and made me question the affable façade put forward by our mysterious host.

I dismissed the matter from my mind until a more appropriate time; right now, the only thing I could think about was how hungry I was – one bowl of vegetable stew in twenty-four hours had done little to fill my stomach.

I piled a variety of starters onto my plate and began trying them in no particular order. Some of the spices were very unusual, but all of them were delicious.

'My compliments to your chef,' I said to Tal Daqar.

He made a dismissive gesture.

'There are few sensual pleasures to be had in Zatuchep,' he told me. 'Eating is one of them.' He frowned slightly and said, 'I do not recognize your accent, despite the obvious Ladden and Vohung influences. What is your native country?'

I was startled by his question; my accent – my Earth accent – had never been noticed by anyone else on Shushuan. Tal Daqar clearly had a very well-trained ear.

'I come from a country called England,' I said. 'It is not on the Thek continent, and until I came here I did not speak the High Tongue.'

'How fascinating,' said Daqar. 'I had no idea any other languages still existed. Tell me more.'

I hesitated, wondering how far this man could be trusted with the real truth – the Vinh are an exceedingly superstitious people (with reason: their gods live among them) and a culturally hidebound one, not inclined to look with favour upon anyone or anything that challenges the established order or their deep-rooted prejudices – when the decision was taken away from me. Luftetmek interrupted our conversation with a question of his own.

'How did you come to this place, Tal Daqar?' he asked. 'These islands have been supposedly deserted since my ancestors left them to found the Empire of Reshek. Technically, you are a trespasser in this city.'

From his tone I gathered he was no more impressed by our host than I was.

'Technically,' Daqar replied good-naturedly, 'you should be dead. Only my intervention saved you. I would hardly have done that had I borne you any ill will.'

Luftetmek frowned, and I smiled to myself; Daqar had not answered the question.

'Many years ago,' our host said, 'I studied to become a Librarian. In the fullness of time, I abandoned the pursuit. I still consider myself a man of learning, but I could not countenance the autocratic mentality of the Mugatih. The love of knowledge is a pure emotion; to dilute it with the quest for power is to debase it. And so, to answer your question, my friend,' (he glanced briefly at Yarissi, as though sensing the true authority in Luftetmek's group) 'I came to this deserted place to continue my studies undisturbed. If I have offended the descendants of the long-dead Kai, then I offer to you, their successors, my apologies.'

Luftetmek appeared not entirely convinced, but he said, 'I take no offence at your presence. No apology is needed. But I am curious on one point. Why would you choose to live in as dangerous a locality as this, when surely there are many places secure from the eyes of men that are less hazardous?'

'I take it you are referring to the charlaki,' Daqar said. 'I had lived here, unmolested, for most of a decade before the charlaki came to Zatuchep. From whence they came I have no idea. I have studied them extensively – though, of necessity, from a distance – and compared them with records of all the known life forms of our world. Nowhere that I have looked have I found anything like them. They are, delightfully, a mystery.'

'Delightfully?' Luftetmek said.

'To a seeker of knowledge,' Daqar replied, 'a mystery – a genuine mystery – is always a delight.'

He raised his goblet and said, 'A salute to mysteries.'

I joined in his toast. After a moment, so too did Luftetmek. His followers echoed him enthusiastically. Yarissi, I noted, did not join in the toast.

I wondered what Zalmetta's place was in Daqar's 'mystery'. She was charlaki, and the only female we'd seen. How was it she served in the house of this man?

Reluctantly, and for the second time tonight, I dismissed the question from my mind. If there really was a Library in Zatuchep, then it was likely that Tal Daqar knew of it, and that it was his real reason for staying here – a fact which Luftetmek seemed already to have picked up on. The important question – to us both – though for different reasons – was how willing he would be to let us use it.

'You say you've been here for over ten years,' I said to Daqar. 'Did you do all this?' I gestured around the chamber at its many appointments, the works of art and such. Even ten years seemed like not enough time for a room such as this.

'These things are of the Kai,' Yarissi answered for him. 'I have seen similar works in the palaces of Reshek.'

'True,' said Daqar. 'Few of the accomplishments of the Kai survive, other than their fine buildings. But I have come across these artefacts in my explorations of the island, and brought them together here so that they should be spared the ravages of time.'

'The Kanaat has taught us that such accomplishments are decadent,' Luftetmek said, without animosity. 'When his rule is secured, the palaces of which he spoke will be stripped, their "treasure" sold to buy food for children who have known naught but hunger. In Reshek, when the Bagalamak have been finally driven from the land that they have betrayed, such luxuries as these will become things of the past. It is not right that one man should live in comfort while another starves.'

'But we are not in Reshek now,' Daqar replied, seemingly not offended by Luftetmek's words. 'And in my house, no man need go hungry. Unless, of course, he chooses to do so.'

'Yet you keep slaves,' I said, gesturing to the men and women who milled about the table.

I was surprised to hear Zalmetta's voice raised in reply; she had re-entered the hall and was standing by the chair at the far end of the table, facing Daqar down its length. 'My master has a perfect right to keep slaves,' she said, 'and their status is not illegal. By what right do you question him?' There was more curiosity than censure in her tone.

'Slavery is offensive to me,' I said, knowing that no one on Shushuan – not even Yarissi and his followers – would understand what I was talking about. 'No one has the right to own another person.'

'What a strange philosophy,' Daqar said, with the air of a man about to get stuck into a serious debate.

Yarissi's reaction was less detached.

'You would undermine our entire civilization with such words,' he said, displaying the first real emotion I had yet seen in him. 'Tear out the foundation and the whole structure collapses. I have heard of this thinking, this "anarchy", but I never thought to meet one of its proponents. Do you have any conception of the world you would create should your beliefs take root? It would mean the end of the Vinh as a race.'

'A society does not have to be built on slave labour,' I replied. 'Free men have as great a stake in the future of their race, but their involvement comes from choice. What choice has a slave? No society has the right to exist simply because a privileged few want to protect their privileges. I thought you at least would understand that.'

I looked around the table, and was startled by the expression I saw on the faces of Luftetmek's men. These men, hardened warriors all, were hanging on Yarissi's every word, their attention absolute.

'You are a fool,' Yarissi said to me. 'And you know nothing of our struggle, or our way of life.'

'Gentlemen, please,' said Daqar. 'You are all tired after your hard day. Say no more until you have had time to sleep on your differences.'

Luftetmek leaned closer to Yarissi and whispered something. The Kanaat frowned, then nodded curtly.

'Very well,' was all he said.

'I have many guest quarters,' Daqar told us, 'few of which have ever been used. Remain here tonight, and in the morning I will do whatever I can to assist you on your way.'

I wondered if Yarissi would speak of his reasons for being in Zatuchep. He didn't.

'Zalmetta will show you the way to your quarters,' Daqar said.

CHAPTER SEVEN

The Library

My 'quarters' were like something from an Arabian Nights fantasy. The style was in keeping with Daqar's palatial dining room, but with even more emphasis on luxury. I could almost understand Yarissi's attitude; few of the people I'd ever met on Shushuan could have afforded a lifestyle that would include a bedroom like this.

We had each been given a separate room, one of Daqar's slaves accompanying each man to offer whatever assistance might be needed or expected. The slave who showed me to my room was promptly dismissed by Zalmetta.

'It is my master's wish,' she told me, 'that I attend to your needs personally.'

'I am a man of few needs,' I told her lightly, not particularly appreciating her tone of voice – more seemed to be on offer here than I was likely to feel comfortable with.

'There is a bathing facility adjoining your sleeping quarters,' she said, apparently ignoring my remark. 'If you wish, I will assist you—'

'No,' I said, 'thank you.'

She studied me with an unreadable expression on her face; I wondered if that was because she knew how to control her features or because I didn't know how to read a charlaki face. Presently she said, 'Do you find me so displeasing?'

I was startled; the question was a touch too honest for the casual nature of our acquaintance. And . . . was it also a touch too accurate? Zalmetta was undeniably beautiful, but the same could be said of a gazelle, or a tiger, or a sunset. Her appearance wasn't the issue. And, of course, even had she been human, there was Mrs Catlin to be considered.

'I find you very pleasing,' I replied, trying to match her directness. 'But I have no need of a slave – temporary or otherwise.'

She regarded me silently for a moment, then gave a slight shrug and said, 'If you need anything before the morning, I will be available.' She indicated a bell rope at the head of the bed. 'Pull this to summon me.'

She turned and left the room without another word. I wondered if I had hurt her feelings.

At the back of my room I found the curtained alcove containing the bath. I was moderately amazed to discover that the bath was fully plumbed in and had running hot water. I stripped off and availed myself of the unexpected luxury. I had never seen such a thing on Shushuan, and wondered if this was an example of Kai engineering or of Tal Daqar's own ingenuity.

I lingered over the bath for an unnecessarily long time, thinking that once I had left Zatuchep it might be a very long time before I got another.

When I finally stepped out and wrapped one of a selection of elegant lounging robes around me, I returned to where I had left my belongings and did a brief stock-check. The sabre was fine, its recent use – probably the first in four years – having done it no harm. I checked both pistols for operation, applying a little light oil from the pouch that contained their ammunition and other accessories. I did not load them. I rummaged briefly through the Vohung field kit, refreshing my memory as to its exact contents. I topped up the water flask from the cold tap in the bathroom, then used the hot-water supply to wash the eating utensils that I had used for my stew earlier in the evening. What I was really doing, of course, was putting off the moment when I was forced to admit to myself that there really was nothing else for me to do but go to bed. I felt uneasy, twitchy, as though afflicted with some kind of premonition of danger. It was probably mindless paranoia, but it wouldn't go away.

I got up and crossed the rug-bestrewn floor to a walk-in closet in which hung a wide variety of garments. They were all a bit antiquated, but perfectly serviceable. They were also, compared to my Vohung outfit, the epitome of luxury.

I picked out what looked like some items of a warrior's casual dress, though to have afforded them he would have had to have been a warrior-prince, and tried them on. The overtunic was scarlet, with enough gold stitching to make up a solid ingot if compressed. It felt marvellous, if a trifle impractical. It fell to mid-thigh all round, and could be worn open or belted. The silk undertunic was black, reminding me of the garb worn by bandits on this side of the continent. There was a sword belt to go with the outfit, though it looked as though it had been designed with a somewhat lighter weapon in mind than the one I was currently carrying. I modified the carrying strap briefly, hung the sabre from it, and belted it around my waist. I'd never worn the sabre this way before, but it felt comfortable. Pistols, however, seemed to have been unknown in the day of my long-dead tailor, so I left the weapons on the small stand by the bed.

I glanced at myself in the eight-foot-high silver mirror that stood to one side of the closet. My Benzan hairstyle seemed incredibly barbaric atop an outfit such as this, but in an odd sort of way it seemed to work.

I turned away and left the bedchamber.

What I was doing wandering around Daqar's fortress-like domain in the dead of night I didn't exactly know. But I couldn't sleep, and somewhere in this ancient edifice there was a Mugaraht, a Library, and my way back to Mrs Catlin. The call of it was not easily resisted.

I wandered at random up and down unadorned and largely indistinguishable stone passages; I found them strangely dark and oppressive, despite their being well lit by more of the fantastic lighting devices I had seen in Daqar's main hall. The impression came, I think, not from the actual strength of the illumination, but from what it illuminated. This building was almost new in Vinh terms, their culture and ancestry stretching back several times the span of all Earth history as it did, yet somehow it and the other buildings in Zatuchep gave off an air of decay and corruption that was entirely absent in many of their older counterparts in other regions of the Thek continent. It was as though civilization in ancient Kai had taken a detour down some uncharted back alley and had never emerged from the other side. It was a dead culture, one that had been drowned in its own poisons. I wondered how successfully the descendants of Kai, Yarissi's Resheki, had shaken off that grim and inauspicious legacy. Given what I had heard of the rule of the Bagalamak I guessed that the influence of the Kai was far from being forgotten.

Eventually I found myself back in Daqar's main hall, and once again I was all but overcome by the splendour of the place. Although I had ended up in the hall quite by chance, I found it impossible to simply turn around and walk out again. I stepped into the room proper and gazed about me at what was, in many respects, a representation of the history of a race. The Kai, for all their seemingly rapid slide into degeneracy and oblivion, had in large part typified the Vinh cultural and social set-up with which I was familiar. There was a quasi-feudal, pyramidal hierarchy to their civilization that differed from human feudalism in one significant respect: the pyramid was one that could be scaled, from bottom to top, by anyone with the will and the strength to attempt it. For a slave to become a king was more than just a fairy story on Shushuan, it was a historically documented fact. Although, it must be admitted, not one that happened every day.

Behind me, a voice said, 'You may find this of interest, Captain.'

I turned to see Tal Daqar standing to one side of the room and gesturing at a collection of statues behind him.

'Forgive me,' he said, 'I did not mean to startle you.'

'You didn't,' I said. 'But I'm the one who should be apologizing. I hope you don't mind my wandering about like this, but I couldn't sleep.'

'I rarely sleep myself,' he confessed. 'And no apology is

necessary. Although my home is, of necessity, heavily guarded, its contents are entirely at your disposal. I am pleased you saw fit to avail yourself of the wardrobe in your quarters. The garments of this ancient city appear to suit you.'

I thanked him – a little self-consciously – then said, 'What were you going to show me?'

'Something that may help you to understand your companions a little better,' he replied.

He indicated a group of statues behind him and I crossed the room to observe them more closely. They were life-size, carved from a white rock similar to marble, and appeared to depict a single individual at seven different times in his life. In the first he was little more than a boy, and was very obviously a slave. In the second he was a young man, and although his garments still suggested servitude of some kind he no longer appeared to be enslaved. The third depicted him in his mid-twenties, and his garments were now those of a free man. In cut and style, however, they suggested a lowly existence. The fourth statue, perhaps the most impressive of the set in terms of its human features, showed the man older again by several years and dressed as a soldier. He carried a long-handled pike-staff, and there was a knife at his belt. The absence of a sword suggested that he was a member of the fyrd, the civilian militia, rather than a career soldier. In no sense was he a warrior. The remaining three statues showed the man growing progressively older by decades at a time. In the fifth of the series he was depicted as a man of some affluence; in the sixth as what looked like a statesman; and in the seventh, incredibly, as a king.

I looked at Daqar, not understanding either the meaning of the statues or their specific significance under the present circumstances.

'You are no doubt familiar,' Daqar said, 'with the traditional Vinh lore on the process of House ascent.'

I hesitated; House traditions were something I had barely touched upon during my last visit. But what he had just said awakened a half-buried memory.

I looked again at the seven statues.

'In the traditions of the Vinh,' I said cautiously, 'the ascending levels on which the hierarchy of individual Houses is based operates on a seven-tier system.'

Daqar smiled, saying nothing.

'Slaves at the bottom,' I said, 'who, if they show particular talents at their given tasks are permitted to buy their freedom by spending a period of indentured servitude as servants to existing freedmen in the House. Once their contract is served – usually between five and ten years after purchase – they become freedmen themselves. If they want to go further, and actually attain the status of a free citizen, they have to spend some years in the fyrd, or in the real army, doing border patrols and such. When they leave the military they can then spend the rest of their lives as citizens or, if they're really ambitious, apply to become members of the city council. And at the head of the city council, and ruling over the first House of the city, is the King.'

'A simplified definition,' Daqar agreed, 'but essentially accurate. Most cities rate no more than a Baron, or Count. A few aspire to Dukedom status, but the capital invariably calls its master "King". Or Emperor.'

'But no one actually utilizes that system any more,' I said. 'The pathways still exist, but the formal structure is only there for public ceremonies and festivals.' I racked my memory. 'The Feast of Gazig, for instance, when freedmen are invited to join the fyrd, or the King's Birthday when slaves can apply for unconditional freedom even if their status is legal . . .'

'All true,' Daqar agreed, 'but with one very important exception. In ancient Kai, the forms were not merely observed, they were enforced. And Reshek is the direct descendant of Kai.'

I looked at him.

'You aren't serious,' I said.

'Perfectly serious,' he said.

'But no one—' I hesitated. Things Yarissi and Luftetmek had said came back to me, as did questions I had entertained about them. Their belief in an antiquity to their race that pre-dated all others—

'The Resheki,' Daqar said, 'consider themselves the only

true, purebred race on Shushuan. As far as they are concerned, they *are* the Vinh, and they regard all other races as corrupt species, not fully human. In time, when this revolution of theirs is over, they will look at the rest of our world and contemplate its conquest.'

I considered the things I had seen in Zatuchep, and wondered how the descendants of its builders could think of anyone else as being degenerate.

'The Resheki,' Daqar went on, 'practice the ancient seven-tier system as rigorously now as when it was first conceived, thousands of years ago. At the age of thirteen their children are all sold into slavery, Houses exchanging them sight unseen in lots four times a year. Parental records are not kept, and it is considered an act of some depravity for a mother to attempt to keep in touch with her offspring. For a father to do so is a capital offence. After three years, each slave is assessed, and if he shows ability, is allowed to rise in status and become an indentured servant. His wages are set by city legislation, and he is permitted to keep one-tenth. The rest goes to pay for his freedom.'

'That,' I said, 'is barbaric.'

Daqar shrugged.

'Once his freedom is paid for,' he continued, 'he must find a sponsor in his House who will nominate him for freedman status. Less than one-quarter of all servants ever actually become freedmen, from what I have heard. After that, continued ascent is much as you have already said. A period in the fyrd, then some years spent directing House affairs as a fully franchised citizen before the desire to rule rears its head. From then on, it is a matter of individual ambition.'

I looked from one statue to another, my gaze lingering finally on the slave boy at the beginning of the progression.

'It's an ugly system,' I said.

'Possibly,' Daqar said, 'but the point is, it shapes and defines every thought these people have. And as bad as the system may be, it is its flagrant abuse by the House Bagalamak that has prompted this revolution.'

It occurred to me I had misinterpreted something.

'You mean,' I said slowly, 'the revolutionaries *want* this system?'

A revolt against the system was a difficult enough concept to grasp where Shushuan was concerned, but with my human perspective this new twist was even harder to comprehend.

'The followers of Yarissi,' Daqar said, 'are fanatical believers in the old ways – and in him. By this system –' he gestured to the statues – 'all men are guaranteed an equal status in the world. No one is allowed to wear the crown of a King who has not worn the shackles of a slave. In some ways, it is the fairest system imaginable. The revolutionaries feel that the Bagalamaks have manipulated the system to maintain their own rule over Reshek.'

'How long have the Bagalamaks ruled?' I asked. The same House had ruled in Benza for over twenty generations, but only because it consistently turned out the greatest warriors and most able statesmen.

'Fifteen centuries,' Daqar said.

Only on Shushuan, I thought to myself.

Daqar took my arm. 'Come,' he said genially, 'there are other things to see in my home, and perhaps less depressing ones.'

I nodded and let him lead me down the length of the room, wondering where we were headed. This way, as far as I knew, led only to the passage that gave access to the city.

'Did you notice this sculpture earlier?' Daqar asked. He was pointing to an abstract of some kind, an Y'nys crystal representation of a man-like figure that seemed rather out of place in this setting. It resembled more than anything a child's stick-figure drawing: a single shaft, six inches thick, formed the 'head' and body, two slightly thinner jointed appendages being the legs; the arms hung from a shoulder yoke that protruded from the body at, from my own perspective, a point just above eye level. The 'head', an eighteen-inch cylinder that was little more than a continuation of the body, contained no recognizably human features, just a sparse cluster of jewel-like nodes and a vertical red bar running down the centre of its 'face'. Its hands were a pair of pincers that owed more to engineering than to biology.

'What is it?' I asked.

'It is called Kziktzak,' said Daqar.

He looked at me.

'Come,' he said at length, 'I think this will interest you.'

He led me not to the end of the room with its huge if insubstantial door but to a point behind the oddly titled stickman statue. The wall that confronted us was as solid and seamless as a single slab of granite.

'Open,' Daqar said. He appeared to be addressing the wall.

For a moment nothing happened, then to my utter astonishment the whole wall seemed to tremble and, with the faint sound of a motor turning, began to rise towards the ceiling. I looked up, and saw the wall being wound onto a roller as though it were no thicker than a sheet of canvas.

I looked at Daqar, more than a little impressed.

'The wall,' he said, 'is composed of a tightly-woven steel mesh. When in place, rods slide through it and gave the illusion of rigidity.'

'One of your inventions?' I asked.

'The original design predates ancient Thek,' Daqar said, 'but this application is my own.'

We passed through the concealed doorway as soon as it had opened sufficiently and Daqar, turning, said, 'Close.' The shutter rolled down again.

'There is a Library circuit built into the device,' Daqar explained, 'that responds to the sound of the words "open" and "close". As a safety precaution, a second device, optical in nature, confirms my identity.' He glanced at me, a little guiltily, I thought. 'It seems paranoid now to have installed such a device,' he confessed, 'but the danger of invasion from the mainland was once a very real one. I suppose, one of these days, I will have to install a simple manual control for the door.'

We were now in a broad, well lit passageway that described a circular, downward path to our right. I had once seen such a corridor before. I felt the hairs rise at the base of my neck, my throat go suddenly dry.

Daqar led the way down the ramp, and I followed in silent expectation. We had made four complete circuits of the unseen chamber that was banded by the corridor before coming to a second door. This one was more conventional in nature and appearance, and Daqar opened it with a simple key.

I knew, before he pushed the door open, what I would see beyond it. But somehow, the knowledge had not prepared me for the emotional impact. I stood on the threshold, eyes slowly rolling back to take in every inch of the fifty-foot-high splendour of the Library.

It was smaller than the one I'd seen in Vraks'has, but no less impressive. It appeared, to both the casual and even the informed observer, to be a mountain of solid crystal, essentially as translucent as all Y'nys creations but with light in a thousand colours trapped forever in its substance. I knew that the physical appearance was an illusion, one that could be shattered by only a single act. The Library was, in fact, a collection of vast stalagmites, only coming together in a single fused mass in the top third of its height. The impression of solidity in its lower two-thirds was caused by the fact that the Y'nys crystal was so prone to distorting and refracting the light that fell upon it, or in some cases fell through it, that the edges of the individual stalagmites blurred into one another and defied all of the eye's attempts to separate them.

I dragged my gaze away from the Library itself and looked around the four-storey-deep chamber in which it stood. As I had expected, I quickly located one of several lecterns that stood some feet back from the device. It was through these that it was possible to communicate with the Library, and through the Library with other Libraries all over the world.

I glanced at Daqar.

'May I?' I said.

'Please—' He gestured to the lectern.

It was a rectangle of green Y'nys crystal set in a wooden frame, supported on two wooden legs. It had no moving parts. The crystal was a solid block, the frame simple rim wood.

How the thing worked was a mystery neither Mrs Catlin nor I had ever fathomed. Functionally, however, the device was simplicity itself.

I picked up the stylus that rested in a small groove at the base of the crystal and drew a symbol on the surface of the lectern. In the written form of the High Tongue, the symbol I had drawn was representative of the Temple of the Thirteen Gods.

The green crystal was suddenly full of light, dozens of intricate lines darting across its surface. I waited until they had settled down and read their message. It said:

THIS SELECTION IS PROTECTED

I smiled. The Thirteen did not want just anyone to gain access to their information. Many of the files in the Libraries were secret, but few were as well guarded as those of Shushuan's Gods.

I wrote:

SHOW ME THE INDEX FOR THE THIRTEEN, then made a sign which the stylus did not illuminate.

More incomprehensible data flowed across the screen before a message was displayed.

ASMINA
KNIGHTS
LIBRARIES
FEYRVAHNEN
PROTOCOL
MAINTENANCE
ACCESS
MARINER

Some of the listings didn't mean anything to me, but that last line sent my brain into a spin that almost made me gasp out loud. The *Mariner* was under protected listing? I wanted to see more, but I was conscious of Daqar at my side, and of the fact that, in the wrong hands, the *Mariner* had immense potential as a weapon. Whether Daqar qualified as the 'wrong hands' was immaterial. The Thirteen had placed a restriction on information concerning my ship, and I wasn't about to argue. In any case, it wasn't to review that particular data that I was here. I placed the stylus against the word KNIGHTS and drew a second symbol which was not illuminated. Celebe had given me these access codes so that I could find her – or at least communicate with her – should the need arise. The fact that the Thirteen had not deleted the codes suggested to me that they were content to allow me this degree of freedom. I doubted, however, that my own interests had figured in their reasons.

The screen scrambled again then said:

QUERY: SPECIFY NAME

I wrote:

CELEBE, and yet another symbol. If Daqar thought his security precautions were paranoid he had nothing on the Thirteen.

The screen scrambled and then cleared. It stayed clear for so long I wondered if I'd done something wrong. Then it lit up with a simple question.

IS THAT YOU, DAVID?

The message was in English.

I smiled, and wrote, in the same language:

IT'S ME. WHERE ARE YOU?

Nothing happened. I frowned. *Something* should have happened. So . . .

Switching to Vinh script I wrote:

THIS IS DAVID SHAW

The screen scrambled and then displayed a message, in English, from Celebe. Now I understood. Her initial greeting had been pre-recorded, as was this message. I had not been speaking to Celebe when I replied, but to the Library itself. And it did not speak English. By identifying myself I had freed this message from its storage system.

I read it quickly, suddenly uneasy.

DAVID
  IF YOU ARE IN THE LIBRARY AT ZATUCHEP
YOU ARE IN CONSIDERABLE DANGER. IT
HAS BEEN SOMEHOW CUT OFF FROM THE

*TRANSPORT SYSTEM IN THE LIBRARY
NETWORK AND I CANNOT REACH YOU
PHYSICALLY THROUGH IT. I AM EN ROUTE
BY THE FASTEST MEANS POSSIBLE, BUT
WILL NOT REACH YOU FOR SOME WEEKS.
EXERCISE CAUTION: TRUST NO ONE.*
   CELEBE

Cut off? How? Not by Daqar, surely. Such an act would require the access powers of a full Librarian. It seemed to me that Celebe might be overreacting somewhat; she had, I thought, grown too dependent on her own Y'nys-bestowed talents. And the mentality of the Thirteen had rubbed off on her. Trust no one? The phrase seemed paradoxical under the circumstances.

I cleared the screen and turned to Daqar.

'My thanks,' I said briefly. 'A message from an old friend, long overdue.'

Daqar nodded. He gestured towards the doorway and I preceded him thither. The notion was still in my head to find out what was in that MARINER file, but not with someone peering over my shoulder.

'My house is large, with much to see,' Daqar said, 'but the hour is late. Perhaps tomorrow——?'

'I'd like that,' I said.

And that, at least, was the truth.

CHAPTER EIGHT

Choices and Consequences

Despite getting only a few hours' sleep I awoke the next morning feeling refreshed and ready to face whatever the day had to offer. I reviewed the more obvious options as I dressed.

First Option: Stay with Tal Daqar until Celebe showed up. He was a gracious host, and his fortress would be a safe place to wait. Also, I was confident that at some point I would be able to gain access to the Library while he wasn't around and possibly find out what was in that MARINER file and why the Library had become cut off from the network.

Second Option: Throw in with Yarissi and his followers. There was a certain appeal to this idea. I had no stake in their revolution, but the only overland route to the nearest fully working Library was through Reshek. If it came to such a trek I would prefer to have both a guide and someone local to watch my back. This option had one drawback: Yarissi wanted access to Daqar's Library, and if Daqar refused it I would be faced with having to live with the consequences of my decision. I hoped, for the sake of all concerned, that it wouldn't come to that.

Third Option: Leave Daqar's house and wait for Celebe in the city above. Ignore Yarissi's cause entirely – and let's be honest, I wasn't likely ever to be a major player in it one way or the other – and trust to Celebe to get me to Mrs Catlin.

I wondered if there was a fourth option. In situations like these, the option you didn't review was frequently the one you ended up *having* to pursue.

I finished dressing and headed for the main hall. I was wearing the Kai outfit from the night before, since for all its ostentation it was comfortable and, it seemed, durable enough for everyday wear. And, after all, Daqar had said I could keep it. As on the previous night, I wore only the sabre for armament.

I met Luftetmek and his men in the main hall, where breakfast was being served. Neither Daqar, Yarissi, nor Zalmetta were present. The meal was being served by several of Daqar's household slaves; the shaving of their heads, I noted, extended even to the removal of their eyebrows. I had heard of this being done in other cities on this side of the continent, the practice serving to make the slaves appear oddly inhuman – which is, of course, the reason for it.

I sat across from Luftetmek, who greeted me with a nod. I let the slaves place a selection from Daqar's larder in front of me – I don't like being waited upon, especially by slaves, but there is a time and a place to voice such objections, and I do not believe that breakfast time at another man's table is either of them – and decided to test out the various options I had contemplated for today.

Round a mouthful of coarse bread and vol's milk cheese I said, 'I saw the Library last night.'

Luftetmek glanced around, as though gauging the distance of the nearest of Daqar's slaves. Then he said softly, 'He showed it to you?'

'Yes,' I replied.

'Did he seem,' Luftetmek wondered, 'secretive at all? Would he share its knowledge voluntarily?'

'He seemed totally open about it,' I told him. I added, hoping the Resheki warrior would follow my drift, 'I see no reason for you to attempt to gain access to it covertly.'

He glanced at me briefly, then said, 'That will be for the Kanaat to decide.'

'And you will abide by his decision,' I ventured.

'In this,' Luftetmek said, 'I will obey him.'

I said, 'He is not a warrior, your Kanaat.'

'He is our leader,' Luftetmek said. There was a hint of

fanaticism in his eyes, but it was not the kind that implied an unhinged mind. Rather, it bespoke a true and genuine devotion. I wondered at it. Yarissi seemed not a particularly exceptional man. Had he, I wondered, performed an exceptional act, and was now reaping its rewards? I reminded myself that Yarissi was not the only Kanaat in Reshek. Perhaps he basked in another man's glory. Perhaps Luftetmek's loyalty was not to Yarissi at all. Perhaps he had merely been charged with Yarissi's protection by the man to whom he truly owed his allegiance. But I remembered the battle in the street, Luftetmek's manner and that of his men. No; whatever devotion there was here, it was to Yarissi. I just wondered why.

(Also, and rather depressingly, I kept remembering something Mrs Catlin had once said: that no matter how long we spent on Shushuan, there might always be some aspects of Vinh psychology that we would never understand.)

From the entrance to the hall I heard Daqar call out, 'Good morning, gentlemen.'

He approached the table with Yarissi at his side, Zalmetta following a few paces behind. The two men moved to the head of the table, and Zalmetta came to sit at my side. She waved away the slave who had been serving me and attended to the task herself.

'I have spoken to my master,' she told me in a businesslike tone, 'and he advises me that my non-human nature places me outside the laws on slavery. I am, therefore, not to be considered his property, but merely a member of his household. You now have no reason to object to my serving you.'

I almost laughed out loud. But . . . she was serious. She really couldn't understand my objection to being waited upon. I was wondering if I could find a way to make her see things from my perspective when I became aware that Daqar and Yarissi were engaged in a dispute of some sort. I turned away from Zalmetta and gave the two men my undivided attention.

'I do not object to your using the Library,' Daqar was saying, 'but I would prefer knowing the nature of your enquiry before permitting you access to it.'

'Why?' Yarissi asked, his tone no less reasonable. 'Surely you cannot claim ownership of the Library? To do so would violate not only the laws of this land but also the ethics of the calling you yourself aspire to.'

'Call it a courtesy,' Daqar said. 'Should your enquiry draw the attention of a genuine Librarian, my security here could be compromised.'

Yarissi glanced at Luftetmek who said, 'Regrettably, that is not something we can allow to concern us.'

Daqar looked pensively at Yarissi. Then he glanced briefly at Luftetmek, as though weighing possibilities. Finally, and for no reason I could fathom, he looked at me. It was a stare that, whilst in no sense hostile, made me feel very uncomfortable. It suddenly occurred to me that no one here had considered Daqar's own agenda, so wrapped up had we each been in our own missions. And, for no immediately obvious reason, I suddenly found myself recalling – and questioning – something Daqar had said on the previous night: he had called me 'Captain', when to my certain knowledge no one had mentioned my rank in his presence.

'Do I take it,' he finally said, 'that my refusal to permit you access to my Library will result in an act of violence on your part? An act directed at either myself, my property, or my slaves?'

Luftetmek said, 'We would regret such an act, Tal Daqar, but our situation is desperate. The knowledge contained in your Library – and only in your Library – means success or failure for our revolution. We cannot permit anything to prevent us from obtaining that knowledge.'

I was pleased that Luftetmek had said what he had, and relieved that Yarissi had been content to let him. It suggested the possibility of a diplomatic resolution to the situation.

'What you have said saddens me greatly,' Daqar said, and he appeared sincere. 'I do not doubt the validity of your revolution – I have studied the history of your country, and I know of the extremes perpetrated by the Bagalamak House. In purely abstract terms, I might almost condone your actions. But when your revolution impinges upon my own activities, when it threatens my security and my ability to pursue my scientific endeavours, then it ceases to have – ceases even to merit – my approval. If you are determined to enact violence upon me and mine, as I see you are, then I in turn must act to prevent you.'

He glanced towards the doorway, and I followed his gaze with a sudden sense of unease. In the doorway, virtually filling it, stood a man. He was dressed in a Kai warrior's garb, not unlike the outfit I was presently wearing, and had a double-edged, unsheathed longsword hanging from a beltring at his side. His head was shaved like that of every other of Daqar's slaves, but that was the only resemblance. In stature, the man was a giant. He stood head and shoulders above the tallest of Luftetmek's followers, and probably weighed as much as any three of them put together. He was as impressive an individual as I had ever seen.

And yet—

He was only one man. And Luftetmek's soldiers all had firearms.

'A redoubtable warrior,' Luftetmek observed calmly. 'Yet surely you do not expect him to overpower all of us?'

'I do not expect Blukka to overpower any of you,' said Daqar, 'unless you attempt to leave, of course. He is here simply to distract you.'

Luftetmek and I were on our feet at the same instant, swords drawn as we spun to survey the rest of the room. His men were a little slower, but not much. The hall, however, seemed to offer nothing of an overtly threatening nature.

Daqar chuckled.

'Kziktzak,' he said, 'please disarm our guests.'

I looked with disbelief toward the statue Daqar had shown me the night before. Its cylinder of a head rotated slowly until the vertical red bar that ran down its length was directed at us. Then the 'statue' stepped off its stone pedestal and walked slowly towards us.

Luftetmek recovered his wits first. To his men he commanded, 'Bring it down!'

Six pistols left their holsters as one. With a precision that was almost choreographed, the men cocked their weapons, aimed and fired. The room shook to the multiple reports, white smoke obscuring our view of their target. The smoke cleared, and the thing called Kziktzak stood unmarked and unharmed. Its head turned a fraction. A slender beam of red light flicked from the centre of its face, catching the pistol barrel of one of Luftetmek's men. The metal glowed cherry-red and the man dropped it with a yelp. In an instant, the beam struck five times more, and all six pistols lay on the floor; one of them lay on a rug that was now burning from the heat.

I was mindful of the fact that the weapon had been directed only at inanimate objects. Whether Kziktzak was 'programmed' not to kill or was just following a particular order seemed irrelevant; it was a weakness we had to exploit. (At what point I had thrown in my lot with Luftetmek I don't know, but the decision was made, and I intended to stand by it.)

'This way,' I said, gesturing toward the more human adversary that Daqar had called Blukka.

Luftetmek shoved Yarissi behind him, barked an order to his men to hold their line, and spun towards Daqar, his sword aimed at the man's throat. Whether he actually intended Daqar's death I didn't know, but it was irrelevant in any case. For all his size, Blukka was incredibly swift. He sprang forward, his longsword drawn, and slashed Luftetmek's blade aside. The weapon flew from the Resheki's hand, narrowly missing one of his own men as it clattered across the chamber. Disarming a swordsman is no mean feat, and Blukka impressed me considerably in that brief moment.

I turned to Zalmetta, unsure of her part in the proceedings, and uncomfortable in any case to have my back to a potential adversary, to find her leaving the chamber by the door behind Blukka. I wondered at her flight, but at least it gave me one less thing to think about.

Kziktzak was moving slowly toward Luftetmek's men, who had drawn their swords and were fanning out around it. Its head would occasionally flick around, the red bar lining up with one warrior or another, but the deadly beam was not unleashed again.

Daqar moved away from the table, seemingly not much

concerned about his safety. His confidence – especially given the fact that he was unarmed – was deeply worrying.

Blukka backed away from Luftetmek, who had now drawn his own pistol, and for a moment the violence was suspended, the whole scene frozen between one moment and the next.

'Tal Daqar,' I said, hoping to restore some semblance of sanity to the proceedings, 'stop this now. Let us negotiate. There is no need for bloodshed.'

'I desire no man's life,' Daqar said. 'But you are a threat. If you would convince me otherwise, lay down your weapons.'

I glanced at Luftetmek. He moved his head a fraction, but the message it conveyed could have been no plainer had he shouted it out loud.

'Very well,' Daqar said, having seen the rejection of his offer as clearly as I had. 'The path you have chosen is set, and no fault of mine.'

I could hear the finality in his voice, and also the regret.

'Kziktzak, Blukka,' he said, 'subdue them. Alive, if possible.'

The creature called Kziktzak moved with incredible speed. Three of Luftetmek's men were unconscious before I had time to blink, and only the battle-forged reflexes of the others saved them from a like fate.

I turned at the urging of some unknown instinct in time to see Blukka bearing down on me, the double-edged longsword aimed at my heart. I threw a wild parry at his blade and leaped backwards, away from the large dining table, making some room for myself. Not far away, I saw Luftetmek looking in my direction with a pained expression on his face. He wanted to help me, as any warrior would, but his first duty was to Yarissi, and Kziktzak would be upon them both in moments. I resigned myself to dealing with Blukka alone, and felt strangely pleased at the prospect.

He circled the table slowly, turning me so that my back was to Kziktzak. This was a tactic not, I thought, designed to leave me open to an attack by the creature, but to keep me distracted by such a possibility while Blukka pressed his own attack.

He came at me suddenly, his blade a hand-held spear that flew for my chest. I leaped back, taking the weight out of his attack – he was, without a doubt, far stronger than I – and parried his thrust, not attempting to re-engage.

I stepped sideways, my sword at arm's length between us, my other hand behind my back in the classic sabre duelling pose. Blukka circled with me, his eyes never leaving mine. His poise was remarkable; I'd fought swordsmen of the minimalist school before, but never anyone this steady. There was no extraneous movement at all, no wasted energy. Even the tip of his blade seemed motionless, a display of control that was as rare as it was intimidating.

I offered a feint, making the slightest blade contact. He didn't fall for it. I didn't attempt to follow through.

Not far away, Luftetmek's men were now down to two, but they were putting up a spirited defence. The Kziktzak creature was a silver blur of movement, but most of its blows were falling on empty space. In the end, I suspected, exhaustion would be the deciding factor in the battle, and Kziktzak would not tire.

Blukka lunged at me. I parried, and his blade seemed to vanish. It was a feint, and a good one. I leaped back, feeling his point open the front of my tunic. It missed the flesh beneath by the thickness of my undertunic. Logically, I should now continue to retreat, overwhelmed by his speed and skill.

I attacked. I almost caught him with a double feint, then tried to capitalize on my near-success by switching styles and throwing three rapid strokes at his head and neck. He parried them all, as I had known he would, so I threw half a dozen more without missing a beat, none of them following any kind of predictable pattern. I'd practised moves like this endlessly, first with Mrs Catlin and later with Tor Taskus, my Benzan colleague and fellow Captain, so that the seemingly disjointed movements could be executed rapidly and with no loss of rhythm. I'd never met anyone who could anticipate the change of line of attack for more than five moves without so upsetting his own timing that he left himself open for a swift *coup de grâce*. Blukka parried

me for over fourteen strokes, by which time it was *my* timing
that was getting shaky.

I disengaged, and found myself on the receiving end of an
attack that was a carbon copy of my own. I was astounded. It
seemed impossible that anyone could learn a tactic so quickly.
Knowing that my chances of survival if I stood and traded blows
were next to nil, I retreated rapidly, but Blukka matched me step
for step and the rain of blows never paused. In a desperate effort to
foil his attack I suddenly stopped and, instead of simply parrying
his next stroke, I thrust against his blade and leaped forward. Our
swords crashed hilt to hilt, our bodies almost touching, and I
shoved against him with all my might. I might as well have
thrown myself against the side of a house, for all the good it did.
Blukka flung me back; my legs connected with a badly placed
chair, and I went flying over it.

For some reason, the giant slave did not press his advantage.
Instead, he stood calmly back, his blade lowered, while I got to
my feet.

I risked a glance around the room. The last of Luftetmek's
men was down, and Kziktzak was now advancing on the warrior
and his leader, neither of whom looked especially hopeful about
their chances. Daqar himself was nowhere to be seen, and the
hall door was now closed and, I assumed, locked.

Blukka and I crossed swords yet again. I kept switching styles,
sometimes attacking with the point, sometimes the edge, never
attempting the same manoeuvre twice. Blukka parried every
move with ease. Once or twice I got close enough to score a
minor hit, but few of them did more than damage his tunic. He
got me with a few similar cuts, neither of us doing any harm,
and I was beginning to wonder how this could ever end. I was
running out of tricks, and I had an uneasy feeling that Blukka
still had a lot of moves up his sleeve.

I heard a sudden crash from the far side of the room, but
didn't dare look around. Blukka, however, seemed to take this
as some kind of signal, because he began to press his attack
with renewed vigour. For the next few seconds I fought
some of the most elaborate and, I think, brilliant swordplay

of my entire life. Formal techniques went out of the window and Blukka and I improvised one attack/defence combination after another. Under any other circumstances, it would have been an exhilarating experience; that I was fencing the greatest swordsman I had ever met was a certainty. What was less certain at that moment was whether or not I could beat him.

From the other side of the room came a sudden and ominous silence. Some sixth sense made me duck as one of Kziktzak's pincer-like hands flashed over my head. Blukka lunged at me from the opposite side, and only speed and brute force allowed me to deflect the blow. Pain exploded in my back, Kziktzak's claw gouging into my flesh, and Blukka's sword lashed sideways at my face. I tried to parry, but Kziktzak had his other claw around my wrist faster than I could avoid it. There was an incandescent flash as the sword struck, and then a roar of thunder as I sank into oblivion.

I was brought back to consciousness somewhat roughly, and found myself sitting on one of the dining chairs that had now been placed in the centre of the hall. A massive pair of hands that could only have belonged to Blukka were holding me by the shoulders. I heard Daqar's voice, from somewhere behind me, saying, 'Place them in one of the larger dungeons, my dear, then go about your duties. I shall deal with our Captain myself.'

My vision cleared as Daqar walked around in front of me, a look of what I would have sworn was genuine concern on his face.

'Blukka, please,' he said, 'there is no need for such force.'

The giant slave's grip lessened by an almost imperceptible degree.

Daqar squatted down in front of me and examined my head. It felt as though a herd of gryllups was thundering through it, though the fact that the top of my skull was still in place at all told me that Blukka had hit me with the flat of his sword and not the edge. I made a mental note to thank him for that — right after I'd done the same for him.

'You put up a remarkable fight,' Daqar said, apparently satisfying himself that the damage to my cranium was minor. 'I've never imagined a swordsman who could give Blukka such a hard time. He is, as I'm sure you have gathered, a rather proficient warrior.'

'For a slave,' I conceded.

Daqar smiled.

'Now, Captain—' he began.

'Who said I was a Captain?' I asked.

'Your friends did,' said Daqar, 'as soon as they told me your name.'

I must have looked puzzled.

'Your exploits with the *Mariner* are famous,' he told me. 'They are recorded in the Libraries. When I became aware of the presence of a Benzan Captain in Zatuchep I despatched Zalmetta to find him — to find you. I had not anticipated your becoming involved with Yarissi and his pantheon of wishful thinkers, however.'

'You set the charlaki on them,' I said, suddenly knowing it to be true.

Daqar did not deny it.

'They had no business here,' he said, 'and the charlaki are easily roused in any case. Had I not alerted them, they would undoubtedly have stumbled across Yarissi's party eventually. Unfortunately, by the time Zalmetta arrived the herd was so aroused that nothing would have calmed them. Luckily, your battle took place close to one of the entrances to my domain.'

'So you already knew I was a Captain before you heard my name,' I said.

'Your appearance, to one who has studied the fashions of the Vohung, gave you away,' he said. 'But there are those who affect such styles who have not earned them. Once I heard your name, however—' He let the sentence go unfinished.

'OK, so I'm a celebrity,' I said, irrationally annoyed at the notion. 'What makes me so interesting to you?'

'The one aspect of your notoriety which is not recorded in the Library,' Daqar said, '– or at least, not in any file to which I can gain access. And that is the one thing which you will tell me.'

I said nothing. Daqar smiled. He seemed genuinely unflappable.

'You will tell me,' he said, 'how to build an airship like the *Mariner*.'

I hesitated, then said, 'But without an airframe . . .'

'That need not concern you,' he told me. 'You need only give me the plans.'

'There are no plans,' I said. 'The Ladden built it, not me.'

'From your design,' Daqar said.

'Following my suggestions,' I corrected. 'But the final design . . .'

'Enough of this,' Daqar said, now displaying a trace of impatience. 'You will tell me everything that you told the Ladden – and as much of what they added as you are able to remember. I will do the rest.'

Daqar's attitude puzzled me more than somewhat. What was he really after? The *Mariner*'s plans were useless on their own, and even if he'd had access to an airframe what did he plan on doing with his ship once he'd built it?

It seemed to me that I should have been in two minds about telling him what I knew; that the fact that the *Mariner* was, in many ways, a military secret, should have vied in my thoughts with the obvious fact that even with his own airship, Daqar was unlikely to be much of a threat to anyone, or at least no more of one than he already was. But, for reasons that were not all clear, I wasn't in two minds. I had already made my decision: there was no way I was giving Daqar anything. Part of it was the mystery over the charlaki and Zalmetta. But a lot of it was just instinct; I didn't trust Daqar, hadn't from the very start, and I wasn't about to be taken in by his softly-softly approach.

I think he saw in my face what my response was going to be, because a brief and fleeting sadness came into his eyes.

'It would grieve me to harm you, David Shaw,' he said quietly, 'but you must understand – knowledge is all I live for:

its pursuit has defined my existence, its acquisition has shaped my life. The accumulation of knowledge *is* my life. Nothing else matters, nothing else has ever mattered, nothing else can ever matter. When I found, in the Library, a record of your *Mariner*, I knew that this was knowledge I must have.'

'You just want the knowledge?' I said suspiciously. 'Just to know how to build an airship? You don't actually—'

'Oh, I shall build one with what you teach me,' he said, smiling like a child at the prospect of a new toy. 'Quite what I shall do with it I have no idea, but I must have it. You see, it is in the making of such a thing that the true knowledge lies. Your plans are only the starting point, but as fascinating as they will be, they are only the seed, the inspiration. What I shall learn from the actual making of the device will dwarf them to insignificance. And when I am done, my airship will be superior to yours in every way, just as yours was superior to its predecessor. Thus does knowledge grow. And grow it must, David Shaw; such is the purpose of the universe.'

I looked long and hard into Daqar's eyes as he said this, and he did not look away. Any doubts I might still have entertained were swept away in that one moment, as a chilling realization came to me: Tal Daqar was potentially the most dangerous man I had ever met. And he didn't even seem to know it.

'Blukka,' he said, 'take our guest to the cell in which we are holding the warrior Luftetmek. I think they will be good company for one another while they each ponder their fate.'

I was lifted bodily from my seat and virtually carried out of the hall.

CHAPTER NINE

Incarceration

—————◦∞∞◦—————

Luftetmek and I could hardly claim that our cell was crowded. Its single vaulted ceiling, six or seven storeys above us, looked down on a circular floor space that could have housed more than a hundred prisoners. The central stone pillar that rose in an eight-foot-thick column met the underside of the roof in an impressive array of buttresses, any one of which looked as though it would have been adequate to the task.

There were no windows in the cell.

In fact, it occurred to me that there were no windows anywhere in Tal Daqar's abode. Or, at least, in those parts I had seen.

The cell was lit, dimly but adequately, by many dozens of lanterns set in niches in the walls, the lowest of which was well out of our reach, whose light output was considerably less than the other such devices I had seen recently. Had these lanterns been as bright as, say, the one Zalmetta had carried when first we met her then our cell would have been too bright to bear. I wondered if these lanterns were old, their power failing.

We were not especially uncomfortable in our confinement. The cell was cold, but tolerable. There was no damp to speak of, and the unevenly flagged floor was strewn with enough straw for us to gather together a pair of makeshift beds. All in all, things could have been worse.

I studied the door which was the only break in the circular wall of the cell. It was several inches thick, sard bound with iron,

84

and had no lock. It was barred from the outside with a beam that it had taken two slaves to lift. I did not expect escape via that route to be a viable proposition.

Luftetmek saw where I was looking and I gave him a humourless grin.

'You kick it down,' I suggested, 'and I'll overpower the guards.'

He laughed, the amusement genuine and unforced.

'You are too gracious,' he said. 'Please, allow me to deal with the guards.'

More seriously, I said, 'If the chance presents itself—'

'Captain,' Luftetmek interrupted, 'while you and I are alone and, I think it is reasonable to assume, in a situation from which death is as likely a way out as any, permit me to speak openly. I have watched you in battle, and know you to be a brave and capable warrior. You appear also an honest man, freely speaking your heart even when to do so is not to your material advantage. You have said that you have business with the Thirteen, so I know that your destiny is already written, yet you seem not overburdened by it, as are many that I have seen. In short, you are a man whom I feel I can trust, at least insofar as our respective missions allow. We are warriors, you and I, and although not of the same country, we are of the same kind. It is possible that, should we escape and then return to my country, my Kanaat may order your death – your words to him regarding slavery were more costly than you may have known. If that should happen, then as his Champion the task of killing you would fall to me. In single combat, you might defeat me; my oath to the Kanaat would not, therefore, allow me the luxury of giving you the opportunity. I tell you this now, because when we leave this cell, I will never again be able to speak of this. Should you and I succeed in an escape, I would owe you my life. The words I have just spoken are as much of that debt as I shall be able to repay. If, knowing this, you choose to leave me behind, I shall understand.'

I sat as he concluded his speech, wondering at the factors that had motivated him to say what he had. I had, in my own mind, questioned his actions on a number of occasions, wondering at the way he placed his Kanaat, Yarissi, above his own personal honour as a warrior. This declaration seemed to suggest that the loyalty I had sensed in him and his men was as real and as deep as I had thought it to be. And, yet again, I found myself astounded that someone as uncharasmatic as Yarissi could command it.

'If we escape,' I told Luftetmek, 'it will be together. And until we are on Resheki soil, I shall trust you with my life. After that, no debt will remain between us.'

He seemed visibly relieved.

'And in any case,' I added, 'if – when – we escape, my own route will not necessarily take me through your country.'

'If it does,' Luftetmek said, 'and other factors do not intrude, you will be welcome in my House.'

Our confinement was tedious in the extreme. We were fed twice a day, as nearly as we could calculate the passage of time, but other than that we were left entirely undisturbed. The monotony alone was an ingenious form of torture.

We did what we could to make the time pass, and to keep ourselves in some kind of fighting-fit condition. The spacious cell gave us plenty of room for exercise, and even for a certain amount of 'road work'. Luftetmek taught me Resheki warrior skills and I taught him those of Earth and the Vohung Kingdoms. We told one another tales of our personal pasts, and of our respective countries' pasts. And listening to Luftetmek's account of the history of Reshek, I came to some slight understanding of the power that Yarissi had over his people, a power that was bestowed upon him freely and without reservation: Yarissi was Kanaat, the One out of the Many, different yet equal, the first and the last. The Resheki believed themselves the oldest race on Shushuan, direct descendants of the First Men who were created by the Old Gods, deities who predated even the Thirteen. Their seven-tier hierarchical society, so rigid in form yet infinitely flexible in execution, had gone unchanged for countless centuries – or millennia if their 'history' was to be believed. It was in no sense a perfect society, but it was as good as many that were founded on more 'moral' doctrines, and had the possibly unique distinction of being acceptable to all members of its various levels and classes, from the highest to the lowest. Which is what made the actions of the Bagalamak family so incomprehensible to so many. They had used their power and influence to subvert the system. They had bred their own line in secret, and had attempted to secure their permanent rule over the land and its people. They had manipulated the country's slave trade, had used politics to cause their own slaves to be manumitted against the natural order, and had saturated the armed forces with freedmen of the Bagalamak House, keeping them attached to the army long after their compulsory tenure had ended, and elevating them to officer status. They had, in effect, used the system for their own ends. To the Vinh way of thinking this was a crime of the most monstrous kind. Not above conquest or the perilous art of brinkmanship where their neighbours were concerned, the Vinh as a race were scrupulously fair and honest in their cultural dealings. They were not a naive race – they were too old for that – but they were, in some ways, an innocent one. Perhaps, to carry the analogy to its logical conclusion, they had evolved beyond childhood and manhood and were now into their dotage, all life's problems simplified by the ever-present spectre of extinction. Whatever the rationale, the nature of the Vinh was one thing, and the acts of the Bagalamak were very definitely another. Rebellion, as I have said, comes hard to the Vinh. It defies all their teachings, all their beliefs – it smacks of the very thing the Bagalamak themselves had done. So generations had to pass before the ancient, half-forgotten title of Kanaat could once again find followers, and the people rise in open revolt. And at their head, speaking not of hellfire and brimstone but of reason and truth – and the Law – was Yarissi. No one who had come as a stirrer of unrest or fomenter of discontent could have caused the Resheki to rise against their rulers, but a man who spoke plainly and simply of a way of life that had been betrayed found that he had the attention of a nation.

Luftetmek's devotion to Yarissi was typical of that of most of his people. He saw not a great leader, or a hero, but a man who, by his very existence, was a constant reminder of what they were fighting to restore. Yarissi's co-leader of the rebellion, the man he had once referred to as Kandirak, served a more practical purpose to the movement. He had spent many years in the Resheki military and, though no genius in matters of strategy or campaigning, was an able field commander with an impressive record of battles won. No one followed Kandirak as they did Yarissi, but he was not without his supporters.

It would be fair to say that Luftetmek and I became friends during those long weeks of imprisonment, and that although we still had our differences a bond grew between us that transcended them.

We should have seen the danger long before it presented itself. But the tedium of the interminable days and nights dulled our wits and we never realized how totally we were playing into Daqar's hands.

It was on the seventy-third day of our imprisonment, with the arrival of the first of our two daily meals, that the change to our established routine took place.

The usual order of things went like this: the bar would be lifted from the door, the door would open, a single male slave would enter carrying our food; outside the door and several paces back from it, two other male slaves, armed with shortswords, would stand guard; the food slave would place our meal upon the floor and withdraw; the door would close, and the bar would rasp back into place.

Today, the food slave carried no food.

'Come with me,' he said simply.

Luftetmek and I looked at one another stupidly. The opportunity for escape was presenting itself, and we had become so institutionalized that we were in danger of letting it pass us by.

The hesitation passed, and I saw in my companion's eyes the glint that told me we were each thinking the same thing.

Luftetmek preceded me through the door, the food slave standing to one side, inside the cell. I started to follow the Resheki warrior, and he and I moved in unison, as we had planned a dozen times. I grabbed the food slave and flung him bodily at the guard on the right of the door, while Luftetmek simultaneously sprang upon the left-hand guard. In seconds, we had overpowered the two men and divested them of their weapons, leaving their unconscious bodies, and that of the food slave, inside the cell. We returned the bar to the door so that, to the casual observer, all would appear normal. Then, moving with all the caution that our haste would permit, we headed for Daqar's main hall, and the only exit that we knew of from his fortress.

We had debated and argued over this one move more than any other. Luftetmek, understandably enough, wanted to free his men. But escape of any description was going to be hard enough. Escape with a retinue, none of whom we had had the opportunity to school in our plans, would be fore-doomed to failure. My own plan was that we two should escape, hide out on the island until the arrival of Celebe, then use her knowledge and powers to effect a rescue of Yarissi and his men.

In very short order we reached Daqar's great hall, and were relieved to find it deserted. Even the Y'nys creature, Kziktzak, was gone from its pedestal. We crossed to the ceiling-high double doors at the far side of the chamber and spent what felt like an age looking for the concealed handle that would open the smaller door we knew to be set into them. Eventually, with much cursing from both of us, the portal gave up its secret and we tore open the slender sardwood panel. Beyond, the smaller hall through which we had first passed on entering Daqar's abode stood silent and empty. In its farther wall, the black mouth of the exit waited for us.

'Can you remember the way from here?' I asked, my voice a stage whisper.

'Barely,' Luftetmek confessed. 'You?'

I shrugged.

We crossed the dimly lit hall and stared down into the darkness that awaited us.

'We'll never make it without a lamp,' I said.

'Wait here,' Luftetmek said.

He retraced his steps and returned a moment later bearing one of the brazier-like lamps that burned constantly in the main hall.

'A little cumbersome,' he said, 'but adequate to the task.'

Using the lamp, we made our way through the narrow switchback corridor leading to the apparently solid stone wall that formed the outer boundary of Daqar's fortress. Once again we searched for long, frustrating minutes before locating the opening device. Once found, however, it was the work of seconds to swing the great stone slab about its vertical axis. Then we were through, and into the maze-like pits beneath the city.

Now, indeed, we were at the mercy of random chance. Neither of us could remember the combination of twists and turns that had brought us here, much less negotiate them in reverse. We wandered the gloomy corridors and passageways for hours, occasionally chancing upon some slight evidence of recent habitation and following it hopefully, though usually finding ourselves at a dead end only moments later.

Finally, and more by luck than judgement, we came to a ramp that led upwards.

'Does this look familiar to you?' Luftetmek asked.

'I don't know,' I said. 'Zalmetta led us down from the street level in total darkness. But this is the first exit we've seen, so . . .'

I let the thought hang in the air for a moment, then set off up the gentle gradient. Luftetmek, lamp in hand, marched alongside me.

I think we were both totally amazed when, moments later, we found ourselves in the very building from which we had made our descent into the city's cellars all those weeks before. There were still the traces of our fight with the charlaki on the stones of the floor and in the nearby doorway that Luftetmek's men had so valiantly defended.

'From here,' Luftetmek said with a laugh, 'I know the way.'

He put down the lamp and we headed out into the street.

Ringing the doorway stood upwards of twenty of Daqar's household slaves. All were armed, and all were looking directly at us. For a moment I believed Luftetmek and I to have been the victims of the most outrageous ill fortune, but then the real truth came to me: they had been waiting here for us.

I heard Tal Daqar's voice call out, 'Gentlemen, surely you have not yet tired of my hospitality.'

He stepped into view, Kziktzak and Blukka flanking him. I considered the possibility of fighting our way out of the doorway, but not seriously. I glanced at the creature called Kziktzak: the vertical bar of its eye, with its deadly ray that could raise steel to red-heat at a touch, was focused upon us.

'Please be so good as to put down your weapons,' Daqar said, 'and then we will take a little walk. I have something to show you that I think you will find interesting. Especially you, David Shaw,' he added cryptically, 'Captain of the *Mariner*.'

CHAPTER TEN

Nightmare

We moved down the broad avenues of Zatuchep with Daqar's guards arrayed in a lens formation around us, their eyes never turning away from the black orifices of the windows and doors of the surrounding buildings. I supposed they were watching out for charlaki, and wondered what they would do if we were attacked – they were less well armed even than Luftetmek's men had been, and probably not as well trained.

We traversed numerous streets without incident, finally coming to an area that appeared to have suffered some great devastation. A broad swathe of demolished buildings cut across at right angles to our path, a tract of debris that extended for as far as the eye could see to left and right. I recognized the region; I had seen it from the top of the tower in which I had intended spending my first night in Zatuchep.

We turned and began to follow the path of destruction, heading deeper into the city. I recalled that in this direction the damage ended abruptly, perhaps half a mile ahead of us, and that a greyish object, impossible to make out from my then vantage point, had seemed to be embedded in the ground at that location.

Long before we reached the object, I saw it, rising up among the ancient buildings like a silver needle, and knew it for what it was.

I saw Daqar looking at me; he knew that I knew, of course. I wondered if he expected me to deny it.

'What is it?' Luftetmek whispered. He could not be expected to know.

'It is an airframe,' I said, 'like the one on which the *Mariner* was built.'

He looked at me blankly.

'Knowledge of your exploits,' Daqar said to me, 'is not, perhaps, as widespread as I may have led you to believe.'

I said nothing. I would neither confirm nor deny any information Daqar might think he already possessed.

As we drew closer to the fallen airframe I noticed something odd. I had assumed, at first glance, that it had somehow been crashed into the ground – a feat that we had been unable to accomplish with either the *Mariner* or the *Freedom*, both of which refused to descend to ground level – and had then become so embedded in the rubble that that was what had pinned it down, just as the *Mariner*'s airframe had been when first we discovered it. But a closer examination showed that the amount of rubble lying on top of the airframe was not nearly massive enough to overcome the metal's natural gravity-defying properties. Which left only one possible explanation: the airframe had been damaged, and could no longer fly. The notion seemed incredible. What power could do such damage? I envisioned some kind of air battle, conducted not with the primitive weapons currently available to the Vinh but with those to which the airframes' inventors must surely have had recourse. Only one incongruous thought intruded: this airframe had crashed into a Kai city, a city of an empire that had not even been born until the makers of the airframe had lain dead and forgotten for centuries.

In moments we were standing in the shadow of the airframe's central spar. It rose above us, tilted at an angle of about forty-five degrees, its two lower arch-like wings partially embedded in the rubble. In that region of the central spar that lay between the forward and aft mountings of the wings, a section perhaps thirty metres long, I had expected to see the black tile-like fixtures that were to be found in the same location on both the *Mariner* and the *Freedom*. On this airframe, they were missing. We had never understood the purpose of the tiles, or worked out how they were attached. Or how they could be removed.

Assuming that the airframe had crashed nose first, then its forward end was totally buried in the substance of the street to a depth of more than twenty-five metres; it was probably embedded in the island's underlying bedrock.

'Using your plans,' Daqar said to me, 'I shall construct a hull around this airframe and fly it to all the corners of the known world – and further. The potential knowledge to be acquired is limitless.'

I said nothing. Daqar was not the threat to the peace of Shushuan that the Librarians had been – possibly he was not a threat at all, except to anyone unfortunate enough to have knowledge he wanted and an inclination not to divulge it – but the mere prospect of granting him the freedom to wander the planet at will sent a shiver through me.

He did seem, however, to be overlooking one rather obvious fact.

'This airframe,' I said, indicating the derelict, 'will not fly.' Maliciously, I added, 'You are going nowhere, Tal Daqar.'

He smiled affably. 'That fact need not concern you, Captain,' he said. 'Your involvement in this project is rather less . . . executive.'

I almost laughed. Daqar was better at this kind of fencing than I was.

'Now that you have seen the airframe,' Daqar said, 'I hope that you will reconsider your position. You have, so far, seen little of my powers of persuasion, and being a rational man I have no desire to have you see more. What do you say, Captain? Can we settle this like intelligent creatures?'

'No, Daqar,' I said. 'Because in your mouth, the word "intelligent" is an insult.'

He looked pained by the comment, but said nothing. Turning from me, he walked away from the crash site and his slaves herded Luftetmek and me after him.

*　　*　　*

Luftetmek was silent as we returned to Daqar's fortress. It was only when he finally spoke that I realized the reason for his silence.

'This Tal Daqar,' he said pensively, 'he wishes you to tell him something?'

'Yes,' I said.

'And you will not?' Luftetmek said.

'No,' I said.

'And he will use whatever means are necessary,' Luftetmek said, 'to extract this information.'

'Yes,' I said.

'Including,' Luftetmek said, 'torturing you – and your friends.'

I looked at him.

'I . . . suppose so,' I said.

I began now to understand why Daqar had imprisoned Luftetmek and me together. It seemed likely, in retrospect, that we had been observed, covertly, during all that time.

'Are we friends, David Shaw,' Luftetmek asked, 'you and I?'

'I consider you my friend,' I said.

'And you think Daqar does not know this,' he observed. It wasn't a question.

I said nothing.

'This knowledge,' Luftetmek said, 'which you will not divulge: Would it endanger your country, your people?'

I considered that carefully before answering.

'I doubt it,' I said.

'But it would make Daqar a dangerous man,' Luftetmek said, '– more so than he is already?'

'I believe so,' I said.

He nodded.

'He is a strange man,' Luftetmek said, 'and I do not trust him, present circumstances notwithstanding. Very well: tell him nothing. We will bear the consequences as warriors should.'

'I had not considered others when I made my decision,' I confessed. 'I should have.'

'One cannot always consider others,' Luftetmek said

philosophically. 'The right choice does not become any less right just because it is harder than we expected.'

I laughed; Luftetmek sounded so like my old friend, Tor Taskus, that they might have been brothers. Which, in a very real sense, they were.

When we reached Daqar's dwelling we were instantly split up. We cast one another questioning glances, no explanation being forthcoming from Daqar or his followers. Luftetmek gave me a grin as he was led away, and made the sign of Shushuan's grim war god, Gazig. I returned it instinctively, and instantly felt a smile cross my own lips – if Daqar seriously thought he could threaten us, he was living in a fool's paradise. I had little doubt that, under sustained torture, I would eventually have to tell him what he wanted to know, but I was confident that by the time my resistance had been that far beaten down I would be in no fit state to offer the kind of detailed technical information he was after. It would be a pyrrhic victory, but as the only one on offer I was willing to take it.

I was returned to the cell that Luftetmek and I had shared, and in only a matter of minutes the loneliness was all but intolerable. This was something I had not anticipated – torture not of the body, but of the mind. Luftetmek would not be tortured before my eyes, but would be kept out of sight, allowing my imagination to run riot.

I paced the cell endlessly, round and around the central column, until I was almost dizzy from the effort and my feet ached from pounding the cold stone floor. It had been early morning when Daqar took us to see the airframe. It was evening before the cell door opened again.

By that time I had abandoned my pacing and was lying on my straw mattress, staring unseeingly up into the cell's vaulted roof. At the sound of the cell door's restraining bar being lifted I sprang instantly to my feet, rushing towards the door. Good sense prevented me from approaching too closely – overpowering the guards a second time was not even a remote possibility – and waited in a fever of anticipation as the heavy portal was swung open.

The food slave entered. He deposited my evening meal, not

looking at me. He left. The door closed, and the heavy bar was slid into place.

I stared at it for several dumbfounded seconds. Then—

'Hey!' I yelled. 'What the hell is this?'

I threw myself at the door, beating on it with all my might, crying out at the top of my lungs for Luftetmek, for Daqar, for the Thirteen Gods to stop their incessant, incomprehensible games. I kept it up for long enough that when I did stop I sank to my knees in exhaustion.

'. . . what . . . the hell . . . is this . . . ?' I gasped, my throat raw.

I heard the heavy sound of the bar being lifted from behind the door. The thick portal swung inwards and Zalmetta stood framed in the open doorway.

'Come with me,' she said.

I arose and followed her.

We walked down the long corridor that led away from Daqar's main hall, then along a transverse passage. At its end was a ramp leading upward. We ascended two levels and then turned in what, if my orientation was reliable, would have been a northerly direction.

'Where are we going?' I asked.

She made no reply, but led me to a partially open door at the end of the corridor. She paused in the doorway, looking back over her shoulder at me. Something in her expression made me wary, on guard: what was going on here? And did it have anything to do with Daqar?

Zalmetta stepped into the room and I followed . . :

Drapes hung everywhere, including around a huge four-poster bed. A stone-railed balcony looked out over the ocean; there was nothing between the room and the balcony except a shutterless arch. Somewhere, incense was burning, filling the room with an almost hallucinogenic scent.

Zalmetta appeared from behind one of the drapes with a pair of wine glasses in her hands. She offered me one.

I took it and raised it to my lips; I was on the point of drinking, when a thought intruded. I flung the glass aside. 'Where is Luftetmek?' I demanded. 'Where—'

Pain cold harsh light *Drapes* hands dragging carrying *balcony* voices complaining grumbling cursing *where?* stumbling between them, trying to find my feet as I was shoved roughly down the corridor outside my cell. Disorientation faded in a familiar realization: *dream*. But I had *smelled* those incense . . .

By the time we reached our destination I was fully awake and walking between my two guards. We three were the only ones in our small retinue. I considered, briefly and abstractly, attempting escape. The idea was never a serious one.

We came to a door set in the stone wall and one of the guards opened it and pushed me through.

What I saw stopped me in my tracks and all but froze the blood in my veins.

I was in a torture chamber. No other name would do, and those two words can scarcely convey the impression that that room made on my senses at that moment. It was not a large room, and many of its appointments were unrecognizable to my untrained eye, but whilst their specific application may have remained a mystery, their purpose, the slow and measured inflicting of pain and suffering on human flesh, was unmistakable.

Yet it was not the instruments of torture themselves that had so horrified me, but what lay on a large stone slab that stood directly before me. The slab was a table of sorts, similar to those found in abattoirs, with drain channels for blood and a raised lip to keep its load from spilling over the sides. The load in question was the remains of a man.

He was impossible to identify. Certainly he had been a large man, muscular, though beyond that nothing was certain. He had been skinned. I tried, not successfully, to convince myself that he had not been skinned alive. His fingers had been removed, as had his eyes and ears. There were other mutilations, some gross, others subtle, all intended to cause pain to a living subject. There were no wounds that, in themselves, could have been regarded as mortal. In effect, the man had been tortured to death.

'I thought you would wish to see the body,' Tal Daqar's voice said.

He was standing at the other side of the room, partially hidden in shadow. The giant warrior, Blukka, stood behind him. I had been so shocked by the sight of the man's body that I had not realized anyone else was present.

I looked at Daqar, who stepped forward into the light of the single roof-mounted lantern. He looked like an undertaker, all professional solicitude and concern.

'—As you were his friend,' he added.

I looked at the body, not yet prepared – or able – to accept the suggestion Daqar was making. The body was of the right size and build, but was so disfigured that it could have belonged to almost anyone.

'He told me nothing,' Daqar said conversationally.

I stared at him, horrified.

'He *knew* nothing!' I yelled.

'You were alone together for over seventy days and nights,' Daqar said. 'Are you seriously telling me that you never discussed with him the reason for my interest in you? Never revealed the secrets of the *Mariner* design?'

'Never!' I cried, not believing Daqar could be so stupid.

I stared at the ruined mess on the slab. The senselessness of it was almost more than I could bear.

'I suspected as much,' Daqar confessed, 'but it was necessary to be sure.'

I looked up and, with a cry of rage and hate, I hurled myself at him. Faster than his great size would have deemed credible, Blukka got between us and fended me off, much as I might have restrained a troublesome child.

'Return him to his cell,' Daqar said.

The other two slaves took hold of my arms and dragged me away; I made several furious attempts at breaking free as I was pulled backwards along the narrow passage back to my cell, but the two men seemed well versed in prisoner control and I succeeded in doing little more than acquiring – and inflicting – some nasty bruises.

They hurled me bodily into the cell and slammed the door

behind me. I flung myself at it, but too late to prevent the bar from being slid into place.

Beaten, I sank to the floor of the cell, my shoulder to the obdurate door, my head hung in defeat and despair.

CHAPTER ELEVEN

Mindgames

———◦◦◦———

I awoke surrounded by silk. Gossamer, spiderweb hangings seemed to enfold me on all sides, and the sheets upon which I lay were as fine and as light as spun cloud.

I sat up slowly, a fog in my mind, unable to recall falling asleep. Beside me, tangled in the moonlit bed linen, lay a black form; milk-white hair was spilled over the pillow that we shared. Her features were indistinct in the colourless light, but the beauty of her face and form were breathtaking. I sensed that I knew her, but her name wouldn't come to my mind.

I arose slowly, brushing aside hangings and looking around the room. The light was coming through an arched casement that gave onto a stone-railed balcony. Like the woman on the bed, the setting was familiar yet tantalizingly vague. I stepped out onto the balcony, a cool sea breeze playing over my naked skin. The view was spectacular; hundreds of feet below, all but invisible in the night, the ocean crashed and roared against jagged rocks and the sheer side of a silver-hued cliff face.

I turned back to the bedroom, moving slowly and silently across the thickly carpeted floor. I noticed the room's appointments and furnishings without really seeing them; until I saw the lectern.

Galvanized into activity I almost ran across the room, batting gauzy drapes aside as I went, until I was standing before the wooden-framed block of Y'nys crystal. I snatched up the stylus from the base of the frame and accessed the nearby Library. It took only seconds for me to gain entry to the file labelled MARINER, and not much longer to locate the 'delete' command.

'David—?'

The voice came sleepily from the bed.

'Just a minute,' I replied.

'David Shaw—'

'Just a . . .'

'Wake up, Captain.'

Disorientation, quickly fading as reality reasserted itself. *Another dream, just another dream.* That had been Zalmetta on the bed; what did it mean? Or was I just succumbing to Daqar's psychological warfare?

I realized that someone had been saying my name in the real world as well as in my dream. I forced my eyes into focus and let out a yelp of startled fright at what I saw.

I was on my feet in a second, my back pressed to the wall of my old familiar cell.

'You cried out in your sleep,' said Luftetmek. 'I thought it best to wake you.'

I stared at him, at his face and hands, at his . . . skin. He was unharmed, unmarked, alive; I reached out and grasped his shoulders, to be absolutely certain that he was not a phantom of my own guilt and grief, that I had not awoken from one dream into another. My hands were shaking uncontrollably.

'I have seen your corpse,' I told him.

'I think not,' he said.

I laughed nervously, and a bit hysterically.

'If not you,' I said, 'then who?'

What poor unfortunate had Daqar so horribly maltreated simply to gain . . . what? The admission from me that Luftetmek knew nothing, an admission obtained under circumstances that would make it believable? The idea that so much pain could be inflicted, so high a price exacted, for so slight a return was grotesque, and gave further evidence of the twisted workings of Daqar's mind. His was a perverted intelligence, a warped and malignant genius, made all the more deadly because it was so focused, so unrelenting. No price, I now realized, would be considered too high by Daqar to get what he wanted.

Was now the time to give it to him, I wondered? Now, before he destroyed something too precious to lose?

I sat on the straw matting at the side of the room and repeated my thoughts to Luftetmek, no longer confident of being able to reach a decision on my own.

'Do nothing,' Luftetmek urged. 'If you give this man anything, it can only serve to increase his ability to inflict harm.'

I wanted to believe him, but nothing seemed as sure to me now as it had before seeing that anonymous body on the slab in Daqar's torture chamber.

The next day, at the time of our regular first meal, our food slave arrived without food but with a retinue of a half-dozen armed guards.

'Accompany me,' he said simply.

Glancing warily at his grim-faced following, Luftetmek and I complied. We were herded back towards the torture chamber. I felt my muscles begin to tense, my fists to clench; whatever happened next, I was resolved not to go meekly to my fate. The heavy door was thrown open, and we were pushed inside.

The chamber had been entirely refurbished. It was now equipped like some kind of dining hall. The stone slab had been replaced with a heavy wooden table; the iron fixings in the wall that had once sported hideous instruments of cruelty now held lanterns to give the room a bright and cheery aspect. Against one wall, a side table stood laden down with the kind of food we had only dreamed of for the past weeks. There were even bottles of sukoki, Ladden wine from the north. I wondered, slightly amazed at the sight, how Daqar had acquired it. I had never seen sukoki outside of Ragana-Se-Tor, the land through which the nomadic Ladden wander.

A handful of slaves, decked out in the livery of squires from ancient Kai, stood adjacent to the side table, and at our arrival two stepped forward and pulled out chairs at either end of the main table.

A slave whose livery was the finest of the lot said, 'Please, masters, be seated.'

Luftetmek and I, too dazed to argue, sat.

The slave – I couldn't help thinking of him as the maitre d' at some upmarket hotel, and the thought sent a hysterical giggle, which I swiftly smothered, to my lips – gestured to his underlings and they began to bring food to the table, placing it in front of us.

'Some wine, master?' the head slave said, offering me a view of the bottle. The glass was unmistakably Ladden in origin.

'Please,' I said numbly.

He poured, and I lifted the goblet to my lips. The taste brought back a flood of memories, and also a series of hacking coughs from my ill-prepared system.

I got myself under control and looked across at Luftetmek. He was as bemused as I.

'Eat, masters,' the slave bade us. 'There is nothing to fear.'

Until that moment, fear had been the last thing on my mind. If it was Daqar's intention to kill us by poison, he was certainly letting us go out in style.

Cautiously at first, then with genuine enthusiasm, Luftetmek and I ate. The food was an absolute delight; the only thing I had ever encountered that could compare was the illusory repast laid for me by the Thirteen when I had first visited their city in the Asmina Valley. That had, at the time, seemed as real as this, even to the effects of the wine. But there was no reason to suppose that Daqar had access to powers like those of Shushuan's gods, so it was reasonable to assume that there was nothing imaginary about the meal we were now enjoying.

I heard Luftetmek mutter, 'This can only be a ploy.'

I glanced at him; his reasoning was a step ahead of mine, but I quickly caught up. 'We're being set up for a fall,' I said, eyeing the slaves warily. 'Good treatment to soften us up, to get our defences down.'

He nodded.

I tried to imagine some benefit to us in not eating the food; other than representing some ambiguous moral victory, I couldn't see any. At the same time, I couldn't imagine any disadvantage to us in filling our bellies.

No one hurried us, but as soon as it became obvious that

we had thoroughly stuffed ourselves the chamber door opened and our armed guards filed inside.

'Come with us,' said their leader.

Neither Luftetmek nor I moved.

'You are merely being relocated,' said the guard. 'You have nothing to fear.'

Something in his manner suggested that that sentence should have included one extra word, and that that word was 'Yet'. There seemed little point in arguing, however, so we allowed ourselves to be escorted from the room.

We were taken deeper into Daqar's fortress than either of us had yet been. The walls around us seemed to darken, to become fetid and damp, the passageway narrowing. The temperature dropped by several degrees, our breath now making clouds of water vapour in front of our faces. It was like the descent into some Nordic Hell.

We came to a door. It was less than four feet high, barely eighteen inches wide. There was a small, barred window set into it, and a heavy iron latch that was secured by a bolt.

One of the guards slid the bolt back and lifted the latch. He pulled the door open — there was barely room to do so in the confines of that cramped passage — to reveal a cell beyond. The cell was on a scale comparable to that of the door: a cube six feet on a side, the floor sloping slightly, away from the door, to a drainage hole set in one corner. Above the hole was a crude water tap and, hanging from a rusty nail, a tin cup. The only other 'furnishing' was a wooden pallet that could, at a pinch, be described as a bed. Other than the door and the drainage hole the cell was devoid of openings; there was no light in the cell.

The guard gestured for me to step through the door. I hesitated, then complied with his 'request'. I had to turn sideways to get through. The door slammed behind me, and I heard Luftetmek's voice raised in objection. We were, it seemed, to be separated once again. There were the sounds of a scuffle, then curses, and then the sounds receded as my companion was dragged away.

A face appeared at the grillework set in the door.

'When my master is ready for you,' the owner of the face said, 'you will be sent for. Until then, make yourself at home.' He laughed loudly at his joke, then moved away from the small window.

From further along the corridor, I heard the slamming of a second door, and suspected that Luftetmek was now incarcerated even as I was.

Footsteps receded into the distance. The silence that followed them was the deepest, darkest, most ominous sound I had ever heard.

CHAPTER TWELVE

Freedom . . . of a Sort

It became impossible to measure the passage of time. The only illumination in my cell was the bit of grubby yellow light that fell through the grillework in the door. My eyes accommodated to it rather quickly, and by it I explored my surroundings. The floor was a seamless slab of stone; the walls were built from blocks of the same substance, the smallest of which was over a foot square. The ceiling was a series of criss-cross beams of heavy black wood.

I was not fed. The water that came from the wall tap was black at first, then brown, and finally a pale, oily yellow. It tasted rather less revolting than it looked.

I tried to exercise, to occupy my mind; I called out to Luftetmek and from some distance away he replied, but conversation was impossible: we would have shouted ourselves hoarse.

Days passed, and still I was not fed. I became weak, disorientated. I drank more and more of the foul water from the tap, trying to keep my belly full. The effect this had on my digestive system is not hard to guess, and not a memory I care to dwell upon.

Days became weeks, and it came to me that I had been forgotten. Some other item of interest had presented itself to Tal Daqar and the fate of David Shaw had slipped from his mind. I became convinced that this tiny, soul-destroying cell was to be the last thing I would ever see: I would die here.

As nearly as I could reckon, I had been in the cell for between fifteen and twenty days when the door opened and one of Daqar's armed guards leaned through the opening. *This is it*, I thought, *the last act in an increasingly meaningless drama*. I could not even find the enthusiasm to put up a struggle.

The guard grabbed me and dragged me out of the cell. I all but collapsed into his arms; he shoved me back, cuffing me roughly. Apathy could not overcome trained instincts, and I lashed out at the guard with all my diminished strength. Weakened as I was, the edge of my hand demolished his throat, and as he sank gagging to his knees I delivered a back elbow into the side of his neck to finish the job. He sank to the stone floor, body spasming in death.

I looked around, expecting a dozen guards to swarm over me. Other than myself and the body at my side, the corridor was deserted.

I tried to stand. The effort left me dizzy; spots of colour danced before my eyes and there was a hollow ringing in my ears. Undeterred, I dragged myself along the passageway in the direction of Luftetmek's cell.

The door was bolted but not locked. I dragged the bolt back and pulled open the door. Inside, Luftetmek lay curled up on a wooden pallet identical to the one in my own cell. For an instant, I thought he was dead. Then his eyelids fluttered, and his gaze met mine.

'Shaw—?' he groaned.

I reached in to him.

'Let's go,' I said.

He took my hand. His grip was weak, but his hand was steady.

'Is this another trap?' he muttered, swaying at my side.

'I no longer care,' I told him.

We retraced our steps to my own cell. The body of the guard was where I had left it.

'One lone guard,' Luftetmek said.

'And unarmed,' I added.

'Why are we even bothering?' he asked.

'Because,' I told him, 'every time he does this, he plays with fire. Eventually, he will get burned.'

Luftetmek smiled, but his eyes were murderous.

'Lead on, David Shaw,' he said.

We reached Daqar's main hall without encountering any opposition – without encountering anyone at all.

'This is it,' I said, leaning on the door handle.

'David Shaw,' Luftetmek said, 'I will not go back to that cell.'

I looked at him. There was steel in his gaze, and an unflinching acceptance of the one thing all warriors know they will one day face.

I nodded. 'Nor I,' I vowed.

I pushed the doors open.

Tal Daqar stood in the centre of the room, beyond the great table and between the rows of statues that lined the chamber, looking at us. Behind him stood Blukka and Zalmetta. Arrayed in a half-circle, flanking the three, were a dozen armed slaves.

Zalmetta's presence rather surprised me. I hadn't seen her since before my imprisonment. Or . . . had I? Events of the last months were now very confused in my memory.

'Gentleman,' Daqar said, smiling at us. 'I knew you would not take long to get here. Please, come and join us.'

I glanced around the room. The creature known as Kziktzak, I noticed, was gone from its place among the statues. I wondered where it was lurking.

'We will not be imprisoned again,' I said.

Luftetmek had been right, and now, perhaps for the first time, I knew it. The only options now were freedom or death.

'Of course not,' Daqar said. 'That time is over. Now we will move along.' He regarded me. 'I will give you your freedom,' he said, '– and your companion's as well – if you will tell me what I want to know. What do you say?'

I heard a sound from Luftetmek, too low to carry as far as Daqar. It was a snarl.

'I have all the freedom I need,' I replied. 'If I should want any more, I shall take it.'

Daqar laughed.

'Magnificent!' he said. 'I had wondered if you could be broken psychologically – I already knew that physical torture would be a waste of time – and now I know. The experiment has been well worth the expenditure in time and materials.'

He gestured to his retinue of slaves and they filed out of the room past Luftetmek and me, leaving us alone with Daqar and Blukka and Zalmetta.

'Come,' Daqar said, 'there is something I think you should see.'

Bemused, Luftetmek and I shuffled forward, both looking out for the inevitable trap. Nothing happened that could in any way be considered threatening.

'Come along,' Daqar said, 'there is nothing to fear. Have I not said that that phase of our relationship is over? I am a reasonable, rational man. You have answered the question I set you, and now it is behind us. It is time to move on to other, bigger issues.'

We followed him towards the exit at the back of the hall. I hated playing into his game in way at all, but I had to know. I asked, 'What question have we answered?'

He laughed. I was learning to hate that laugh.

'You are not that obtuse, Captain,' he said. 'You know what question.'

'If this is another ploy,' I said, 'to discover the plans to the *Mariner*—'

'Nonsense,' Daqar said. 'That is no longer anything that need come between us. The only thing I ever wanted from you was to learn if you could be made to give me the information. It never actually mattered to me whether or not you did so, since it was readily available from another source. I *did* need you to assist me in gaining access to that source, and for that I thank you.'

Too confused to speak, I followed him out of the hall and down the passage beyond.

We emerged into the street and Daqar led us in the direction of the downed airframe. I glanced nervously around, looking for any sign of the charlaki roaming the ruins around us.

As though sensing my thoughts, Daqar said, 'We will be

quite safe so long as Zalmetta is with us. The charlaki will not attack one of their own.'

I remembered the battle in which I had first met Luftetmek and Yarissi and his followers. Zalmetta's appearance had not prevented further bloodshed on that occasion.

The bright sunlight was giving me a thundering headache, but I did my best to ignore it as I followed Daqar towards the trail of destruction that led to the airframe.

As soon as we turned the corner and faced in the direction that the ship had taken during its long-ago descent, I froze in my tracks, not believing what I was seeing.

Ahead of us, already visible even at this distance, was a half-constructed copy of the *Mariner*.

I walked slowly, dazedly forward, trying to comprehend what I was seeing, trying to understand how I could be seeing it.

The airframe had been unearthed and propped up at either end by wooden towers, its weight supported on its lower wings that still rested in the rubble. Other towers, less imposing in sheer scale, had been constructed to facilitate easier access for the workers who were assembling the hull. I recalled that Hareg of the Ladden had used a similar tower during the original construction of the *Mariner*.

As we drew nearer, I saw that my initial appraisal had been in error: the airship was considerably more than half finished. I looked more closely at the craft, picking out details. Through an open section of the hull, I could see that the interior was almost entirely open plan, and the twin propeller shafts that were the ship's drive mechanism had a certain crude, unsophisticated appearance to them. For a moment I couldn't work out why that should be, and then I had it: the device was as Hareg and his people and I had first designed it, before all the work that we had done after the *Mariner* was airborne. Whatever plans Daqar was working from, they were the oldest that could possibly exist. But where had be obtained them from? And what had he meant by that remark earlier, when he thanked me for gaining him access to them?

I caught Daqar looking at me; his smile seemed to suggest that he was reading my thoughts.

'Have you had any strange dreams lately, Captain?' he asked mysteriously.

I didn't know what he was talking about, and I felt too weak from hunger and too miserable from all my days of captivity to play his stupid games.

'No matter,' he said dismissively. 'Let us inspect my handiwork, and you can tell me if it matches your own.'

I laughed maliciously, heedless now of any consequences to my words or actions.

'It's a joke,' I told him. 'Compared to *my* ship, this is a pitiful copy cobbled together by a bad craftsman.'

Daqar's expression registered, for the briefest of instants, a fury like nothing I had ever seen before. Had he spoken at that moment, it could only have been to command my destruction. Whether or not he would regain mastery of his emotions in time to spare my life became academic, for the street suddenly rang to the harsh report of a pistol shot. One of Daqar's slaves was flung through the air, blood fountaining from his neck, his head almost detached from his body.

Everyone in the street turned in the direction from which the shot had come – the fact that no two of us were looking in the same direction was evidence of the multiple echoes being thrown back by the high-walled buildings all around us.

A second shot shattered the brief, startled silence, and a second slave went down, as neatly dispatched as the first.

I felt Blukka's giant hands grab me by the shoulders; I had no idea what was on his mind, and no inclination to find out. With an adrenalin-born strength I tore myself free of his grip and shoved him backwards. A third pistol shot took him through the shoulder – I think my shove had probably, inadvertently, saved his life – and he staggered back from me, his other hand going not to the wound but to the hilt of his broadsword. I admired his singlemindedness, but I didn't intend giving him the chance to gain the upper hand. I kicked him in the right knee, driving him down to the rubble, then again in the solar plexus. He grunted, stunned, but obstinately refused to collapse.

Two of Daqar's slaves advanced on me, and both went down

to the unseen gunman in rapid succession. It seemed that my safety was foremost on the gunman's agenda. Or . . . my freedom?

I threw a hasty glance at Luftetmek – he was surrounded, and his captors looked rattled enough to kill either of us on the spot and worry about their master's displeasure later.

'Go!' he hissed, sensing my indecision. 'I cannot leave while Yarissi is still a prisoner.'

I edged away from him, and from Daqar's men.

'Stop him!' Daqar yelled.

To Luftetmek I yelled, 'I'll be back!' and turned and ran back down the rubble-strewn street. I heard footsteps behind me. Then came the crack of the pistol again, and the footsteps ceased.

I ran blindly through the city streets, not yet able to orient myself in the unfamiliar territory. My only concern at that moment was to put as much distance as I could between myself and Daqar. Elaborate plans beyond that simple goal could wait.

I turned a corner, skidding on the loose debris that littered the street, my legs trembling with the unaccustomed effort after so many weeks of Daqar's relentless tortures. In front of me, scarcely a dozen yards away, stood a small herd of charlaki.

I froze, almost falling over, unable to get my balance.

None of them had seen me. Yet.

I tried not to breathe, tried not to think, tried to exude an air of simply not being there.

One of the charlaki turned and looked at me. Its eyes, like ovals of liquid amber, stared at me for long, unblinking seconds. Then it opened its mouth and let out the blood-chilling howl of its kind.

Flight, I knew, was useless. A charlak can outrun almost anything of Shushuan. And whilst I would have stood an outside chance of defeating one in a hand-to-hand battle – a slim outside chance, to be sure – there was no way for me to take on the half-dozen that I now faced.

As one, the other animals in the herd turned and surged toward me, a tide of living death.

The air was suddenly filled with a sound I had never heard before. It was like the hunting cry of the charlaki, but was less a challenge than a wail of abject torment. It was, I think, the most mournful sound I had ever heard. The creatures stopped in their tracks, bodies quivering with bloodlust, and slowly, to my astonishment, they began to back away from me. The sound came again, a heart-rending cry of loss and grief so primal that human words could not express it. One or two of the creatures glared at me, a trace of regret, of wistful longing on their suddenly disturbingly human faces, and then the whole group turned away and slunk off into the buildings around me.

I felt as though every muscle in my body relaxed at once. I almost sank to my knees in relief.

After a moment, I began to look around in an effort to work out where I was. From the roof of a nearby high tower, sunlight glinted off something bright and shiny. I shaded my eyes and looked more closely. From that rooftop, most of this quarter of the city would be visible, including the site of Daqar's shipyard.

I began to make my way towards the base of the tower. It featured the usual broad storey-high stairway leading up to its main entrance, the steps flanked on either side by terraces that might once have been hanging gardens but were now an overgrown tangle of weeds and grass.

I climbed the steps and entered the building. The interior was better preserved than others that I had seen; frescos and murals, though faded by the passage of the centuries, could still be seen on its walls and ceilings. The subject matter was as decadent and, in some cases, as repellent as the other remnants of late Kai 'art' that were to be found in the city, and I wasted no time in perusing it. Instead, I found the inclined ramp at the back of the structure that led up to the roof and began to ascend.

Moments later I stepped out into the open air once more and moved around the shell-like structure that shielded the upper part of the ramp from the weather.

At the far side of the roof, lined up on its low parapet, lay a half-dozen pistols. Beside them was a sack of ammunition and several containers of powder and primer.

And standing in front of them, facing me, was the one responsible for my current freedom.

Her armour shone brightly in the sunlight.

She smiled as I approached.

'Hello, David Shaw,' she said.

'Hello,' I said, 'Celebe.'

CHAPTER THIRTEEN

Renewing an Old Acquaintance

<hr/>

I helped Celebe carry the pistols and their assorted accessories down into the level immediately below the roof. I realized, as we did so, that they were the weapons that Yarissi's men had carried, the men who had died in the battle with the charlaki. I was astounded at the level of accuracy Celebe had been able to achieve with them: from the bore size and barrel length such accuracy should have been impossible. But then, Celebe – and her masters – specialized in the impossible. I also noted, rather ruefully, that the ammunition pouch I was carrying was almost empty.

'How long have you been in Zatuchep, Celebe?' I asked.

I could not imagine the weapons having lain in the street for the past six months. But if Celebe had been here all that time, why had I not heard from her sooner?

'I came to the island in the last days of the month of J'tel,' she replied.

I glanced at her.

'It is now the middle of V'reth,' she said.

I did a quick mental calculation; she had been on the island for about forty days. That seemed to me a long time.

'When first I landed,' she said, '– having come by boat from Reshek – I discovered the crew of the boat belonging to Kanaat Yarissi. They had docked in the same place that I had, which was no coincidence as it is the most easily accessible port on the northern coast of the island. The crew told me where Yarissi and his people had gone, and why they were on the island.'

'You didn't know?' I asked, surprised.

She shook her head.

'I had been out of touch with the Valley and my fellow Knights for some months,' she said, 'ever since setting out overland to meet with you. There are few Libraries in Reshek, and none of them would have shortened my route.

'I followed Yarissi's trail to Zatuchep and discovered the site of a battle. The bodies had been partially devoured, making identification impossible. Also, the elements had done their work, and I chose not to tarry. I did, however, salvage these few weapons, the only ones that were still serviceable. Most of the ammunition was ruined. Shortly after that I discovered a herd of charlaki in the neighbourhood, which explained the condition of the bodies. My enhanced senses told me much about the creatures, their artificial nature not least.'

I nodded. 'I had been wondering about that,' I said. 'I supposed them to be the survivors of some ancient experiment.'

'One out of three, David,' Celebe said. 'Yes, an experiment, but not ancient – and not survivors. A better word might be rejects.'

I must have looked puzzled.

'Daqar created them,' Celebe said. 'He has discovered on this island a huge treasure trove of malleable Y'nys, a substance that is so rare even the Knights, whose armour is made of it, do not know of any deposits still in existence.'

'*Malleable* Y'nys?' I said.

I had watched Celebe's armour mould itself to fit her form after it had been removed from her taller, more full-bodied predecessor. It had not occurred to me that the armour was made of a different kind of Y'nys crystal to the Libraries themselves; I suppose I had simply ascribed the transformation to some programmed function of the substance.

'The ancient Y'nys, it is believed,' Celebe said, 'were made from living Y'nys crystal. The substance survives today as malleable Y'nys. When in contact with a sympathetic living host, the crystal becomes quasi-organic, though it is far more durable than human tissue, and possessed of greater powers.'

I nodded; I had seen the powers of a Knight, and of a Librarian.

'What Daqar has done here is an abomination,' Celebe said. 'He has created a forced fusion between Y'nys and flesh. He has built Y'nys skeletons and grafted onto them the flesh of living charlaki.'

'Living?' I said. 'You mean they're a true species? But their skin—'

'Their coloration is a consequence of the grafting process,' Celebe said.

'Daqar told me,' I said, 'that the charlaki were an unknown species.'

'True charlaki are, indeed, rare,' Celebe said. 'I can only speculate as to their origins, but today there are perhaps only a dozen tribes left on the planet, and they tend not to live in regions frequented by humans. In their natural state, they are a gentle, peaceful race.'

I shook my head. What was Daqar that he could do something like this? I thought of the months I had spent as his prisoner, and of his psychological manipulations of me, attempts at gaining a knowledge he apparently already had. He had just wanted to see if I could be made to crack. And he had been willing to sacrifice months of his time, and the lives of several of his slaves, to answer a question that could not possibly be of any practical value.

'What is he?' I asked Celebe.

She shrugged.

'A scientist,' she said. 'Perhaps the ultimate scientist. Bereft of conscience, devoid of feeling, a slave to knowledge. He is as without mercy as he is without malice. He cares nothing for anyone, and would probably lay waste the continent simply to test a trivial hypothesis. I think you have seen something of this aspect of his character, yes?'

I shuddered.

'Yes,' I said, 'something of it.'

We stacked the arms in a small chamber on the building's top floor. There were provisions there from which Celebe offered me bread and cold meat and milk. I accepted them gratefully.

'Much has happened during the last four years,' Celebe said. 'Would you like to hear of it?'

'I would,' I said. 'How is Benza? Are the Kingdom still safe?'

'Very much so,' Celebe said. 'And as part of a plan to keep them that way your old friend, Tor Taskus, was dispatched to the lands south of Asmina with a force of a thousand men to seek out the home city of the Librarians. He located it many days' march beyond the Lost Kingdoms, those few Vohung countries that were cut off from their cousins in times past. The Librarians, who use the city only as a central meeting place and seldom actually live there, were actually rather relieved at Tor Taskus's arrival. Though immensely powerful, they are relatively few in number, and had feared massive reprisals for the actions of their late leader, Rohc Vahnn. It seems that he had had few supporters among his own people for his plans of world domination. They reported that his whole personality had changed in the year leading up to his attempted conquest, and that only Sonder and a handful of others had willingly gone along with him. It seems that he began to change at about the same time that he discovered how to teleport himself without needing to use one of the Libraries. His fellow Librarians expressed the opinion that the use of this power had unhinged his mind, and agreed to make no attempts to duplicate the feat. Tor Taskus gained from them a further assurance that from now on they would be more forthcoming with their considerable knowledge and would use their skills for the betterment of the condition of their fellow men. I suspect that the known involvement of the Thirteen in Vahnn's defeat was no small factor in helping them reach that decision.'

'And was Tor rewarded for his efforts?' I asked. Tor Taskus had been as good a friend to me as any man who had ever lived. It would please me greatly to learn that he was doing well.

'He is now a Lord,' Celebe said. 'He commands the main force of Benza's armies.'

'Excellent!' I said, genuincly delighted. 'What of Hareg of the Ladden? Is he back in Ragana-Se-Tor, or does he still dwell in the Kingdoms?'

Without Hareg and his skilful people, the *Mariner* would never have been built.

'He dwelt in Benza for over a year after your departure,' Celebe said, 'working on both the *Mariner* and the *Freedom*, carrying out repairs and then redesigning parts so that they would function more efficiently. Your ship, I am sure you will be pleased to know, is no longer quite so badly affected by adverse weather conditions as it once was.'

I laughed, remembering how the Vohung winter had incapacitated the *Mariner*'s drive mechanism.

'But Hareg is Ladden, and a nomad,' Celebe said. 'He wearied of always seeing the same horizon, and when last I heard had made his way back to his own lands.'

I nodded, hoping my one-time enemy would find what he was looking for. He had done the right thing by his former slaves, myself included, both legally and, by Vinh standards, morally. His reward for such behaviour should be in equal proportion.

'P'nad is well,' Celebe said, anticipating my next question. 'Joshima placed him in temporary command of the *Mariner* in your absence, though when you did not return he felt obliged to give the post to a fully fledged Captain.'

'P'nad deserved to command the *Mariner*,' I said. 'He was my lieutenant. And none of Benza's Captains would know her half as well as he did.'

'Which is why Joshima made him a Captain,' Celebe said.

I stared at her. She laughed. I recalled that toying with my emotional responses had always been a favourite hobby of hers. I put it down to her Gallic origins.

'Of course,' she added, 'P'nad could not become a ranking Captain overnight. But he is now, I think, well placed in Benza's hierarchy. He is popular among her warriors, and his natural diplomacy has earned him many friends.'

'What of the others?' I asked. 'S'nam – how is he?'

'Well, the last I heard,' she said, 'though no longer in Benza. He yearned for the land of his birth, and now that he was legally free, he departed soon after P'nad's promotion.'

I nodded, remembering how much S'nam had missed his old country.

'You recall Hol Krexus,' Celebe said.

I stiffened at the mention of that name. Hol Krexus, Captain, bully and woman-beater. His death at my hands was one of the few about which I felt no guilt or remorse. The man had been a disease.

'His family have declared Blood Feud against you,' Celebe said. 'Joshima was most annoyed to hear it, especially given the amount they owed him in unpaid taxes. To ensure your safety upon your return he drew up papers to have you officially adopted by one of Benza's Houses, thereby discouraging anyone from taking up the Feud.'

'Which House?' I asked, startled.

'His own,' Celebe said.

I stared at her, open-mouthed.

'I am a member of the House of the Duke of Benza?' I said in disbelief.

'I believe,' Celebe said, 'you are now one hundred and sixty-third in line for the throne.'

She grinned, and I found myself laughing. I had come to Shushuan six years ago and become a slave of the Ladden. Now I was in line for the throne of the Vohung Kingdoms.

Mention of Hol Krexus put me in mind of another 'acquaintance'.

'What of Droxus?' I asked.

'He still resides with the Thirteen,' Celebe said, more than the hint of a tremor in her voice. Celebe, better than anyone, knew what it meant to be in the power of Shushuan's Thirteen Gods.

She shook her head and leaned towards me.

'And now that we have dispensed with the trivia,' she said, 'why do you not ask me the question you really want me to answer?'

I took a breath, steeling myself.

'Mrs Catlin—?' I said.

Celebe laughed, rocking back on her heels.

'Mrs *Shaw!*' she said. 'You married her, do you recall?'

'I recall,' I said wryly.

It had been a Jandtzian wedding, entirely legal and proper by Vinh law though having no real meaning in the Kingdoms, where marriage is unknown. But somehow, to call her 'Mrs Shaw' seemed bizarre.

'She, too,' Celebe said, 'is now of the House of Joshima, due to her relationship with you. She has been given the legal Vinh name "Linna", as the Ladden called her during her time with them. And,' she added, her smile now a genuine one, 'she is well, and waiting for you.'

I closed my eyes, mouthing silent words of thanks to all the gods I knew. And then, aloud, to Celebe.

'She is in the Kingdoms?' I said. 'In Benza?'

'Far from it!' Celebe said. 'She is in Ragana-Se-Tor.'

'What?' I cried.

She was . . . here? On this side of the continent? She was separated from me by only the land of Reshek? By nothing more than a single country? I had envisioned having to battle my way across the Plains of Ktikbat, or to attempt to exploit the arcane powers of a Library. But all I actually had to do was cross the short stretch of ocean leading to the mainland and then *walk* to her? A mere two thousand miles?

'It occurred to her,' Celebe said, grinning at my excitement, 'that you would return to Shushuan in the same place that you and she had first arrived here. So, being the woman she is, she petitioned Joshima to dispatch the *Mariner* there with her aboard. She would locate the valley in which you had made your first advent and set up a camp there to await your return.'

'And Joshima agreed?' I said.

I knew Mrs Catlin was persuasive, in much the same way that an avalanche is 'persuasive', but even so . . .

'He declined,' Celebe said. 'But he did agree to send the *Freedom*, and a small troop of warriors and slaves to be her escort. The *Freedom* was to serve only as transport, however; it could not remain with her once the valley had been located. And although Joshima was willing to have it return at intervals to see if you had returned, he warned her that the intervals would not be frequent. I think once a year was his best offer.'

'She accepted,' I said, already knowing the answer; Mrs Catlin was the most wilful woman I had ever met. And the bravest, the most loyal, the most wonderful – what can I say? I loved her. Love her. Will always love her. Have, I think, always loved her.

'Naturally,' Celebe said. 'This was, perhaps, two years ago.' Her face became serious. 'David,' she said, 'the first two years were bad for her. She . . . did not take your enforced departure well. She was very depressed, very angry; she frightened me at times. Few in Benza dared approach her, though P'nad seemed always welcome. He, I think, helped her to get through those days. And then, as might be expected, she began to look for things to occupy her time, to make the waiting not so hard. She worked in Benza's library, much to the scandal of the city's scribes and scholars, and eventually earned the respect of them all.

'In time, when pragmatism had, to some extent, won out over despair, she hit upon the idea of returning to Ragana-Se-Tor. She planned a long stay there, just in case the Thirteen were in no mood to hasten your return, and as I said, Joshima gave her what little aid he could.' She laughed ruefully. 'I think he was willing, by then, to do anything to be rid of her for a while. And, too, he had shared her sadness at your absence, being not unmindful of the debt that he and all those in the Vohung Kingdoms owed to you.

'And so there she waits,' Celebe said, gesturing expansively towards the north. 'And does not even know that you and she are once again upon the same planet.'

I smiled.

'She will know soon enough,' I vowed.

Celebe became serious.

'David,' she said, 'I know how eager you are to be reunited with her—'

'Eager isn't even close to how I feel,' I said. 'It's been four years, Celebe – four *years*! I don't intend waiting any longer.'

'Be that as it may,' Celebe said, 'I am in Zatuchep on a mission of my own, a mission that is, and can be, my only priority. Until it is accomplished I cannot help you.'

'You've already helped me,' I said. 'I'll do the rest myself.'

She nodded.

'There can be nothing to keep you on this island now,' she agreed.

I hesitated, suddenly overwhelmed by guilt. My feelings for Mrs Catlin had swamped my memory of recent events.

'I can't leave,' I said, the words like a knife in my heart.

Celebe said nothing.

'I have friends here,' I said, 'who are still in Tal Daqar's power. I can't desert them.'

Luftetmek, at least, I could not abandon.

'There are more here in Tal Daqar's thrall than you know,' Celebe said. 'The charlaki, for all that they are a made race, are living creatures. Their natural development has been frustrated by Daqar, who uses them as a guard force within the city. Also, the female you know as Zalmetta – the only altered female charlak in existence at this time – has been particularly diverted from the path of her true nature.'

'In what way?' I asked.

'The aggressive nature of the altered charlaki is sex-linked,' Celebe said. 'The males all become violent when they reach maturity. In the females, this does not occur. Instead, their mental faculties increase considerably – almost in quantum leaps. Some of these faculties are hypnotic in nature, including an almost mystic control over their male counterparts. Daqar has introduced drugs into Zalmetta's diet – unbeknown to her – to subdue her higher reasoning powers. Had he not, she would not have stayed in his power. David, she is not human, and therefore not bound by Vinh slave law. And she is rational, therefore not claimable as property. In full possession of her thoughts, she would leave Daqar in an instant.'

'Why?' I asked. 'Surely, with him, with his intellect and his access to the Library network, she could have anything she wanted.'

Celebe gave a grim laugh.

'David,' she said, 'Daqar is a monster.'

I looked at her, not understanding.

'Zalmetta,' she said, 'is not.'

Realization dawned slowly. I had very badly misjudged the charlaki woman; I had indulged in the worst kind of prejudice: guilt by association.

'You know a lot,' I said to Celebe. 'How?'

'I have gained access to Daqar's Library,' she said. 'He does not yet know it, though I will be unable to keep my actions secret for much longer. He keeps detailed, meticulous notes on all his experiments. Zalmetta is his third female. The others all died, as a direct result of the drugs he uses to control their minds. It was from his notes that I learned of your own fate. David, it was not easy for me to leave you in Daqar's clutches like that, but I knew your life was not in danger, and as I said, I am here on a mission of my own. When I learned that Daqar intended showing you his airship – another psychological test, I gather – I realized that here was an opportunity to free you and, indirectly, to further my own aims.'

'Very generous of you,' I said dryly. I can never quite bring myself to trust Celebe – she is too close to the Thirteen for that – but I also never hold a grudge for those things she has been obliged to do and of which I do not approve. She has her motives, and I have mine; we occasionally walk the same road, and I am content to leave it at that. I worry, occasionally, what will happen on the day, the perhaps inevitable day, when we walk down that road in opposite directions, and find ourselves confronting one another, with no way to avoid the conflict. It is not a pleasant image.

'So,' I said, yielding to the fatalism that the moment seemed to call for, 'what do we do now?'

'We free your friends,' Celebe said. 'Then you and they leave this island with all deliberate haste.'

'And you?' I asked.

'When I am certain you are safe,' she said, '– or sooner, if necessary, though I would hesitate to place your life at risk, David – then, in order to end the threat of Tal Daqar forever, I will destroy this island entirely, and every living thing upon it.'

CHAPTER FOURTEEN

Last Bid for Freedom

In the moonless half-light of a billion nameless stars, Celebe and I stood with our backs to the ocean and stared up the sheer north face of Daqar's fortress. Behind us, and a long way down, the turbulent waters threw themselves at silver and black rocks, their rage uncontainable, their patience indefatigable. We stood upon damp, naked stone, four storeys beneath our objective. Even in daylight, I could have hesitated to attempt what we were contemplating.

Despite my previous belief to the contrary, Daqar's fortress was not devoid of windows. Thirty or more feet up the otherwise featureless wall in front of us, an open casement let onto a wide, stone-railed balcony. It had never occurred to me, when I was a prisoner in Daqar's fortress, that all of the rooms I had seen were above ground level. The seeming absence of windows had fooled me into thinking that much of it was below ground, in the maze-like network of subterranean tunnels that lay beneath the city.

I wondered why the balcony looked familiar. I was certain I had never seen it before.

Beside me, Celebe uncoiled the rope on my grappling hook. We had visited my 'grave' before coming here, and had retrieved much of my equipment. Most of the bladed weapons that I had brought – the axe, knife, and katana – were hanging from my belt. In a pouch slung over my shoulder were Celebe's half-dozen pistols and the meagre supply of ammunition for them. Conspicuous by its absence was the Desert Eagle. It had been at Celebe's suggestion that we had acquired the weapons we had, and due to her veiled warnings that I had left the Eagle and other more technological artefacts behind. I was still mindful of what she had written in her letter to me, and had no desire to introduce any Earthly anachronisms into Vinh culture, however tempting the idea might have been.

We had tied cloth around the claws of the grappling hook, but it was still going to make a far from silent contact with that stone railing. Celebe spun the hook on its rope and cast it overhead. It caught on the first try, and with somewhat less of a clatter than I had feared.

'After you,' Celebe breathed in my ear.

I grasped the rope and began to climb.

It was a difficult ascent, the sheer side of the building offering no purchase to my feet. But I was in no mood to be baulked, not after all those weeks in captivity. I went up the rope virtually hand over hand.

I cleared the stone parapet and peered in through the half-open shutters, letting my eyes adjust to the darkness within the room. It was as spacious as all the apartments in Daqar's abode, but numerous silk hangings gave it a cosy, snug atmosphere, whilst at the same time hinting at a depressingly familiar decadence . . . *I had seen this room before, but where?*

Half-hidden behind a translucent drape was a four-poster bed, big enough to sleep four people in comfort. Lying on it, tangled in silk sheets, was a black form; a mass of white hair trailed over a wide pillow.

I heard Celebe alight behind me, but I was barely conscious now of the realities of this situation, because the memories were all coming back, and with them a guilt that was almost unbearable. If those memories were true, then the mystery of where Daqar had got the plans of the *Mariner* was no mystery at all.

Moving like a man entranced, I walked stiffly around the hanging drapes, knowing what I would find on the far side of the bed.

'David—?' Celebe hissed, her tone a curious mixture of

warning and confusion. She was right behind me, but the dark form on the bed was faster than either of us. She was on her feet before I had covered half the distance from window to bed, and with a single leap had delivered a kick to my chest that sent me reeling. I crashed through anonymous bits of furniture, picking up some serious bruises in the process, and was still trying to work out what had happened when I felt her slender yet incredibly powerful arms around my throat. Blackness welled up, consciousness fading in a thunder of blood. Then the pressure was gone and I was gasping for air, my hands tearing at my collar as though it were choking me.

I glanced around, dazed, and saw Celebe moving purposefully away from Zalmetta's unconscious, naked body. I looked past them both, to the other side of the huge bed. As I had expected, there was a Library lectern standing in the corner of the room.

Celebe reached down and helped me to my feet.

'It was me,' I said miserably. 'I thought it was only a dream, but it was real. I accessed the *Mariner* file, and Daqar got all he wanted—'

'Peace, David,' Celebe said. 'I told you Zalmetta possessed hypnotic abilities. Even diminished as they are by Tal Daqar's drugs, they are formidable. If it helps, you may console yourself with the knowledge that he had to trick you in order to gain the information he wanted. I assume you did not access the file in order to turn it over to him?'

'No!' I said. 'I intended erasing it.'

Celebe gave me a wry smile, and I tried to return it, though without much success. I rubbed my throat, feeling bruises beginning to form where Zalmetta had throttled me.

'That is one tough lady,' I observed, 'and fast.'

'Fast and tough,' Celebe scoffed, 'but no lady.'

She threw a prudish glance at the charlaki woman's naked form and I smothered a laugh. As worldly as Celebe may have been, deep inside her was still a prim little French girl named Ailette. In many ways, I was glad.

She bent down over Zalmetta's unconscious body and lifted her onto a nearby settee. I kept a straight face as she cast a sheet over the charlaki's form and then sat down beside it. She took Zalmetta's head in her hands and felt at it like a phrenologist, but I knew that what she was doing was a little more scientific than that. She was 'looking' at what damage Tal Daqar had done to the creature's mind.

'Celebe,' I said, 'there's something I'm not absolutely clear on.'

'What?' she asked.

'Is Zalmetta,' I asked uneasily, 'alive?'

Celebe glanced at me. 'David,' she said, 'this is not the time for a metaphysical debate.'

'Please, Celebe,' I said, 'I need to know. Are the charlaki truly living beings?'

She sighed. 'Their skeletons are malleable Y'nys,' she said, 'which is, by your standards, not a truely organic substance – it is not carbon-based, as is all life that you know. Her flesh and organs are living, having been removed from the original creature that she was before Daqar altered her. Her mind has been enhanced by contact with the Y'nys, just as mine was, though not to as great a degree. In her natural form, she would be no more intelligent than the males you met before. David, she is undeniably intelligent, but as to whether she is alive, or sapient, I do not know. I am proceeding under the assumption that she is, but that is only an assumption.'

I nodded, not much wiser.

'And what you're doing now,' I said, 'is interfering with her brain?'

Celebe's voice carried a trace of exasperation as she said, 'I am undoing the damage Daqar's drugs have done to her brain.'

I nodded again.

'I don't like it, Celebe,' I said. 'Interfering with a living creature. It isn't . . . right. It's the sort of thing the Thirteen do as a matter of course. Even when it's well meant, it isn't right. Everyone should have the freedom to choose.'

'When I am done here,' Celebe said, her voice now cold, 'Zalmetta will have that freedom. Until then, she has not.'

I could see Celebe was getting angry – she didn't like some

of the things the Thirteen had made her do any more than I did – so I didn't pursue the argument.

Zalmetta began to stir in Celebe's hands.

'The damage is not permanent,' Celebe said. 'Reversing it will take only a few moments.'

I felt the hair stir on my scalp and arms as energies passed from Celebe's Y'nys armour into Zalmetta's body, unseen energies of unguessable power.

Zalmetta's eyes opened, the glittering ovals devoid of expression. Then, slowly, a look of astonishment and finally of horror filled her beautiful countenance, twisting her finely wrought features into a mask of dismay. She looked like someone waking from a nightmare and finding that the reality is no better.

'It's all right,' Celebe said softly, 'no blame attaches to you. But you know now what you must do.'

Zalmetta nodded slowly.

She looked across at me, seeing me for the first time.

'David,' she cried, 'I did not mean to attack you. I did not recognize you—'

'It doesn't matter,' I said.

'And the other things I have done—'

Her face was haunted, her eyes shining with an emotion beyond my understanding.

'What's going on?' I whispered to Celebe. 'What have you done?'

'The charlaki are an instinctively peaceful race,' Celebe said. 'I am using that aspect of her original personality to counter Daqar's corruption of her natural instincts. Her Y'nys conversion will help her in this; being emotionally neutral, the Y'nys can be used to amplify the emotions of its host – or, as Daqar has done, to subvert them. David, I am not manipulating her. Please keep out of my way while I do this.'

Zalmetta's expression now settled into one of grim resolve. On a human face, I might have expected to see an element of vengefulness, but there was nothing like that on the charlak's. She looked up at me.

'I will help you,' was all she said.

'If you do,' I promised her, 'I will take you away from Tal Daqar.'

'I ask nothing,' she told me. 'But I will willingly accompany you.'

'Clothe yourself,' Celebe told her.

Zalmetta arose, holding the sheet around herself, and went to the closet at the side of the room.

To Celebe, I said, 'Can you do this to any of Daqar's, uh, creations?'

'Not this effectively,' Celebe said. 'Zalmetta is, I think, the most intelligent of his followers. If Daqar should attempt to reconvert her, she will now have something with which to fight him. But as to the others – possibly Kziktzak could be saved, being the most nearly pure Y'nys, but Blukka and . . .'

'Blukka is—?' I gasped, then, 'He's not a charlak!'

'Blukka is a *human* conversion,' Celebe said. 'Daqar used the charlaki in his recent experiments only as a variation.' She glanced at me. 'Everyone on this island, with the exception of Tal Daqar and his visitors, is a creature of his making. Did you not know?'

I felt as though reality was unravelling around me. Blukka? A half-Y'nys creature? No wonder he had beaten me so soundly when we fought; I had been treating him like a human opponent.

From the far side of the room, Zalmetta said, 'I am ready.' She was 'dressed' in the same diaphanous silks and gold accoutrements she had worn when first I saw her. Celebe's expression – what little of it could be seen below her helm – was pure Ailette, but I just said, 'Then let's go.'

And so it was that the three of us presently found ourselves moving furtively down through Daqar's dwelling to the prison level – which, I now reasoned, was actually on the ground floor. Everything about the man, from the layout of his fortress to his 'servants' and his own genial image was a lie.

We came to Luftetmek first, as I had intended. He was back in our original cell, and with him were the rest of his men. It seemed that, after my escape, Daqar had lost interest in his

Resheki prisoners, and no longer felt the need to keep them isolated.

Of the nine men in the cell, Yarissi had fared the worst. He had visible signs of physical torture on him, and the imprisonment had left him weak and frail. In his eyes, however, there burned the same cold fire that I had seen there at our first meeting. I wondered how much vital information Daqar had gained from his inability to break Yarissi's spirit.

I gave the axe to Luftetmek and the knife to one of his men. The pistols we shared out as best we could, but given the paucity of ammunition for them I didn't expect their presence to be of much help. Then, with Yarissi being half-carried by two of his followers, we made our way through the fortress back towards Zalmetta's room; the thought uppermost in my mind as we went was how we would get Yarissi down that rope.

We were halfway along the passage leading up from the second floor when things went completely awry.

I heard a cry of alarm from behind us, and turned in time to see one of Daqar's servants disappearing down a side passage, his cries still audible even as they receded. Now things could get really messy; as poorly armed as we were, and with two whole levels between us and freedom, I didn't give much for our chances.

On a sudden impulse, I turned to Zalmetta and said, 'Where does Daqar store the weapons he took from the prisoners?'

'On the floor below,' she said. 'The room is locked, but I have a key.'

'Lead us there,' I said, 'as fast as you can.'

We changed direction and headed for the ramp that led down to the first floor. We encountered a group of Daqar's slaves, armed with swords, at the head of the ramp. Not wishing to announce our presence through the use of firearms, Celebe and I took the brunt of the attack, using sheer aggression as a counter to the fact that we were outnumbered on the weapons front by about three to one.

I dispatched one man in the first exchange, letting his own

momentum carry him past me even as he collapsed in death, knowing that Luftetmek was at my back and would take advantage of the situation. An instant later, he was fighting at my side, the weapon of the downed slave in one hand and the axe in the other.

For all their Y'nys-enhanced metabolisms, Daqar's regular slaves were not warriors, and although they pressed us hard it was only a matter of minutes before we had finished the last of them. With our troop now somewhat better equipped, we moved on down the ramp.

We encountered no more resistance in reaching the armoury, but as Zalmetta opened the door for us I could already hear the sound of more of Daqar's slaves approaching.

'Move swiftly,' I said to Luftetmek. 'We haven't got much time.'

I took Zalmetta and Celebe to one side, giving Luftetmek and his men time to retrieve their weapons and ammunition.

'We aren't likely to make it out the way we came in,' I said. 'That only leaves the main hall.'

'Daqar will undoubtedly expect us to try that route,' Celebe said.

'I'm open to alternatives,' I told her.

We each glanced at Zalmetta.

'There are none,' she said.

I nodded.

'Let's do it,' I said.

Luftetmek called my name, and as I turned he threw something to me. It was my sabre. He also held the belt containing my pistols and their accessories.

'Yours, I believe,' he said with a grin.

I slung the sabre over my shoulder and buckled the belt around my waist. I loaded both pistols and shoved them into their holsters.

'Is everyone ready?' I asked.

I heard Yarissi say, quietly to Luftetmek, 'Does this youth now command here?'

Luftetmek paused, not looking at me, then said, 'Within

these walls, he commands. Once outside Zatuchep, he and I will have equal standing. And I follow you, Kanaat.'

Yarissi smiled, saying nothing.

Luftetmek turned to me, cocking the hammer on his pistol.

'We are ready,' he announced.

'We're going to do this on the run,' I said. 'Zalmetta will lead, Luftetmek and I will be right behind her, then Yarissi and his men, with Celebe bringing up the rear. We stop for nothing. Work in pairs; if one man is hurt, his partner helps him. But we keep moving. Yes? Then let's do it.'

A thought occurred to me as we threw the armoury door open, a question I should have asked Zalmetta: how many men did Daqar have in his household?

Coming down the corridor towards us, from the direction in which we needed to go, was a seemingly endless tide of slaves.

Retreat was not even an option; it was advance or die – perhaps, realistically, advance *and* die.

It was Luftetmek who gave us the impetus we needed. He pushed Zalmetta to one side and emptied both of his pistols into the front rank of the oncoming slaves. At such close quarters, a pistol ball that did not hit bone could not be stopped by mere flesh. Five slaves collapsed, one struck by a ricochet off his neighbour's Y'nys skull. The psychological effect was even more telling than the physical; Y'nys skeletons notwithstanding, these human hybrids were not as formidable as their charlaki counterparts, and Luftetmek's volley had rattled them badly. Those few that still had the heart to press their attack found themselves having to climb over the bodies of their fallen comrades to do it.

Luftetmek barked an order to his men, and six pistols were levelled at the second rank of slaves. The report as all six fired simultaneously was thunderous in the narrow corridor, the air now filled with greyish-white smoke and the stink of gunpowder.

'Advance!' I yelled.

We threw ourselves forward, and so effective had been the

blow to our foes' confidence that they actually gave ground before us, despite outnumbering us by who-knew-how-many to one.

Luftetmek and I now took the point, our swords clearing a path through our enemies that brooked no opposition. The slaves were all armed with swords and knives and, in a couple of cases, spears, but they were not warriors, and their bladesmanship was primitive, to say the least. Of course, they didn't need much skill in these conditions, just a willingness to stand and fight and wait for us to tire ourselves out. And as fearful as they were of such a prospect, they were on Tal Daqar's orders, and their fear of him was the greatest of all. In the end, however long it was in coming, they could not help but be victorious.

Our brief moment of glory soon faded, and the slaves began once again to advance. Luftetmek's men worked in rotation with their leader and me, allowing each man a few moments' respite as another came forward to take his place, the confines of the passageway not allowing for more than two or three men to fight side by side on either hand.

Behind me, Yarissi had reloaded the pistols of one of his men. As I fell back briefly from the front line he pushed forward to take my place. A sword edge lashed out, and the gun in his right hand clattered to the floor, a cry of pain escaping his lips. He blasted the swordsman with his second pistol before staggering back, clutching his forearm from which blood was spurting, the sword having passed right through it. There was a blur of motion at my side, and Zalmetta was clutching Yarissi's arm in her slender fingers, pinching the wound shut.

A second man on our side went down, his skull cleft almost to the chin by one of the stronger slaves, and I hurried past his slumped form before the gap in our defences could be exploited. I impaled the offending slave as I did so, driving up inside his ribcage until my point exited behind his left shoulder. It was too extravagant a blow, prompted by an unexpected rush of adrenalin, and I paid the price for it. The blade jammed, and a second slave lunged at me with his spear. I twisted sideways, taking the point through the fleshy part of my hip instead of my abdomen as he had intended, and only a backward slash from

Luftetmek saved me. The slave collapsed, his head following him at an unnatural angle.

I pulled the spear from my side, surprised and relieved that the flow of blood that accompanied it was controllable.

The battle was rapidly going against us now, with little hope for a change in our fortunes, when I heard a voice whisper in my ear, audible even above the din of swordsteel. It was Celebe's voice.

'Step aside, David,' was all she said.

I sidestepped, parrying an attack from in front of me at the same time, and risked a glance behind me to see what Celebe had in mind.

What I saw gave fresh meaning to my concept of horror. Behind us, to a distance of thirty feet or more, the corridor was carpeted with the bodies of the slain. And as I watched, those broken and bloody corpses struggled slowly to their feet and, haltingly, like the marionettes of a bad puppeteer, they turned and shambled towards us.

Beyond them, standing alone in the passage, her head bowed, stood Celebe. Her armour, in the darkened corridor, glowed with a sickly radiance.

'Luftetmek,' I gasped, 'pull back!'

The Resheki warrior needed no second urging, and as he and his followers flattened themselves to the sides of the corridor, our erstwhile foemen shuffled leaden-footed past us and fell upon their living comrades.

What followed was slaughter of a kind I had never imagined. The dead slaves were insensible to harm, and their Y'nys skeletons made it impossible to dismember them, which would have been the only practical way of stopping them. Worse was to follow, for as each of the surviving slaves was cut down, he would rise up again and turn upon his fellows.

I glanced at Celebe; her fists were clenched to her bosom, as though in an act of intense concentration – or prayer. If the latter, I pitied her soul.

Unable to watch further, I turned to the task of tending our own wounded. Zalmetta had bound Yarissi's arm, using bits of clothing from those around her, and had fashioned a sling for him. We had lost one man in the battle, and two others had sustained minor if bloody wounds. My own injury was now beginning to pain me, and my side was growing stiff. Zalmetta tended to me with the same silent efficiency she had shown all along. I wondered at her thoughts, her feelings. Were they human in nature, or charlaki?

Or Y'nys?

That, most of all, troubled me. The Thirteen, I had become convinced after meeting them, were powerfully connected to the long-dead Y'nys race, and I trusted nothing that involved them. What part did this enigmatic female play in their unguessable plans?

The battle, if it could be dignified by such an appellation, had moved away from us, and Celebe was inching slowly forward. Her face, the little of it that could be seen below her helm, was sheened with sweat. I had never seen her sweat before. Her armour's glow was dimming, and the Y'nys crystal of which it was constructed had lost its translucence, become greyish and dull. I had seen it do that once before, when its previous wearer had died.

I caught Celebe in my arms as her knees buckled. She was heavy, but not as heavy as her appearance would have suggested. I ground my teeth against the pain as I felt my side tear, and then other hands were there as well, helping me. We lowered the Knight of the Thirteen to the floor of the passage and I stared into the triangular lenses of her eyes, behind which the light had almost gone out.

'Ailette—?' I breathed.

I had seen Celebe die once; I couldn't bear to lose her again.

'David,' she sighed.

'Why did you do it?' I said. I wanted to yell, to tell her nothing was worth this kind of sacrifice. But I couldn't bring myself to raise my voice to her.

She laughed softly.

'Don't grieve yet,' she said, her voice steady and, I

thought, a little stronger. 'The strain was considerable, but endurable.'

'Why did you do it?' I asked again.

I could see her armour changing, its dullness becoming a wash of rainbow colours that hung on the very edge of visibility.

'If I had attacked them physically,' she said, 'I would have been overwhelmed. Their bones are stronger than my armour, and there was no way to know how many of them there were. What I did was . . . difficult, but more likely to succeed.'

I stepped back as she slowly pushed herself back to her feet. She smiled at me, Ailette Legendre briefly surfacing and looking at me through the eyes of Celebe.

'I shall not forget your concern, David,' she said, her voice a whisper that only I could hear.

She glanced down the corridor. The way to Daqar's hall was now clear.

'Come,' said Celebe, 'there is not much time.'

CHAPTER FIFTEEN

The Power of Celebe

In the great hall, Celebe pointed towards the now familiar exit and said, 'Leave the city as quickly as you can. I will delay for as long as I may in what I must do, but not so long that I am prevented from accomplishing my mission.'

I nodded, knowing that Celebe would be implacable in this. It was the Will of the Gods, and Celebe was Their instrument.

'Will you join us?' I asked.

She shook her head: no.

'If I am successful,' she said, 'I will have freed the Library's travel facility long enough to make my escape that way. If not, there will not be time to leave by any other route.'

I hesitated.

'Go, Captain,' Celebe urged, 'before Daqar's reinforcements arrive.'

I took her hand in mine. The armour, I noted, though not for the first time, was warm to the touch. It seemed almost that I could feel a pulse.

'May the Bright Lady watch over you,' I said.

'And Gazig protect you, Warrior,' said Celebe.

She turned to the concealed entrance to Daqar's Library. Unseen energies passed between her and the mechanism, and with a shriek of protesting metal the doorway opened before her. Without a backward glance, she strode through the opening and out of sight.

I turned away.

'Let's go,' I said to the others.

'The Knight will not accompany us?' Yarissi asked. His face was ashen, his limbs trembling from the exertion of getting this far.

'Tal Daqar has to be stopped,' I said. 'That's her job. Ours is to get off this island while we still can.'

'I do not understand . . .' he said.

'You don't need to understand,' I snapped, 'you just need to do it. Now come on!'

Luftetmek laid a hand lightly on my arm. We exchanged a wordless glance, and after a moment I offered him a resigned nod. Together we led the way out of Daqar's fortress.

It was almost dawn when we struck out from Zatuchep across the hilly countryside towards the cove where Yarissi's ship was waiting.

Leaving the city had been a nerve-racking experience, dodging the aimlessly roving bands of charlaki, and the less aimless patrols of Daqar's slaves. But Zalmetta was an excellent guide, and her presence among us meant that any charlaki who did chance to glimpse us tended to give us a wide berth.

We passed close to the location of Daqar's airship, and I got the biggest shock of the night as we did so. The ship was gone! I could hardly credit the evidence of my eyes, and found myself speculating wildly about where it had gone, and why. There was no time to pause to investigate, so all I could do was hope that this unexpected development would in no way interfere with Celebe's plans.

My second shock came when we sighted Yarissi's ship. It had never occurred to me to wonder what kind of vessel to expect, but somewhere in the back of my mind I had been visualizing a kind of Elizabethan sailing ship, all tall masts and flapping canvas. What I found myself confronted with was about two thousand years older than that, and was very obviously not intended for use on the high seas. The ship was about eighty feet long, and perhaps ten feet wide in the beam. It had a single mast with a square sail, and in place of a rudder it had a side-mounted steering oar. It had other oars as well, because in addition to its sail the ship was rigged as a galley. Given its design, I suspected that the mainland was closer than I had previously thought.

My speculations were interrupted by the voice of Yarissi from behind me.

'The time has come, Captain of Benza,' he said, 'for you and I to settle the matter of your status.'

I turned to face him. Luftetmek stood at his side, looking uncomfortable. The other six warriors in his party were lined up behind them. Zalmetta stood off to one side, looking slightly puzzled.

'Very well,' I said.

I unslung the sabre.

'Wait—' said Luftetmek.

He turned to face Yarissi and spoke with him at length in tones too hushed for me to hear. I looked away to one side, as though unconcerned. If it came to a fight, I wanted those six warriors as rattled by my self-confidence as possible. In reality, of course, I would stand no chance. Individually, none of them was a match for me, not even, I suspected, Luftetmek, although I knew it would be close with him. But against them all I wouldn't last two minutes. I knew Zalmetta would back me up, or at least I hoped so, but if Luftetmek was even half as good as I believed him to be he would take her out before the fight even started.

Presently, Luftetmek stepped back and Yarissi looked at me once again. I waited, then returned his gaze. He seemed resolved, but not happy.

'Your only desire,' he said, 'is safe passage to Ragana-Se-Tor?'

I nodded: yes.

'You have no interest in the affairs of Reshek,' he said, 'and no intention of involving yourself in our current difficulties?'

'None whatsoever,' I assured him.

He glanced at Luftetmek, who met his gaze unflinchingly. I knew that Yarissi's next words would seal my fate one way or the other.

'Very well,' the Kanaat said, 'you may accompany us to Xacmet, the Resheki capital. There, we will draw up papers that will grant you safe passage through our lands. But understand this, Captain: should you encounter the followers of the Bagalamak, they will treat you as our ally, and thus as their enemy. In truth, there is no such thing as "safe passage" through Reshek at this time.'

I reslung the sword and stepped forward.

'I accept your generous offer,' I said. 'For the rest, I will trust to the Will of the Thirteen and my own abilities.'

I offered him my left hand, swordsman style, since his right was currently in a sling; I knew he was no warrior, but I couldn't dismiss from my mind the memory of how he had gained that injury, and the gesture I made now was intended as a genuine compliment. I saw Luftetmek smile, and after a moment Yarissi did too. He took my outstretched hand in a grip that was surprisingly firm.

'And now,' I said, 'we must hurry. Whatever Celebe has planned, I don't think we want to be anywhere near here when it happens.'

Three hours later we were on the open sea connecting Kai to the Thek mainland. The sun had long passed its zenith and was low on the horizon to my left. I was watching the island intently, deeply concerned for Celebe. If she did not escape, I would never even know it.

'David Shaw—?'

I turned to see Luftetmek approaching me down the narrow length of the boat. As I did so, I was suddenly conscious of an intense heat on my back, and an ink-black shadow leaping from my body across the boards of the boat. Luftetmek's face reflected a dazzling light and he threw his hands over his eyes.

'Gazig's immortal blood!' he swore.

I turned, one hand raised to shield my eyes. A pillar of incandescent light, tens of miles high and still rising, stood where the city of Zatuchep had once been. It was spreading outwards as well as upwards, consuming the island to one side and encroaching upon the ocean on the other. Steam rose in a vast cloud behind the pillar of light, and between the island and our boat I could see a mighty swell beginning to rise.

I looked back into the body of the boat. The men at the oars had stopped rowing.

'Row!' I yelled.

No one moved, each man's gaze fixed with incredulity and fear on the southward horizon. I ran down to the rowing station and yanked the lead man to his feet. I shook him until his teeth rattled and finally his eyes fixed on mine.

'As you value your life,' I said, 'row.'

He nodded, his face still sick with fear. I pushed him down again and he took hold of his oar.

'Row,' I yelled at the man behind him.

Two or three of the oarsmen were trying to pull, but it was a disjointed effort, and was doing little to advance our progress.

From the stern I heard a voice say, with more composure than I could muster at that moment, 'Cease rowing.'

Yarissi moved between the banks of oarsmen until every eye was on him. Then he turned and said, 'Row.'

Every oar went into the water.

'Captain,' Yarissi said to me, 'would you be so good as to set the beat?'

I had noticed the absence of a hortator, or timekeeper, on the boat, and had put it down to the fact that this was not a war galley and was thus unlikely to have more than one speed.

'Slow time,' I said, and began to call out the cadence. As soon as everyone was pulling in time I said, 'Increase,' and picked up the pace.

I glanced at Yarissi. He was looking to the south. He turned to face me.

'A little faster, I think, Captain,' was all he said.

'Maximum beat,' I called, and the men rowed faster, keeping time to the beat as I called it out.

I could hear a strange, rushing sound, seeming to come from nowhere yet filling the air all around us. I felt the hair stir on my body, an itchy sensation creeping across my skin.

'Faster!' I yelled, calling out a beat that my own Marines would have been hard pressed to sustain for long.

Yarissi's voice behind me said, too calmly, 'Never mind, Captain.'

I turned. The only thought that came to me was, *where did the horizon go?* Then I saw the white water at the top of the wave just before it hit us.

CHAPTER SIXTEEN

Things Get Worse

>===<

'David. Wake up, David. David. Wake up. David. David!'

I opened my eyes. I seemed to be going up and down on some kind of slow-motion rollercoaster. In addition, I was being shaken roughly by the shoulder. And even though my eyes were now open, all I could see was fog.

I shrugged off the offending hand and rubbed my eyes. I tried opening them again, in time to get a face full of salt water. I spat it out, coughing, and discovered pain in my chest.

'Move cautiously, David,' said the voice, which I now recognized as Zalmetta's. 'I think you were struck in the ribs, so you may be in some pain.'

'That,' I winced, 'is an understatement.'

I looked around. Zalmetta and I, together with two warriors and one of the ship's sailors, were lying on a fair-sized section of the ship's hull. Not far away, clinging to the remains of the mast, were Yarissi, Luftetmek, and three sailors. Beyond them, in the water, swimming towards us, were five or six unidentifiable figures; from the way they moved I guessed them to be sailors. We seemed to be the only survivors.

'We have a problem, David,' Zalmetta said.

I laughed, stifling a groan as my ribs protested. 'Is this your day for understatements, or something?' I asked her.

The humour, it seemed, was lost on her. 'Look up there,' she said, gesturing skyward.

I turned my head, finding new aches in my shoulders, and

stared in the direction she was pointing. About a mile away, and skimming almost along the surface of the ocean, was Daqar's airship. That its movements were purposeful and directed was obvious. That it was looking for us was, it seemed, under the circumstances, likely.

'He got away,' I said numbly.

'He left Zatuchep before our escape,' Zalmetta said. 'I am sorry, I should have told you. But—' She shrugged helplessly. 'He was still my master.'

'If he captures you,' I said, 'he will make you his slave again.' I looked at her pointedly. 'You understand what I am saying?'

There was a level of fear in her expression as she looked at the circling airship that told me she knew exactly what I was saying. Even so, she forced herself to look at me and say, 'That airship is your best – perhaps your only – chance for survival.'

'Personally,' I said, 'I'd rather take my chances with the ocean than end up in Daqar's clutches again.'

I said it for her benefit, but it was the literal truth. Even if she hadn't been with us, I would not have accepted Daqar's aid. Better to drown than to be at his tender mercies again.

'He sees us!' Luftetmek called.

I looked to the airship again, and sure enough it was now bearing down on our position. I wondered how he was flying it so low with no ballast weights visible. Its lower wings were almost in the water.

'What weapons have we got?' I called.

Luftetmek waved his pistol, which might or might not have been in working order after a dunking in the ocean. My own pair would be in as dubious a condition, likewise those of the other two warriors with me. And that, apart from our assorted swords and knives, seemed to be it.

Daqar's ship came to a halt directly above us. The hull was still only partially completed, but its drive section was obviously fully functional. I wondered how many crewmen he had, and how well armed they were. Zalmetta had said that Daqar had left Zatuchep before our escape, yet it was inconceivable that he could have known of the impending destruction of the island by

Celebe. So this must have been a simple test flight, a shakedown before completing the construction of the hull. That made sense: access to the drive was less easy with the hull in place. If I was right, then it was unlikely Daqar had more than a single watch on board.

A belly hatch opened, and a rope ladder was flung out. Then a second and a third. Men began to descend. They were slaves, armed with swords and knives; wielding them, hanging from those ladders, would not be easy. Was it possible we might actually have a chance?

The man descending the ladder that fell between Zalmetta and me was the first to reach us. He swung around, one hand held out to us. Obviously, he did not expect anyone to refuse aid under these circumstances.

I met his gaze, my sword leaving its sheath with a whisper of steel.

'Leave this place or die,' I told him.

He looked at me in disbelief. I jabbed him in his outstretched arm, drawing a trickle of blood. He snatched the hand back, glaring at me. Beyond him, the men descending the aft ladder had reached their objective, placing them almost within reach of Yarissi and Luftetmek, whose battered mast was drifting steadily toward us.

The man above me went for his sword. I ran him through.

From above I heard a voice call out, 'Bring me the Benzan Captain. Kill the rest.'

So, I thought, *Zalmetta has become expendable*. Not that it made a difference to our plans, but it did rather vindicate my position where Daqar's 'help' was concerned.

Men now swarmed down the rope ladders, which whipped about under the extra weight so ferociously that it became increasingly difficult to avoid their attack. Several of them actually leaped into the water, attempting to outflank us as we struggled to fight off our airborne attackers. Luftetmek and the other survivors put up a valiant defence, but I was the object of this attack and it seemed I had my work cut out for me. Only the fact that they were trying to take me alive gave me an edge.

I managed to get a footing on the planks of the bit of hull that was our life-raft and then, with those extra few feet of reach, I was able to take the fight to our enemies. I slashed and cut wildly at the slaves as they came down the ladders, hacking sections out of the ladders themselves so that the slaves could not reach us so easily. The sea around me was scarlet with blood, and the bodies of Daqar's men bobbed grotesquely on the discoloured waves.

A lucky blow from a sword hilt caught me across the temple and I staggered on the decking, my balance deserting me. A second impact, aimed for my chin but taking me instead in the shoulder, sent me into the water, and only years of training kept me from dropping my sword in blind panic. Instead, I kicked with my legs and broke the surface of the water, thrashing about wildly at unseen targets. A rope fell around me, instantly tightening and jerking me roughly out of the water. It had encircled my right arm, making it impossible to use my sword, and was also partially around my neck. The pressure of it was sending waves of dizziness and nausea through me, and I knew that unconsciousness was not far away.

Something slammed into me, but I was too weak now to fight it. The rope swung sickeningly, spinning around under the added weight, and then I was falling, the object which had hit me wrapping itself around me with what I now identified as a pair of very strong arms. We hit the water, and then I was being dragged back towards the comparative safety of the raft. I got my eyes open in time to see Zalmetta, a knife held between her teeth, hauling me onto the decking. The air suddenly rang with a volley of gunshots, followed by the sound of bodies falling into the sea all around me. I got a grip on the makeshift raft and looked up. Luftetmek's men had managed to load their pistols and, miraculously, most of them were still able to fire. I didn't know how big Daqar's crew complement was, but he had already lost eight or nine men, with a half-dozen more nursing debilitating injuries, and I didn't see how he could sustain these kinds of losses for long.

My thoughts were prophetic, for at that instant the ship began to rise, the ladders being pulled up into the belly hatches with the survivors still clinging to them. The ship surged forward and, as it continued to rise, turned its prow northwards. The last view I had of it was its twin propellers, still accelerating, as it faded into the distance.

I turned my gaze to Luftetmek and Yarissi. Luftetmek was sitting astride the mast, sword still drawn, his arm bloody to the elbow. There was a nasty-looking wound running across his chest, and his face was pale. I felt my heart sink at the sight – he needed medical attention, and quickly, if he was to survive.

I called out to one of the sailors who clung to the mast.

'How far to Reshek?' I demanded.

He looked around at the circular, featureless horizon. Then he shrugged, pointed, and said, 'Thirty torbiks that way.'

I hoped he was right, because Luftetmek's only hope lay in our reaching the mainland before he bled to death.

We transferred everybody to the remains of the ship's mast, tore up the section of hull to make crude paddles, and then set out northwards.

The going was slow, painful and infinitely dispiriting. Zalmetta was tireless, and the surviving sailors had the fatalistic bent necessary to keep them going long after exhaustion should have claimed them. Even Yarissi took his turn, though his efforts were little more than a token gesture.

Zalmetta made Luftetmek as comfortable as possible, binding the wound as best she could with bits of our clothing, her knowledge of human anatomy and the rudiments of first aid being quite considerable. Once she had completed her ministrations she turned Luftetmek over to Yarissi, who kept a constant watch over his Champion, ensuring that the warrior remained conscious and renewing his dressings as often as our primitive resources would allow.

We had no food and no water, and only the most rudimentary means of establishing our course and position.

Twenty-four hours after the attack by Tal Daqar's airship, we sighted the coast of Reshek.

*   *   *

We landed on what appeared to be a desolate stretch of infinitely wide beach, nothing to either east or west offering much hope for the medical help that Luftetmek very urgently needed.

'There is a town five torbiks inland,' said one of the sailors. 'It has a doctor who once plied his trade on the ocean. He is used to sewing up men with wounds such as this.'

'Luftetmek won't survive a journey like that,' Yarissi said.

I turned to the sailor. 'Can you find the town,' I said, 'and bring the doctor here?'

'Of course,' he replied.

'Do it,' I told him.

He glanced around once, as though orienting himself, and then moved off as fast as his weary limbs would carry him.

A thought occurred to me as I watched him go. I turned to Yarissi, who was kneeling beside Luftetmek's supine form.

'Can we trust him to return?' I asked.

Yarissi looked up at me; there were times, and this was one of them, when something in his gaze frightened me.

'Yes,' was all he said.

CHAPTER SEVENTEEN

Reshek

———◦◦◦◦———

It was some hours before the sailor returned. By then we had carried Luftetmek off the beach and into the limited shelter afforded by a group of stunted trees growing in the nearby grasslands. He was no worse now than he had been for the past hours, but no better either, and in a quiet corner at the back of my mind I was preparing myself for the possibility of his not surviving another night.

When the sailor returned he brought with him the promised doctor who, despite being very old and unbelievably wrinkled – and of a disposition that would have made a gryllup blush – he was one of those rare and talented people who was so adept at his chosen trade that he radiated confidence like a tangible force. Now, for the first time, I believed Luftetmek had a chance.

Less welcome were the others who accompanied him to our makeshift camp. There were three of them, warriors, clad in the drab grey tunics of Reshek – but with a difference: each man's accoutrements, from helmet to boots, were a polished, glossy black. Even the hilts and guards of their swords had been enamelled to match. There was an unpleasant ostentation in this form of self-decoration, a hint of something corrupt in the men who aspired to it. That it was a badge of office of sorts I sensed from the very first, and soon had it confirmed.

'Who commands here?' asked the first of the three, whose accoutrements marked him as a lieutenant of some kind.

'This is Luftetmek, Captain Champion of the Kanaat,' said

Yarissi, which seemed to me an odd way to answer the question, given Yarissi's own status.

'And you—?' the lieutenant asked him.

'I am Yarissi,' the Kanaat replied.

The lieutenant hesitated for the briefest of instants before bowing to the Kanaat.

'Greetings from Kanaat Kandirak,' said the Lieutenant. 'He has left standing orders at all coastal prefectures that you be hastened back to Xacmet upon your return from your great mission. Any assistance I can render—'

'Who are you?' Yarissi asked. 'I do not recognize your uniform. And what means "prefecture"?'

I was getting uncomfortable with the way this was going. Under the lieutenant's studied courtesy there lurked a thinly veiled contempt. And things in Reshek, it seemed, had changed in Yarissi's absence.

'Kanaat,' the lieutenant said, 'I am second sub-prefect Gelmek. My uniform is that of the recently formed filinta, a special body within the regular army answerable only to Kanaat Kandirak. We were formed following the fall of House Bagalamak when it was learned of their many plots to infiltrate the regular army. A great many traitors to . . .'

'House Bagalamak has fallen?' Yarissi said; he seemed stunned.

'It no longer exists, Kanaat,' Gelmek said proudly. 'All references to it are being expunged from our histories. It will be obliterated from the memory of man.'

Yarissi tried in vain to rally his thoughts.

I asked, 'What of these prefectures?'

The man looked at me as though seeing me for the first time.

'What are you?' he asked.

I considered ignoring the insult, not rising to the obvious challenge. But not seriously.

'Captain of Benza,' I replied. Adding, 'What were you?'

He saw my hand resting lightly on my sword hilt. He glanced around the camp; we were all worn out and in no fit state to fight, but there wasn't a friendly eye directed at him. I think he knew his life hung on his next words.

'I meant no insult,' he said blandly. 'We do not see many foreigners in Reshek these days.'

It wasn't quite an apology, but I decided it was enough. I tucked my hand into my belt and felt the level of tension in the air ease a little.

'Must I repeat my question?' I asked, smiling thinly.

He seemed to wonder which question I meant, then said, 'Following the discovery of the traitors in the military, and their many sympathizers in the ruling Houses, Kanaat Kandirak found it necessary – though regrettable – to create the filinta, using only picked men whose loyalty to the Kanaat was beyond question, and then declare martial law. To facilitate the change of leadership in the outlying regions, he divided up the outer country into prefectures, each under the direct control of the Captains in the filinta, who were now known as Prefects. The rank of Captain,' he added, giving me a nervous glance, 'being associated as it was with the old ways and all that they stood for, has now been abolished.'

'Martial law?' Yarissi said.

He was visibly shaken by what he had heard, and on top of his exhaustion and the torture he had suffered at Tal Daqar's hands I did not think he would be up to making any big decisions in the near future. I began to worry about my own position, and that of Zalmetta. Zalmetta! The lieutenant – my apologies, the second sub-prefect – had not yet seen Zalmetta, who was hiding behind us in the shadows. How we were going to explain her was a question I didn't feel up to addressing right at that moment, but I knew that in the next few minutes I was going to have to do just that.

The doctor chose that moment to look up from what he was doing – which was to sew up the worst of Luftetmek's lacerations – and say, in a voice like someone sharpening a knife on a coarse stone, 'This man needs carrying. Who's up to it?'

The sub-prefect looked at the doctor with obvious distaste and said, 'My men will tend to that task.' He cast a furtive glance at Yarissi and added, 'It is the least we can do for the Kanaat's Champion.'

If Yarissi was supposed to be impressed by the man's devotion then the comment was wasted. The Kanaat wore the aspect of a man who has just managed to convince himself that the inconceivable had not only happened, but that it had proved a dozen times worse in reality than in even his worst nightmare.

'We must return to Xacmet with all possible haste,' he said. To the doctor he said, 'How soon will my Champion be fit to travel?'

I was so used to the adulation shown by Yarissi's followers for their Kanaat that the look on the doctor's face as he turned to answer was genuinely shocking. He detested Yarissi, and with a vehemence that fairly leaped across the space between them.

'I'm an old man,' he spat, 'not a miracle worker. He'll mend at his own pace. All I can do is help. And I'd do that for any man, whatever his rank.' He paused, then added, 'Even a slave.'

This seemed to be some kind of particular insult, but in what way I couldn't begin to guess. Gelmek, it appeared, was better informed, and smothered a grin. Then, as though realizing this was not an appropriate response, he cuffed the old doctor viciously across the head.

'That's enough of your tongue, old man,' he snapped.

'Let him be,' Yarissi said, a weariness in his voice that was in no way physical. 'Slave I am, and slave I remain, until this land of ours is once again governed by the law, and not the whim of a degenerate ruling House.'

'That day is here, Kanaat,' Gelmek said proudly, while I tried to take in what Yarissi had just said. 'Under Lord Kandirak's rule—'

'Lord—?' Yarissi all but yelled.

'Uh, yes Kanaat,' said Gelmek, blushing scarlet. 'The Kanaat decided, uh, that as leader – I mean, co-leader – of the new ruling House . . .'

'What House?' Yarissi demanded.

'House Tchelnet,' Gelmek said, his voice almost a whisper. Yarissi glanced at me.

'Kandirak's family name,' he informed me, although I had already guessed as much.

'Your House too, Kanaat,' Gelmek said, sounding pleased for Yarissi. 'With the abolition of the ruling Houses, your own, uh, contract became void. Lord Kandirak – as was his legal right – purchased it from the office of the Slave Master. You and he are now of the same House, making your alliance all the stronger.'

Yarissi said nothing, but I could read his thoughts in the very set of his body. He and Kandirak were of the same House, but Kandirak was its master and Yarissi was, incredibly, no more than a slave. I couldn't fathom any of it. Luftetmek was a warrior, a Captain, yet he – and his men – followed a slave? How could it have happened? What monstrous tyranny had the Bagalamaks perpetrated on their race that a slave could raise an army and overthrow them?

Yarissi turned once again to the doctor, who was nursing his head. I couldn't say I blamed him; that slap would have shaken *me* up.

'How soon?' was all he asked.

The doctor glanced at him, then at Luftetmek. He sighed.

'Ten days,' he offered.

I saw Yarissi draw a breath to protest, to argue. Then, as he looked down at Luftetmek, he let the breath out again.

'Very well,' he said.

Gelmek said, 'We could leave your Champion at the town, Kanaat, and go on . . .'

'No,' Yarissi said. 'I will not abandon the one who has been my most loyal follower. We will wait until he can travel.' He looked at Gelmek, and the steel was back in his eyes. 'And then,' he said icily, 'we will visit my Lord Kandirak at Xacmet.'

The town of Abeyz was a fishing community, and to say that it had seen better days was a brutal understatement. The harbour was all but choked with the wrecks of various ships and boats, scarcely a handful still plying their trade. Few of the populace seemed to be in work, the narrow cobbled streets rife with beggars – and others, those whose method for seeing that cash changed hands followed a more direct route. Not that there seemed to be much cash in evidence, or material wealth of any kind. I kept looking around for any sign of a well-to-do landholder who could be blamed for this level of poverty, but everyone in Abeyz seemed to be existing on much the same level. There were a few of Gelmek's filinta prowling the streets – usually in groups of three or four – but despite their shiny accoutrements they seemed no better off than their fellow citizens.

The doctor lived in a one-storey hovel close to the docks, and it was there that we took Luftetmek. Yarissi wanted to stay with his Champion, but the doctor's abode was scarcely big enough for two men, let alone three. Satisfying himself that Luftetmek was in good hands – something I had been convinced of from the old man's first appearance – he let Gelmek lead us off to another part of town. This, it seemed, was where the Prefect and all his sub-prefects, and second sub-prefects, and under sub-prefects, and . . . well, just about everyone in his household, it seemed, all of whom had 'prefect' on the end of their title, lived and, for want of a better word, worked.

It was no more hospitable, and certainly no grander, than any other part of the crumbling town, but here at least there was an air of businesslike efficiency, of purpose, of a grand scheme unfolding. I took one look and decided I would rather sleep elsewhere.

Zalmetta stood at my shoulder, her expressionless eyes taking in her surroundings, her face and body giving away nothing of her reaction to what she saw. It occurred to me that this might be her first experience of the world outside Zatuchep, or at least her first opportunity to interact with that world. I wondered how the reality compared to the data she had undoubtedly studied in Daqar's Library.

As to how that reality reacted to Zalmetta herself, we had Yarissi to thank for finding the explanation of her that had eluded me. No sooner had one of Gelmek's men spotted her – and drawn his sword, a startled oath on his lips – than

Yarissi stepped forward and turned the tables rather neatly in our favour.

'Trouble her not,' he had said, a rare note of imperious command in his voice. 'She is blessed of the Thirteen, and must not be molested. You recall the reason for my mission to ancient Kai?' Gelmek had nodded, eyes wide with superstitious awe. Yarissi made a gesture towards Zalmetta that was at once a revelation and a benediction. Gelmek stared at Zalmetta as though suddenly finding himself in the very presence of one of the Thirteen. I smothered a smile; I had not expected Yarissi to be such a showman – or such an actor.

Now, standing in the courtyard of the Prefect of Abeyz, I prayed for Yarissi to show the same kind of fervour here. If he did not, I anticipated having to fight my way through the twelve hundred miles of Resheki territory that lay between me and Ragana-Se-Tor. Not a pleasant prospect, but better than the only alternative that Shushuan had ever offered me under previous, similar circumstances.

The Prefect, when he finally emerged, was a bit of a shock. I had been expecting a warrior of Gelmek's ilk, but instead I now found myself confronted by a short, somewhat rotund individual with an unruly ruff of white hair and the kind of florid complexion that suggested too close an affinity with red wine and potent cheese. Smiling broadly, and sweating profusely, the Prefect rushed up to Yarissi and took him by the hand.

'Kanaat!' he enthused. 'A pleasure, a true pleasure – and an honour, oh yes, a real honour – to meet the architect of our glorious new future! If we had but known you were coming I could have prepared a feast, a banquet – and games, like those once famous in Xacmet itself, though not of course as degenerate as those of the Bagalamak, oh no, nothing like that. Plays perhaps, or a circus – there are Travellers in the region, possibly I could send out riders . . .'

I was struggling to keep a straight face as this impromptu speech rambled on and on, and the puzzled look Zalmetta was giving me didn't help matters – she, it seemed, could read my facial expressions a lot better than I could read hers.

Yarissi finally managed to disentangle his hand from the Prefect's and, with a diplomacy that was remarkable after all he had learned in the past hours, cut short what looked like turning into a marathon address.

'Such celebrations, my friend, are premature,' he said gently. 'But I thank you for the warmth of your greeting, and look forward to the day when the future of which you speak is an everyday reality. For the present, we have travelled far and under circumstances not entirely pleasant. If you could show us to our quarters—'

'Of course, of course,' the Prefect enthused. 'This way, please, everyone, this way—'

He led us through a ramshackle loggia that ran most of the full length of the front of his domicile – actually, it was little more than a wooden awning atop a dozen irregularly shaped stone columns, but I could imagine that it had looked better at some time in the past, say five or six centuries in the past – and into the dimly lit and not very well maintained interior. If this was the 'glorious future' of which he had spoken so animatedly I dreaded to think how bad things had been before this new Golden Age.

We came finally to a large, sparsely furnished chamber on the first floor, irregularly partitioned into individual sleeping areas. I gathered these were the Prefect's guest quarters. I could only assume a lot of his guests had been staying away lately.

'I hesitate to mention such a matter to you, Kanaat,' the Prefect said, suddenly looking even more self-conscious than ever, 'but ever since the declaration of martial law we have had to impose a curfew upon the populace. Civil unrest and all that, enemies in every quarter, never know who might be spying for the traitors in the military, that sort of thing. We would not dream of applying it to you, of course, but for your own safety – accidents will happen, and so forth – perhaps you could confine yourself . . .'

'Say no more,' Yarissi said. I couldn't help but think he meant it literally.

It took another ten minutes of bowing and scraping for the

Prefect finally to leave us alone, and when he was gone we all stood and looked silently at one another for some considerable time.

Hours later, I lay on my bed and stared up at the spider-infested ceiling, unable to sleep. I had killed as much time as I could in cleaning my weapons and, as far as possible, stripping the pistols to make sure the salt water had not damaged them. After that, and perhaps the least appetizing meal I had ever been offered, there was very little else to do. No one felt much like conversation, though the four sailors – who were not, it turned out, natives of Abeyz, but were from a larger town to the east – exchanged a few desultory comments on the mess that the country seemed to have got itself into while they were away. One of them seemed to decide that remarks of this nature might not be entirely appropriate with the Kanaat sitting not ten feet away and shushed the others to silence. After that, there wasn't much left to do but turn in for the night. Yarissi's two remaining warriors, as though deeply conscious of Luftetmek's absence, gave him a close-order honour guard and, apparently, set up a rotating watch for the remainder of the night.

I must have drifted off at some point, because the next thing I was conscious of was waking up. And in that brief moment of transition between sleep and wakefulness, as my mind free-associated all the jumble of memories that had been crammed into it during the last few years, three disjointed yet inextricably linked thoughts came to me, and with them the solution to one of my more recent puzzles: Mrs Catlin – and Celebe – had expected me in Ragana-Se-Tor, at the place where she and I had first come to Shushuan; the would-be conqueror Droxus had told me that the rift between worlds could be made unstable by certain natural occurrences, such as tectonic activity; and during the winter following my return to Earth, there had been a minor earthquake in the north of England. I woke up smiling; it seemed that not even the 'omniscient' Thirteen knew everything.

(It was hours later that I realized how inappropriate that

smile had been: the first thing I had encountered on this visit had been a message from the Thirteen, left right where they knew I would find it.)

'David—?'

I looked around, startled, and became aware of what it was that had awoken me. Zalmetta was standing at the entrance to my cubicle, eyes glowing in the half-light. I noticed, not for the first time, her disconcerting ability to become almost invisible in anything but direct illumination.

'May I speak with you?' she asked.

I sat up uneasily, but I could hardly refuse to hear her out.

'Certainly,' I said, putting more warmth into my tone than I actually felt.

She moved to the bed and sat down on its edge; I thought I detected a hint of tension beneath her natural grace and poise.

'Your customs confuse me,' she said, apropos nothing that I could think of, 'and at times do not appear to conform with those of the known Vinh races.'

'*My* customs—?' I said; I had thought she meant human customs generally.

'I have studied the habits and social mores of the Vohung Kingdoms,' she went on, 'and you appear an atypical example of a Benzan.'

I stared at her, lost for a reply.

'You are,' she said, 'monogamous?'

'Now, look—' I began; this was getting seriously strange.

'Were you not,' she went on, 'I would not need to speak of this. You see, I believe I owe you an apology, for things I did while still under the influence of Tal Daqar.'

I was struck by an odd dichotomy in her manner; she displayed no *need* to apologize, as though she was speaking entirely for *my* benefit, yet her sincerity was undeniable.

'You may recall,' she said, 'certain dreams—'

I felt my fists clench at the memory of how I had been tricked into betraying the plans for the *Mariner*.

'Yes,' she said, 'I see you do. They were not, in fact, dreams, though you were never fully conscious during those times. It was my master's desire that I seduce you—'

'What—?'

'Be at ease,' she said, almost laughing, 'I had no intention of doing so – David, forgive my bluntness, but I find you no less repulsive than any other male of your species. I respect you as a sapient being, but I could never think of you in those terms.'

'Oh,' I said, trying not to sound too crestfallen.

'Surely you do not regard me—?' She seemed genuinely startled.

'I find you extremely beautiful,' I told her. 'But it makes no difference what I think, because you were right: I *am* monogamous.'

'I sensed it from the first,' she said, 'and used that as my excuse to Daqar. Your loyalties run deep, David; you know of my mental powers?' I nodded. 'They are more instinctive than intellectual, but they are seldom wrong. I knew that only through trickery or misdirection could my master's aim be achieved. I took a part of his seduction plan and wove a trap of my own for you. By taking you from your place of incarceration to one of peace and serenity, and with my presence used only as a mental cue rather than as an overt promise, I was able to lower your resistance to the point where you behaved in an uncharacteristically reckless fashion—'

'Not *that* uncharacteristic,' I muttered.

'And it is for this,' she concluded, 'that I offer my apologies. I was as much a pawn of Tal Daqar as you were, but if I had simply done as he had asked, his plan would undoubtedly have failed. Instead, I protected myself at your expense. I am, truly, sorry.'

I looked long and hard into her featureless eyes, and she didn't look away. After what should have been an embarassingly long time, yet somehow wasn't, I shrugged.

'I accept your apology,' I said. 'Frankly, I don't believe you have anything to apologize for, but I accept it anyway.'

I wanted to add that I was relieved she had made the choice she had; Daqar, I was convinced, would have found some way to get what he wanted anyway, but at least this way no further harm had been done to Zalmetta's mind. I couldn't forget the things I had once thought about her, beliefs held and felt for no better reason than her association with Daqar himself; Celebe had set me straight on those matters, and my rashness of judgement still bothered me. All of this I wanted to say, but I didn't. Because, in truth, I now found myself remembering something else: how little Celebe could be trusted to know the whole truth in these matters. Once again, as had been the case when first we met, we were both pawns in the games of the Thirteen, Celebe's 'Knighthood' granting her no more power of free will than that possessed by either Zalmetta or myself.

CHAPTER EIGHTEEN

The Fate of the Bagalamak

It was five days before Luftetmek was well enough to travel again, and at that he was far from recovered. Had not Yarissi's need to reach Xacmet been so pressing I do not think he would have subjected his Champion to the rigours of the journey so soon. I think Luftetmek knew this too, and he vehemently protested that not only was he well enough to travel but that anyone who questioned it was welcome to take him on in single combat to prove it. None of us felt inclined to accept.

I had my own reasons for wanting to get underway as soon as possible, but any suggestion of my going on alone was out of the question. Aside from the nightly curfew, I had no papers and no legal status. Both of these could only be obtained in Xacmet, where the Slave Master for this region would officially decide my place in Resheki society. This was common practice when visiting a foreign land uninvited or with no letters of introduction. Of course, unless a state of war existed between the two countries in question it was unlikely that a free citizen, especially one with the rank that I could claim, would be in danger of losing his freedom. The problem with Reshek at the moment was that everyone in the country was presently undergoing a re-evaluation of his or her status – and that, it appeared, included visitors.

When we finally set out northwards – Xacmet lying some two hundred miles to the north-east, but not easily accessible in a straight line from Abeyz – our party consisted of Yarissi, Luftetmek, the two surviving warriors from their original party, myself and Zalmetta, and a pair of Gelmek's filinta. To travel without at least one of these representatives of what I was already coming to think of as the Secret Police would have been to risk summary imprisonment should we be spotted by any of their wandering patrols. Not even Yarissi's presence would afford us any protection, since he had no means of official identification, and in a country like Reshek his actual physical appearance would not be familiar to everyone.

Before we left I spent some time talking with Gelmek, ably assisted by such liquor as could be obtained in Abeyz, and found out something of the mood in the country. Yarissi's original plan, to re-establish the old traditions, was still widely regarded as the only possible future for the country, but the realities of the new regime as typified by the filinta and the constant proclamations of Kandirak and his more militaristic Prefects were sitting well with no one. There was little likelihood of a revolt against the revolt, as it were, but that was due more to the effect of Kandirak's iron-fist-in-a-chainmail-gauntlet approach than to the actual will of the people – it was difficult to rally support for a cause when informants lurked in every group and a visit from the filinta was tantamount to a death sentence.

That said, one of the things we noticed during our journey was the constant unrest and, in some towns, actual armed conflict, with the filinta and their supporters on one side and the Old Guard, for want of a better term, on the other. These reactionary elements, clinging to titles and offices that Kandirak had unilaterally abolished, might have succumbed with little or no resistance to Yarissi's brand of revolution, but faced instead with a fight-or-lose-everything situation they had chosen to fight. And some of the general populace, perhaps as a response to the more excessive acts of Kandirak's followers, had joined them.

For Yarissi, these scenes were heartbreaking. He seemed scarcely able to believe the changes that had occurred in Reshek in the short time he had been away. That so much could have happened so quickly was almost inconceivable.

Everywhere that we went, whether in sprawling cities or isolated farming hamlets, we encountered the most grinding poverty I had ever seen. Meat was a forgotten luxury, and crops died in the fields while men fought running battles across the landscape. Retribution followed hot on the heels of any act of sedition against Kandirak's rule, and every act of retribution brought fresh resistance from the dispossessed and disenfranchised ex-Lords of the old ruling Houses. It was insane, an internecine strife that could only end in the desolation of the whole country.

But as bad as things were, nothing could have prepared us for our eventual first sight of the Resheki capital, Xacmet. It was a mighty white-stone-walled metropolis, ten times the size of a Vohung city, its simple yet elegant buildings ranging from single-storey chalets to towers nine and ten storeys high. That it had known greatness was undeniable; that it was currently experiencing the antithesis of all things great was equally as certain. Yet it was not the strangely dishevelled look of the city that brought us up short, our eyes wide with disbelief and horror, but the monstrous thing that had been enacted upon the long, straight road leading up to the main gate.

From our slightly elevated vantage point, perhaps two miles from the city itself, the road stretched straight and white ahead of us, and on either side of it, to a distance of a mile or more from the main gate, were gibbets. I tried to count them, but gave up when I realized their number ran to three figures. Yarissi sank to his knees, staring with eyes that shed unheeded tears, for the bodies that occupied the cages hanging from those grotesque posts were not all warriors, nor even all men, but included a fair number of women and children as well. The tiny form dangling from one gibbet could not have been more than a year old.

At my side, Luftetmek found his voice.

'Who—?' he said, the word almost choking him.

'The Bagalamak,' said one of the filinta matter-of-factly.

I said, my voice an involuntary whisper, 'There must be hundreds.'

Yarissi looked up.

'Two hundred and eleven,' he said numbly.

I knew he hadn't counted them.

'Every free member of the House,' he added.

'Of course,' said the filinta.

I heard the rasp of steel at my side. Luftetmek had drawn his sword.

'The filinta did this?' he asked softly.

'It was our duty,' said the filinta, a note of wariness in his voice.

I think I was the only one who might have moved swiftly enough to stop Luftetmek. I wonder, now, whether my failure to do so was deliberate.

He wiped his sword on the man's tunic, rolling the head aside with his foot.

The other filinta looked at him, sweating, not daring to move. Luftetmek was wielding his sword left-handed, and he was in visible pain, but the black-and-grey accoutred young officer had no doubt as to the abilities of Yarissi's Champion.

'I will turn my back,' Luftetmek said to him, 'but not for long. If you are still here when I turn again, you will die.'

He turned to Yarissi.

'Rise, friend,' he said gently, 'there is work yet to do.'

'Had I known,' Yarissi said, his voice a strangled whisper, 'that any of this would follow, never would I—'

'Enough of that,' Luftetmek said. 'Yours is not the blame. Kandirak has overstepped his legal bounds with this. The people will rise up at your slightest word.'

'More death?' Yarissi cried. 'No! Never! Not in my name! It was to prevent this that I spoke up at all! You should have beaten me to silence, not followed me. Were you mad? To follow a slave?'

'Only a slave could say the things you have said,' Luftetmek told him, his voice reasonable but with an edge in it – his faith in Yarissi was a rock. 'Only a slave could see the things you saw. Only a slave could know what was wrong with our society. Only a slave could show us the way. Because only a slave could be trusted to speak the truth, and for too long our people had hidden from the truth. Only a slave, Yarissi. Only you.'

I hadn't taken my eyes off the filinta all through this exchange, and now I saw an incredible thing. The young man suddenly tore off the black leather trappings of his office, flinging them from him as though they had been serpents twined around his body. He pulled the black-handled sword from its black scabbard and hurled it a considerable distance from the road. Then he threw himself at Yarissi's feet.

'Kanaat,' he wept, 'I have failed you! Let your warrior strike. Give me back the honour I have shamed.'

Yarissi looked down at him as though his words had been spoken in a foreign language, their meaning lost on him. Then he said simply, 'What is your name?'

'Kanaat, I was Usak, of the House Adapazir,' the man moaned. 'Now I am nothing. End my misery, Kanaat.'

'No, Usak,' Yarissi said, 'end mine.'

The man lifted his head to see Yarissi's hand held out to him. 'Be the first man to shed no blood in my name,' he said, 'particularly not your own.'

'Kanaat?' the man said, struggling to understand.

'Live for me,' Yarissi said, 'and earn the honourable death you seek. I will not give it to you.'

His hand was still extended, but I thought it trembled slightly. I wondered if Usak of the House Adapazir knew how important his answer would be to the future of Reshek.

Slowly, he reached out his own hand, and the two men rose together.

'Now,' Yarissi said, 'I believe we have business with my master.'

The only practical thing to do now was to march purposefully through the ranks of the victims of Kandirak's pogrom and thence into his own presence. After that, it would be up to Yarissi. That was the only practical thing to do. Nothing else made sense or would serve any purpose.

Luftetmek and I moved to opposite sides of the roadway and began to cut the bodies down.

Most were dead. A few of the younger men, probably the

Bagalamak's military offspring, still lived, as did others who, under the circumstances, should not have. One child, a girl of perhaps eleven or twelve years, was in startlingly good health, and a man who must have been on the high side of ninety was able to stand unaided once we had freed him. These, however, were the exceptions.

We had cut down thirty or more before we were challenged. A group of filinta, twenty strong and riding gryllups caparisoned for battle, galloped up alongside us, their leader hurling all manner of abuse at us as they did so.

'You rebellious dogs!' was one of his less obscene bits of invective. 'You will die by slow torture for this.'

Yarissi's voice, harsh but controlled, cut through the man's tirade.

'No man dies by torture in my Reshek,' he snarled.

The leader of the filinta wheeled his gryllup to face Yarissi, a sulphurous oath on his lips. Watching the colour drain from his face provided one of the day's better moments.

'Kanaat,' he said, leaping from the saddle. 'We thought you dead! Lord Kandirak had declared a period of mourning for . . .'

'Enough,' Yarissi snapped. 'Cut down these people and lead the survivors to the city. Then attend me in the Kanaat Hall.'

The man looked around, indecision and several kinds of trepidation written on his sweating countenance.

'But, Kanaat,' he protested, 'they are being executed—'

'No longer,' Yarissi said. 'Do as I bid; it is the law.' The filinta glanced around at those of us in Yarissi's group, apparently seeing for the first time one of his own men, now devoid of his insignia. For some reason, that sight seemed to unsettle him most of all.

'As you will, Kanaat,' he mumbled.

He gestured to his men, and with some obvious reluctance they fell to and began cutting down the remnants of House Bagalamak.

'Lord—'

The wavering, ancient voice was that of the aged Bagalamak. He was addressing Yarissi.

'I am not a Lord,' Yarissi said. 'I am a slave.'

The man appeared puzzled.

'You command here?' he said.

'By the will of the people,' Yarissi said.

The man seemed unable to comprehend.

'I am Kanaat Yarissi. Who are you?'

The old man recoiled as though struck. Then he recovered himself and, with a venom that was shocking to behold, he spat at Yarissi.

'Burn in Hell,' he swore.

Yarissi said nothing. He glanced at Luftetmek, the warrior's hand resting lightly on his sword hilt. Then, with still no word being said, he turned and headed up the road toward Xacmet.

CHAPTER NINETEEN

The Hall of the People

—◦◦◦—

I was conscious of being watched from a dozen shuttered windows as we entered the city. No one was on the street, which was littered with cracked masonry and other refuse. Unlike the majority of cities in the Kingdoms, Xacmet boasted sidewalks for pedestrians, raised several inches above the cobbled road. There was blood on several of the sidewalks, and the walls of nearby buildings were pock-marked with bullet holes.

As I looked around, I noticed that the young Bagalamak girl was trailing along behind us. Of the rest of the survivors, there was no sign. I hung back until she was alongside me.

'You should not follow us,' I told her.

She looked at me, dry-eyed and without expression.

'I have nowhere else to go,' she said.

'Your family—'

'I have no family,' she said. 'By order of our new emperor I am outcast. Yarissi is the only future I have now, and I will follow him.'

The word which she used for 'follow' had, in the High Tongue, only a prosaic meaning; she was not speaking of 'following' Yarissi in the way that Luftetmek followed him. I gathered from this that the feelings she had for Yarissi were not sympathetic.

It troubled me that she did not cry. If my estimate of her physical age was correct, then her mental – or emotional – age was far in advance of her years. I wondered how long she had hung at the roadside.

'I am David Shaw,' I told her, 'a Captain of the city of Benza.'

She looked at me with a thinly disguised distaste

'An outlander,' she said, the word acquiring whole new levels of contempt on her lips. 'Bad enough I am in the debt of a slave, but to an outlander as well—'

I resisted the urge to take her across my knee and beat some manners into her. Instead, I said, 'In my country, it is regarded as common courtesy to respond to an introduction by reciprocating it.'

The child laughed, a barking, ugly sound that made my skin crawl. But then her expression abruptly changed, and it seemed to me that she might be recalling something and that the recollection had made her regret her rudeness of a moment ago. Seeming to grow in stature and composure, she turned to face me.

'I ask your pardon, Warrior,' she said, using the polite form of the High Tongue that was reserved for equals, 'and give you my thanks for saving my life. I am—'

The rest of her answer was drowned in a clatter of gunfire. I threw my body over hers, feeling bits of stone pepper my side, realizing how close the shots had been. Luftetmek and his warriors were all returning fire, and I scooped the girl up in my arms as we all ran for cover. An alley close by seemed like the best bet, and in seconds we were in the semi-darkness that it afforded. From its far end, the sound of running feet and cries of 'Death to the Kanaat!' told us we had probably made an error of judgement.

Zalmetta was at my side.

'Give me the child,' she said.

'No!' the girl screamed, looking at the charlaki woman in horror.

'Go with her,' I snapped. 'She will protect you.'

Shoving the struggling child into Zalmetta's arms, I drew my sabre and pushed past Yarissi to confront the new enemy.

Luftetmek, who was in no shape for prolonged swordplay, guarded our backs while the rest of us took the brunt of the attack.

Our foes were armed with swords and spears and axes but, thankfully, no pistols or bows. We met their charge with a solid wall of steel and muscle, and though they outnumbered us by better than three to one we were warriors and they, for the most part, were not. Also, we were fighting for our very lives, and that tends to tip the scales in any battle.

Yarissi's two warriors were magnificent. Neither one was a great swordsman in the classical sense, but under conditions such as these they displayed a rare talent for brawling. In a matter of minutes, and with no losses on our side, we had fought our way to the far end of the alley. Luftetmek had done a good job in the rearguard, and the unarmed Usak had never left Yarissi's side. A quick, nervous glance at Zalmetta told me that both she and the child were safe, for which I gave silent thanks to the Thirteen.

'Which way?' I asked Yarissi.

He seemed to be weighing options.

'With the direct route blocked, the alternatives are either long or perilous,' he said, '– or both. Luftetmek—'

'Yes, Kanaat?' the warrior replied, still standing watch some yards away, two pistols tucked into the crook of his bandaged arm and a third covering the alley behind us.

'Would you choose the Plaza, or the Street of Coins?' Yarissi asked.

Luftetmek scowled; neither option, I sensed, would have been his first choice. I was beginning to get some sense of just how dangerous a place Xacmet had become; the city was virtually divided up into armed camps, with no one certain which of his neighbours were friends and which foes.

'The Street of Coins,' Luftetmek said.

Yarissi turned to me.

'Put up your sword,' he said. 'The Coins offers more likelihood of a firefight than a close-quarters battle. But Luftetmek is right; the Plaza will be too crowded, and once I am recognized we will be as impeded by friends as by foes.'

I sheathed the sabre and drew my pistols, priming and cocking them. Glancing quickly out of the alley at the narrow street beyond, I gave Yarissi's warriors the signal to move out.

I was no expert at this kind of urban warfare, but even I knew that the biggest danger in moving a group of men through streets like these was one of spacing. Get too strung out and you ran the risk of being split up; get too close, and an ambush would wipe out the whole group before you could get off a single shot in reply.

Luckily for us, Yarissi's men were more experienced than I was. They kept us moving, using the buildings to provide whatever cover was possible, and despite one or two moments that fairly invited an ambush, we reached our destination without incident.

Because we had come at it by one of its lesser side entrances, the first glimpse I had of the Kanaat Hall was not especially impressive. Certainly there was a sense of considerable size and grandeur, but nothing specific, nothing that hinted at the real significance of the place. All of that ended as soon as we were inside.

On the island where Zatuchep had stood, we had seen hints of the former glory of the Kai Empire, vague images distorted by the later degeneration of their culture. In Xacmet, in the Kanaat Hall, we came face to face with the reality. The Resheki, it seemed, had embodied all that was best in their island forebears, and in this Hall those qualities had found the ultimate means of expression.

The chamber in which we stood was not that much bigger than Tal Daqar's hall had been, and in truth it was probably not as well appointed. But to stand in it was to feel humbled. I look back now on that first glimpse that I had of it and try to pin down one single facet of its appearance that so profoundly affected me, but I find that I cannot. It was rather like the feeling one sometimes has upon entering a very old cathedral; men had gathered in this place not merely because it was convenient to do so, but for a very specific purpose: they had come here to worship. But this was no religious edifice, and their worship had had nothing to do with Shushuan's pantheon of deities.

The men and women of Reshek had come here to bend their collective knee to The Law, to the very underpinning of their ancient culture. And in every aspect, the building had grown to reflect that fact. Its decorations, whether vast, panoramic friezes or sumptuous hanging tapestries, all reflected the tiered, multi-level society that had been maintained and preserved by the activities that had gone on in this place.

'This was once the Hall of the People,' Yarissi said quietly. 'It was law court, temple, schoolroom – it was the heart of our country. Then the Bagalamak came to power. They closed the Hall, boarded it up, scattered its offices about the city, removed from us the centre of our being. We took the Hall so much for granted, assumed so readily that what it stood for was eternal, that we could not conceive of these things being lost. We forgot that the building was more than merely a symbol.' He glanced at me, perhaps wondering if I understood. 'The heart is only a pump,' he said, 'and not the seat of our feelings, as the poets would have us believe. But tear out the heart, and the body dies. What matter then where the feelings truly lie?'

I looked around the Hall. There was a magnificent simplicity to the architecture which the ornate appointments enhanced rather than contradicted.

In stark contrast, however, was the use to which the Hall was currently being put. Refuse and street debris littered the floor; folding tables and cheap, poorly made camp chairs had been set up in small clutches all across the broad central aisle; filinta stood, bristling with weapons and bad attitudes, behind every desk and pillar and doorway; and on the walls, sometimes over the top of the original murals and vistas, revolutionary slogans and propaganda had been scrawled.

'Come,' Yarissi said, 'let us find Kandirak.'

It was the work of moments to accomplish this task, and one of the biggest surprises of the day for me when we did so. I had been building up a mental picture of Kandirak for some time now, based on fleeting comments from a dozen sources. None of what I had imagined now confronted me in the flesh.

Kandirak – Lord Kandirak, I should say – was not so much

holding court as sitting in attendance on proceedings that scarcely seemed to touch him. A vast, crudely built throne had been set up on a square platform at one end of the Hall's central aisle; ringing the throne were upwards of a dozen filinta, of medium rank if I was reading their insignia correctly, all armed with heavy-headed Resheki war spears. Sitting on the throne, a half-empty bottle of some kind of liquor at his side, his eyes half closed, was Kandirak. I placed him in his mid-fifties, a heavy, corpulent individual, his jet-black hair pulled back from his face and tied in a single queue that hung over his left shoulder and reached almost to his ample waist. He wore silk robes, cut like a warrior's but in a style many generations out of date. He was armed, if the word could be so applied, with a slender dagger whose hilt looked as though it contained a Duke's ransom in diamonds, rubies and sapphires. The rings that adorned most of his pudgy fingers would have ransomed the rest of the Duke's household.

I was surprised. Yarissi's grip on the people of this troubled land was almost Messianic. How could the recumbent lump now confronting us have done so much to undermine that grip in so short a time? Or was I missing something obvious? Given my past record on Shushuan this seemed a not entirely unlikely possibility.

Scattered around the podium at irregular intervals, officials in the new regime were doing the actual business of Kandirak's court. I couldn't identify all the activities that were going on, but they seemed to include such mundane and diverse tasks as the issuing of licences and visas, permits and proclamations, the collecting of taxes and fines, the settling of minor disputes, the appointment of Prefects and other court officers, the entabulation of new legislation, and other similar and esoteric dealings. It was all terribly prosaic, the matter-of-fact atmosphere given an unpleasant edge by the preponderance of weapons in the various groups: everyone, it seemed, bore arms here, a state of affairs I had encountered in no other country on the Thek continent.

We approached the podium. Our presence in the Hall had not gone unnoticed, and I saw a messenger whisper something to Kandirak as we drew near, his gaze flitting nervously from his somnolent master to Yarissi and back again.

Kandirak seemed not to have heard his messenger, but no sooner had Yarissi reached the foot of the podium than the Lord of House Tchelnet opened his eyes and bestowed upon the Kanaat a smile of such utter insincerity that it might have been the result of surgery rather than emotion.

'Yarissi!' he cried, as though announcing it to the Hall at large. 'You have returned from the dead!' In a more normal tone he added, 'Or so they are saying.'

'My Lord,' Yarissi said, bowing.

'Away with such nonsense,' Kandirak said dismissively, settling more comfortably on his throne. 'Your counsel has been much missed by the people. Now that you have returned, I think it will best serve our great cause if you were to address them as soon as possible. There is unrest everywhere. Your soothing tones will, I think, cool some of the hotheads who are making trouble for our cause. I have in mind a tour of sorts, taking in the out-lying prefectures . . .'

'Lord,' Yarissi said, 'I have returned to Xacmet, and here I shall stay – until certain very troubling matters have been explained to me.'

Kandirak said nothing for a time. He studied his fingernails, then picked at his teeth with one that seemed to take his fancy. Finally he looked at Yaarissi.

'I think not,' he said. 'Your part in our great revolution is best categorized as informative, not investigative. You know the old laws better than any man alive, and you serve our cause best by imparting that knowledge to our followers. They need to be reminded of the rightness of our revolution, lest they be swayed by the backward-thinking few who still cling to the ways of the Bagalamak. Better that you leave the executive tasks to those more suited to them.' He added, as though prompted by his conscience towards total honesty, 'There are those who have expressed the opinion that it is not . . . appropriate for a slave to issue orders to free men.'

Yarissi, for the first time since I had known him, seemed beside himself with rage.

'I have never ordered any man!' he yelled. 'Each man who has followed me has done so freely and willingly – yourself included, Kandirak.'

'And so it will continue,' Kandirak said blandly. 'Now, you are obviously tired from your long and arduous journey—'

'Do not dismiss him,' Luftetmek said from behind me. His tone had the effect of ice water on Kandirak.

Luftetmek pushed past me to stand beside Yarissi.

'You forget yourself, warrior,' Kandirak snapped.

'Never,' Luftetmek said. 'I am Luftetmek, Captain, Champion to Kanaat Yarissi, ruler of the new Reshek.'

'You would put a slave on the seat of the mightiest empire the world has ever known?' Kandirak scoffed, but there was a look in his eyes that I did not like – Luftetmek was walking a tightrope here, and I did not think he fully appreciated his danger: the room was filled with filinta, and none of them seemed entirely pleased to see Yarissi.

'No,' said Luftetmek. 'But I would follow one against a self-styled emperor. In case you have forgotten, my Lord, it was to do away with emperors that we overthrew the Bagalamak. I see no need to replace one tyrant with another.'

I was surprised that Kandirak did not rise to this bait, especially given his mood. Instead, he smiled inscrutably and beckoned to one of his aides. A brief, whispered conversation ensued, and then the aide was waved away.

'Ah, yes,' Kandirak said, 'the Bagalamak. I gather you did not approve of their disposition, *Captain* Luftetmek.'

Yarissi put his hand on Luftetmek's arm.

'That,' he told Kandirak, 'was my decision.'

'But Kanaat,' Kandirak said, 'you have already told us that no man is under your command, that each of your followers is free to follow his own path. Is that not true?'

Yarissi said nothing.

'So,' Kandirak continued, '*Captain* Luftetmek chose, of his own free will, to interfere with the lawful execution of the enemies of our great country. Tell me, Kanaat Yarissi, where stands the law on such an issue?'

Yarissi seemed unable to speak. Luftetmek stepped forward, unslinging his sword. On the podium, twelve blades sang from their scabbards.

'The penalty,' said Luftetmek, 'is death.'

I glanced around. Everywhere, at exits, along the walls, in the spaces between the many tables, filinta stood, alert, hands on sword hilts, ready to move in an instant. I was glad there were no firearms in evidence, but it was a minor advantage under the circumstances. If Luftetmek intended going down fighting, the odds were so hugely against him it wouldn't have mattered if the filinta had been armed with wooden clubs. If he did decide to fight, now was the time for me to decide if I would help him. If I did not, could I use that fact to influence Kandirak in the matter of providing me with safe passage to Ragana-Se-Tor, something Yarissi was clearly no longer able to offer? The question was purely accademic, something to mull over as I unslung my own sword and moved around Yarissi to flank Luftetmek. I caught the confused gaze of Yarissi's two warriors, neither of whom, I imagined, had ever envisioned a situation such as this. They exchanged a brief glance, then formed up on either side of me, making a square with Luftetmek. Yarissi and Usak, and Zalmetta and the child, were now excluded from what would come next – at least, until the four of us had been dispatched.

Kandirak smiled down at us from his throne, unruffled by the sudden air of tension that had settled on the Hall. At a word from him a lot of men would die in a very short space of time. I wondered how much that bothered him – if it bothered him.

'If this is your preferred method of execution—' he drawled.

'It will do as well as any other,' Luftetmek said.

He unsheathed his sword.

Kandirak raised his hand lazily.

'Wait!' cried Yarissi.

Kandirak looked at him pityingly, his hand still raised. 'This,' he said, 'is the law. Will you dispute with it?'

Yarissi looked around, almost frantic. Then he seemed to see something that brought a sudden, almost unnatural composure to his face. He seemed to grow where he stood, and I received the absurd impression that everything around him, the people, the furnishings, the very walls of the building itself, took a step back, leaving him alone in the centre of a vast and empty space, his person inviolate. I looked about, wondering what he had seen that could cause such an effect. For an instant, I couldn't work it out. And then I realized. In the Hall, between the ranks of the black and grey filinta, the ordinary men and women of Reshek were looking directly at Yarissi, and the strength of the whole nation seemed to be pouring through them and into him.

'This is not the law,' Yarissi said softly, his voice not remotely that of a slave. 'I will speak the law.'

Kandirak hesitated. He was not the fool his appearance might have suggested, and he knew the power of the Kanaat. Then his eyes narrowed craftily and he said, 'Do you place yourself above the law, Yarissi?'

'When you invoke the law,' Yarissi replied, 'it is my name the people whisper. I will speak the law.'

'This man must die,' said Kandirak, indicating Luftetmek. 'And because of their actions, so too must those who stand with him.'

'You invoke the law,' Yarissi said, 'then hear the law. Any man who interferes with a lawful execution must himself face death.'

'Such is the law!' Kandirak cried, rising to his feet in triumph.

'Unless—' Yarissi cried.

All eyes were on him now.

'Unless,' he repeated softly, 'he acts in accordance with the instructions of his ruling Lord. In which case, the sentence of death can only be imposed through trial by combat.'

Kandirak seemed puzzled, uncertain.

'Is this relevant?' he demanded. 'Luftetmek did not act in accordance with my wishes—'

'Ah, but, Lord, he did,' said Yarissi. 'You are my master, and before I left upon my recent mission you agreed that I should speak for us both until such time as I returned to your presence. Since Luftetmek was charged with executing my wishes – even though I had no power to command him in any matter – and since I could not know under what circumstances the Bagalamak had been executed, he was merely acceding to my own unvoiced desire when he set them free. And in so doing, my Lord, by your own direction, he was also obeying you.'

Yarissi smiled.

Kandirak frowned. His thoughts were plain for all to see: was Yarissi bluffing? Was this a true interpretation of the law? Or just an act of desperate grandstanding?

Presently, Kandirak smiled, though it was as strained and artificial a smile as that first one he had bestowed upon Yarissi.

'Very well, Kanaat,' he said. 'Trial by combat it is.'

This seemed to me a pyrrhic victory at best. Luftetmek was in no shape to fight. Come to that, none of us were, not after everything we'd been through lately.

'And,' Kandirak went on, 'since Luftetmek is your Champion, and his skill well known, I think it only fair that we pit him against an equally worthy opponent.'

Better and better, I thought. There had to be an alternative to this.

Luftetmek was preparing himself for combat. I could see him withdrawing into the privacy of his thoughts, his movements becoming measured and ritualistic. He was removing all distractions from his mind, blocking out everything that was not relevant to what he was about to do. I was loath to interrupt such preparations, but there was no way for him to fight a duel in his condition.

'Luftetmek,' I said quietly, 'let another fight in your place. The law will allow that, surely?'

He seemed surprised that I had spoken, and a little annoyed.

'It is my fight,' he said. 'I will fight it.'

'Don't be so bloody stupid,' I hissed. 'You'd be committing suicide.'

He looked at me, and a genuine smile crossed his lips before he smothered it.

'Your concern is appreciated,' he said. 'I will fight.'

I stepped back from him, recognizing that further entreaties would be useless. Instead, I turned to Yarissi.

'Can't you speak to him?' I asked. 'Make him see sense?'

Yarissi seemed puzzled.

'This is his choice,' he said. 'I do not think he would thank me for interfering.'

'Damn it, you manoeuvred him into it,' I said. 'You and your blasted law—'

'The alternative would have seen you dead as well,' Yarissi said, a bit annoyed. 'And Luftetmek's death under those circumstances would have dishonoured his name for all time. This way, he keeps his honour. And, if the Gods will it, his life as well.'

From the podium, Kandirak said, 'My Champion—'

We all turned to look. Standing next to Kandirak, and towering a head or more above him, was Blukka.

CHAPTER TWENTY

Crime and Punishment

———◆◇◆◇◆———

A moment of stunned silence followed Kandirak's announcement, and then it seemed as though every voice in the Hall was
speaking at once.

The members of Kandirak's court seemed as startled by
Blukka's appearance as we were, making me suspect that whatever
unholy alliance the self-styled Lord of Reshek had struck with
Blukka's master it was one to which only he was privy.

Of Daqar himself, or any other of his followers, there was
no sign. Nor had we had any glimpse of his airship on the way
here, either outside the city or within its walls. Such a vessel,
even given its inexplicable ability to come to ground, could not
easily be hidden in a metropolis like Xacmet. Perhaps Blukka was
alone here, left behind by Daqar for some unguessable purpose.
If so, it gave us our one and only chance to avoid falling again
into that madman's clutches.

Behind me, Yarissi and Zalmetta were engaged in a furious
tête-à-tête, Zalmetta evincing a real and genuine fear at the
unexpected appearance of her former colleague. The prospect
of being returned to Daqar's service was clearly a terrifying
one for her. Behind her, the Bagalamak child was looking
on with confusion and a degree of annoyance; she had her
own reasons for being here, and none of this was a part of
her agenda.

I put my hand on Luftetmek's arm.

'This is no longer a simple matter of choosing how to die,'

I told him. 'Lose to Blukka, and we are all doubly endangered. Let me fight in your place.'

Luftetmek looked at me. I think he was amused.

'Think you so little of my skills, David Shaw?' he asked.

'You are still recovering from an injury,' I said. 'On the best day of your life you *might* beat Blukka.'

He held my gaze for a moment, then shook his head.

'I am sorry, David Shaw,' he said, 'but this is not about me – or you. It is about the difference between a Reshek run by Kandirak and one run by Yarissi. If we must all perish to preserve what is right, then so be it.'

Kandirak's voice rose above the general hubbub.

'As the accused's master,' he said, 'the choice of weapons is mine.'

I cursed silently. Yarissi's manoeuvring was looking less and less like a victory with each new twist. Kandirak could read Luftetmek's physical condition as well as any of us, and obviously intended exploiting it to the fullest.

'I nominate war axe and shield,' Kandirak said.

Our fate, it seemed, was sealed. I would miss Luftetmek, for however many minutes I survived him.

The weapons Kandirak had chosen were brought in by a pair of his filinta. The axes were not unlike those I had seen in Vohung: single-headed with a balled spike for counterbalance. The handles were perhaps two feet long, terminating in leather wrist thongs. They were a weapon I had had some experience with, but not one I favoured. The shields were shorter than Vohung cavalry shields and broader. They comprised iron frames covered with timber and hide, capable of deflecting an arrow or, if used skilfully, the blade of an axe. I wondered how much experience Luftetmek had had with such weapons.

As the two opponents were being divested of their current weapons I leaned close to Luftetmek and gave him what little help I could.

'Blukka can match you skill for skill,' I said, recalling my duel with him. 'Even if he's never used these weapons before, his artificial intelligence will let him learn so fast you'll never be able to keep up. But there's one thing you have that I think he lacks: you've got an emotional stake in this fight. Use that. Use your anger, your desire to stay alive, to prove Kandirak a liar, to continue Yarissi's fight—'

'Step back, outworlder,' said one of the filinta. 'You may not interfere in this.'

I let myself be led to one side. The central aisle had been cleared, and Blukka was walking slowly towards Luftetmek. The war axe looked like a child's toy in his huge fist. The shield on his other arm was barely large enough to protect his great barrel of a chest. Facing him, Luftetmek looked like an infant, his own weapons seeming strangely out of proportion in comparison.

With no hint of a warning, Luftetmek attacked. It was the most devastating charge I had ever seen, and against a human foe – any human foe – I think he would have been instantly victorious. There was no pattern to the rain of blows he flung at Blukka, no art or skill to his attack, but merely a savage, unrelenting outpouring of naked, mindless aggression. Blukka's shield was battered out of shape in seconds, the surface rent and cracked in a dozen places. During the whole fusillade of blows, the giant slave never once had an opportunity to counter-attack, his own axe hanging useless from his right hand.

There is a moment in any such attack when the aggressor will pause, even if only for a heartbeat, to assess the success or failure of his strategy. At that moment, he is susceptible to a counter-attack, and perhaps more vulnerable than he ever will be again during that particular combat. A good opponent will wait for that moment and then exploit it.

Blukka and I, it seemed, read Luftetmek's attack in the same way. The moment of hesitation came, and Blukka swung his axe into the vacant space.

But Luftetmek had fooled us both. The hesitation had been a feint, a ruse, designed to draw the counter at the moment when Luftetmek, and not Blukka, could most profit from it.

He blocked the blow without missing a beat of his own attack, and his axe buried itself briefly in Blukka's left thigh. But the sheer strength behind the slave's blow had taken Luftetmek by surprise, and although his own strike landed, it was not as devastating in its effect as he had intended. Reeling from the impact of Blukka's clout, he all but tripped and fell, his grip on his own axe failing and only the leather thong around his wrist keeping him from being disarmed. The head of the weapon was jerked from Blukka's flesh, blood trailing after it, and the two men backed warily away from one another. Blukka was limping, but Luftetmek looked half dead from the exertion of his attack.

For long moments they circled one another, and I began to wonder why Blukka did not attack. From my own experience with him I would have expected him to duplicate Luftetmek's own opening strategy, relying on his superior speed and strength to succeed where Luftetmek had failed. I could only guess at his reasons for not doing this, and at that I was relying on the validity of my own speculation from before the battle began: Blukka had no emotions to speak of, and his brain – primitive by human standards – could not deal with the style and nature of Luftetmek's attack.

As though sensing his adversary's hesitation, Luftetmek attacked once again. His strategy was different this time, consisting of a dozen or more standard axe-fighting techniques that any trainee warrior would be taught. Blukka's unfamiliarity with them, and his rapidly improvised defences, seemed to please Luftetmek, who began to add more sophisticated moves, building up complex compound attacks and watching Blukka's response. I wanted to warn him, to remind him of how fast the slave could learn – Luftetmek was, in effect, teaching Blukka how to fight with these weapons. This was the tactic I had tried in my own fight with Blukka, and it had almost cost me my life.

There was no advance warning of the next sudden change in direction of the battle, but when it came no one could have missed it. In the space of a single exchange, Luftetmek went from being the aggressor to fighting a fierce defensive battle as Blukka began to throw all of his techniques back at him. And Blukka had twice Luftetmek's strength.

In seconds, the Resheki Captain's shield was in tatters, his arm so weak from Blukka's attack that it could barely hold up the bedraggled remains. Blukka's attack continued at the same dogged, relentless pace; a human, in the same circumstances, his adrenalin level rising, would have intensified his attack. Blukka, it seemed, was in no such hurry.

Whilst the majority of my thoughts were taken up with an almost unbearable anticipation of Luftetmek's impending defeat – and, it was logical to assume, death – there was a corner of my mind that couldn't help but regard Blukka's performance dispassionately, analytically. What he was doing, allowing for minor variations, was a replay of Luftetmek's own previous attack. Certainly Blukka was stronger and faster, and Luftetmek's poor response was colouring the slave's attack to a degree, but in essence the two attacks were all but identical. And in three more passes, Luftetmek would die . . .

Two more passes . . .

One more . . .

The counter that would have been Luftetmek's last never came. Instead, he abandoned every pattern that the past minutes had established and simply took the full force of Blukka's stroke on what little remained of his shield. The impact drove Luftetmek to his knees, the head of Blukka's axe embedded in the battered shield; the giant slave was off balance by the tiniest degree, his unchecked momentum sending him forward further than he had intended. Luftetmek pulled furiously with the straps of his shield – and Blukka was sent flying past him, the Resheki Captain's outstretched leg sending his foe crashing to the floor. Luftetmek turned, axe swung high, and threw the finishing stroke at Blukka's head. The axe caught Blukka a glancing blow to the forehead, ripping a hideous wound in his scalp, and was deflected by the Y'nys crystal beneath. Blukka struck his opponent a single savage blow with his massive fist, and then their positions were reversed, the slave, his face pouring blood, straddling Luftetmek's barely conscious form, the axe raised to strike.

Movement in my peripheral vision caused me to glance briefly away. I shielded my face as, less than a foot from it, Zalmetta fired one of Yarissi's pistols. The report boomed around the Hall like a peal of thunder, and the shaft of Blukka's axe was smashed in two by the impact of the ball projectile.

Blukka looked in our direction, a puzzled expression on his redly streaming face. Zalmetta was already pointing a second gun directly at the slave's throat. And Blukka now knew – as did everyone else in the Hall – just how good a shot his erstwhile colleague was. What he couldn't know – but what I suspected – was that Zalmetta was incapable of killing. She was bluffing, but doing a very good job of it.

A dozen voices cried out at once in response to her act, and few of them were raised in her defence. Some of the warriors present, those not in the garb of filinta, saluted the skill that the shot had demonstrated, but they did so silently. On the podium, Kandirak wore an expression that quickly changed from irritation to sardonic pleasure. *Let's see Yarissi defend that*, his malefic grin seemed to say.

Beside me, unflinching, her gaze never leaving the equally motionless Blukka, Zalmetta muttered, *sotto voce*, 'This has made matters worse, yes?'

'Probably,' I replied, 'but thanks anyway.'

'You are welcome,' she said.

Blukka rose slowly from his place atop Luftetmek's chest, casting aside the remains of his weapon as he did so. Then, still facing Zalmetta and the cocked pistol, he backed slowly away, arms out at his side.

'Tell us, Kanaat,' Kandirak cried from the dias, 'what is the penalty for *this* crime?'

Yarissi glanced from me to Zalmetta and back again. Zalmetta was still watching Blukka, but the pistol was now aimed at the floor. I noticed, though I doubt anyone else did, that she had unobtrusively lowered the hammer.

'You well know,' Yarissi replied, his voice leaden. 'The penalty is death – without appeal.'

'So be it,' Kandirak said, gesturing to his men to take Zalmetta.

This is it, I thought. I glanced quickly at Luftetmek. He had not moved since Blukka had struck him. I couldn't tell if he was breathing or not.

The filinta advanced on us in an unbroken circle. Blades rasped from scabbards, unblinking eyes regarded us for any sign of weakness. We were outnumbered by better than twenty to one, and not all of our number were armed.

I felt Yarissi's hand on my shoulder, and glanced at him. He was shaking his head.

'Not this way,' he said simply. 'Too much is at stake, for Reshek and, I think, for you. Let us live to fight another day.'

I felt torn. What he said was true; if I died now it would achieve nothing, and it would mark a stupid end to four years of grim and bitter waiting. But to surrender Zalmetta and Luftetmek – and the nameless Bagalamak child as well – to our enemies would be a burden too heavy for me to bear. Better a swift death in battle than that kind of guilt—

'Kandirak,' Yarissi said, 'there is an alternative – one within the law, and one that will set the seal on your rule.'

The words, I sensed, were ripped from Yarissi's heart, and spoke greatly of his feeling for Luftetmek. I felt I had judged him too harshly over his suggestion of trial by combat: to a Vinh, such a thing would not have seemed quite like the betrayal it had seemed to me.

Kandirak seemed intrigued, but not entirely convinced of Yarissi's good intentions.

'Say more, Kanaat,' he suggested.

'The creature Zalmetta is not of our race,' Yarissi said, 'and is ignorant of many of our laws.'

'Ignorance is no defence,' Kandirak said.

'True,' Yarissi said, 'but it is a mitigation at sentencing. If ignorance is proved, death need not automatically follow. As *supreme ruler* of Reshek, you have it in your power to commute the sentence.'

Kandirak seemed to like the idea, reinforcing as it did his own power.

'Commute to what?' he asked.

'Lifetime slavery,' Yarissi said, 'with no possibility of manumission.'

To the Resheki, who regard slavery as, if you like, a career starting point, this notion would be horrifying. And as a punishment it would seem far worse than death. One of the reasons for the apparently irrational support that the institution of slavery has among the men and women of this oldest of countries is the notion of its transience, its lack of enforceable permanence. Every slave in Reshek looks forward to the day when he or she will earn, or win, their freedom. To take away that fundamental right was to rob their society of its very foundation. It shocked me that Yarissi, of all people, should advocate such a thing.

'So be it,' Kandirak laughed. 'You see, Yarissi, I can be merciful. Slavery it is. But the creature you call Zalmetta is already slaved to our new ally, from whom our Champion, Blukka, is on temporary loan. Upon our ally's return, the animal woman is to be returned to him. But since the law must be served, someone must bear the consequences of her crime. As the self-styled Captain of Benza is allied to the creature he shall suffer her fate.' Kandirak glanced around the Hall. 'Oh, yes,' he said, 'and the traitor Luftetmek also.' He glanced at Yarissi, smiling that terrible humourless smile. 'I believe that concludes today's business. Prefects, take them away.'

The filinta advanced again, this time with an arrogant confidence that made me furious.

'David—?' Zalmetta muttered, visibly dismayed by these developments; the pistol, I noticed, was cocked again.

I threw a glance at Luftetmek; he was struggling to his feet, swaying drunkenly.

I looked at Yarissi.

'Sorry,' I said, 'but no deal.'

I yelled the war cry of Benza and charged the nearest filinta. He was dead before he knew what had hit him. The two on either side of him were sent reeling from sword strokes as I broke through the line, laying about me with complete abandon. I was surrounded in an instant, but no one seemed able to lay a blade on me. I parried and slashed faster than the eye or hand could follow, working entirely on instinct and reflex. There was no time to plan, no time to think, and no time to give the slightest consideration to the possibility of defeat. The circle around me tightened, and then the man in front of me seemed to explode as something hit him from behind. It was Luftetmek, wielding his war axe like a bludgeon. I swung my sword around me in a wild circle, clearing a space to Luftetmek's side, until we stood back to back, ringed by our enemies.

No one came to our aid. Yarissi's two warriors, together with Usak, were forming a wedge in front of the Kanaat, presumably just in case, in the mêlée, a convenient dagger should remove Kandirak's rival from the political scene.

Zalmetta and the child had vanished, as had Blukka. I suspected the two facts were not unrelated.

Above the noise in the Hall Kandirak's voice rose like the bellow of a bull.

'Yield, fools,' he roared, 'or die before leaving this place.'

Yarissi called out, 'Shaw, do as he says. I promise you—'

'Slavery!' I yelled back. 'Never!'

I didn't know what Yarissi was plotting, but I did know slave law. If Luftetmek and I were sentenced to the fate Yarissi had proposed, no power on Shushuan could free us. And I knew, first-hand, what being a slave on this planet was like.

'Ready, Captain?' I said to Luftetmek.

'Ready, Captain,' he shot back.

'Follow me,' I said, and we each gave one last desperate war cry as I charged the massed ranks of warriors in front of me.

CHAPTER TWENTY-ONE

Departure

It was like running headlong at a wall of steel. Individual warriors went down before me, but for each one that did two, three, four more were there to take his place. And despite my attempts at appearing to know what I was doing, I had no plan whatsoever. There were doorways in the wall ahead of us, but where they led I had no idea. Basically, this was your classic blaze-of-glory swan song.

Luftetmek was doing a sterling job of guarding our retreat, but I was rapidly losing ground. One of my opponents got through my guard with a half-hearted thrust and clipped me in the shoulder. I lopped a chunk off his own deltoid in return but in doing so left myself open to a better-aimed stab from one of his colleagues. He gave me a superficial but potentially incapacitating cut across the right side of my ribcage, and got out of range again before I could respond. Luftetmek jostled me from behind, overbalanced by the efforts of his own foemen, and I took a blow to the head that left me momentarily stunned. I was conscious of blood dripping down my face, of men pressing in around me – and then the Hall was filled with the sound of gunfire and a space had opened up in front of me. I shook my head fiercely; at the far end of the Hall, Zalmetta was standing in an open doorway and picking off the men who were directly between us. Not one of the injuries was fatal, but all were incapacitating. And she was reloading so swiftly between shots that her hands were a blur.

I didn't know where she'd come from, or how, and I didn't

care. I grabbed Luftetmek's sleeve and together we raced towards our deliverer. Very few of the surviving filinta tried to stop us; Zalmetta shot the first to make the attempt, and the others lost heart.

'Out of the door and go left,' she snapped as we reached her.

The door gave onto a long corridor. Luftetmek and I ran, or rather staggered, down it. Behind us, we heard Zalmetta cursing fluently in the High Tongue, apparently hurling abuse at our would-be captors in an effort to forestall pursuit. I wondered how much ammunition she had left.

At the end of the corridor we came to a chamber in which were two people. One was Blukka. He was unconscious on the floor. The other was the Bagalamak child.

Zalmetta joined us on the run.

'Did you do that?' I asked, indicating Blukka.

'It was necessary,' she said, appearing flustered, unhappy with her role in events.

'Let's get out of here,' I said.

'I know the way from here,' Luftetmek said. 'Few havens will exist in Xacmet for us now, but I think I can still find a few friends willing to defy Kandirak's tyranny.'

Zalmetta said, 'Go; I will catch you up.'

She kneeled at Blukka's side and cradled his head in her hands; her fingers seemed to search his skull like those of a surgeon. It occurred to me I had seen someone do that before . . .

I was surprised that we were not more hotly pursued as we made our way through the back corridors of the Kanaat Hall. Zalmetta caught up with us as we reached the door leading to the street and provided a partial explanation.

'After I had rescued you,' she said with no hint of irony, 'Yarissi started talking again. He persuaded the warriors in the Hall, the ones not in the filinta, to rally round and guard your retreat. He said Kandirak had had no right to order your deaths the way he did just because you objected to slavery.'

'A subtle legal point,' Luftetmek said sceptically.

'I think,' Zalmetta said, 'he was merely giving us time to get away, and did not expect to be taken seriously. But you know how it is: when he speaks people listen.'

Luftetmek led us out of the Hall and down a half-dozen back alleys before stopping at the door of an unremarkable little house in a street of similarly unremarkable dwellings.

'This was a safe house in the old days,' he said. 'Only Yarissi and I and two others know of it.'

Inside, the house displayed considerable evidence of its lack of use. I heard the scurryings of tiny rodent feet as the door opened, letting in light for perhaps the first time in months.

We all crowded into the small main room of the building, sinking wearily to the floor in the absence of any furniture. I felt as though we'd been on the move for days, though in fact it was only a few hours since we had arisen and marched towards Xacmet.

'I gather events proceeded apace while I was unconscious,' Luftetmek said, referring to the less than agreeable conclusion to his battle with Blukka.

I explained Yarissi's ploy to save our lives, and my own rejection of a lifetime of slavery under Kandirak. To my surprise, Luftetmek appeared dismayed by my choice.

'Slavery for life,' he said, 'can only be imposed by the ruling monarch. And "for life" means either for the life of the slave, or the life of the monarch. Any monarch who dies in office will have his rulings reviewed by his successor. Frequently, as a gesture of goodwill, the successor will reduce all such sentences and free the slaves, usually on his birthday, or the anniversary of his coronation, or some public holiday. Clearly, Yarissi intended this for us when he made the suggestion.'

'But for that to happen,' I said, 'Kandirak would have to die while still in office.'

Luftetmek nodded.

'He'd have to be assassinated,' I said.

Luftetmek regarded me. The idea did not seem to disturb him greatly.

'I'm sorry,' I said. 'I guess I blew it.'

'The damage is worse than that,' he said. 'By fleeing, you

have made us both runaway slaves. Yarissi's plan now has a new obstacle: as runaways, we are automatically under sentence of death. Only our master can revoke that sentence. And our master is Kandirak.'

I put my head in my hands. This was just like old times.

'Suppose he's killed before we're caught?' I suggested.

'Then our ownership passes to his successor,' said Luftetmek. I nodded.

'Let's try not to get caught,' I said glumly.

Luftetmek laughed.

'Good advice under any circumstances,' he observed.

We stayed in the safe house for the rest of the day, and all the day and night that followed. Luftetmek brought food on the morning after our arrival but that was the only time any of us ventured out.

And then, at last, it was time for a parting of the ways.

'I dare not return to Yarissi,' Luftetmek said. 'To do so under these circumstances would place him in an impossible position.'

'Where will you go?' I asked.

'To the east,' he replied. 'There are many poor settlements along the coast, places where Yarissi's dream means more to men than Kandirak's insane lust for power. I will find a welcome there, and I will do what little I can to be worthy of it.'

He didn't add, *Until Kandirak is dead and I can return to Xacmet.* But we all knew it was what he meant.

'What of you?' he asked me.

'North,' I said, 'and Ragana-Se-Tor.'

'Where your woman awaits you,' Luftetmek said with a grin. 'I hope you find what you are looking for.'

'And I hope the same for you,' I said.

I glanced at Zalmetta.

'I will accompany you,' she said.

'And I,' said a voice from behind her.

The Bagalamak child stepped into view.

'I do not think it would be wise to follow me,' I said. 'Perhaps you should go with Luftetmek.'

The Resheki Captain gave me a doubtful look.

'She will never be safe in Reshek,' he said.

'Where I go,' I told him, 'the gaze of the Thirteen tends to follow. The child is not likely to be any more safe with me.'

'At least with you,' Luftetmek said, 'there is an element of chance. In Reshek, should anyone discover her identity it will mean instant death.'

I felt like I was being backed into a corner, and I didn't much like it. But it was hard to argue with his reasoning.

'Very well,' I said. The child gave me a regal nod, as though my approval were no more than a formality. 'But I think I shall live to regret it,' I muttered.

We left the safe house at dawn, when the curfew was lifted and the filinta on the streets were fewer in number. We had contemplated breaking the curfew, but had dismissed the idea as impractical and foolish. Even in broad daylight, the way turned out to be not without its share of risks. Several times we were accosted by Kandirak's stormtroopers, always with the same demand: papers. Of course, we had none. What we did have were two potent swordsmen, a half-dozen pistols, and a charlaki superwoman. In any other Vinh land that I knew, that would not have been enough – not after the first few encounters, anyway. But in any other Vinh land the filinta would never have been tolerated. And something of that feeling persisted in Xacmet, even in the quarters where Kandirak found greater approval than did Yarissi. When the filinta who had stopped us began to cry for aid, they found it conspicuously absent. Only other filinta would rush to their support, and we had timed our journey so that none were likely to be within earshot.

Several fraught hours later we found ourselves on a bleak hillside several miles beyond the north wall of the city. There were no patrols out here, though I knew that as we moved further from the capital we would encounter them again – usually when it would be to our least advantage.

'Your way lies there,' Luftetmek said, pointing. 'Beware of

patrols and large, industrious towns and cities. Yarissi's message is listened to most keenly by the underprivileged.' He held out his hand to me. 'If the Thirteen will it,' he said, 'we will meet again. Until then, go with Gazig.'

I took his hand.

'May the Lord of Blood favour your cause,' I said. It was the right thing for one warrior to say to another, but I couldn't help adding, 'And may the Bright Lady watch over you.'

I hoped the qualification wouldn't offend him, and judging by his wry smile it didn't.

He raised a hand to Zalmetta, who returned the gesture. The Bagalamak child offered a polite bow, which was not inappropriate but seemed, at this place and time, somewhat incongruous. Luftetmek returned the bow with no hint of mockery. And then, without a backward glance, he turned and strode off down the hillside towards the east. I watched his progress for some minutes, then turned away.

'Time to move on,' I said to no one in particular.

We headed in the direction Luftetmek had suggested, keeping up a steady though fairly brisk pace. I knew that I could march twenty miles in a day, and I didn't doubt that Zalmetta could match me, but what of the child?

And speaking of the child, now that I had had time to think about it her choice to accompany me seemed an odd one. If, as she had once said, her future in Reshek lay in Yarissi's hands, would it not have made more sense to go with Luftetmek?

She was walking alongside me as these thoughts went through my mind, so I was slightly startled when she said, 'You are wondering why I chose to follow you rather than the renegade Luftetmek.'

Recovering my composure after my astonishment at her seeming telepathic abilities I said, 'Yes. And you owe that "renegade" your life, just as surely as you owe it to me.'

'I am aware of that,' she replied. 'And to answer your question, Luftetmek was correct when he said my place in Reshek would not be safe at this time. To stay with him, at a time when he is unlikely even to be able to protect his own existence, would have been foolish. So I chose to accompany you, which seemed the lesser of two evils. In time, when this treasonous revolt has been crushed, I shall return.'

I was curious, so I asked, 'And do what?'

'Claim the throne of Reshek,' she said simply.

I stopped and looked at her. She stared up at me with perfect candour, her green eyes carrying no hint of duplicity.

'Who are you?' I asked. It seemed about time that I knew.

'I am Ylyrria Muti,' she replied, 'last surviving heir to the House Bagalamak.'

'You were not the only survivor,' I reminded her.

'I am the last of the Emperor's Inner House,' she said. 'The others were all killed before being hanged at the roadside.'

I said nothing. What could I say?

Zalmetta said, 'You have a beautiful name, child. *The fire of the dawn*. It suits you.'

More ancient Thekkish, I thought. But Zalmetta was right. With her red-blonde hair, the name was singularly appropriate.

To me, Ylyrria Muti said, 'Instruct your creature not to address me directly. I will tolerate your own lack of courtesy, but not that of an animal.'

I glanced at Zalmetta. She might not have heard Ylyrria's insult, for all the response she gave. Annoyed on her behalf, I said to the child, 'Why were you not killed with your kin?'

She ignored my tone and said, 'I am female, and a child. They did not expect me to live. And even if I had, they did not see me as a threat.' Her face darkened with a momentary rage, quickly contained. Through clenched teeth she said, 'That was their mistake.'

Despite her frequently insufferable attitude, I reminded myself that this was a child who spoke. The things she had seen and endured over the past days would have left most adults scarred for life; the miracle was not that she had survived this well, but that she had survived at all.

'Let's keep moving,' I said. 'We've still a long way to go.'

CHAPTER TWENTY-TWO

The Road North

The Resheki landscape was like nothing I had ever seen on Shushuan. There was an almost primeval aspect to some of it, and it was easy to imagine that it had gone unchanged since the dawn of time. Of the green fields and wooded hillsides that typified the Vohung lands there was no sign. Instead, there was a wild, untamed, feral countryside that was at one moment dense forest and the next bleak and lifeless desert. And what desert! The surface of Earth's Moon could not have been more devoid of colour or any hint of moisture. Nothing lived in those regions, neither plant nor animal, and we ourselves made a point of skirting them, even though to do so was to add days to our journey.

It was easy, after experiencing their country, to see why the Resheki people considered themselves the oldest race in the world. The only time I had ever seen anything as primordial as this was when the Thirteen had caused me to witness the illusion that their Valley was still in its prehistoric infancy. Fortunately for our current journey we did not encounter any of the beasts that I had imagined seeing on that long-ago day.

What we did encounter were poverty-stricken villages, looted and ravaged hamlets, towns racked by civil unrest, and – once – a city that burned against a midnight skyline. The stream of dispossessed souls who trudged silently past us on the road that night were like men and women bereft of all joy; and whatever conflict had originally split them, they were now united in their grief and loss.

We travelled northwards for better than a month, the going frequently arduous, and we went hungry as often as not. But we managed on the whole to avoid any serious encounters with the troubled populace.

That changed the day we crested a low hill and found ourselves facing our first truly insurmountable obstacle. Lying across our path, from west to east as far as the eye could see, was a river. And what a river. A quarter of a mile wide it was, and with a current that looked formidable even from this distance. I stared up- and downstream, fighting a sense of despair – we would die if we attempted to ford that torrent, I was certain of it. To the west, towards the interior of the continent, the river ran unbroken to the horizon. To the east . . . I shaded my eyes against the mid-morning sun, blinking and looking away, then staring again into the middle distance.

I touched Zalmetta's arm. 'Do you see that?'

She stared off into the east, the light not appearing to give her any discomfort.

'It is a ferry station,' she said.

'You're certain?'

'I would not have said so otherwise, David.'

The ferry, if such it was, lay several hours' walk from our present position, on the other side of a stretch of rocky terraces. Between here and there, the river ran a set of rapids that were short but steep – and as deadly as any I had ever seen.

We made good time across the uneven terrain, keeping as far back from the river bank as was practical, and presently it became obvious that Zalmetta had been correct. The ferry was a heavy wooden platform, railed, that was docked against a weather-beaten wooden structure at the water's edge. Ropes crossed the river from the ferry to a point on the far bank, which was visibly closer at this point of the river. Also, the current here was clearly less ferocious, though given the mass of the ferry itself I suspected the river was still quite deep.

On the ferry itself, eight men, naked except for loincloths, sat hunched up by the grab rails, four on each side of the ferry. I looked more closely; each man wore a broad belt of what looked like leather, and from each belt ran a length of chain that was affixed to a metal ring set in the ferry itself. The men were slaves; the ferry's motive power was now obvious.

It was a little after noon when we reached the structure that apparently served as the ferry station. Its wooden boards, bleached now of all colour, might once have been brightly painted – spots of colour could still be seen in the cracks between them – but routine maintenance had obviously become a forgotten art in this part of the empire.

There was only one door in the front of the two-storey building, and it was open. Inside it was as dark as the bottom of a well. Walking through that door, going from direct sunlight to shadow, we would be blind for several seconds. I glanced around the side of the building, Zalmetta and Ylyrria looking at me curiously: there were no windows. I stood in front of the open door, about ten feet back from it, and shaded my eyes.

'What are you doing?' Ylyrria asked.

'Hush, child,' Zalmetta admonished her.

I could still see nothing inside the building, but that didn't change anything.

I called out, 'Hello, the ferry!'

There was no reply.

'You have customers!' I called.

Still no reply.

I looked around both sides of the building once again; there was no way to get to the ferry itself without going through the station. I drew one of my pistols and, unhurriedly, loaded it. I threw it to Zalmetta. Then I loaded the second and threw that to her as well. I unslung the sabre and removed the strap, tying it around my waist. I didn't unsheath the blade.

'It's a lovely day,' I called out. 'Very *dry*! Nice day for a fire.'

After a moment, I heard movement inside the building. Whispered voices, raised in argument, carried indistinctly through the open door. Then, one at a time, four men emerged. They were scruffy, dirty, their garments rags. All sported beards and looked several years overdue for a dental check-up. One of them, the one that I instinctively knew to be the leader – he had emerged last – wore a patch over one eye, and his face, above and below the patch, was horribly scarred.

The first two men began to circle around me, and I resisted a smile at the expressions on their faces – they had never seen anything like Zalmetta before, and were torn between keeping one eye on me and another on her. I heard the snap of a pistol hammer being cocked, then a second, and the two men froze in place.

None of the four carried firearms. And only the one-eyed leader carried a sword. The other three were armed with knives; one – the third man – carried a battered war axe.

'Tonoko da,' I said politely to the leader.

And waited.

Presently he said, 'Da tono,' and offered a black and gap-toothed grin.

'We require passage across the river,' I said.

He looked me up and down. Then he leaned to one side and looked past me at Zalmetta and Ylyrria. Straightening up, he spat on the ground between us.

'Ferry's closed,' he said.

'We will be happy to pay,' I told him.

This, actually, was only half true. None of us was carrying Resheki currency, but Zalmetta's gold jewellery would, I was confident, be acceptable as a medium of exchange.

'You will pay,' he said, 'but the ferry is still *closed*.'

He barked the last word, and instantly the two men who had been circling sprang upon me. They were good; had Zalmetta been possessed of human reflexes, they would have reached me before she could react. Instead, two pistol shots rang out, and each man took a bullet through his knife arm.

The axeman was as swift as his comrades, but speed only counts for so much. I sidestepped his roundhouse swing and planted the sheathed sword in his belly, hard. He doubled up, gasping, and I clubbed him with the weapon's guard. He didn't get up.

Between the leader shouting 'Closed' and the axeman hitting the earth at my feet, only three or four seconds had elapsed.

I looked swiftly from one to the other of the men who flanked me, each of whom was nursing a bleeding forearm. Both men backed away from me.

I met the one-eyed gaze of their leader. He gave me that ugly grin again, this time with no hint of amusement.

'I am Nazar,' he said, drawing his sword. 'In times past, I was an officer in the Emperor's Guard.'

I acknowledged the challenge in his words. I unsheathed the sabre.

'I am David Shaw,' I told him, 'Captain of the city of Benza.'

'You are far from home, Benzite,' he said, using an insulting form of the name of my city. He obviously expected it to anger me, and make me careless. I decided to oblige him.

'You stinking gryllup-spawn—' I cried, pretending to rush impetuously forwards.

He leaped into the opening I had provided, a lethal thrust aimed at my heart. I believed, in that second, that his words on introducing himself had been true, that he had indeed been one of the Emperor's Guard. But that, I guessed, had been long ago. I avoided the thrust and caught him across the throat as we passed. He sank to the grass, staining it scarlet as his life departed.

I turned slowly to the remaining two men.

'Leave now,' I advised them.

They fled, in opposite directions, neither one looking back.

I wiped the sabre on the grass and sheathed it. Zalmetta handed me back the pistols.

'Thank you,' I said.

'I do not like causing pain to humans,' she told me. 'Each time I do it, it becomes more difficult. I tell you this so that you will not come to rely on me too heavily in these situations.'

'I understand,' I said.

We entered the ferry station, still wary for a possible trap, but the building was deserted. It was also little more than a hollow shell. Once, possibly, it had been some kind of trading post, but the inside had been long ago gutted by its erstwhile occupants, leaving only the sad echoes of its former identity. In this, it was in no way atypical of the rest of Reshek.

We took the ferry across the river and then spent an hour setting free the eight slaves. Ylyrria was not slow to show her disgust at our behaviour, but I ignored her.

'You now have two choices,' I told the men. 'Flee, and possibly die as runaways. Or stay here and run this station.'

'As . . . free men?' one asked.

I hesitated, then said, 'As whatever you want to be. Chained to this raft, you would die in a matter of days. At least now you have some element of choice.'

We left them still debating what they would do next. Listening to them, I guessed it would be hours before they even started to reach a decision.

The days of walking once again turned into weeks. The landscape changed again and again, by turns green and lush then grey and lifeless, sometimes as flat as the Plains of Ktikbat and then as rolling and hilly as the lands around Benza. We would pass through belts of woodland, the trees some variation of conifer that were more blue than green, and emerged from them to find ourselves at the edge of a desert, or a sheer precipice that could not be circumnavigated, or, once, by a vast blue lake that challenged the horizon on three sides.

Yet for all the delays, all the detours and frustrations, we managed to keep plodding on. A day in which we could cover twenty-five miles due north would be followed by one that took us to east or west and saw us barely a mile closer to our objective by sundown.

I hadn't expected to find a border that could be recognized as such between Reshek and Ragana-Se-Tor, so when, better than forty days after leaving the ferry station, we found ourselves confronted by the remains of an Y'nys city, I took this as our first step into Ragana-Se-Tor.

'There are a few Y'nys cities in Reshek,' Zalmetta pointed out.

'Humour me,' I suggested.

She shrugged.

We took a few hours to explore the ancient city, Ylyrria in particular being fascinated by its construction. It's not easy to explain what it is about these cities that gives such an impression of alienness, of their builders being not merely non-human, but non-humanoid. Part of it is the obsession with circles – the buildings are all cylinders or domes, the streets interlocking or concentric circles, the city 'blocks' all following the shape of the buildings that make them up – but that's only part of it. The seamless stone of which the whole city is built, every building and street flowing into every other with not a hint of a join, is another factor, as is the preponderance of windows and doors in places where no human would put them. But the real source of the impression is undoubtedly subliminal, below the threshold of consciousness, and perhaps beyond the reach of language. Whatever it actually was, whether one thing or a combination of many, it was as real and as tangible in this city as it had been in Hippom Ather, and the similarities were so intense that the memories they evoked were an ache inside me.

I was hoping, rather foolishly, that we would find a working Library in the city. To no one's surprise, we did not find one. We pressed on, leaving the city as deserted as we had found it.

If that ancient edifice had not constituted proof of this being Ragana-Se-Tor, then what we encountered four days later did. What we encountered was the Ladden.

CHAPTER TWENTY-THREE

The Ladden

———◆◇◆◇◆———

There was a whole tribe, upwards of fifty individuals, slaves included, moving at right angles to our projected course. They were a mile or more away from us, and at our present relative speeds we would miss one another by better than an hour. I decided, for a number of good reasons (and several rather more dubious ones) to change course and intercept them.

I was conscious, as I did so, of an irrational fear at what I was doing. When Mrs Catlin and I had first come to Shushuan we had fallen in with a tribe of Ladden, and had done our best to fit in with their nomadic lifestyle. This had been a logical thing to do, since we needed the Ladden as guides and teachers. It had also been our first mistake. As passing strangers, we were relatively safe from harm at the hands of the Ladden, who were not a malicious or aggressive race. But by becoming *de facto* a part of their tribe we placed ourselves at the mercy of their laws. And because we were unable to earn our keep in any other way we ended up as slaves. There was no danger of that happening today, not under circumstances such as these, but the fear of confronting the race that had once caused me a great deal of misery was not one I could easily ignore.

Of course, this tribe would not be the same one Mrs Catlin and I had met all those years ago. Hareg's former people did not march this far south.

The Ladden slave who was on point spotted us early on and called a halt to the march. He was an impressively built individual, with coppery-red hair and a neatly trimmed beard. He wore the short kilt favoured by most Ladden male slaves, and at his left ankle was the grey band that ensured his obedience. To the casual observer, the anklet was a ring of cold iron, perhaps an inch in cross-section, seamless but otherwise unremarkable. In fact, it was composed of an ancient Y'nys substance that, when activated by a mutahiir, or control rod, could inflict intense pain, or bring about a hideous and protracted death. I had once worn such a band, and I had seen the effect it could have when set for lethal force. As a means of slave control, it was particularly effective.

It was my guess that this individual was the head slave of this group. As such, he would be prized by the Ladden themselves, and would have absolute control over the other slaves. But, at the end of the day, he was no less a slave than they. And the power of life and death would not rest in his hands, but in those of the nominal leader of the tribe.

The column of men and women gathered together as we approached. Armed slaves made their presence known – the Ladden do not do their own fighting – but they would not attack us unless ordered to do so. We were, after all, free, and they were just slaves.

The Ladden tribes are loosely organized, and have no leaders as such. Each tribe has a nominated spokesman who deals with such matters as might fall within the purview of a leader, but being a somewhat hedonistic, carefree race, the Ladden keep their formalities to a minimum.

As was appropriate, I said nothing to the slave, and for his part he chose not to address me. Under other circumstances, I might have greeted him, just to see his reaction. And, it must be admitted, out of a sense of mischief for which I have been repeatedly punished over the years. Today, however, the stakes were too high for that kind of self-indulgence.

One of the Ladden stepped forward. He was typical of the breed: not especially tall, with a good physique and an intelligent face. His dark hair was neatly trimmed and he was clean-shaven. His only garment, a simple loincloth, was threadbare in places and showed signs of several repairs. The Ladden, great artists and craftsmen by anyone's standards, were entirely lacking in sartorial pretension.

'Tonoko da,' he said, offering the common greeting.

I was glad he had spoken first. It indicated a desire to treat us as equals. Some of my tension evaporated.

'Da tono,' I replied.

'You are strangers in Ragana-Se-Tor?' the man said.

'We are travellers from a far land,' I said. 'We are bound for the lands that border the market town of Vraks'has.'

'That is a good distance,' the man observed. He glanced at Zalmetta. 'Your pardon,' he said, 'but is that a charlaki woman? Her colouring is most odd.'

I was startled; how did a Ladden know of the charlaki?

'She is,' I replied, cautious not to reveal too much.

'Is she your property?' the Ladden asked.

This was not a question a native Vinh would take offence at – natural charlaki are, after all, regarded as animals by those few who are familiar with them – and I tried to keep that in mind when responding. (Knowing the Ladden, the question was probably intended as a preamble to making an offer to purchase Zalmetta.)

'She is a free woman,' I said, 'who travels with me by choice.'

'A free charlak?' the man observed, clearly surprised. 'An interesting notion.' He looked back at me and smiled. 'I am Chaymek,' he said. 'Will you share our camp tonight, and tell us of your travels?'

'Gladly,' I replied.

Chaymek turned to the red-haired slave.

'We will camp early,' he said.

The slave nodded and turned away, calling out orders to his people.

Ylyrria Muti stepped up to my side. There was a look of disdain on her face as she regarded the Ladden.

'Do we need this diversion?' she asked. 'What possible benefit can we gain from associating with these savages?'

'The Ladden know this country better than anyone,' I said. 'They can give us directions to where we're headed. A few hours lost now could save us days later on. Also, once we reach Hippom Ather I'm not certain of the way to the place where we're going. Someone in Chaymek's group may know that region well enough to provide us with a map.'

I saw Zalmetta watching the Ladden with a wariness that surprised me. I recalled the remark made by Chaymek, and my surprise that he had known Zalmetta was a charlak.

'Have your people had dealings with the Ladden?' I asked.

'There is a charlaki tribe in Ragana-Se-Tor,' Zalmetta said. 'It lives in a secluded valley that I had thought unknown to the Vinh. It troubles me that this is no longer the case.'

'You'll be safe with me,' I told her.

'I believe so,' she said. 'But Chaymek and his like will never regard me as anything but property.'

'I am sorry for that,' I told her.

She looked at me strangely, but said nothing.

That night we sat around one of Chaymek's camp fires and swapped travellers' tales with our hosts. I had introduced myself as Yaved Tor, a Vohung corruption of my true name, but had offered no rank and no city of origin. Among certain of the Ladden my name was known, and not necessarily guaranteed to earn us a friendly reception. My companions, of course, were under no such restrictions.

It was a convivial evening, and reminded me of the early days of my first experience with the Ladden, before Hareg had made slaves of Mrs Catlin and me. I recalled Hareg; once an enemy, later a reluctant ally, and finally a friend. It would be difficult to overstate the importance of Hareg's involvement in my life.

One of Chaymek's people was able to furnish the directions I had been hoping for, and sketched out a map for us of the route we needed to take. Of course, 'sketched' is a relative term; a cartographer could not have done a better job, nor an illuminist a more attractive one. Everything the Ladden made, no matter how prosaic its function, was a work of art. It had been their skill and craftsmanship that had made the *Mariner* possible.

Late into the night, with Ylyrria fast asleep and Zalmetta curled up close by, I found myself standing on the edge of the camp and staring out into the darkness. Ragana-Se-Tor is a beautiful country; its name, in ancient Thekkish, means *The Garden of Forever*. Overhead, the nearer moon was a pale yellow crescent, perhaps a little smaller than Earth's Moon might have appeared in the same phase. I searched the heavens and, with a little difficulty, found the two smaller and further moons. It was only their motion that singled them out from the clusters of stars around them. The stars, of course, were much further away; I wondered if our own sun were visible from here. I had often speculated on the location of Shushuan. Did it lie in our galaxy, or even our universe? Or was it in another place, another time, separated from our reality by more than mere distance? I doubted that I would ever know.

I gazed northward. Far away, on the pale horizon, I could make out the jagged tips of mountains, probably the same mountains Mrs Catlin and I had seen on our first night on Shushuan. I wondered if, somewhere in the far distance, she too was standing out under the stars tonight, and looking southward. It was a strangely comforting thought.

CHAPTER TWENTY-FOUR

Vraks'has

We took our leave of the Ladden the next morning. The map they had provided included all the known trails where bandits could be expected. These particular markings were largely speculative, of course, especially in the more northern regions, but we planned the remainder of our journey to avoid crossing those trails whenever possible.

The other thing the map showed was that we would be likely to reach Vraks'has before we reached Hippom Ather. This came as a surprise, since Vraks'has lies some hundred and fifty miles northwest of the ancient city. The reason was that the Market Town lay due north of our current position, and the way to Hippom Ather was made virtually impassable by the presence of a vast cliff; the very cliff, in fact, that formed the southern boundary of the valley that was our ultimate destination. The only way to get there in a straight line would have meant a rock climb that only an experienced mountaineer would have attempted. Had I been alone I might have risked it, since it would have cut many days off our travel time. But there was no way that Ylyrria could be expected to undertake such a task, and in truth it would have been a foolish risk to take under any circumstances. Also, I had a reason for wanting to visit Vraks'has first, though I had not yet voiced it to anyone.

The way was much easier now than it had been in Reshek. Ragana-Se-Tor is a country in name only, being more of a region as far as political and legal divisions are concerned. There is no capital and no centralized government. What few large cities there are are autonomous, and usually walled and heavily defended. By contrast, the many market towns – such as Vraks'has – were entirely cosmopolitan. Their rulers tended to be of the town council variety, composed of merchants and businessmen. The law in such towns, with the exception of those few topics covered by ancient tradition, such as slavery, theft, and blatant acts of personal violence, was pretty much whatever the council said it was, and there was usually a paid police force on hand to enforce the council's rulings. I had had one run-in with such a body, and now found myself hoping that the memory of Vraks'has's 'police chief' was not an especially long one.

We did our best to avoid the strongholds, having no desire to have to explain ourselves unnecessarily. But we actively sought out the market towns and other similarly open settlements. Here we were only marginally noteworthy as far as our appearance and purpose were concerned. Locals, bandits, Ladden and foreign travellers rubbed shoulders without a second glance, and although Zalmetta did draw one or two curious stares, no one accosted or attempted to molest us.

It was late spring in Ragana-Se-Tor now, and I was beginning to envy Zalmetta her almost non-existent garments. My own tunic was becoming intolerably warm and uncomfortable during the long days, and I found myself longing for the Benzan garb I had abandoned so long ago in Zatuchep. Paradoxically, Zalmetta herself seemed entirely unaffected by the various climatic changes. Whatever the weather, she was never discomforted, either in appearance or in fact.

As for the child, Ylyrria, she seemed actually to revel in the warm sunshine and occasional refreshing showers of cool rain. Her energy was boundless, though her perennial moodiness was never entirely eclipsed. She troubled me, but as our destination drew steadily nearer it became impossible for me to think of anything but the reunion that lay ahead. I found myself sometimes laughing for no good reason, and it was a rare day that did not see a definite smile on my face.

The landscape now offered few insurmountable obstacles, and the map of the Ladden kept us fairly safe from bandits.

But the journey was not entirely without incident; there were rivers to be crossed, cliffs to be scaled or circumnavigated, belts of dense woodland to be hacked through, and men and beasts to be contended with. It was nothing compared to the time we had spent in Reshek, but there were few days that passed entirely uneventfully.

None of us was sad to see the squat wood-and-stone buildings of Vraks'has when they finally appeared on the horizon.

'How long will we remain here?' Zalmetta asked as we crossed the plain that led to the city.

'One night,' I replied.

'You will consult the Library here?' she asked.

I had eventually spoken of my reasons for wanting to visit Vraks'has. There was risk involved, but I needed to know if Celebe still lived, and the Library was likely to have that information. The problem, of course, was that if Daqar was somehow monitoring the Library network he would learn of our location as soon as I accessed the system.

'Yes,' I said. 'I have to.'

'I understand,' she said.

'I don't,' Ylyrria said irritably.

'I have to know about Celebe,' I said. She knew that; I had explained it at some length. She was just being perverse.

'Why?' she demanded.

I wanted to ignore her, but somehow I couldn't. It hadn't been my choice to have her come with us, but once the decision had been made it had left me with an inevitable sense of responsibility. Last of the Bagalamak and a regular pain, she remained only a child.

'Celebe is my friend,' I replied, 'and I don't know if she's alive or dead. I have to know.'

'What good will it do?' Ylyrria asked, not unreasonably. 'What good will it do you or her? You can't help her. You can't go to her. And even if you could, you wouldn't. You've already got one unfinished mission. Why don't you stick to that, get that finished, get that done with, before you start going off on some other stupid quest?'

Zalmetta put her hand on the child's arm. She shrugged it off; as far as Ylyrria was concerned Zalmetta was just a freak of nature, and the child deeply resented it when the charlaki woman spoke to her or touched her. Zalmetta kept trying, though I wasn't sure why.

'Ylyrria,' I said, in as reasonable a tone of voice as I could muster, 'it doesn't matter whether or not I can do anything. I just have to know.'

'No matter what the cost,' she said.

'No matter what the cost,' I confirmed.

With a child's theatricality she turned and looked slowly towards the north. 'No matter what the cost?' she asked again.

I looked at her intently, trying to read her thoughts. It was a wasted effort. I wondered if I puzzled her as much as she puzzled me.

'Understand this,' I said. 'I do not trust Celebe, and I have no great love for her. But Ailette Legendre was a good and true friend, and I owe her my life in more ways than I can ever repay. If she lives, I need to know. Because if she lives, her life and mine are inextricably linked. That's not my choice, but as long as the Thirteen Gods are still in Asmina, it's the reality we both have to live with. And as long as you're travelling with me, it's the reality you'll have to live with, too. I hope you can understand that, because I don't intend explaining it again.'

I pointed to the buildings in the distance.

'That's where I'm going,' I said. 'You're welcome to join me.'

That night, the three of us sat at a table in a low-ceilinged room at one of Vraks'has's cheaper hostels. The room, which could comfortably have seated thirty or forty people, now contained at least twice that number. Traders and travellers from all over Ragana-Se-Tor were in evidence, as were leather-clad bandits and half-naked Ladden. I knew that the latter would hate a place like this, but business was business, and the dealers who trafficked in the wares needed by the Ladden would all be here, and would be more likely to offer generous terms after downing several bottles of the local brew than they would standing stone-cold sober in the market square.

There would be no trouble tonight, despite the fact that hereditary enemies stood, armed, shoulder to shoulder. Vraks'has would not tolerate any activity that might harm its trading capacity, and everyone here knew that. Still, old habits die hard; I sat with my back to the wall, the entire room visible to my gaze.

'This is truly disgusting,' Ylyrria said, rather more loudly than was absolutely necessary. A couple of heads turned, then their owners smiled good-naturedly and went back to their own meals.

'What's wrong with it?' I asked her, in a rather more hushed tone.

She gestured with her eating utensil, a cross between a fork and a knife that was popular on this side of the continent; in the Kingdoms, by contrast, 'eating utensils' were the pink dangly things attached to the end of your hand.

'The hu is overcooked,' she said, 'the s'tahm is nearly raw, the m'rehn are cold, and as for the g'hak . . .'

'Mine is fine,' I told her. 'Would you care to swap?'

'You have no taste,' she informed me.

'Maybe not,' I snapped, 'but for the money we're paying I have tremendous gratitude.'

She smiled condescendingly. 'Peasant,' she said.

I heard a soft chuckle from Zalmetta and looked at her in surprise. It was the first time I had ever heard her laugh. And I wasn't quite sure what had prompted it. Not for the first time, though perhaps more forcibly than before, I was made aware of how beautiful she looked. Alien, but beautiful. She still drew looks from passers-by, but at least in a place like Vraks'has she was able to show herself safely.

Still smiling, she asked, 'How went your visit to the Library?'

I had consulted Vraks'has's Library while she and Ylyrria had secured our lodgings for the night. They had used up half our funds doing so, funds garnered in Vraks'has itself by selling off Zalmetta's gold armbands and rings at the market square. We had been given a fraction of their worth, but it was a buyer's market and we were desperate – even on Shushuan, some things could only be obtained with hard currency. If we stayed at the inn for many more nights I envisioned having to unpick the gold thread on my antique tunic.

'It was a wasted journey,' I told Zalmetta. 'If Celebe lives, no record of her whereabouts exists in the Library network. The destruction of the Library at Zatuchep has been noted, but without explanation. The resultant explosion and destruction of the island are mentioned by several observers, but again there is no '

'How came you by this?' a man's voice said at my side.

I looked up; the sheer carelessness I had displayed is not seeing the man's approach was something I would berate myself for at length – but later.

He was a bandit; black leather garments sewn with iron plates, steel-backed gauntlets and greaves; a conical helmet with a chain-mail mask and collar dangled from his left wrist. His only weapon was a sabre, worn across his back in the local fashion. And he was pointing at my own sabre, which lay on the table in front of me.

'It was a gift,' I said, my tone neutral, 'from a defeated opponent.'

The man raised an eyebrow; his hair was jet-black, tied in a knot on top of his head. A braided queue hung over his right shoulder, where it would not entangle his sword. He had a thin moustache, and a wispy strand of beard hung from his chin.

'What became of this . . . opponent?' he asked.

'When last I saw him,' I replied, 'he was walking away into a snow storm, following his brethren who were similarly defeated.'

A thin smile crossed the man's lips.

'I believe,' he said, 'it is time for the "gift" to return to its rightful people.'

'I think not,' I said.

'You would dispute with me?' the man asked, his smile unchanged.

I looked around the room. No one was paying us any attention.

'This is Vraks'has,' I said simply.

'I care not,' the man said, matching my tone.

'But I,' I said, 'do care.'

I knew from unhappy experience what happened to people who engaged in open warfare on the streets of this town, and I didn't intend letting anything delay me when I was this close to my objective.

'Then give me the weapon,' the bandit said.

I reached out slowly and took hold of the hilt of the sabre. It was bound in red leather, wound around two shaped sections of sard wood, themselves sandwiching the steel core that extended into the blade itself. The basket guard and cross-piece were separate units, fitted in place and retained by the small pommel. It was a fine weapon, and one for which I had an uncommon, possibly unhealthy, affection.

I looked up at the bandit.

'Let us step outside,' I said.

He stepped back from the table, casually so as not to draw attention from those around us to his true intent, and I arose to face him.

'After you,' I said.

'Please—' he said, gesturing for me to precede him.

'No, no, I insist—' I said.

From the table I heard Ylyrria mutter, 'Outlanders—' but not so loudly that the bandit could hear.

To the bandit I said, 'I will go first. You will not attempt to follow until I reach the door, where I will wait for you. We will then step outside together. Agreed?'

The bandit nodded slowly.

'Should you change your mind,' I said, 'my colleague will shoot you in the back.'

The bandit glanced at Zalmetta, who laid one of my pistols on the table in front of her. From the look in her eyes, no one would have doubted the truth of what I had just said. No one but me, and I doubted it mightily.

The bandit nodded.

By now a few of the hostel's clientele had begun to take notice of what was occurring, and the disapproving looks I was getting were not helping matters. But they did impress upon me one very important insight: if I handled this wrong, I would be unlikely to see Mrs Catlin again for a very long time.

I turned and walked towards the door. Once there, I looked back at the bandit. He glanced briefly down at Zalmetta, then sneered at her and walked towards me, showing us both how little he feared the charlaki woman's marksmanship.

'Do you believe in the Gods?' I asked the bandit as he drew abreast of me in the doorway.

'Of course,' he replied.

'So do I,' I said, and pushed him roughly out into the street. I slammed the door behind him and threw the bolt that was its only visible form of lock. I heard his cries of rage and ignored them. I turned and raced back to the table.

'Back door!' I yelled. 'Now!'

Zalmetta scooped up Ylyrria, who let out a furious curse of protest, and the three of us shoved our way through the press of bodies that stood between us and what I hoped was the back way out. Behind us, I could hear the bandit pounding on the front door, his cries of fury reaching us in disjointed snatches.

'The food wasn't that bad!' Ylyrria shrieked.

Behind us, a new sound drowned out the bandit's pounding and cursing. It was the sound of laughter. I guessed the transient population of Vraks'has thought this was the best floor show they were likely to see tonight.

An hour later we were walking out onto the open trail that led from the Market Town to Hippom Ather.

'I'm hungry,' Ylyrria said.

'There will be bandits on this trail,' Zalmetta said.

I kept walking, ignoring them both.

CHAPTER TWENTY-FIVE

Despair

———◦◦◦◦———

Hippom Ather, the Summer Home of Hareg's old tribe, was deserted. Assuming the Ladden still used it, which seemed likely, it was too early in the year for them to have arrived yet. They travelled mostly in the spring and autumn, when the weather was not too unbearable. The last time I had been here, they had delayed leaving at the end of summer and had then been caught in a freak spell of bad weather while still on the open trail.

We wasted no time in the ancient Y'nys city, but pressed on across the savannah beyond in the direction of the river valley that was our ultimate destination.

The going was difficult now, with heavily wooded hills to hack our way up and muddy crevasses to be waded through. It was slow and frustrating going, but at least we were now safe from any possibility of attack. No predators – human or otherwise – were to be found in this region, though there was no shortage of wildlife, as we discovered on the frequent occasions that we disturbed a nest or blundered across a watering hole.

Gradually, the landscape changed once more, and suddenly things began to look familiar. I had been here before.

We emerged from a tangle of undergrowth and found ourselves on the bank of a broad, slow-moving river. The River. *The* River. We were here. This was it. We had made it. I felt my knees try to give out on me, and it was only through an effort of will that I stayed upright.

'Permit me to guess,' Ylyrria said behind me. 'We now have to cross that, yes?'

I nodded, not able to speak.

'Imagine my delight,' she muttered.

I found my voice.

'But not here,' I said. 'There's an undertow. And it's moving faster than it looks. We need to move upstream. It's narrower and there are places where . . .'

My voice trailed off, the memories too intense. Presently I said, 'We'll cross further upstream,' and left it at that.

We trudged upstream for perhaps another half-mile before I stopped again.

'Here,' I said. A thought occurred to me. 'Ylyrria, can you swim?'

'Yes,' the child replied, apparently affronted that I should think her incapable of anything.

'Hmmm,' I said sceptically. 'Well, even so, perhaps you'd better stay close to me.'

She looked up at me with those grown-up eyes in a child's face. I wished, I truly wished, that I knew what thoughts lived behind those eyes. The moment passed as she asked mockingly, 'Can *you* swim?'

I resisted the temptation to throw her into the water and let her take her chances. Instead, I started to prepare myself for the swim. I removed my sandals and slung them about my neck, tying them to the strap of the sabre. I tucked the pistols into the waxed bag that contained their accessories and slung it with the sabre. Then, with a last glance at Ylyrria and Zalmetta, I waded into the river.

It was deep. And the current, though not swift, was strong. I began to swim. Ylyrria swam along at my side, arms and legs working with a speed that put my own efforts to shame. But I was shifting more water with each stroke than she was with any ten of hers. We were just about staying abreast of one another.

Zalmetta, however, moved through the water like a shark. She was a marvel to watch; she actually swam rings around Ylyrria and me – literally. She was revelling in her physical prowess, enjoying the moment as much as her natural cousins would have. I think I had never seen her enjoy anything so much, and found myself strangely pleased for her.

We lost an hour's walking distance to the current, but we made the far side without incident. We crawled up onto the grassy bank and lay panting; even Zalmetta was breathing hard. She seemed almost to glow with vitality.

A little later, dripping wet but not uncomfortable in the warm spring air, we got up and continued along the bank.

Early the next morning, we spotted the face of the cliff that marked the southern boundary of the valley. It was from a fissure in that cliff face that Mrs Catlin and I had first stepped onto the surface of Shushuan.

The pace I set from that moment on was gruelling. We became strung out in the undergrowth, Ylyrria lagging far behind with Zalmetta in the middle trying to keep both the child and myself in sight. It was foolish of me to place us at risk of getting separated in this way, but I was driven now by feelings and needs over which I had no control.

At noon, I emerged into the small clearing that led up to the cliff itself. Carrion birds wheeled about in the sky overhead. The drone of thousands of insects was heavy in the air, and clouds of them hung over the clearing like a miasma. The camp, large enough to suggest it had been here on a permanent basis for quite some time, lay scattered across the clearing, its tents and cooking fires and pens hinting at a population of perhaps thirty men and women.

I could see, from where I stood, about a dozen warriors, men of Benza, gathered together around one particular tent. The men were dead, the tent hanging in tatters from its wooden frame.

Elsewhere, a half-dozen slaves could be seen, tied hand and foot in a ring. Their throats had been cut.

In the pens, three gryllup lay in the dust, as dead as their masters.

All the tents in the clearing had been ripped apart, their contents scattered across the ankle-height yellow grass.

Numb, unable to react on any level to what I was seeing, I walked slowly forward, towards the remains of the tent that was ringed by the fallen warriors.

Some of the men, I noted, were in full armour; others did not even have on their hauberk. The attack, whatever it had been, had come swiftly, unexpectedly. The armoured men had perhaps been on sentry duty at the time. The men's wounds appeared to be mostly sword-inflicted, but one or two had strange burn marks that at first I couldn't identify or understand. Then I made an obvious connection in my mind, and a single word explained the marks: Kziktzak.

I stepped over the fallen warriors, startled at the sight of one of them and the realization that, once, I had met him, in Benza, and was angry with myself that I could not now recall his name. I pushed aside the remains of the tent flap and entered, terrified at the prospect of what I might find.

It had been the tent of a single person, a woman by the appointments, and one with a passion for learning. There were scrolls and books in abundance, now scattered and trampled. A chest of clothing had been overturned, its contents a now unrecognizable heap of bright colours on the ground beside it.

I looked around the tent slowly. There was no body. And other than the vandalization of the contents, there was nothing to suggest that a struggle had taken place.

I turned and walked out of the tent. Ylyrria was standing to one side of the clearing, her eyes missing nothing. Zalmetta was walking between the bodies, checking each for any sign of life.

She glanced at me. Neither of us spoke.

I turned and looked up at the cliff face. The narrow crevice was just visible, about twenty feet up the rock, as was the small ledge that abutted it. I looked at it for a long time, my thoughts uncertain. Presently, I realized that I was looking at something other than the sheer rock, something on the lip of the ledge, a mark, a discolouration. It seemed fraught with significance.

I ran my hands through my hair, trying to regain control of

my actions. My fingers encountered the three narrow braids that identified me as a Captain in the army of Duke Joshima, ruler of Benza. That thought, for some reason, seemed to drag my mind back from the abyss that had been threatening to claim it. I was facing despair like none I had ever known before, but now, suddenly, I was facing it on terms I could deal with. There was a job to be done, and I was the only one who could do it. So—

'This was Tal Daqar's doing,' Zalmetta said, interrupting my grim reverie.

I glanced at her, saying nothing. She indicated the fallen warriors. 'Some of these men were killed by Kziktzak,' she said. 'In any event, no other explanation makes sense. There are no tracks leading into the clearing: the attack came from the air. The ship would have been mistaken for your *Mariner* when first spotted, so no defensive measures were taken. By the time the mistake was realized, it was too late.'

I nodded. She was echoing my own thoughts. I crouched down in the grass, examining the numerous overlapping footprints that the battle had left. After a while I said, 'Here.' Zalmetta looked. The footprint I had found, left partially in a smear of blood, was not human.

'Kziktzak,' Zalmetta said. She looked around, and for the first time I saw anger on her face. 'Curse Tal Daqar,' she said softly. 'Curse your gods, and curse your Celebe for showing me a truth I cannot live with.'

I didn't know how to answer her. Celebe's culpability in any of this was problematic. If Zalmetta's current situation was a part of the plans of the Thirteen, then it was unlikely Celebe was privy to those plans. The Thirteen did not always explain to Their minions the reasons for the things They made them do.

I changed the subject. 'There's blood up on the cliff,' I said. 'I'm going to take a look.'

It had been hard to get those words out. I could think of only one person who would have any reason to go up into the cliff, and the prospect of what I might find there was almost paralysing me.

I removed my sandals and outer tunic and slung my sword

behind me out of the way. Then, slowly, I began to climb the inclined face of the cliff.

It took only moments to reach the ledge. I immediately unslung my sword and drew the blade, casting the scabbard down to Zalmetta. Then I bent down to examine the dark stain I had spotted upon the rock. It was indeed blood. It was dry, possibly a day old. That seemed to fit the condition of the bodies in the camp. I straightened up and addressed myself to the gap between the rocks. I had grown in stature since the last time I had squeezed my way through this crevice, and it took some effort to force my body through the narrow cleft.

Once through, I found myself in semi-darkness, and took the time necessary for my eyes to adjust. Ahead of me, only partially lit by the sunlight coming through the crack, was a familiar tunnel. Slowly, I began to inch my way down it.

The tunnel ended in a vertical wall of rock, at what I guessed to be the location of the Blind Spot when the rift was in operation. I turned my back to the wall and looked back along the length of the tunnel.

Now that my own shadow was no longer obscuring the floor, I could see a clear, somewhat broken trail of blood leading back towards the entrance. I stepped to one side and examined the wall behind me. There was a faint bloody patch at what, on a shorter person, would have been shoulder height. I looked more closely; the centre of the patch was marked by a tiny chip in the stone. I looked down at my feet, kicking through the dust and small stones that lined the floor. Nothing presented itself. I moved away from the wall, searching in the half-light with eyes that were growing increasingly used to the level of illumination.

Presently, ten feet or so away from the wall, I found what I was looking for. It was the quarrel of a crossbow. It was broken in several places, the iron tip bent at an angle, and the shaft was smeared with blood.

I hurried out of the cave and clambered back down the cliff. Zalmetta was waiting, a look on her face that might have been concern.

'She was in the cave—' I began.

'Dead?'

'She was in the cave,' I repeated, 'when the attack happened. She was wounded. But she isn't there now. They took her.'

'That would be consistent with the conditions in the rest of the camp,' Zalmetta said.

I didn't know what she was getting at, and said so.

'Consider,' she said. 'Why would Tal Daqar take your woman?'

'How would I know?' I snapped. 'Revenge against me for the part I had in blowing up his island, maybe. Or more likely he wanted the knowledge that she could give him.'

'And yet he waited until the day before our arrival here to make his move,' Zalmetta pointed out, 'even though he must have reached this place many days ago.'

'That makes no sense,' I said.

'It does,' Zalmetta persisted, 'if you accept that it was not the woman he wanted.' I motioned for her to say more. 'He was here long before the attack,' she said, 'with lookouts posted to watch for our arrival. When we were within a day's march of here, he attacked.'

Realization dawned slowly. 'It's me he wants,' I said. 'It's always been me. He's snatched Mrs Catlin to ensure I'll follow him. That's why he waited until we were so close, so that the trail would still be fresh enough for us to follow. But . . . where does it lead? Where will he go now?'

'Back to Xacmet.'

I was being really slow today. 'For Blukka,' I said.

She nodded, her expression pensive.

'You know something of how my former master's mind works,' she said, 'so you will not baulk at accepting what I am about to suggest: he is puzzled by you, by your loyalty to your woman and your beliefs. Possessing no such feelings himself, he cannot fathom them in others. With you, he had the perfect opportunity to test the full extent of those feelings, and he will continue to do so until he finally loses interest – no price, no sacrifice in either time or materials, will be too great for him to pay as long as the question occupies his mind. In short, David, neither you nor your woman will be truly safe so long as Tal Daqar lives.'

'We must get back to Xacmet,' I said. 'If only there was some way to get there ahead of him—'

'It would make little difference—'

'It would make *all* the difference! It would be the one thing he couldn't expect, and it would give us the tiny fraction of an advantage that might make the difference between beating him and being in his power again.'

'If it is truly that important—'

'It is.'

'Then there is one way we could possibly get there ahead of him.'

'At this point,' I said, 'I'm open to any suggestions.'

'The Library at Vraks'has,' she said.

CHAPTER TWENTY-SIX

The Benefits of Victory

This was a plan I did not like, but it was also one to which I could offer no alternative.

Zalmetta's Y'nys-augmented chemistry would not let her access the Library's travel system, but it was that system she was now suggesting we use. Which meant we would need help. We would need a Librarian. Or a Knight. The former would demand a price for his aid; the latter would place us too much under the control of the Thirteen.

And all of this assumed that there was a Library reasonably close to Xacmet, something about which I had no idea.

We made good time getting back to the Market Town, and it was early evening when we entered the red-brick building that housed the Library. Few people were about; from other parts of town we could hear the sounds of merrymaking and boisterous partying, but around the Library itself an appropriate air of seriousness prevailed.

We descended the spiral ramp that led down to the chamber of the Mugaraht itself, and found no one else around. That suited me perfectly; for all that the Librarians were supposed to be more open in their dealings nowadays, I had no illusions about whom I was dealing with. If things got unpleasant, I didn't want any innocent bystanders getting caught in the crossfire.

I approached one of the lecterns that ringed the great mountain of crystal and picked up the stylus that lay in the shallow groove below the screen.

On the green crystal surface I wrote one word:

LIBRARIAN

There was a protracted pause before the screen offered a reply.

SPECIFY THE NATURE OF THE ASSISTANCE YOU REQUIRE, it said.

I wrote: TRANSPORTATION

The pause was longer this time. Then the screen said PLEASE IDENTIFY YOURSELF

This, I guessed, was not the machine talking. I was now conversing with an actual Librarian. (I suspected no one had ever asked a Librarian for transport through the Mugarahts.)

I wrote DAVID SHAW OF BENZA, CAPTAIN OF THE MARINER

Almost instantly the screen said WAIT

I looked up at the Library, knowing – or at least guessing – what was about to happen. Almost immediately the front of the Mugaraht seemed to open before us, and a man stepped out of the 'solid' wall of crystal.

I gazed at him in mute astonishment. Not for what he had just done, but for who he was.

'Sonder—?' I gasped.

It couldn't be. I had seen Sonder killed, ripped limb from limb over the Asmina Valley.

The Librarian stepped forward. And I realized my mistake. The man did indeed strongly resemble my old master, but now that I studied him more closely I could tell that he was not the same man. For one thing, he was much older than Sonder had been, or would have been were he still alive. His hair was white, whereas Sonder's had been scarcely grey. But the resemblance—

'I am Mohred,' he said. He looked directly at me, his eyes like flint. 'I believe you knew my son.'

I nodded slowly, unable to read his expression.

He took a step towards me, his eyes – Sonder's eyes, in a face thirty years older – locked on mine. If he felt I had had any part in his son's death – which, in all honesty, I had not – then my own life expectancy could now probably be measured in seconds. I harboured no illusions about the power this man could undoubtedly wield, and I knew that neither I nor my companions could hope to stand against him.

Suddenly, so suddenly that it actually made me jump, he fell to one knee in front of me, his head bowed.

'I am yours to command,' he said, the words emerging through clenched teeth.

'I . . . don't understand,' I said.

Not rising, he said, 'The woman Linna is known to you?' It was barely a question; obviously he already knew the answer.

'She is my wife,' I said.

He made a face, hiding his distaste quickly; marriage is regarded as a barbarous custom in some parts of Shushuan.

'When my people were put on trial for the acts of Rohc Vahnn and his followers,' Mohred said, 'she spoke in our defence. It was she who proposed that we should be utilized by the Vinh peoples rather than being punished as many of Vahnn's victims wished. Few there were who would listen to her, but then the Knight of the Thirteen, the Lady Celebe, added her voice to the argument, and people began to listen. My people owe their freedom to the woman Linna. We offered her a place as a Librarian, but she declined.' He looked up at me. 'We are each now pledged to aid her whenever we can. For the death of my son, I would gladly reduce you to your component atoms, even though I know you were not directly to blame. But for the death of Rohc Vahnn, who corrupted a young and impressionable boy and tore him from the heart of his family, I can never adequately repay you. For the debt my people owe to Linna, I put my life and my skills at your command.'

To say the very least, I was stunned. I had had no idea that Mrs Catlin had been so involved with the events Celebe had related to me during our time together in Zatuchep. But there was no denying the obvious sincerity of what Mohred had just said.

'Get up,' I said to him. 'No man kneels to me. If you will aid us, and take no payment, then do so as an ally, not as a servant.'

He arose. There was an incredible dignity in him, which his previous obeisance had done nothing to diminish.

'Very well,' he said. 'What do you wish of me?'

'What functional Library is nearest to the city of Xacmet in the country of Reshek?' I asked.

Mohred turned to the lectern. He didn't touch the device, but instantly data began to scroll across its surface. Presently he said to me, 'There is a Library three days' ride from Xacmet.'

'Can you take us there?' I asked.

He held up a hand, still studying the map that was being displayed on the lectern's screen. I could read most of what was being shown, but not all. Parts of the Library network remain untranslated from their original tongue, one older even than the Thekkish language from which present-day Vinh speech is derived.

'It is not quite that simple,' he said. 'The Resheki have ever been an insular race, and even my people have had few dealings with them. The Library in question is abandoned; no one has consulted it in generations, much less attempted to travel through it.'

'But it *is* functional?' I prompted.

'The travel mode works,' Mohred replied, 'but that does not necessarily mean it can be used. If the Library has been built around – as has this one, for example – and the building has collapsed through neglect, it could have buried the Library in the process. If that has happened, and rubble lies across the travel surface, you will be crushed as soon as you materialize.

'Further,' he went on, 'the region in question is . . . inhospitable. Parts of Reshek are desert—'

'We know,' I said. 'But three days isn't . . . Wait a minute. A desert? Three days' ride from Xacmet? We saw no sign of it.'

'Xacmet was settled in the distant past by desert nomads,' Mohred said. 'They walked out of the west – explorers, according to some legends; exiles, according to others – and built Xacmet on the first fertile land they found. The desert has since retreated some miles, due in part to the diversion of certain rivers by later generations of Resheki, but remains as inimical to life as ever it was. The Library stands, I would estimate, one day's ride into the desert itself.'

'One day,' I said briskly, not wishing to face the prospect of any further delays. 'No problem. Anything else?'

He glanced at me. He seemed strangely nervous.

'Is that not enough?' he asked half-heartedly.

'You're stalling,' I said, suddenly wary – was this a trap? Was Mohred keeping us here for some reason? 'What's going on, Librarian?' I snapped, ignoring his power to do me an irreparable amount of harm if he so chose. 'What's the real reason for all these delaying tactics?'

He looked, I thought, embarrassed by my question.

'Reshek,' he said, as though the word itself were an explanation.

'Go on,' I urged.

'It is a bad place,' he said. He wouldn't meet my gaze now, and suddenly I knew why. He was afraid.

'Bad—?' I prompted.

'It is said,' he went on, 'that no man is safe in Reshek. That Death stalks that land, and Her hand may come to rest on any man at any time, regardless of his station or his power.' He glanced at me, his face colouring. 'There is good reason for Librarians to shun Reshek. It is not by chance that we seldom go there.'

'Superstitious rubbish,' I said, trying not to sound as contemptuous as I actually felt.

I might have expected him to respond angrily. The fact that he didn't impressed me with the true depth of his feeling.

'Once,' he said, 'we tried to establish a foothold in Reshek. Our historical records, which are known to only a handful of our people, tell of what occurred.' He glanced nervously at the Mugaraht. 'The Y'nys,' he said, 'are not entirely without power in the world, even now. Their ghosts, it is said, still walk in Reshek.'

Some of what he said, I knew, was true: I had been to Asmina. But outside the Valley the Y'nys were little more than a fond memory of Shushuan's past glory; only their indestructible artefacts remained to influence the present, and few of those were truly understood or put to good use. And as for ghosts—

'Mohred,' I said, 'are you taking us to Reshek, or not?'

He gave me a look that was full of reproach.

'Of course I am,' he said. He added, 'I just wanted you to appreciate the possible consequences.'

'We thank you,' I said. I glanced at Zalmetta and Ylyrria. 'If you two want to wait here until . . .'

'We stay together,' Ylyrria said abruptly. From the looks she was giving Mohred I guessed she didn't trust the Librarian any more than I did.

'I agree with the child,' Zalmetta said.

'It's late,' I told them, 'and we have no provisions. We'll get a good night's rest and in the morning we'll . . .'

'I will provide the necessary provisions,' Mohred said.

'It's not necessary—' I began.

'It is,' he assured me.

I relented. I knew what it was like to be in Mrs Catlin's debt. She would never press the issue, but somehow you always felt as though the debt could never be repaid – ever.

'We'll meet back here tomorrow,' I said.

Mohred nodded. He walked back towards the Library and, as silently as he had come, he vanished.

CHAPTER TWENTY-SEVEN

Sirens

The next morning we stepped out of the Library in Reshek and, it seemed, straight into a blast furnace.

I heard Ylyrria's stifled gasp, a barely whispered 'Gods below—' and knew how she felt.

Sweat soaked my body in the first seconds, the sun so hot and bright it seemed to have moved about fifty million miles closer.

I shaded my eyes and tried to look around without squinting. I didn't succeed.

The Library stood in the open air atop a very isolated and rather high butte. Other, similar features dotted a landscape that wouldn't have looked out of place in some medieval version of a Catholic Hell. The stone was blood-red, veined with black and silver, and was about as dessicated as could be imagined. The land seemed to suck the moisture from my very body, the shimmering air helping it along.

Mohred reached into his bag of supplies and produced voluminous headgear for us all. We pulled it on with mumbled but heartfelt thanks.

'The way lies there,' the Librarian said, pointing.

He was indicating a wall of rock that lay across our path, a good day's march away. Beyond it, I assumed, was the more fertile land leading to Xacmet.

'We'll never climb that,' I muttered.

The cliff face was higher even than the butte on which

we stood, and extended across the landscape like an artificial horizon.

'There is a way,' Mohred said. 'It is old and little used – no one in their right mind would come here – but it *is* passable.'

I nodded. This was more than I had expected to have to face. I was already so thirsty I could have downed a flagon of water. How would Ylyrria cope with a whole day's march through this?

'Zalmetta,' I said cautiously, not wishing to offend the child, 'perhaps you and—'

'This way!' Ylyrria called from the far side of the Library. I watched as her head disappeared below the flat top of the butte.

So much for that idea, then.

We followed her, Mohred bringing up the rear, down a narrow, tortuous defile that effectively split the butte in two, yet which was all but invisible until you were actually in it. The air inside was old and stale and, if possible, even drier than it had been outside. And the descent took hours.

When we finally emerged into what had, I assumed, once been a river valley, we were all just about on our knees. Even Zalmetta was flagging, a sign which, frankly, terrified me.

'We'll rest a bit,' I said.

No one argued.

The butte afforded us a little shadow, though the air was no cooler, and we collapsed like four beached fish.

'I can see why your people gave up on this place,' Zalmetta said to Mohred.

'No,' Mohred muttered, 'you cannot. But you will.'

When we could stand again we drank some of our water ration and, following the Librarian, set out along the ancient river bed toward the cliffs that loomed in the distance.

The sun was finally starting to set when we saw the figure standing on the trail ahead of us. Mohred froze, his whole body rigid. The rest of us looked at the object of his apparent terror, more puzzled than anything.

At this distance, perhaps two hundred yards, the figure appeared to be that of a human – or rather Vinh – female. In the rapidly failing light I made out dusky skin and a mass of black hair, a single almost diaphanous gown covering her from throat to ankles yet leaving her arms bare. Her feet were also bare. How I could make out that one particular detail, or why it seemed worthy of note, I have no idea.

'What is it?' Ylyrria asked.

I was struck by her odd choice of words.

'Look away,' Zalmetta said, an edge in her tone.

I tried, and couldn't.

'Mohred—' I breathed; the air had suddenly gone from my lungs.

The Librarian seemed entranced, unable to speak or move.

'Look . . . away . . .' Zalmetta said, her voice strained.

The young woman was closer. Yet . . . she hadn't moved. Or, I hadn't seen her move. Yes, that was the logical answer: I hadn't seen her move.

Her face was lost in shadow, the sun almost below the horizon, her gown suddenly opaque in the twilight. Every contour of her body was outlined by it.

What happened next – what happened to *me* next – I wish to relate very accurately. Once before, in the presence of the Thirteen, my feelings had been manipulated by a vision, a vision that had taken on the form of Mrs Catlin and had forced me to confront certain emotions that I had not wanted to confront. What happened now, in the valley to which Mohred had brought us, had nothing to do with feelings, and nothing to do with Mrs Catlin.

I looked at the body of the young thing that was, once again, closer to us without having had to go through the necessity of actually moving, and I was overcome with lust. The paralysis left me and I stepped forward, around the motionless Librarian, towards the woman, because I had to have her, there, right there, right then, and *nothing* else mattered. I forgot where I was, who I was, why I was here. Only one thing mattered, and I had to have it *now*.

The slender body glided forward, its naked feet seeming barely to caress the earth beneath them, its graceful arms reaching out to me. I heard an animal sound, guttural and not pleasant, a snarling almost. The dim realization that the sound was coming from my own lips was somehow unimportant.

I pulled the slim creature into my arms, my hands rough on its smooth skin, my body seeming to burn. I tore at its gown, the light almost gone now, its body a tantalizing silhouette in the darkness. I felt its breath on my face, sweet and impossibly tantalizing, felt the soft contours of its shape against me, sensed its own urgent need.

Moonlight washed the scene in silver as the last daylight faded and died. The mass of black hair crawled back as though endowed with a serpentine life of its own and the light caught what was beneath it for the first time. There was no face, only a gaping maw ringed with needle-like fangs. A tongue like a serpent writhed around the jagged edges of the orifice, the fangs moving closer to my face. Thoughts flooded my brain; the thing was going to eat my face off. It was going to feast on my living flesh, keeping me alive, somehow, until the last morsel had been swallowed.

And I didn't care. The desperate need was too intense, saturating my brain with chemicals that turned horror into pleasure, fear into desire, terror into delight.

(I felt my hand, the fist clenched so tightly the bones of my fingers seemed to be cracking, curled around the hilt of my sabre, the blade whispering from its sheath.)

A smell like the sewers beneath an abattoir hit me in the face. The thing's tongue licked around my neck, tracing the throbbing veins and the clenched muscles. It slid over my jaw, moving towards my mouth.

(The blade cleared its sheath, the steel quivering as my hand shook. The muscles in my back seemed to go into spasm as I drew my arm back, tensing for the blow.)

The creature drew back, a sad frown crossing a face that was suddenly that of a young and incredibly beautiful woman. She smiled at me, her hands stroking my shoulders, massaging away the tension, sending waves of pleasure through the muscles and nerves. Her body moved against mine; blind passion made me groan out loud. She drew her lips closer to mine, her eyes closing, her breath quick on my face. I closed my own eyes . . .

Something ripped the sword from my unresisting fingers. Pain exploded in my head as I was pulled backwards by the hair so roughly that great handfuls of it came away in the process. There was a *whoosh* of air as the sabre flashed past my face and then a heavy, wet sound, followed by the feel of something hot and fetid hitting me in the throat.

I opened my eyes. Zalmetta was at my side, the sabre in her hand, dragging the now headless creature off my body. Its tentacle-like arms were still hanging onto me, each one terminating in a three-clawed 'hand' that was sunk into the flesh of my back. The pain, which a moment ago I had been oblivious to, was now intense. Shaking from head to toe, I ripped the sinuous arms free and pushed the creature away from me. Its body, which I had been so convinced was that of a young woman, now stood revealed as a lumpy, misshapen boneless mass. Its lower limbs were like its upper, making me wonder how they had supported it. They were more like the tentacles of an octopus than legs.

I looked at Zalmetta. She was breathing hard, amber eyes glassy with horror and . . . something else.

'What were you *doing*?' she cried. 'Couldn't you *see* . . . ?'

She whirled suddenly.

'*Ylyrria!*' she cried.

I turned, my vision rushing in and out of focus uncontrollably, and looked where she was looking.

Mohred hadn't moved. He was like a statue, with a faint, beatific smile on his lips. Six of the creatures were crawling around and over him, caressing his armoured body as though it were the most wonderful thing they had ever seen. Of Ylyrria there was no sign.

I shook myself, snatching the sabre out of Zalmetta's hand. I drew both pistols and thrust them at her, slinging the ammunition pouch around her neck.

'Find Ylyrria,' I said, my voice that of a stranger.

She looked at me sharply.

'Do it,' I snapped. 'I'll help Mohred.'

She hesitated, then nodded jerkily. I suspected that whatever power of illusion these creatures possessed, Zalmetta was not entirely immune to its effects.

I ran towards Mohred, yelling the war cry of Benza as loud as I could – and trying to keep the tremor out of my voice. I was hoping that the creatures would run from a direct assault. Instead, they looked up from the Librarian, faces gaping at me, and an avalanche of sensation battered me to my knees. The power of one of those creatures was enough to cloud a man's mind; this many combined could wring the life out of it.

They moved away from Mohred, six scantily clad sirens that were the answer to a thousand adolescent fantasies. They danced towards me, arms outstretched, circling me as I kneeled on the hard-packed desert sand. Their bodies gyrated and whirled around me, drawing closer and closer with each pass, the power of their minds intensifying and leaving me too stupefied even to think, much less act.

One of them slid an arm around my neck, its face moving down towards mine. An explosion shook the night, the sound going through me like an electric shock, and the beautiful face in front of me was suddenly a nightmare visage of needle teeth and writhing tongue.

I let out a howl of frustration and, not daring to pause for thought, laid about me with the sabre. I swung the blade again and again, right and left, time after time, hacking and slashing everything that was within range, not stopping until my sword arm was numb from the effort, and my body was splattered with something that was warm and wet, yet was somehow not quite blood.

When it all ended I didn't know, but I found myself kneeling amid a pile of bodies, none of which could have passed for anything remotely human. I glanced across at Mohred. The Librarian still hadn't moved a muscle. Beyond him, Zalmetta was leading Ylyrria by the hand back towards us. Both were blood-spattered, the child's garments torn and grubby. They each carried one of my pistols; it had been a pistol shot, I suddenly realized, that had broken the creatures' hold over me.

I got slowly to my feet, leaning heavily on the sabre. Mohred turned and looked me in the eyes, his gaze seeming to come back from a place none of us would ever see.

'This is what you were afraid of,' I said, my voice painfully hoarse.

He nodded. There were almost tears in his eyes. What ultimate fantasy would a Librarian see, that he would let Death eat him alive? I shuddered, somehow glad that my own imagination seemed to exist on a more basic level. Although, that said, it was a bit galling to realize just how lowbrow my tastes appeared to be.

'We must leave this place,' Zalmetta warned. 'I have heard of these creatures, but I had thought them the stuff of legend. If all I have heard is true, these deaths will only serve to make the next attack the more effective.'

'Mohred,' I said, trying to inject a businesslike tone into my voice, and missing by several levels of magnitude, 'where is the closest shelter?'

He answered promptly, but his voice was a million miles away.

'There is none,' he said simply.

'How far to the cliffs?' I asked.

'Half a day,' he replied.

'Then it's up to you to protect us,' I told him.

He seemed to come down to earth then, but his only reaction was a barking laugh that held no humour at all.

'Protect you?' he jeered. 'I cannot even protect myself! I have told you, Death walks this land, and not even Librarians can stay Her hand. Those creatures are the spawn of the Y'nys, they—'

'Death be damned,' I snapped, a real anger driving out the last traces of the manufactured emotions planted in me by the creatures. 'There's nothing supernatural going on here, just some very unhealthy biology. And I doubt very much that the Y'nys have got anything to do with any of it.'

He looked at me, not understanding.

I stepped forward and whacked the edge of my blade against his arm, the steel ringing on the armour under his robes.

'They're just animals,' I said, putting all the contempt into my voice that I could muster. 'What are you scared of, Librarian? What can they do to you that you're so scared of?'

He took a step back, his expression running the gamut of a dozen emotions, all except the one I was after.

I hit him again, harder this time, putting my weight behind the stroke. It was like laying into a stone pillar, but he was starting to get the message.

'Don't—' he said, his hand raised to ward me off.

I cracked his bare knuckles with the flat of the blade.

He cried out in rage, the air suddenly full of thunder. A heaviness descended on the valley, and a wind seemed to pick up around us.

'What's wrong, Mohred?' I asked. 'Are you . . . angry?'

He glowered at me, flickers of lightning dancing in the air behind him.

'You . . . insect!' he roared.

I laughed.

'Better than being scared, isn't it?' I yelled, the wind now a howling gale around us.

His eyes held mine for an eternity, the air between us charged with static electricity. And then, suddenly and completely, everything was still, and the Librarian was rocking on his heels with silent laughter.

I felt sweat trickle down my body. One of these days, I told myself, I really must learn to think before I act, because one of these days things aren't going to work out and I'm going to end up dead. And probably a lot worse besides.

'How did you know?' he asked. 'How could you know?'

'I didn't,' I told him. 'I just got mad, and the fear went away.'

He nodded, still smiling.

'But if they come again—' he said.

'You protect us,' I told him, 'and we'll protect you.'

He seemed about to burst into laughter again, but instead he just said, 'Very well.'

We looked at one another for long moments, and a thought came to me. 'It's the armour—' I said.

He looked away, flustered.

'They . . . they are drawn to it,' he said. 'It amplifies their power—'

'Of course,' I said. 'Y'nys.'

'The charlaki woman was able to resist,' Mohred said, 'because her Y'nys is inside her – they couldn't sense it. They thought she was just a woman. Had they realized . . .'

'They'd have done to her what they did to you,' I said,

He shuddered. I decided he'd been through enough for one night so I let the matter drop. I beckoned to Zalmetta and Ylyrria to come closer – they had backed off a considerable distance during the last few minutes.

'We have to watch out for each other,' I said. 'Whatever those things are, they're only animals, and their effect is weakened when they have to divide their attention. If they come for us again, be ready.'

Everyone nodded, but there was a fair amount of doubt on their faces.

'Now let's go,' I said. 'We'll march through the night. I want to be on those cliffs by this time tomorrow.'

Mercifully, we did not sight the strange creatures again that night, and according to Mohred we would be safe from them once we were on the high ground of the cliffs. That knowledge gave us all the added boost we needed to make good time throughout the following morning, and by noon we were making our way up the rocky trail that led away from the valley floor and towards our destination. None of us looked back.

CHAPTER TWENTY-EIGHT

Return to Xacmet

————◆◇◇◆————

I sat on a narrow ledge far to one side of our camp. The night was cold and bright, and I had wrapped my blanket around me. In front of me, the hills and plains of Reshek were laid out in a grey-and-silver patchwork; directly below, hundreds of feet down, the base of the cliff was littered with boulders that looked no bigger than pebbles. The silence, the sheer sense of aloneness, was indescribable. And yet, oddly, there was no attendant feeling of loneliness.

I sensed rather than heard movement further along the ledge. Since it came from the direction of the camp I was not overly concerned, but under the blanket I let my hand stray to the hilt of my sword.

Zalmetta rounded the curve of the rock face and sat down beside me. She let her feet hang over the edge of the narrow precipice, leaning forward to survey the depths below. Heights don't bother me, but I'm not reckless about them either; I tend to give them the same respect I would anything that has life-threatening potential.

'Does death not frighten you?' I asked, for I knew that she was capable of fear.

'No,' she replied. She paused, and I think she smiled before adding, 'Not my own, at least.'

I settled back against the rock, feeling strangely warm and happy. We faced unimaginable odds, perils that could only be guessed at, yet I was content. If death was to be our fate, I would at least have one chance to see Mrs Catlin again. Nothing else seemed important.

'I am concerned for the child,' Zalmetta said.

'Ylyrria? In what way?'

'I do not fully understand human emotions, and I have never before known a human child. But she seems . . . odd. How do you regard her mental state?'

Reluctantly I said, 'It troubles me, too. After all she's been through . . . She hasn't cried, has she?'

'I have not observed it.'

'She should have. She's got something inside her, something so dark and personal that it occludes everything else; whatever it is, I think she's clinging to it as a means of retaining her sanity. Children do that, I think; fixate on one aspect of their situation and block out everything else.'

'I must take your word for this,' Zalmetta said. 'Do you have any idea what it is that she has "fixated" upon?'

'No,' I said, 'and that's what bothers me. If she were an adult—'

'Yes?'

'I just had a thought,' I said, 'and not a pretty one. The mental state I've just described, in an adult, would describe Tal Daqar.'

Zalmetta was silent for a moment, then she said, 'This brings up another subject that I must speak of. In Xacmet, during our escape from the Kanaat Hall, you observed me to pause by the unconscious body of Blukka.'

I recalled the incident, and said so.

'I had hoped,' she said, 'to do to him what the Knight of the Thirteen had done to me, to free him of the influence of Tal Daqar.'

'Were you successful?' I asked.

'I was not,' she replied. 'There was insufficient self-awareness left in his mind for me to reach. There was, however, enough consciousness remaining for me to . . . manipulate him, slightly.' She seemed to tremble at the memory, as though horrified by what she had done.

'What did you do?' I asked.
She told me.

The next day saw us walking through semi-desert and scrub,
all of which was sheer bliss after the previous day's experiences.
On the morning of the second day we were actually in green
farmland. The 'three days' ride' of which Mohred had spoken
turned out to be closer to six, due partly to the fact that we had
no gryllups but also, perhaps more tellingly, to the rugged and
uneven nature of the terrain over which we had had to travel.

We spotted Xacmet late in the morning of the seventh day.
It lay to the north-east, a handful of miles away across a rocky
and broken landscape. From the highest outcropping that we
could find we stood and surveyed the scene before us.

On the more level plain that lay to the east and south of the
city, two armies fought for control of the city. One, composed
mostly of filinta, was obviously Kandirak's. The other, a motley
assortment of peasants and fyrd militia, appeared to be led by
a mixed bag of nobles and assorted regular soldiers. As to who
their actual commander was, I could only speculate.

The battle was almost entirely infantry-based, with what little
cavalry there was being poorly employed. There were no archers
in evidence, and scant use seemed to be being made of firearms.
Bladed hand weapons of every kind were in evidence, and a great
many improvised weapons too. The fighting was steady rather
than fierce, with neither side, it seemed, expecting to win the
day. As much as anything, they seemed simply to be testing one
another's strength. Casualties were mounting up on both sides
and white-robed non-combatants moved through the fighting,
tending to the fallen. These men – not Librarians, despite their
appearance – seemed indifferent to the origins of their patients,
tending those from both sides indiscriminately.

'What is going on here?' Mohred asked, gazing down at
the battle.

'At a guess,' I ventured, 'this is the counter-revolution of
Reshek's reactionary old guard. Kandirak's attempt at investing

himself as the new Emperor has not made him any friends among the country's established noble Houses. The big question, though, is: what part does Yarissi play in all this?'

'No,' Zalmetta said, 'the big question is: what happens when Tal Daqar arrives and sees all this?'

I looked at her.

'I am only speculating,' she said, 'but if it was me, and I saw my "ally" under attack like this I would be forced to question just how important my alliance with him was. And frankly, under the circumstances, I think I would decide that it wasn't important at all. And I would sail right past.'

'And leave Blukka?' I said.

'Yes,' she replied, 'without hesitation.'

This was not good. It was a contingency I had never thought to allow for.

I turned to Mohred.

'How far would you be willing to help in bringing this battle to a conclusion?' I asked.

'I am a scholar,' he replied, 'an academic. I am not a soldier.'

'But you possess the full powers of a Librarian,' I said.

'Certainly,' he agreed, 'but I am no fighter. I have had no martial training, and frankly it is something for which I have no natural aptitude.'

'David,' Zalmetta said, 'you are overlooking something.'

'I might have guessed,' I muttered. 'What am I overlooking, Zalmetta?'

'Ending this battle will serve little or no purpose,' she said. 'By a reasonable estimate, it will be eight days before Tal Daqar arrives here. By then, the battle could have started all over again. What needs to be done is to bring about an end to the cause of the battle.'

'You're talking about ending the revolution,' I said.

'I suppose so,' she agreed.

I heard a whispered curse behind me and turned to see Ylyrria glaring furiously at us.

'How dare you?' she hissed. ' "End the revolution"? What

gives you the right . . . ? Who are you to . . . ?' She seemed on the point of incoherence, but then she blurted out, 'This is not your country; these are not your people; and this is not your fight. These are *my* people, and I think they might like to have some say in how their affairs get settled.'

'You're right,' I said.

She frowned at me, still angry but now also confused. I gave her my most winning smile. She frowned even harder.

'So what are you going to do?' she asked.

'Let's go down there and ask them,' I said.

She looked across at the battle. Then she looked at me.

'Go down there?' she said.

'Like you said,' I told her, 'it's their country. And their revolution. Let's ask them how they want it settling.'

'Which side do you plan on asking?' she demanded, not a little sarcastically.

'Good question,' I said. 'Which side would *you* ask?'

She opened her mouth to speak, then apparently thought better of it and closed it again. Presently she said, 'Well, not Kandirak's scum, that much is certain.'

'Right,' I agreed. 'So let's find out who's running things on the other side of the fence.'

CHAPTER TWENTY-NINE

Council of War

The battle concluded indecisively, both sides quitting the field in good order and giving one another room to gather up their wounded. Sentries were posted, on the one side atop the city wall and on the other at the perimeter of a makeshift encampment a couple of miles out on the plain. The sense of a timeless ritual being enacted was both surreal and somehow slightly mystical.

'They don't exactly go at it, do they?' I muttered to no one in particular.

I saw Zalmetta giving me a quizzical glance, and it occurred to me that Vinh behaviour was probably as alien to her as it often was to me.

'They make war the way they do everything,' I said. 'The rules were laid down centuries ago, and no one ever thinks to question them.' I hesitated, remembering Rohc Vahnn and his merciless tactics against the people of Vohung. '*Almost* no one,' I amended. I frowned as the memory prompted other recollections. 'And yet I've seen them fight as though they mean it,' I mused. 'In the Kanaat Hall, when Luftetmek fought Blukka . . .' Zalmetta said nothing, so I pursued the line of thought myself. 'There are rituals for everything,' I speculated, 'and sometimes those rituals are more intense. Other times, like now, it's more a matter of just going through the motions.'

Zalmetta shook her head, a very human gesture. 'It is more than that,' she said. 'This battle is unprecedented in Resheki history. There has never been a civil war in this land. The two factions, now that violence has become a reality, are unsure how to proceed. So they fall back upon what they know. They are trying to find their way, to establish who is the incumbent and who the challenger. Each feels that his side is the true Reshek, yet each knows that to the other he is the outsider, the enemy. Neither yet knows how to deal with that. When one side achieves the ascendancy, that side will, in the eyes of both, be the defending side, the true Reshek. Consequently, neither side wishes to sustain untenable losses; thus, both sides move slowly. Left to themselves, they will continue thus for months, perhaps years, until the land around them can no longer sustain two such armies. If that happens, and despair becomes a factor, the end will not be long in coming.'

'You are well informed,' Mohred observed.

'My master was a learned man,' she replied. 'To serve him was to have access to many books, and, of course, the Library. I have also had many weeks in which to observe the Resheki first-hand. I believe my assessment to be accurate.'

He nodded. 'As do I,' he said.

'Good,' I said.

They all looked at me.

'Let's tip the balance,' I said.

We headed across the plain toward the rebels' encampment.

We picked our way carefully through the former field of battle. The white-robed physicians were doing their best with those that the retreating armies had left behind, but the main reason they had been left behind was that there was very little that could be done for them. None of us felt able simply to ignore what was happening, and we offered what little assistance we could. Mohred was probably the most useful, since his powers were capable of arresting potentially fatal injuries before they became actually fatal. Zalmetta was versed in anatomy, and aided the physicians with the more difficult cases, while all that I could do was to act as a stretcher-bearer and occasional hand-holder.

When I could find the time, I looked anxiously at Ylyrria. This wasn't something a child should have to see. But she seemed to be dealing with it as well as any of us, offering comfort to those for whom nothing more practical could be done. I saw her stroking the head of one young soldier, himself scarcely more than a child, until presently he ceased to breathe and his eyes clouded over.

I reached out to her.

'Let him sleep,' I said.

She looked up at me, eyes dry and with an expression so alien it frightened me.

'He's not sleeping,' she said simply, still stroking his head. 'He's with Gazig.'

'I know,' I said. 'Let him be.'

She nodded and moved silently on.

It took us almost two hours to cross the plain, and by then we were in the company of the physicians and those of their charges that had survived.

'Who commands your army?' I asked one of the men.

'Kanaat Yarissi,' he replied.

'Yarissi is here?' I asked, startled.

The man shook his head.

'He resides at Lord Kandirak's pleasure,' he said archly. 'But still do we serve him.'

'Who is your field commander?' I asked.

'I follow Baron Reddak,' he said.

'Baron Reddak rules this host?' I asked.

Getting a direct answer out of the average Vinh is akin to pulling teeth.

'The old lords now follow Captain Luftetmek,' the man said, 'but only until such time as Lord Kandirak is deposed.'

This, finally, was good news. If Luftetmek ruled this camp, there was at least a chance he would listen to what I had to say. But . . . I considered the man's choice of words carefully. The High Tongue is a beautiful language, almost entirely devoid of dissonance and artifice, but its nuances are subtle and its meanings not always obvious.

'The old lords follow the Captain,' I said cautiously, 'but they do not serve Kanaat Yarissi?'

The man laughed without humour.

'They serve only themselves,' he replied. 'I follow Baron Reddak as he follows Luftetmek. But when this is over, my allegiance will be to the Kanaat, regardless of what my Baron says or does.' He looked at me, a sudden thought apparently occurring to him. 'Who do *you* serve, stranger?'

'My Duke,' I replied. 'But I follow Luftetmek.'

He smiled, relieved.

'I am glad,' he said. 'I would not have liked to have had to kill one who had been so solicitous of my people this day. How are you known?'

'David Shaw,' I replied, 'Captain of the city . . .'

'Of Benza!' the man cried, his face suddenly excited. 'By Gazig, I should have known! Your companions, your hair—'

'You know me?' I said puzzled.

'All who follow Captain Luftetmek know you,' the man enthused. 'We have standing orders to offer succour and aid to you and your companions whenever we meet you. Tell me, how fares your quest? Have you yet been reunited with your woman?'

It was more than a little disconcerting to have so much known about me by a total stranger, and one who, it seemed, was not unique in that respect.

'Not as yet,' I told him. 'I must speak with Captain Luftetmek. Where can I find him?'

'Follow me,' said the man. 'I will take you.'

The camp was a bustle of activity as we passed through it. Soldiers of every type were in evidence, from fyrd militiamen in civilian dress, armed with farming implements crudely converted into weapons of war, to warrior nobles in full chain- and scale-mail armour bearing broadswords and cavalry shields. The latter were invariably surrounded by flocks of camp followers, all eager to gain favour with the prospective rulers of the new Reshek.

I saw traders and merchants, the inevitable profiteers and the honest businessmen, parasites to the misfortunes of others or purveyors of a much needed service for an equitable price. It was a fine line to tread at a time such as this, and I suspected as many would fall to the wrong side of it as would uphold the dubious honour of their various professions. Of one particular profession, whose honours have ever been of the nebulous variety, I saw very many exponents. They called out to me as we passed, displaying their wares provocatively. I resisted the urge to blush, and instead tried to find something else to look at. I saw Ylyrria gazing at the half-naked young women, her interest only casual, and I made a gesture at Zalmetta that the charlaki woman failed entirely to understand.

'The child,' I hissed.

Zalmetta gave me a puzzled look.

'Can't you find her something more . . . appropriate to look at?' I asked.

She clearly didn't know what I was talking about.

'They are only whores,' she said. 'What is inappropriate? Would you rather I showed the child the hospital tent?'

'No, of course not,' I said. 'But, I mean, really . . .'

Our guide led us through the outer fringes of the camp to a place that seemed to be almost at the exact centre of the circle described by the palisade wall. Here we encountered a wood-framed structure that had the appearance of a makeshift keep. It wouldn't have stood up to an hour's worth of determined assault, but knowing what I did of Vinh battle tactics I doubted that its structure was functional. It was built to a design that was older than living memory, the reason for the design lost in the mists of antiquity.

A sentry stopped us. He leaned casually on a mighty-looking spear, pushing his conical helmet back from his eyes. I looked at the spear curiously. It was unlike the slim javelins I had known in Benza, yet was not as hefty as the axe-headed halberds I had encountered in Ragana-Se-Tor. With weapons development so much a thing of the past on Shushuan, it was always startling to find something unfamiliar.

'This,' our guide said grandly, gesturing to us, 'is David Shaw and company.'

The sentry straightened up slowly, eyeing us.

'Including the Mugatih?' he asked, tipping the head of his spear in Mohred's direction.

'He is my ally,' I said.

The sentry seemed unimpressed. In any other country on the Thek continent, his discourtesy to a member of the caste of Librarians would have spelled instant death, or at the very least a period of unparalleled pain and suffering. Mohred, however, gave no indication that he had even heard the man's comment.

'Wait here,' said the sentry.

He disappeared into the structure. A moment later he re-emerged.

'Shaw may enter,' he said. 'The others of his party will be made comfortable in the tent of the Captains.'

I glanced at my companions. What was said in the next few minutes would affect all of us, but I could hardly dismiss Luftetmek's orders in his own camp. I thought for a moment that Ylyrria might say something, but the moment passed and she merely looked away. No one else offered any objections, and I breathed a sigh of relief, glad that they hadn't elected to put me in a difficult position. I wondered if I'd have been as reasonable in their place.

The sentry held open the canvas flap that was the structure's only visible entrance and ushered me in.

Within, Luftetmek and a dozen nobles were engaged in a heated debate. Yarissi's Champion was just as I remembered him, even to his nondescript grey tunic and close-cropped hair. Those around him provided a striking contrast, with their ornate battle dress and shoulder-length hair. It was slightly disconcerting to realize that, at present, I resembled them rather more than I did Luftetmek.

At the moment that I entered one of the nobles, a tall, black-haired individual in blue scale-mail hauberk and a flowing scarlet cape, was making a point with which many of his fellows seemed to be in agreement.

'Today's battle demonstrated our superior powers in the field,' he said, an observation for which I myself had seen no supporting evidence. 'My Captains and I have studied the situation, and we believe that another twenty or thirty such engagements will see Xacmet restored to the ruling Houses.'

The other nobles nodded wisely at this sage counsel. Luftetmek seemed less convinced.

'And how many men will die during these engagements?' he asked.

The tall noble seemed prepared for this question.

'Of regular soldiers,' he said, 'we can expect less than one thousand casualties; of those, perhaps a quarter to a third will be fatal in nature. By our estimates, Kandirak's forces will sustain three times that number, and with a higher proportion of deaths.'

'What of the fyrd?' Luftetmek asked.

Now the noble appeared puzzled.

'What of them?' he asked.

'What will their losses be?' Luftetmek asked.

The noble glanced uncertainly at his fellows. They seemed as incapable of dealing with this question as he was.

'What does it matter?' he asked at last. 'They serve only to act as shields to our professional soldiers in any case. So long as the warriors survive in the numbers we have predicted, the victory is assured.'

Luftetmek was furious, but no one in the tent seemed capable of seeing it, much less understanding the reason for it.

'The fyrd,' he said, 'are what this war is all about. It was for them that Yarissi—'

'Yarissi be damned!' the noble spat. 'Let the peasants dream their dreams of a new world; we fight to restore the *old* world.'

Luftetmek leaned closer to the noble, his eyes narrowed and his teeth clenched.

'Repeat those words outside,' he said softly, 'and see how long you live.'

The noble sneered in Luftetmek's face, but his own countenance had paled and there was sweat on his forehead.

'Twenty to thirty battles,' Luftetmek said, 'is too many.'

'No one will give you a better figure,' the noble said irritably.

'I will,' I said.

All heads turned toward me. Luftetmek alone smiled at seeing me

'How many battles would you take to end this?' he asked.

'If he offers less than fifteen,' the noble said, 'he is a liar. Or a fool.'

I ignored him.

'How many, David Shaw?' Luftetmek asked, straining to keep the desperation out of his voice.

I smiled grimly, not liking the consequences of what I was about to propose.

'One,' I said.

CHAPTER THIRTY

The Arrow

———⟩○◦○⟨———

Against a barrage of objections Luftetmek elected to confer with me alone. Assuring his visibly doubtful nobles that they would be present at any decision making, he claimed that all he wanted for the moment was to renew an old acquaintance and, for his own peace of mind, establish the military bona fides of my proposal.

As soon as we were alone he rounded on me with a grin and clasped my hand in his.

'I never thought to see you again, my friend,' he said. 'But no one is more welcome in my camp.'

'I hope I can live up to the welcome,' I said wryly. 'I gather the counter-revolution has proved itself useful to your own plans.'

Luftetmek made a dismissive gesture at, it seemed, everything outside the confines of his own tent.

'Those fools have no idea of what will happen after Xacmet falls,' he said angrily. 'They think their followers will willingly embrace a return to the old ways, with some other House taking the place of the Bagalamak. What is more likely is that as soon as Yarissi is liberated not a one of those Lords will still be alive to see the sunset.'

'A grim prospect,' I observed, not pushing too hard – Luftetmek's position in all of this was not yet entirely clear to me.

'Not one I look forward to, I must admit,' he said. 'But if even one of them had the brains that the Thirteen gave to the average vol-worm they'd realize what their likely fate was to be and do something about it *now* while there was still time.'

'What could they do?' I asked.

'Support the Kanaat in *fact*, rather than merely paying lip service to him,' Luftetmek said. 'Yarissi has no intention of abolishing the old Houses; if anything, he supports the system of House rule. But he wishes that rule to be by the standards and practices of our ancestors, not through tyranny or fear, as the Bagalamak – and Kandirak – would have it.'

I wondered whose belief in the events that would inevitably follow the fall of Xacmet was the truest; I hoped, in many ways, that Yarissi's dream would come true, but I had seen the country-wide consequences of what the perversion of that dream could bring, and was not entirely convinced that the dream was tenable. On the other hand, the alternative was always worth fighting against.

Luftetmek looked at me intently.

'Can you really show us a way to end this in one battle?' he asked.

'Before I answer,' I said, 'you must know that I have my own reasons for wanting Xacmet to rest in your hands.'

'I had already suspected as much,' he said. 'Does this involve your woman? And Tal Daqar?'

As swiftly and succinctly as I could I brought him up to date with what had happened since last I saw him.

'When Daqar arrives,' I said, 'he must not suspect that Kandirak does not still rule. He *must* feel safe, he *must* set down at Xacmet, Mrs . . . Mrs Catlin *must* . . .'

He put his hand on my shoulder. I was shaking so badly I couldn't speak. It was some kind of delayed shock, I knew, hitting me now when I least needed it.

Luftetmek pulled up a chair and pushed me into it. Then he crossed the tent to a wine rack and pulled out a bottle. He opened it, poured two generous goblets, and handed me one. I drank half of it in one swallow, paused for breath, and downed the rest. Luftetmek refilled the cup and sat down opposite me.

'Can you do what you have said?' he asked me again.

I nodded, regaining control of myself.

'I can show you the way,' I said, 'but I can't make your people obey me. You and I are going to have to work together on this, Luftetmek, and it's going to mean forgetting everything you ever thought you knew about warfare—'

'These are the days for new ideas,' he said. 'I will do anything to prevent the kind of slaughter those . . . Lords propose. Of course, convincing them to go along with it might be less straightforward.'

'What I have in mind,' I said, 'will require all the firearms you can muster.'

'Fire—?'

'I know it's not the way things are usually done around here,' I said, 'but—'

'No, you misunderstand,' he interrupted. 'I have already considered the usefulness of such weapons, but their effectiveness is minimal in an open battle such as this. Their range is so limited that each weapon would be capable of no more than a single effective shot before the enemy was upon us. And the next time they attacked they would also bear firearms. The killing would be made worse, and we would be no nearer victory.'

'Your logic is flawless,' I said, 'but you are forgetting one thing. If my plan succeeds, there will be no second battle.'

He seemed stunned.

Warfare among the Vinh is primitive in more ways than the immediately obvious. The rituals and traditions that surround it have caused it to revert to its prehistoric roots, when the purpose of armed conflict was not to annihilate the opposition but to demonstrate one's own strength, thus driving off the enemy without placing oneself at undue risk. Shushuan is so underpopulated that the borderlands between its warring peoples have grown larger than the populated lands they separate. Wars of expansion have almost no meaning. As a consequence, the idea of *having* to win a war, of one's very survival depending upon it, has almost died out.

'How many pistols have you?' I asked.

'Hundreds,' Luftetmek replied, his tone subdued. His eyes

were haunted. He was too intelligent not to understand what I was proposing. 'Perhaps a thousand at most.'

'Ammunition?'

'Considerable. Many thousands of rounds.'

'But no muskets?'

'Muskets?'

'Long-barrelled weapons, with greater range.'

'No. No . . . muskets.'

I took another drink. The alcohol was propping up my wounded confidence, but I didn't want to overdo it.

'What about gryllups?' I asked.

The sudden change of subject seemed to snap Luftetmek out of his stupor.

'The nobles each have their own stables,' he said, 'and some of their Captains also. Perhaps three hundred beasts between them.'

'It's less than I would have liked,' I said pensively, 'but—'

'A man on a gryllup is still only a man,' said Luftetmek. 'What difference does it make that he is taller?'

'A gryllup has other advantages,' I said.

I thought carefully about the figures he had just given me. What I was contemplating had been proven effective countless times in the history of Earth's military past, but even so I felt overwhelmed by the sheer scale of what I was contemplating.

Luftetmek seemed to be reading my thoughts, because he said, 'Say what is on your mind, Shaw. If I think you have gone mad, I shall tell you.'

I laughed without humour.

I took a long drink of wine and set the cup aside.

'Your people,' I said, 'make war by phalanx. That means two great masses of soldiers charge at one another and try to overwhelm each other by sheer brute force. That's why your nobles claim it will take so many engagements for a victor to emerge. In theory, you could win a war like that in a single battle, but when it was all over you'd be hard pressed to know who'd won and who'd lost. What I want to do is to remove the brute-force element and substitute a scientific approach; the application of *enough* force, in the right place; manoeuvrability; making the enemy do what you want him to do, instead of just hitting him head on; misdirection; tactics—'

'My friend,' Luftetmek said uneasily, 'this is war we are planning, not simple swordplay between two men—'

'The theory is as valid for one as the other,' I said. 'Only the numbers are different. Look—'

There was a commotion outside the tent, the sound of voices raised in anger. Then one of the nobles from Luftetmek's party came striding in, a sentry reeling in his wake.

'We will not be excluded any longer, *Captain*,' the man barked, making Luftetmek's rank sound like an insult. 'Will you invite us in, or must there be bloodshed?'

'There is no need for violence of any kind,' Luftetmek said easily. 'Please, we were just about to send for you.'

He didn't give the insult time to sink in before gesturing magnanimously for the man and his companions to rejoin the discussion.

The confrontation that followed was far from pleasant. The task that lay before Luftetmek and me was thankless beyond all measure, but since the hasty plan I had been putting together existed only in my head there was no way to avoid it.

Just getting the assembled nobles and Captains to acknowledge my existence was hard enough, only some judicious twisting of the known facts about the war in Vohung during my first visit to Shushuan swaying them in my favour – to listen to Luftetmek tell it, I had won the battle against Droxus and his entire army single-handed. Once we had established my credentials, the next hurdle facing us was the task of getting our audience to actually listen to me. It did not start well. The opposition to virtually my every utterance was something I had already anticipated, and had thought myself prepared for, but I could not have been more wrong.

It was not so much their inability to grasp the bigger concept – a fight to the *finish*, a blitzkrieg – that irritated me, but rather their obstinate refusal to comprehend even the most simple notion, the most rudimentary tactic. As far as they were concerned, if great-great-great-great-grandfather didn't do it that way, then neither did they. Much as I loved the Vinh as a people – and I did love them, for their honesty, their loyalty and their fierce, uncritical friendship – there were times when I would cheerfully have had many of them drowned at birth.

'That won't work,' was the objection I heard the most often.

'Why not?' was my naive response.

'Because that isn't the way it's done,' was the staggeringly logical answer.

After an hour I should have been getting stuck into the details of the various aspects of the battle plan I had been devising. Instead, I was still fielding objections to the very nature of the plan itself.

'You can't do that with gryllups,' said one of the nobles.

'You can't use firearms like that,' said one of the Captains.

'Infantry can't manoeuvre like that,' said another of the nobles.

'What's this business with the flags?' asked another of the Captains.

'Why do we want to get men into the city?' asked another of the nobles.

'How can you fight if your fyrd aren't at the front?' asked another of the Captains.

'The fyrd won't fight at all without a few gryllups behind them, biting their lazy behinds,' said the first noble.

'This just won't work,' said virtually everybody.

Luftetmek looked at me. I looked up at the roof of the tent.

In the end, Luftetmek and I adopted the only approach that was left to us.

'If this fails,' Luftetmek said, 'what have we lost?' He looked around the assembled nobles and Captains and warriors. 'If this fails, it's just one more battle. But if it doesn't fail, it's victory.'

'It will fail,' someone called.

'And we'll be the laughing stock of the empire,' another called.

'If,' Luftetmek yelled, 'this does fail, you will still have won one victory.'

All eyes were on him, their curiosity aroused – mine, also.

'If this fails,' he said, 'I shall step aside as leader. One of you may take my place.'

I glared at him in disbelief. For all the confidence I was beginning to feel in our plan, I would not – could not – have asked him to stake so high a personal price on its outcome.

'Agreed!' shouted one of the nobles.

The cry was taken up by many others, but not, I was surprised to note, by all.

'But—' Luftetmek called, and waited for silence before continuing. 'If you accept my pledge, then you yourselves must pledge yourselves to David Shaw's plan. If you do not obey his instructions in every particular, then the bargain is broken, and however many battles it takes to defeat Kandirak, it is I who shall lead our armies on the day of victory.'

One of the nobles, one of those who had not taken up the earlier call, said, 'Agreed.'

The others looked at one another, questioningly. Then, one by one, sometimes grudgingly, sometimes with evident relief, they all agreed.

Luftetmek looked at me and grinned.

'Now,' he said softly, 'it's up to you.'

The meeting broke up soon after. And for all the frustrations and false starts, I actually felt good about it. There were factions among the nobles and Captains that were willing to accept Yarissi's revolution, though clearly they only intended showing their hand once the revolution had proved a success. These factions had embraced the plan Luftetmek and I had laid before them, and in so doing had helped persuade their less enthusiastic colleagues to do likewise. Many facets of the plan that had been only half-formed in my mind at the start of the evening were now full-blown and already being put into effect. One of these – the means of taking Xacmet once Kandirak's army had been defeated in the field – had been giving me a particularly bad time. Luftetmek, I was delighted to discover, had already gone a long way towards solving the problem. I quizzed him on it as we left the tent and strode through the camp.

'You're sure about the location of the ammunition stores?' I asked.

'Shaw,' he replied, 'I was Yarissi's Champion. I know every place in Xacmet which has any military significance whatsoever.'

'But if they moved it—'

He laughed.

'It would be an undertaking too large for Kandirak's indolent soul to contemplate,' he said.

I knew he was right, and not just for the reason he had stated.

'I will round up some men,' he said. 'I have no stomach for robbing the dead, but in the case of the filinta I will willingly make an exception.'

I spent the rest of that evening going about the camp on numerous errands. I had a pass signed by Luftetmek giving me carte blanche to enlist anyone I needed, and I put it to considerable use.

I met up with Zalmetta and the others and told them of our plans.

'Mohred,' I said to the Librarian, 'I know you don't want to involve yourself in this fight . . .'

'It is not my fight,' he said.

'Understood,' I said, 'but you are not averse to helping me in a non-combative fashion?'

'Of course not.'

'We need three hundred lances,' I told him.

He raised an eyebrow.

'Heavy ones,' I added.

He nodded. All Librarians were historians to a degree; he would know what I wanted.

I looked at Zalmetta.

'We need signalling devices,' I said. 'Flags on high poles. Can you do anything?'

'I can,' she said.

'We need about six different colours,' I said, 'two flags of each colour.'

'Ylyrria and I will attend to it,' she said.

I saw the child bridle at the prospect of manual labour. 'I trust,' she snapped, 'that you will be helping in this?'

'I'm going to have my hands full with a task of my own,' I told her. 'Now let's move: I don't know how much time we've got.'

Ylyrria lingered as the others moved away. I looked down at her, wondering what she wanted to say that she couldn't say in front of an audience.

'You have a plan,' she observed.

'Yes,' I said.

'A desperate one,' she suggested.

'Yes,' I said again.

'Should it fail,' she said, 'it will mean the end for your quest. You will not be reunited with your woman.'

'That's a reasonable assessment of the situation,' I confessed.

'And in the process,' Ylyrria said, 'you will have doomed Luftetmek's counter-revolution.'

I thought she was misreading Luftetmek's plans, but I let that pass.

'Probably,' I conceded, not without some reluctance.

'But you are going to do it anyway,' she said. There was a fire in her eyes that looked as though it could ignite at any moment.

'I'm open to suggestions,' I told her.

'No, you are not,' she said. 'You have made up your mind and nothing is going to change it. Right or wrong, you are committed.'

'Is there a point you're reaching for?' I asked.

'Yes,' she hissed, 'and it is this: you are staking the welfare of *my* people on your personal ambition. You are obsessed, and you care nothing for those who get trampled while you pursue your selfish quest. Will you argue the point?'

I looked at her long and hard: no child, not even a Vinh

child, should harbour such thoughts. But whatever my feelings, this was no time to deal with them.

'No argument,' I said smiling.

She glared at me, then turned and walked away, her back rigid.

I watched her go with a sense of relief; if she'd pushed any harder, I might have had to agree with her, and right now that was a luxury I couldn't afford. Once before I'd staked thousands of lives on a plan whose acceptance I'd had to fight for every step of the way, and the safety of Mrs Catlin was what had kept me going back then. Now it seemed as though I was doing the same thing again. I remembered a conversation I'd had with Celebe right before that other battle, when she'd asked which meant more to me, my adoptive city or the woman I loved. I hadn't been able to answer her then, a fact that seemed significant to her. If she'd asked me now whether I cared more for Mrs Catlin or the thousands who would fight and probably die very soon, I still wouldn't have been able to tell her.

I wished Celebe would turn up before the battle. It played on my conscience that I didn't know her fate, even though there was nothing I could do about it either way. And, too, I needed to hear her approve of my plan, or at least not disapprove. She was of Earth, but well versed in the ways of Shushuan. Of all the people I knew, her insight would have been the most valuable.

(There was also the little matter of how much interest the Thirteen Gods were taking in all of this, but that was an issue I simply daren't let myself consider.)

Evening turned to night, and the night was long and eventful. But with all the things we needed to accomplish, it was far from long enough. Luftetmek and his small group of volunteers returned shortly after midnight, upwards of fifty uniforms and their assorted accoutrements bundled up in their arms. All of the garments were bloodied, but their tell-tale black accessories were still clearly visible. I marvelled at Luftetmek's part in this plan; the concept of a 'fifth column' was, so far as I knew, unknown among the Vinh. When this was all over, a Reshek with Luftetmek in it would be a military force to be reckoned with.

PAUL WARE

By the time of their return, the camp was already being divided up into specialized groups. Mohred had recruited scores of helpers to assist him in the production of our lances. He had applied some marvellous lateral thinking to the problem and come up with an ingeniously simple solution: he had dismantled the rear part of the palisade that surrounded the camp. The palisade itself was a redundant legacy of Shushuan's once-inventive past; there was no room in present-day military thinking for the concept of a full-scale siege. I wondered if the men who had erected the palisade had ever stopped to consider why they were doing so.

As fast as the lances were being completed Mohred was instructing his slightly bemused cavalry in their usage. In the narrow streets between the tents, numerous cavalry charges made life interesting for anyone walking about the camp. I would have liked the opportunity to practice for real, en masse on the open plain. But the slaughter this battle would produce would be horrific enough without giving Kandirak's troops advance warning of our tactics. I was counting on our being able to catch the enemy totally off guard and thus keep the number of deaths to the barest minimum. Not that I was fooling myself; what I had proposed to Luftetmek was nothing short of a bloodbath, and only the knowledge that, left to themselves, his nobles and Captains would have enacted an even worse scenario gave my conscience any kind of comfort.

As for what I had been doing for the past few hours, I had spent the first of them wandering the camp and recruiting Luftetmek's best marksmen. These were few and far between, so I made up the numbers with anyone who already owned a pistol and knew one end of it from the other. I eventually assembled something close to the one thousand men Luftetmek had promised me, and then set to work teaching them how to shoot in ranks. Like everything else I'd done today, it was slow work. To the Resheki, the pistol was a one-shot weapon in any battle; after that shot, the pistol was forgotten. The first thing I showed them was how to reload at high speed. I think a few of them thought I was a magician, and that what I had done was some kind of sleight of hand. Then one or two of the brighter ones copied

264

me, and a degree of enthusiasm swept across the group. In a few minutes, everyone seemed to become infected by it, and suddenly I knew that *this* part of the plan, at least, had a chance. As soon as everyone had grasped the reloading idea I set about showing them how to sustain a rate of fire that was three times faster than their fastest man. It was a simple, ancient idea, of course, but one long forgotten on Shushuan. The influence of the phalanx on military thinking was far-reaching.

Morning eventually came and we were nowhere near ready. We had expected this, of course. The preparations I had in mind would take days to complete. But we had a little surprise in store for Kandirak's troops today.

As we had known they would, the filinta and their followers marched out of Xacmet and onto the plain beyond the city. It was several hours after the dawn, with the sun breaking through some straggly cloud cover but not providing much in the way of warmth or good cheer. The army marched out to the middle of the plain and stopped. Its commanders were visibly puzzled. The gates of our stockade were shut, and the camp appeared lifeless.

Presently, a group of about twenty mounted officers rode to within bowshot of the palisade. They were effectively safe from a pistol ball at that range, and I knew that there were no archers in Luftetmek's following, the bow not being a Resheki weapon.

From their markings I knew the twenty to be filinta of middle rank. I thought it significant that not one of Kandirak's generals was willing to risk his safety.

The leader of the group called out for our commander – which, under the circumstances, seemed a bit presumptuous – so we sent a man from the fyrd up onto the palisade wall. The reaction of the filinta was predictable enough, and included some highly imaginative threats and one or two references to the parentage of our leaders that, frankly, defied the laws of genetics.

Behind the gate, Luftetmek and I and several others tried to contain our laughter at the exchange – our fyrd volunteer was a born stand-up comic, with a dry delivery that was as natural as it was hilarious – until eventually the filinta abandoned their efforts and rode back to their army.

The militiaman descended from the wall and faced us.

'Now do we fight?' he asked.

Luftetmek and I exchanged glances, then cracked up again.

'No,' Luftetmek managed to say, 'we do not.'

The man was as puzzled as the filinta had been.

'We fight,' I said, 'when we are ready. And then, we fight to win.'

He frowned. I could almost see the thoughts evolving in his mind, concepts that were so simple and yet so hard to grasp. I had seen this kind of mental blind spot many times before – and not just on Shushuan – but I had no time today for guiding anyone through it. We split up, each of us facing a dozen tasks that needed completing before sundown, and the fyrd man returned to his own group.

For two days we kept Kandirak's men waiting. Once our own troops had grasped the concept of not actually having to go out and fight just because the enemy wanted them to they were able to derive vast amusement from the situation. Working in shifts, they took their turns atop the palisade wall, calling out taunts and insults to the filinta, challenging the courage/parentage/intelligence of their enemies as they saw fit. Kandirak's men tried to respond in kind, but they couldn't seem to grasp the tactics that this new type of warfare called for. To them, an insult was a challenge to do battle. Yet we stayed in our stockade and ignored their replies. It must have been very confusing for them.

On the evening of the third day the filinta retired to Xacmet. I found Luftetmek.

'It's time,' I said.

He nodded.

On the morning of the next day, we would leave the camp. Kandirak's troops, seeing us take the field, would rush out to attack us. Had they had any grasp of our tactics they would have stayed put, giving us a taste of our own medicine. But their frustration would not let them do that, and so they would play into our hands. Or, at least, that was the theory. I knew that many of Luftetmek's nobles and their followers still did not like or understand the orders Luftetmek and I had given them for the following day, but I believed that they would all fulfil their part of the plan. The only thing left to wonder about then, of course, was whether or not that would be enough.

The warriors of Benza, my own city, were renowned throughout the Kingdoms for their berserker fury in battle, but that was a technique that had evolved because of Benza's relatively diminutive size and the consequent small size of its armed forces. In Reshek, a vast country with no contiguous enemies to speak of, such a concept had never been necessary. And whilst I knew that the people of this country counted many great warriors amongst them, the two sides in this conflict were equally matched. What we needed, over and above the tactics I had tried to set in place, was a psychological edge over Kandirak's people, and I had no idea how to provide such a thing.

The night before the battle was a very relaxed, casual time. The strangely peaceful nature of the past days – both unexpected and thoroughly appreciated by Luftetmek's camp – had generated an air of confidence about the day to come that no one was trying very hard to undermine.

Entertainment on Shushuan is very much a do-it-yourself affair for most peoples, since travelling players and circuses and fairs are few and far between. Soldiers and warriors particularly – and not peculiarly to Shushuan – are adept at entertaining themselves. So I was not surprised, wandering the camp under a canopy of stars in a cloudless sky, to find numerous groups of men and their assorted camp followers singing songs or telling stories, regaling one another with tales of their prowess – true or otherwise – both in battle and in other pursuits. And, of course, there were many in the company that night who, for all their optimism, were treating this as their last night among the living. Their pursuits, naturally enough, tended towards the more basic, and a great deal of money changed hands in one particular tent that night.

I found Zalmetta and Mohred and Ylyrria sitting among a largish group of warriors, all common soldiers, mostly fyrd militia, around a camp fire beside which a woman was dancing. She was clearly a slave, and that irritated me, but I decided that now was not the time for that particular argument. A group of warriors were playing musical instruments, a wild and very unearthly melody to which the woman danced. Slave or not, she was fairly spectacular to behold. I gathered that a lot of men in the crowd shared my opinion.

'She's good,' I observed as I joined them.

Zalmetta's eyes were lambent with more than just the reflected firelight.

'She is magnificent,' she said. 'I never imagined humans could look so . . . feral.'

'She's a zhyratta,' said Ylyrria.

We all looked at her. Myself, I thought it must be past her bedtime.

'They're a tribe from the north,' the child said knowledgeably. 'They make good slaves. Especially the women.'

I felt irritated at her superior tone, and her automatic assumptions about a concept I found obscene.

'Why is that?' I asked.

She bridled at the tone in my voice, but said simply, 'Everyone says so.'

I almost laughed, but didn't. I didn't want to hear what that particular laugh would sound like.

'What is wrong with you?' she snapped. 'Must you hold a contrary view on every subject?'

'No,' I said, 'not every subject. But I prefer to think for myself, not be spoonfed my opinions by faceless people whom I've never met and who probably know no better than I do how this world is supposed to work.'

I saw Mohred looking at me strangely, but he said nothing. Ylyrria gave me the evil eye for a moment, then turned her back on me and watched the zhyratta dancer. One day, she'd pull that particular manoeuvre on the wrong person and get a knife between her shoulders for her trouble.

I sat with them for a while, then got up and moved on. There were others in the camp that I wanted to look in on and only a limited number of hours available to do it.

Hours later I was still walking the camp. My official duties – checking on my 'artillerymen' – were finished now, but I couldn't face the prospect of sleep just yet. I had purchased a flagon of ale from a vendor – at a price that, in Benza, would have bought a whole cask – and was now wandering aimlessly about the camp, the flagon half drained, and my spirits not much improved.

I was not the only one still abroad this late, and it seemed that all those who shared my insomnia also shared my mood. We greeted one another wordlessly in passing, Captains and warriors and fyrd and nobles alike, all made equal in the moment.

I was passing a large, wood-framed tent, offering a silent salute to the sentry on duty – he was no doubt standing guard over some lord or other lest his devoted followers cut his throat while he slept – when I became conscious of a blur of movement, little more than a flickering shadow in the light of the stars and the moon and the camp's few lanterns. Why I knew that death followed that shadow I cannot say, but perception and action followed one another so rapidly as to appear simultaneous. I threw myself to the ground, and heard the dull thud of a swift object striking wood. The sentry cursed, and I looked up to see the quivering shaft of an arrow protruding from one of the uprights of the tent. It had passed through the space that, an instant before, my body had occupied.

I leaped to my feet, and the sentry and I both made a brief but thorough search of the immediate vicinity. We found no trace of the would-be assassin, and returned to study the arrow in the vain hope it might give us some clue as to the identity of its sender.

The sentry pulled it from the wood and peered at it. While

he did so, I retrieved my ale flagon from where it had fallen. A little liquid remained, and the sentry and I shared it with a fatalistic toast to the all-seeing Thirteen, who surely had been watching over me this night.

'This is most strange,' the sentry said.

'What is?' I asked.

'The arrow,' he said.

'What is strange about it?' I asked.

He showed it to me, and it seemed the world slowed about me, the air suddenly very cold and still.

'It is Vohung,' the sentry said.

CHAPTER THIRTY-ONE

The Battle

———◄►◄►◄►———

Early the next morning, as preparations got under way for the day ahead, I found a few minutes to mention the previous night's events to Luftetmek.

'Strange,' he said, 'I did not think there were any archers in the camp.'

'There is at least one,' I told him wryly.

Having only a single arrow to work with as a clue to the identity of our would-be assassin there was little likelihood of our finding him before the battle began. And I would now be facing that battle with the prospect of dying not at the hands of the enemy but at those of a supposed ally.

The division of Luftetmek's forces began early. Our fifty 'filinta', complete with battle wounds and an officer who was seemingly a virtual stretcher-case, left the camp at the crack of dawn, heading around the plain to a point just south of Xacmet's main gate. Despite their hideous-seeming wounds, they moved with the practised ease of born warriors. Which was precisely what they were. The fifty were the cream of Luftetmek's most trusted and loyal followers. And all of them had served in Xacmet's city guard. They knew the city better than anyone.

Shortly after their departure, I saw Luftetmek moving through the ranks of the main body of his men; he didn't seem to be saying much, but each man he passed suddenly beamed from ear to ear. It was incredible to watch. I wondered what he could possibly be saying to prompt such a reaction.

Around me, I heard orders being called out, men beginning to assemble in their formations. The cavalry trotted off towards the opening in the rear of the palisade wall; my own troops, the thousand or so artillery, were lining up on either side of the main gate. In the middle of the camp, the largest single body of Luftetmek's following, the infantry, were dividing up into their separate companies; they had three score of commanders, sixty nobles and Captains to command upwards of six thousand men. I heard armour rattle onto limbs that might soon be rent and torn. I heard men curse and laugh and grumble and, somewhere, sing. I heard the creak of the palisade gates being opened more fully, the sounds of the plain beyond, the wind, the cries of birds, the rustlings and snarls of animals, which were gradually drowned by the other, different, more immediate sounds from within the compound.

Luftetmek had returned to his tent briefly and now re-emerged, clad in the full panoply of war. His weapons were those of a simple infantryman: spear, sword and shield. But his bearing and his carriage were those of a born leader. Yarissi had chosen well in making this man his Champion.

He carried his helmet in the crook of one arm, and looked up and down the massed ranks of his soldiers. Nobles and Captains stood, slightly lost without their customary gryllups, awaiting the call to arms, and although some of them tried to pretend that it was not Luftetmek for whom they were waiting to give that call, an equal number were visibly pleased to be following him into battle. I found myself surprised, though not for the first time, that men of previously high standing in Resheki society were so willing to acknowledge the type of revolution that Luftetmek and, to a larger extent, Yarissi stood for. Surely, I reasoned, if Yarissi were to succeed in his goals, their way of life would be changed forever, and not to their benefit. Or was I missing something? Something that was so obvious to these men, and yet to which I seemed oblivious?

Luftetmek marched to the main gate and ascended the narrow stair leading to the palisade's inner catwalk. He peered across the plain beyond the camp, nodded, and turned to face those of us who stood, in our thousands, inside the gate. Every eye was upon him, and every voice was stilled. The sense that something irrevocable was about to happen was almost unbearable.

'For Yarissi—' Luftetmek said quietly.

The roar of approval was deafening, as was the pounding of men's fists on shields and armour, the feet stamping, the voices crying out the name 'Yarissi!' over and over in sheer unbridled, unalloyed ecstasy at what that name meant to them. If I had wondered how Luftetmek might provide his troops with a psychological advantage that day, he had answered me with those two simple words.

He leaped to the ground and, at the head of his army, marched out onto the plain. I had objected, briefly, to Luftetmek placing himself on the front line, but he had overruled me flatly and would hear no arguments on the subject. In retrospect, I was not surprised that he had so chosen. On Shushuan, as once on Earth, it was not the case that the leader of a mighty army sat at some remove from the fighting and directed his troops like the pieces on a game board. Rather, he was the leader because he led. His men would not follow him otherwise. It seemed to me significant of a great many things that Kandirak had chosen not to take the field in defence of his city, that he had left the task to his generals and the filinta.

It took some considerable time for the infantry to quit the stockade, but by the time they had the dawn was still only a smudge of red on the horizon, and Xacmet a black shape against a pale sky. It was unlikely that Kandirak's lookouts – if he had placed any – would be able to observe our movements yet.

When the last of the infantry were a hundred yards beyond the gate I turned to my own lieutenants. There were five of them, for the artillery would operate as six separate companies, comprising some hundred and sixty men each.

'Move out,' I said.

We kept low and moved as stealthily as a thousand men could move, three companies to either side of the plain. Even when the men of Xacmet spotted Luftetmek's infantry, they would not spot his artillery. At least, not until we wanted them to.

Shortly after our own departure, if all was going according to plan, the cavalry would have left the stockade and headed into the woods to the north of the plain. From there they would take up their predetermined position and await further orders.

For a considerable period of time our forces had the plain all to ourselves, and once we were all in position there was nothing we could do but wait. I'd known lonelier moments in my life, but not many.

Soon, sooner even than I had expected, the gates of Xacmet flew open and Kandirak's horde came charging through them.

I smiled.

This had been the one element of our plan that we could not control. I had been counting on the sheer frustration that must have ruled in the camp of the filinta for the last three days to drive them into our arms as soon as the opportunity presented itself. A more seasoned army, with better generals, would have suspected our motives in taking the field now, and so openly. But Kandirak's followers were not that sophisticated, nor that professional.

In a single mass the filinta and their followers surged across the open plain, a phalanx of bodies whose only 'strategy' was to swarm over the enemy and smother it. Today, if all went well, we would teach them a thing or two about tactics.

I began to turn towards the palisade wall far away to our right, when something at the front of the advancing forces caught my attention – or, rather, someone. The someone was Kandirak. For an instant I doubted the evidence of my eyes, but once I had accepted the startling truth of what I was seeing I felt a pang of real doubt for the outcome of today's battle. This was one contingency that none of us had thought to allow for, and consequently one that could, conceivably, upset all our carefully laid plans.

I cast a feverish glance at the palisade wall; no one back at Luftetmek's camp could possibly be aware of Kandirak's presence, and it was from the camp that all the signals for the battle would come.

At that instant, a flag went up on the top of the palisade wall. It was a green flag, the colour that represented Luftetmek's infantry. An instant later, a red flag went up alongside it.

I turned to stare at the ranks of men in the middle of the plain. Would Luftetmek obey the signal, as we had planned, or would he see Kandirak and decide—

The battle cry of 'Yarissiii!' could be heard right across the plain, and a great cloud of dust went up as Luftetmek led the charge. This was it, then: we were committed. Whatever Kandirak's presence meant, it would not affect our own plans. I just prayed we had not underestimated the man.

From my vantage point I could see what Kandirak's men could not. As Luftetmek led the charge, the ranks behind him did not all follow immediately. Each rank held back before joining the attack, creating a space between each row of men. To the enemy, the charge would appear to be that of a solid body of men, a phalanx like their own, and according to Resheki battle tactics there was only one way to defeat such a charge: charge at it even harder.

The two armies met with a clash of steel that rolled across the plain like discordant thunder, a rattling, clattering crash of blades that was almost melodic, its harshness muted by distance but made no less terrible by it.

Luftetmek's front rank met the charge, held for an instant, and fell back.

Kandirak's army charged on, the self-styled Emperor of Reshek leading the attack with a vigour that was astonishing to behold, particularly so considering his reputation for dissoluteness and decadence. I thought I saw, in that brief moment, something of the reason for his rise to power and the hold he had over his followers. Somewhere in his degenerate soul there still lived the heart of a warrior.

Rank after rank of the rebel army gave ground before Kandirak's onslaught, the men racing back through the open ranks behind them, back towards the palisade wall. They would never reach it. But it didn't matter, because that was not part of the plan.

Kandirak's army was almost as strung out now as ours had been when the charge began, and it was showing no sign of slowing down. I looked again toward the palisade wall. A moment later, a blue flag, the colour for the artillery, was raised aloft.

'Take your positions!' I cried.

My men sprang from their hiding places. In three ranks, they faced Kandirak's army as it sped past them; the front rank raised their pistols. I glanced briefly to the east and saw two other companies of artillery assume the same stance. Across the battlefield, to the north of Kandirak's army, I knew that three more companies were copying our action.

On the palisade wall, a red flag was raised.

'First rank, fire!' I cried.

The crackle of gunfire was almost deafening; white smoke, like a blanket of fog, settled over the plain. As soon as they had discharged their weapons the first rank fell to their knees and began to reload.

'Second rank, fire!' I cried.

It was impossible now to see through the smoke, but we knew where the enemy was and we knew also that only the enemy was in range of our weapons. We had caught Kandirak's forces in a crossfire, the limited range of our pistols guaranteeing the safety of our own men. We had, in effect, made our limitations work to our advantage.

The men of the second rank now fell to their knees and began to reload. Most of the first rank, I was pleased to see, had already completed their own reloading.

'Third rank,' I cried, 'fire!'

I looked up to the top of the palisade wall, which was just visible through the outer fringes of the smoke. The red flag remained aloft. From the top of the wall, our signal men would watch Kandirak's troops until a given number had fallen, and only then would the red flag come down.

'First rank—' I cried.

The men arose.

'—Fire!'

We completed the whole sequence a second time, and then a third, and still the red flag was up. I wished I could see through the smoke, to get some idea of how well our tactics were working. Then again, I was glad not to have to see the consequences of our actions.

I looked to the palisade wall again, and the flags were down.

'Cease fire!' I cried.

Silence settled over the plain, as though the billowing white smoke were a real blanket and it had smothered the opposing army. Then, slowly, haltingly, sounds drifted towards us. Men could be heard, cursing or weeping or crying out in pain. And occasionally, though disjointedly, giving orders to those still able or willing to follow them.

On the palisade wall, a yellow flag now flew with the red. From the woodland on the northern side of the plain, three hundred gryllups charged towards the Resheki army.

'Move out,' I ordered my men.

We abandoned our position and moved at a slow trot towards the city in the distance.

Behind us, Luftetmek's cavalry hit Kandirak's forces with their heavy lances and wreaked a new kind of destruction upon the disorganized army. Luftetmek's orders to the cavalry had been simple: charge – once – and stop for nothing. To their credit, his mounted warriors obeyed as well as the conditions would allow. Taking a slightly diagonal path into the body of the enemy troops, they used their lances to devastating effect in the first, battering-ram moment of impact, and then drew their swords to slash and hack a way out into the open once more.

On the far side of the plain, I saw the other three artillery companies moving to form up with my own trio. If our cavalry charge was insufficient to convince Kandirak's troops that retreat was not an option, then I suspected that a wall of a thousand flintlocks might change their minds. At all costs, if today's plan was to succeed, Kandirak's city must be denied to anyone who might return to defend it. Winning the battle on the open plain was only winning half of it.

It took some considerable time for the gryllup cavalry to cut their way through the massed ranks of infantry, but I was relieved to see that when they did finally emerge they had lost very few of their number. Once clear of the press of bodies the mounted rebels spurred their animals away from the fighting.

I watched closely as Kandirak's badly wounded army tried to make up its mind what to do next. Parts of it wanted to press the attack, unable to accept – or believe – that defeat was staring them in the face. Other parts wanted to retreat, which was the more sensible option. But mostly the confused and badly led foot soldiers who made up the bulk of Xacmet's forces simply didn't know what they wanted to do. I wondered where Kandirak was, and what he was doing. I wondered, briefly, if he was dead.

In the far distance, hardly visible now, two signal flags went up: one red, the other green. A mighty roar rose from Luftetmek's infantry, deafening even at this remove. The earth seemed almost to shake as Yarissi's Champion led the second charge, and this time, I knew, the charge was in earnest.

I watched as the two armies converged, Kandirak's forces still in disarray and unprepared for the fight Luftetmek would give them.

'First rank,' I cried, 'ready—'

I heard the order echoed by my five lieutenants. Over three hundred men aimed their pistols at the flank of Kandirak's phalanx.

The armies met, our infantry ripping through the front rank of filinta as though they had been made of straw.

'—Fire!' I said.

We were at the extreme limit of the range of our weapons, but the psychological effect alone was devastating to Kandirak's forces. Again and again the artillery roared, the men working in ranks as they had before, so that there was barely ten seconds' respite between volleys.

On the palisade wall, a yellow flag was flying. I peered into the distance, through clouds of smoke and dust, and saw two columns of cavalry forming up along the north and south edges of the plain. The army of Xacmet was now surrounded. A moment later, a single flag flew over Luftetmek's compound. The flag was white.

'Cease fire!' I cried.

The crackle of gunfire dwindled and died, and then we all stood and watched as, for long minutes, the battle between the two armies continued. Even though our artillery had ceased to fire, none of Kandirak's forces attempted to close with us. On and on the battle raged, neither side giving or expecting quarter. I glanced at the city behind us: why hadn't we had the signal yet? What was taking so long? Had our 'fifth column' met with resistance we had not anticipated? If so, and it became necessary to besiege Xacmet in earnest, then now was the time to devise new strategy, before events overtook us and today's battle went for nothing. I looked back to the plain, wondering again what had happened to Kandirak – and the air shook with a terrific explosion. The main gate of the city and most of the wall surrounding it was blown to fragments, debris raining down for hundreds of yards all around.

No signal flag was needed now; where the two armies met, bit by bit, man by man, Luftetmek's forces began to pull back. Kandirak's men did not press them. Slowly, like the creeping of some unnatural fog across the landscape, a grim stillness came over the plain. The silence was not absolute – the rattle of arms, the cries of the wounded and dying, these remained – but it was profound.

From this far away, and with the thousands of men that stood between us, it was impossible for me to discern the figure of Luftetmek, but I knew what he would be doing. He would be advancing, probably alone, into the no-man's-land that now existed between the two armies.

Bits of Xacmet's gatehouse were still raining down onto the plain, and everyone was noticeably jumpy.

'Holster your weapons,' I called, not wanting an accidental shot to distract Luftetmek now.

I could no more hear what he was saying than I could see him, but I knew what the words would be. Our own 'filinta' had gained access to Xacmet, disguised as casualties from the battle, and had put the torch to Kandirak's store of ammunition. There was now no way to defend the city from our attack. And no way for the defending army to return there as long as our artillery barred their way.

Basically, Luftetmek was offering to accept the filinta's unconditional surrender.

The waiting was almost more than my nerves could stand. I knew that Luftetmek was prepared – perhaps even expecting – to fight again, and we had made plans and laid down strategies in the event that such was the case. But I was hoping desperately that those plans would never be needed.

Finally, after over an hour of a verbal dispute that none of us could influence, we saw a flag go up on the palisade wall. The flag was red and white, and it flew alone.

A mighty cheer went up all around me, but all I felt at that moment was a deep and intense relief. The army of Kandirak, whether still led by him or by one of his underlings, had surrendered.

I turned to my men, and found myself smiling in spite of my feelings.

'Now,' I said, raising my arms for quiet, 'we march on Xacmet!'

CHAPTER THIRTY-TWO

Betrayal

It took hours to coordinate the next move in our plan. It was necessary to secure and disarm Kandirak's entire army, and to sequester its leaders so that, should they change their minds about their surrender, there was nothing they could do about it. During this uneasy period we discovered something that added to our troubles: Kandirak was among neither the dead nor the captured. Somehow, during the battle, he had escaped. His whereabouts were a mystery, and his capture a priority.

It was the middle of the afternoon before we entered Xacmet, and early evening before our encampment there was secure. Fighting was still going on all through the city, pockets of resistance holding out to the bitter end. Kandirak's filinta found themselves with few allies among the indigenous population, but those few they did find were fanatical in their loyalty and extremely zealous in their defence of the black-clad warriors.

In the quarter surrounding the former site of the main gate, however, it was Luftetmek who ruled, and whose forces controlled the routes into and out of the city. It was only a matter of time, then, before the rest of Xacmet was his.

Now that a haven of sorts had been created, the non-combatants in Luftetmek's camp had begun to make their way into the city. With them came Mohred, Zalmetta and Ylyrria. I was pleased to see the Librarian, since I once again had need of his talents, but I was less enthusiastic about the appearance of the other two. Xacmet was still a war zone, and the fighting was far from over. I would have been happier if they had stayed at the camp until this was all over.

Luftetmek was busy organizing patrols and suchlike, coordinating with his various Captains and other commanders, so I took Mohred on one side and told him what I wanted from him. He gave me one of his long-suffering looks, as though this were some kind of affront to his scholarly dignity or something. Then he nodded resignedly. I gave him a grin and returned to advise Luftetmek that we were ready.

On foot, Luftetmek, Mohred, I and a hundred hand-picked warriors advanced upon the great doors of the Kanaat Hall. The doors had been locked and barred against us since our arrival; it was logical to assume that the last of Kandirak's surviving lieutenants were within. It seemed almost obscene, in light of the events of the past hours, to entertain any personal considerations where the final outcome of this battle was concerned, but uppermost in my mind at that moment was a single thought: after this confrontation, only one more obstacle stood in the way of my reunion with Mrs Catlin. Perhaps Ylyrria had been right when she had said I was obsessed. My actions seemed scarcely more noble than those of the people I was fighting against.

At a gesture from me, Mohred stepped up to the giant double doors. He looked up at them, hands by his sides, face impassive. A hint of a breeze seemed to rush up the avenue behind us, tugging at our cloaks and tunics, yet when it reached the motionless Librarian it left him untouched. There was the sense of a gathering of energies around us, and a faint, almost imperceptible sound, like the buzzing of a swarm of bees very far off. I felt the hairs on my forearms stir.

Mohred's arms swept up and forwards, and with a roar like cannon fire the two huge doors flew from their hinges, the near-indestructible sard wood from which they had been fashioned centuries before smoking and blackened by the force of the arcane energies the Librarian had hurled against them.

They crashed to the floor of the Hall, raising dust in vast clouds all around. And then there was silence, as though the whole city had been shocked into immobility, as though the buildings themselves now held their breath.

Into that vast silence, a single sound intruded. Mohred's Y'nys-shod feet, invisible beneath his flowing robes, clacked mutedly over the stone flags of the street as he stepped aside from the now-open doorway. He looked at Luftetmek and me. Luftetmek strode forward, the rest of us following.

The Hall was not deserted, but it had an air of emptiness and disuse that was exaggerated by the nature and demeanour of its occupants. They stood at the far end of the central aisle, upwards of a hundred filinta in full battledress. Similarly attired, and standing upon the dais beside its vast wooden throne, was Kandirak. He was leaning heavily on a mighty two-handed broadsword, and both the weapon and his own person were bloodstained. Most surprising of all in his appearance, however, was the look in his eyes: it was not the look of a defeated man.

On the dais with Kandirak were two men. On his right, resplendent in his ancient Kai robes, stood Blukka. His face was as impassive as ever, but like Kandirak he held a naked sword in his hands. The man on the other side of the dais was Yarissi. He wore slave chains and appeared haggard, half-starved. I wondered if Kandirak had planned to have him appear thus, perhaps hoping to anger Luftetmek into making a rash and ill-considered move. If so, he succeeded only in the first part of his plan. Luftetmek's fury was a tangible presence in the room, but he controlled it. I saw his eyes flit briefly across the ranks of filinta that stood in front of the dais. All were armed with sword and spear. At close quarters, the effectiveness of the spears as missile weapons would be limited. As hand-held weapons, they would be formidable. I could see no firearms in evidence.

'Ah, the slave army,' Kandirak said, smiling. 'And their slave leaders! How appropriate.'

'Surrender now,' Luftetmek said, 'and we may spare your life.'

Kandirak laughed; he was too confident, too relaxed. What were we missing?

'Strange,' he said, 'I was about to offer you the same opportunity. Do I take it you decline my generosity?'

'If you kill every man here,' Luftetmek warned him, 'your defeat is no less certain. You are beaten, Kandirak. Let no more die for your lost cause.'

'Ah,' Kandirak said, 'you appeal to my better nature.' He leaned forward, his face hardening. 'What a pity I do not have one.'

'Once,' Luftetmek said, 'you were a warrior.'

'Once,' Kandirak said, 'I was a child. I grew up. Now, lay down your arms. I have had enough of this foolishness.'

'If that is the way you would have it—' Luftetmek said.

'It is,' Kandirak said.

Luftetmek turned to his men.

'Take him,' he said.

From the back of the Hall, behind us, from the open doorway, a voice was raised above the sudden rattle of arms.

'Do nothing!' it boomed, unnaturally loud even in the echoing vault of the Hall.

Virtually every head turned at the sound of that voice, and its owner strode imperiously forward. Men were swept aside as he passed, invisible hands parting them as effortlessly as a breeze parts smoke.

I stared dumbfounded as Mohred marched to the front of our forces. What had possessed him? I had not asked him to act further on our behalf. By his own admission he was no fighter. What did he hope to gain by this?

'Mohred—' I said, reaching out to him.

The air was torn from my lungs, my knees giving way beneath me. I barely felt the harsh impact of the floor as I hit it, my vision a mass of black spots on a background of swirling colour.

As if from a vast distance, I heard the Librarian say, 'Fool! Killer of my son! Did you think I did any of this for you? Cretinous simpleton! Too long have I waited for this.'

Something hit me, repeatedly; all around, I heard screams of pain and terror; I was conscious of an incredible heat, and sounds like the impact of lightning bolts. And then, mercifully, nothing.

CHAPTER THIRTY-THREE

Reunion

———◦◦◦◦———

'Let it be written,' Kandirak cried, 'that on this day, the Empire of Reshek was born anew!'

The men at the long tables raised their drinks and shouted their approval. The feast had been going on for some time now, and few of those present were anything close to sober. Or, at least, few of those at the tables. There were others in the Hall, myself for one, who were not so much at the feast as casualties of it.

We were once more in the Kanaat Hall, but it was now changed beyond all recognition. The official, businesslike furnishings that had once stood before the dais of the city's ruler had gone, and in their place were rows of dining tables, at which Kandirak's chief filinta now sat and ate and drank at his victory celebration. At the far end of the Hall, opposite the dais, a group of musicians had assembled, and throughout the evening they had been beating out a variety of Resheki folk tunes and anthems. Under other circumstances, I might have found them enjoyable.

Luftetmek and I, together with others of Luftetmek's troops, had been put in chains and variously beaten and kicked by Kandirak's revellers, all in the spirit of celebration, of course, until eventually the men had tired of this entertainment and we had been dragged off to one side and chained to the pillars that lined the central aisle of the Hall.

Kandirak himself seemed more animated than I had ever seen him. He had not partaken of the feast, so I could only put his mood down to the intoxication of power. And, indeed, his power in Reshek now seemed incontestable.

It was five days since that last fateful confrontation, when Mohred had shown his true colours and the beginning of the end had come for Yarissi's revolution.

Much had happened in those five days, though Luftetmek and Yarissi and I had learned of most of it only after the fact, and then only in parts.

For three days following our defeat by Mohred I had been kept in total isolation. I had awoken in chains. I was naked except for a thick leather belt that was padlocked around my waist, my wrists manacled to it. A wooden beam, six inches thick, was forced through the crook of my arms and across my back, then chained in place around my forearms. Perhaps feeling that this was insufficient in itself to restrain me, I was also locked in a cell. The cell was about four feet square and four feet deep. A double door of heavy wood, barred on the outside, filled one wall. Through a small, iron-grated window, a certain amount of grubby light was admitted.

As small as my cell was, I quickly discovered that I was not its only occupant. Furtive scurryings and half-heard twitterings told me that if I wasn't careful I would end up as something's lunch. I would occasionally feel the touch of a furry body, small and somehow incredibly repulsive, and at such times I would yell and curse furiously, my voice the only weapon I had with which to drive the creatures away. I am not actually disgusted by rats or other rodents, nor afraid of them beyond the normal fear each of us has of anything that can do us injury. But I had not come this far, and endured this much, to end up as an entrée on some murine menu.

For three days I was left in that stinking cell. I neither saw nor heard another human soul in all that time; I was not fed, nor given anything to drink. And because of the size of the cell, I was incapable of moving sufficiently to ease the incredible cramps that were developing in my body. But if it was Mohred's intention that this imprisonment should break my spirit, or reduce me to a gibbering wreck, then he was a fool. After the mental tortures heaped upon me by Tal Daqar, this was a picnic. The physical pain and discomfort was excruciating, but it was *only* physical.

What was torturing my mind, and was nothing to do with Mohred – other than indirectly – was the mess I had made of the battle against Kandirak. The thing had been won, and I had thrown our victory away because of a stupid error of judgement. How could I have been so gullible as to trust Mohred, a Librarian – Sonder's *father*? Once again I had acted on an impulse, an impulse that had prompted me to *want* to believe what I *needed* to believe, and once again others had paid the price.

On the third day, when I had just about run out of ways to castigate myself, the cell doors were dragged noisily open and I was pulled out into the corridor.

I bit down on an ear-splitting scream as my legs were straightened and the muscles worked vigorously. My knees and ankles were like fire, my hips locked into a permanent crouch.

At the same time that this physical abuse was going on, someone else was hosing me down and using some kind of scrubbing brush to remove the stink of the past three days from my body. I didn't know which of the two was the worst.

Presently I was hauled to my feet between the two men who had taken me out of the cell, my legs buckling instantly, the weight of the beam across my back seeming like that of a whole building. Supporting me between them, the guards half-carried me along a narrow corridor that was lit by flickering oil lamps, the walls, floor and ceiling bare of any ornamentation. The floor felt like ice underfoot.

My awareness of my surroundings faded in and out as the pain in my body throbbed constantly. But gradually it came to me that the floor beneath my feet had become carpeted, the level of illumination was greatly increased, and, in fact, I was now being held still: we were no longer moving. We had arrived. But where?

I looked up, blinking away tears of incredible pain, and found myself face to face with Mohred.

He put a hand on my shoulder, and I couldn't stop the muscles jumping spasmodically in response.

'Painful?' he asked.

I didn't even try to respond.

The hands that had been supporting me let go, and I fell to the carpeted floor.

'I have waited for this moment,' Mohred said conversationally, 'for over four years. My only regret is that it cannot go on forever.'

I tried to look at him, but I couldn't even lift my head.

'Tomorrow,' he went on, 'Tal Daqar arrives. And with him, the woman Linna.'

I made a supreme effort and managed to turn my head. I looked up at the Librarian and wished him dead. I wished the power of the Thirteen to smite him where he stood. I wished for an ounce of strength, and a sword, or a knife, or a club.

'I will let you live,' he said, 'just long enough to watch her death.'

He gestured to the two guards. They picked me up by the arms. In Benza, in practice with Tor Taskus and his fellow Captains, I had learned seven different ways to kill using only my feet. Each of them, however, required that I be able to lift at least one foot more than an inch from the floor.

'Give him back his clothing,' Mohred said, 'and place him in the main prison cell.'

I spent the next two days incarcerated with Luftetmek and Yarissi and the men who had entered the city following our victory on the plain beyond its walls. Not all had been taken. A handful of common soldiers, mostly artillery, had managed to escape. They had stayed within the city and attempted to mount a guerrilla campaign against Kandirak. That they had had any success at all was a measure of how much support Yarissi's name could still elicit within the city.

I looked around the Kanaat Hall at those assembled today. They were the pick of Kandirak's filinta, men who followed him not for an ideal or for the future of Reshek, but for the power they would wield in the kind of country he would create for them. They were mercenaries in all but name, and the name of Yarissi meant nothing to them.

A movement behind the pillar to my left caught my eye. I glanced around, and saw Mohred entering the chamber via one of its side doors. He looked around briefly, spotted me, and walked over to stand in front of me.

He looked troubled, distracted.

'I am not a vindictive man,' he said, which was, I thought, a strange admission. 'Say the word, and I will kill you now. It will be swift and painless.'

'Mohred—' I said.

'Yes?'

'Go to Hell.'

He was visibly startled, then angry; but, above all, there was still that air of preoccupation, as though I had ceased to be the centre of his attention. Given his earlier comments, and the depth of the hatred I had sensed he felt towards me, I wondered what could possibly have happened to cause such a shift in his attitude.

'You are a fool,' he said, 'and you will die the death of a fool.'

'Better a fool,' I said, 'than a traitor.'

That seemed to get his attention.

'How can you call me traitor?' he demanded.

'You work it out,' I said dismissively. 'I have no time for you.'

I looked away from him, my mind seemingly on other, more important matters. He shrugged and walked away.

I was astounded. Two days ago my defeat had been the centre of Mohred's existence. What had changed?

The Librarian crossed the Hall to the dais. Seeing him, Kandirak arose.

'Let the traitor be brought in,' he said, which brought a rousing cheer from the assembly.

Mohred ascended the dais, and moments later Yarissi was dragged into the room, his body weighed down with enough chains for five men.

Those at the tables jeered and mocked him, heaping all manner of abuse upon him as he was led roughly to the foot of the dais.

I watched the men in the Hall as they abused the man that all Reshek had once hailed as its saviour. I wondered if any of them had, in the past, for their own purposes, supported Yarissi.

I looked at Kandirak. If Yarissi possessed some indefinable quality that spoke to men's better nature, then what Kandirak possessed was its antithesis. His followers were no less zealous than Yarissi's, but the forces that drove them were entirely selfish and malevolent. It was almost as though the primal forces of good and evil had been made manifest, and the people of Reshek given a simple choice. I didn't agree with everything that Yarissi stood for, nor with all the things he hoped to bring about; but if Kandirak were the only other option then that, for me, was no option at all.

'Kanaat Yarissi,' Kandirak said. 'You have betrayed the great and noble cause that once you espoused. Can you deny the charge? Will you deny the charge? Or will you meet your fate as a man?'

Yarissi looked up at him; he was pale and haggard, but the fire in his eyes was undimmed.

'I am a slave,' he said simply. 'My denial would serve no purpose, since in law my word has no meaning. I am what you chose to make me. I have ever been what others have chosen to make me. My life has had no other purpose.'

'Fine words,' Kandirak said, 'but as bereft of value as your worthless life.'

He gestured to the guard.

'Chain him to the next pillar,' he said.

The guard obeyed. I wondered what Kandirak had in store for us. Perhaps he intended lining the avenue outside the city with gibbets again.

'And now,' Kandirak said, 'bring in the last of the Bagalamak.'

I stiffened in my chains. I had not known if Ylyrria had been with those who were still at large.

Escorted by two guards, flanked by them but otherwise unrestrained, Ylyrria Muti walked into the Kanaat Hall.

The men at the tables watched in silence as the child passed them by, her eyes fixed straight ahead on Kandirak, her expression unreadable. She had been dressed in the traditional robes of a Resheki woman of high birth, her wrists and throat adorned with slender chains of gold. Her hair, which had been brushed and combed, was held back by a gold band encrusted with jewels. If she truly was the last of her line, then effectively she was now ruler of House Bagalamak, and she looked every inch the part. But in this context, in this place, and at this time, her appearance filled me with apprehension. What monstrous game was Kandirak now playing?

She stopped at the foot of the dais and looked up at Kandirak. If she felt any fear, it did not show on her face or in her deportment. I wondered, briefly and furiously, if she had been drugged.

'You are the last surviving heir to the title of the Bagalamak,' Kandirak said.

'If you say so, Lord,' Ylyrria replied.

'My decree that all your House should die,' Kandirak said, 'has troubled me of late.'

I glared at him. Did anyone in the Hall believe a word of that? From the looks on their faces, it seemed that perhaps they did. Or, at least, that they were mindful to let it be seen that they did.

'I am pleased,' he went on, 'that fate has given me an opportunity to make amends for my rash action.'

He arose and stepped down from the dais. To my astonishment, he got down on one knee in front of the child, so that his face was level with hers.

'Will you honour my House,' he said, 'by consenting to become a part of it?'

I felt a blind rage build inside me. The only legal way for a free person to change House allegiance was by the Vinh equivalent of marriage, but by every custom and tradition that there was Ylyrria was too young even to consider such a thing.

'I would be honoured by such an arrangement,' I heard Ylyrria say.

I was dumbfounded. Was this the same girl I had known for all these months? What possible inducement could Kandirak have offered her to provoke so meek an acquiescence to a proposal that she would once have greeted with open scorn and contempt? And yet, for all her fire and all her strength, she was only a child. Perhaps, as any child might, she had simply tired of the role she had been playing and had decided to try a new game. As plausible, and even probable, as the explanation might seem, I felt compelled to reject it. Child though she was, Ylyrria was not fickle. Or was I simply imposing my own prejudices and expectations upon her? She had never been slow to let me know that her agenda and mine were far from complementary, that they were, in many respects, antagonistic. If the throne of Reshek was truly where she saw herself, then perhaps this new alliance was not merely logical but actually desirable.

Kandirak had arisen and resumed his place upon the dais.

'Fetch a chair for our new sister,' he ordered.

Within moments an elaborately carved chair was brought forth and placed next to Kandirak's throne. He gestured to the child, and she ascended to the dais and sat upon the chair with a complete absence of self-consciousness, a princess in every sense of the word.

Kandirak leaned back in his throne, surveying his audience. The throne itself was a monstrosity, obviously newly created for him. Its bulk was ink-black sard wood, which meant, given its size, that it must have weighed half a ton or more. The wood was upholstered in dark purple leather, the colour looking like dried blood in the diffuse sunlight that filtered into the room. The arms and wings were inlaid with bits of gold and precious stones, some in random paterns, others arranged to suggest fabulous beasts or heroically proportioned warriors. The whole ensemble suggested an imagination that ought to have been humanely destroyed.

'I think it is time for some entertainment,' he announced.

Cheers rang through the Hall, but from their tone I didn't like to contemplate the nature of the entertainment that would follow.

'Bring in the creature,' Kandirak ordered.

I looked over to the far end of the Hall, already knowing

what I would see. Bound with heavy ropes, her ankles locked into a hobble-bar, Zalmetta was driven into the Hall by two spear-carrying guards. Despite her bonds, they seemed wary of her, unsure of their ability to control her. Her shock of white hair was in wild disarray, her wide eyes sparkling with a deadly light. For all her natural pacifism, I sensed a fury in her that matched the one in my own heart.

Walking in the hobble was almost impossible. A fiendishly simple device, it was merely a two-foot-long iron bar with an anklet at either end. Even if her arms had been free for balance she would have struggled to walk upright. Bound as she was, it was a marvel that she could even stand, with the guards prodding her as they were.

She moved slowly, stiffly forward, her gaze taking in her surroundings in one swift glance before finally settling on Kandirak. Baring her teeth in a feral snarl, she moved more swiftly forward.

As she passed me, I could see evidence of the physical ill-treatment she had recently received, scratches and bruises on her arms and face and legs. Under the mass of ropes that bound her torso, her arms behind her, her garments hung in tatters.

Before she could get within ten feet of the dais one of the guards thrust the butt of his spear in front of her and tripped her. She fell, but not heavily, not clumsily, as he had intended. Rather she rolled gracefully over and was back on her feet all in one fluid movement. The guard, startled, ran forward. He put himself in front of her, as though to block her way. Zalmetta launched herself forward and, in a move that was as crude as it was effective, headbutted him in the middle of his face. He went down like a rock, gushing blood, either deeply unconscious or stone-dead. The other guard sprang forward, his spear raised to strike, but Zalmetta swivelled on one well-planted foot and the guard's thrust went past her, the point of the spear striking sparks off the floor at her feet. In a single graceful motion she ducked, twisted, and threw her head up and back, catching the guard under the chin and catapulting him six feet into the air. He hit the floor and didn't get up.

Zalmetta whirled to face Kandirak, shaking her hair back from her face. He was smiling down at her, unconcerned by her show of force. I thought she would attack him, hopeless though such an attack would have been. Instead, she straightened up, staring unblinking into his face, and said, 'Free me and I will serve you without question.'

I was stunned. Had everyone gone mad? What had happened during the five days of my incarceration?

'Why would you serve me?' Kandirak asked, smiling. He appeared genuinely curious, as though her offer had been quite unexpected.

'Tal Daqar is here,' she said, 'is he not?'

'He will join us presently,' said Kandirak.

'He will make me a slave,' she said. 'I would rather die. You, however, are a third alternative.'

'Remain in Reshek,' Kandirak said, 'and you will still be a slave. I could not permit a creature such as yourself to roam free.'

'You speak only of physical slavery,' Zalmetta said. 'What Tal Daqar will do to me will enslave my soul.'

Kandirak allowed a frown to cross his brow; he appeared to be considering her offer seriously.

'I will accede to your request,' he said, 'on one condition.'

'Name it,' said Zalmetta.

'That no matter what occurs here today,' Kandirak said, 'you will neither speak nor act unless I so direct.'

'So be it,' Zalmetta agreed.

The two guards were stirring. I suspected it would be some days before they ceased to feel pain.

Kandirak called for some of those at the tables to take the men away, and for others to release Zalmetta from her bonds. They did so – warily – and then she stood passively before the dais, facing Kandirak.

'Place yourself behind one of the pillars,' he told her, 'where you may observe events without being seen.'

She nodded.

'Attempt to escape,' he said, 'and I shall have you killed instantly.'

'I understand,' she said.

She moved to stand behind a pillar at the far side of the Hall from me. I wished, rather desperately, that she had come to stand behind my own pillar. I wanted to talk to her, to find out what had been happening to turn both her and Ylyrria into willing followers of Kandirak. I could understand Zalmetta's predicament – to a degree – but were things really this hopeless?

On the dais, some kind of debate was raging between Mohred and Kandirak. It was impossible to make out what was being said, but from their expressions I gathered that the Librarian was attempting to urge Kandirak to some course of action and that his suggestions were not meeting with much success. As I watched them, I had a sudden flash of intuition: Mohred wasn't trying to persuade Kandirak to do something, he was trying to persuade him *not* to do something. I felt a cold shiver run through me; for no good reason, I suddenly knew that my own fate was inextricably tied up in what Mohred was saying.

Heedless of the consequences, I called out, 'Listen to him, Kandirak. He speaks the truth.'

Both men looked at me, Kandirak with annoyance, the Librarian with surprise.

'Gag that fool,' Kandirak ordered.

'Gag us all,' I cried, 'but listen to the Librarian. *He knows!*'

Mohred was glaring at me now with stark terror etched in every line of his face. Whatever it was he knew, he was now convinced I knew it too. I just wished that I did.

One of the guards succeeded in getting a gag in my mouth and tying it securely. He almost got away with all his fingers intact.

On the dais, Kandirak waved angrily at Mohred for him to be silent. Fuming, the Librarian stepped back.

A deathly hush suddenly fell over the Hall, even the sound of the musicians trailing uncertainly away. All eyes turned towards the main entrance.

'Ah!' Kandirak exclaimed. 'Our guests.'

Into the Hall strode Tal Daqar. Behind him were Blukka and

Kziktzak. Not a man in the Hall was able to take his eyes off the seven-foot-tall Y'nys creature. Its stick-like body moved with the easy grace of a living thing; its vertical red slit of an eye turned slowly to survey the whole room. It fixed on me and stopped. That faceless face was incapable of registering any expression, yet I knew that I had been both recognized and targeted. If the creature chose, it could sear my body with its deadly ray without even breaking its stride. I wondered, sweating, how much independence of action Tal Daqar had granted it.

It looked away from me. I breathed again.

'Tal Daqar,' Kandirak said, 'honoured ally of the Resheki people, join me in my feast.'

Daqar looked around the Hall. I wondered if I alone read the veiled contempt on his face. To one such as himself, who prized intellect above all else, this scene must have represented the antithesis of everything he believed in.

'You honour me,' was all he said.

He joined Kandirak upon the dais, Blukka and Kziktzak flanking him.

Kandirak addressed the Hall.

'Thanks to the timely arrival of our new ally,' he said, 'the last of the traitor army that had been encamped outside our walls has now been taken. This has left your emperor with a dilemma: how to dispose of several thousand criminals in a manner that will be both fitting to their crime, and efficacious to the populace of our great city.' He glanced at Daqar. 'Once again, our ally has come to my aid. He has a suggestion that I think will satisfy all concerned.'

Daqar smiled thinly. He tipped his head to Kandirak, declining the implied invitation to reveal the suggestion himself.

'In ancient times,' Kandirak said, clearly pleased at being allowed to continue, 'criminals were disposed of in something called an arena. Here, men would fight to the death, sometimes against other men – criminals like themselves – or against wild animals. This was considered a great form of entertainment in those days, with whole cities turning out to watch. I think it would be not inappropriate to restore the practice – for this one occasion, at any rate.'

'No!' cried Yarissi. 'It is barbaric! You cannot!'

Kandirak looked at him coldly.

'I can,' was all he said.

Luftetmek said, 'No one will fight. Our people will not make war on one another. You will have to get your entertainment elsewhere.'

To my surprise, it was Tal Daqar who replied.

'They will fight,' he said. 'They will fight Kziktzak.'

'At odds of thousands to one?' Luftetmek said. 'Even your creature is not that powerful.'

'It is precisely to test that contention,' Daqar said, 'that I have suggested the match. I have . . . certain plans. Kziktzak is central to them. Knowing his limitations – or lack thereof – would be useful.'

'But first,' Kandirak said, 'I believe there is a smaller conflict to resolve.'

He looked at Mohred. The Librarian shifted uneasily; he flicked a glance in my direction, not meeting my eyes.

Kandirak, visibly irritated by Mohred, gestured to a guard at the far end of the Hall, and a figure was dragged struggling into the chamber. She lashed out at the guards – she was not chained, or bound – and they fended her off, laughing.

I felt my knees go weak; I almost collapsed against the pillar behind me.

She spun to face the Hall, her eyes narrow and blazing. Her hair, waist-length and a rich red-brown, swirled about her. She was dressed as a Benzan noble woman. Her wide-necked chemise was finest silk, the full sleeves fastened at her wrists with bracelets of gold. Her ankle-length, layered skirts were brocaded cotton and finest woven wool. Her bodice was elaborately embroidered with fanciful patterns suggestive of exotic flowers; the leaves and blossoms were precious stones. About her throat was a slender choker set with diamonds. On her feet were finely tooled leather slippers. On the third finger of her left hand was a simple ring of yellow gold. It was not an ornament. It was a wedding ring.

And on its inner surface, inscribed in the flowing cursive script that was the written form of the High Tongue, were two names. One of them was mine.

'Bring the woman here,' Kandirak ordered.

The room seemed to be spinning around me. I wanted to cheer, to curse, to weep, to laugh, to sing.

She turned to the ruler of Reshek and fixed him with a look that could cut diamond. (Few people can accurately read her expression, but I read it now: behind her bravado, and a very real courage, there was fear. She was too intelligent not to know the danger in which she stood.)

'This,' she told Kandirak, 'is an act of war.'

'Of course it is,' he replied. 'Reshek is at war with the world; we would not wish your backward land to feel left out.'

She flicked her gaze to Mohred. I knew what she was doing; she was looking for an ally, any ally.

'Who are you?' she demanded.

She had not moved from the far end of the Hall, and was completely ignoring her guards.

'I am Mohred,' the Librarian replied, his words falling like lead weights. 'Sonder was my son.'

'You have my sympathy for your loss,' she said. 'Why are you here?'

Rallying somewhat, Mohred said, 'You killed my son. You must pay . . .'

'I killed no one,' she snapped. 'Sonder died at the hands of the Thirteen. Are you allied to this warmonger?'

'I . . .' He hesitated, then said, 'For the moment, I am.'

'More fool you,' she said scornfully.

She looked around the room. There was a lot to see, and before her gaze could reach me, one of her guards nudged her with his spear and she wheeled to face him.

'Do that again, boy,' she hissed, 'and I will take that toothpick away from you and make you eat it.'

The guard hesitated, perhaps remembering what Zalmetta had done to two of his colleagues, then made a tentative gesture that was half invitation, half challenge, and seemed to suggest that, in her own time, she might like to approach the dais.

She acknowledged the gesture and walked calmly down the length of the Hall. The two men followed her like an entourage. Reaching the dais, she pointed a finger at Tal Daqar.

'This man is a murderer,' she stated. 'With no declaration of war, he slew the men who constituted my honour guard from the court of Duke Joshima. If there is any justice left in this land, you will have him bound over to stand trial.'

'There is justice here,' Kandirak said darkly.

She looked at him.

He pointed to himself.

'I am the justice in Reshek,' he said. 'I am swift and I am terrible.' He smiled suddenly. 'But I am fair. I have heard your charge, and I find it to be not without substance. Very well; we will try the matter here and now.'

'I have no witnesses,' she said. 'All were slain.'

'You need none,' said Kandirak.

She looked puzzled.

'This will be a trial by combat,' Kandirak told her.

'Ah,' she said, smiling.

I felt myself in the grip of emotions I could neither name nor understand. Too much was happening, and all of it was outside my control. The responses I felt I should have been making had been cut off from me, leaving a void that nothing could fill.

'My Champion,' I heard Kandirak say, 'will be Blukka.'

The giant slave stepped forward.

'And who is to be mine?' she asked.

'I believe he is known to you,' Kandirak said.

I saw Mohred give me another nervous glance. What was going through that devious mind of his, and why was it troubling him so much?

Mrs Catlin was looking round the room in a puzzled fashion. 'No one here is known to me,' she said. 'At least, no one I can imagine would be willing to champion me.'

Kandirak waved an arm vaguely in my direction. Mrs Catlin followed the gesture. Her eyes passed me by, no recognition in them, and then suddenly snapped back to stare me full in the face, her look of shocked disbelief an eloquent testimony to my present appearance.

She turned her gaze slowly upon Kandirak.

'Set him free,' she said quietly, her voice like the blade of a knife.

'Of course,' Kandirak said. 'He cannot fight chained to a pillar.'

I felt my bonds being released, and as soon as my hands were free I tore the gag from my mouth.

Mrs Catlin took a step towards me, her eyes bright and a smile playing about her lips. An almost tangible attraction seemed to be in the air between us, a force drawing us together. And all I wanted, all I had ever wanted, was to yield to that force, to surrender to it . . .

But I couldn't. Not here, not like this. With the pillar behind me, I couldn't back away, but I stepped sideways, a hand out in front of me to ward her off.

'Not now,' I heard myself say, the words coming out in English. 'Later, not now—'

The smile was still on her lips, but it was frozen there now, a triumph of muscle control over emotion. She was hurt, and I was responsible. But there was no way for me to explain, even if I'd known how; this was all I'd lived for for over four years, and now I was rejecting it. What was wrong with me?

I circled away from her, keeping ten feet of floor between us, and turned to face Kandirak.

'If I beat Blukka,' I said, 'what then?'

He laughed. 'You will not,' he said.

'If I do—' I persisted.

'Then you will have proved the woman's case and she will be free,' Kandirak said.

I gave Mrs Catlin a half-glance, not meeting her eyes. She wasn't looking at me, and from the expression on her face you would have thought we were strangers.

To Kandirak I said, 'Do I get choice of weapons?'

Kandirak laughed, and seemed on the point of saying no.

Then he cast a sly glance at Tal Daqar and said, 'By all means. It is your woman who is, after all, the injured party.'

I winced at the phraseology. 'I choose pistols,' I told him.

Kandirak called out, 'Clear a space!' and the men at the tables moved aside as far as the pillars that framed the main aisle of the Hall.

One of the filinta stepped forward with a pair of pistols and offered them to me. I took them both.

'I think,' Kandirak said, 'that one pistol *each* is the tradition.'

'You did give me choice of weapons,' I said, 'and if you recall, I said "pistols": plural.'

Kandirak scowled. *What*, I suspected he was thinking, *was the lesser evil?* Concede the point, or risk being proved wrong if he argued?

'Quite so,' was all he said.

A second filinta carried a pair of pistols to Blukka.

I watched him as he loaded them: his movements were measured, precise; they were the movements of a machine.

I loaded my own pistols and said, 'Let's get on with this. I've got plans for later.'

I cast Mrs Catlin a glance as I said this, and our eyes met. I didn't look away, and neither did she. Something passed between us, something beyond the artificiality of language, and I think there was a flash of understanding, or at least the beginnings of it, of why I was behaving so badly towards her. Neither of us was given time to explore the sensation, for at that moment Blukka was stepping silently down from the dais to the floor of the Hall.

I called out to Kandirak, 'Are there any rules to this?'

'None,' he replied. 'Except that you will fight Blukka without assistance.'

'To the death?' I asked.

'As you say,' Kandirak replied.

I found a space in the Hall that suited me and then turned to face the dais. I crossed my wrists in front of me, the pistols pointed at the floor.

'Except,' I said, 'Blukka isn't alive. Is he?'

Kandirak seemed surprised. He glanced at Tal Daqar.

'He lives,' Daqar said.

'Truly?' I asked.

'Truly,' said Daqar.

'But you made him,' I said.

'I . . . fashioned him,' Daqar said. 'But I did not "build" him in any mechanical sense. I brought the various elements together, no more than that.'

'So the fact that he's full of Y'nys crystal doesn't count?' I asked.

'Not in the way you are trying to imply,' Daqar said. 'Kziktzak is a construction, a thing. Blukka is a living being.'

'With no mind,' I said.

'He has a mind,' Daqar said.

'But no will of his own,' I said.

'No,' Daqar said.

'No soul,' I said.

Daqar hesitated.

'No,' he said. 'I do not believe so.'

'Thank you,' I said. 'That's all I wanted to know.'

I raised my right arm, aimed, and fired, all in a space of time scarcely long enough to measure. I had gone for speed more than accuracy, and as a consequence missed my intended target by well over an inch; the shot took Blukka in the throat, the pistol ball tearing out one side of his neck. The giant slave reeled, dropping one of his pistols and clamping his huge hand over the spurting blood vessels in an effort to staunch the flow. Still staggering, he turned to me and raised his remaining pistol.

I stood motionless and stared down the barrel of the pistol, waiting. I could see Blukka's finger, curled around the trigger, the knuckle almost white with effort, the pistol aimed squarely at my head. I watched impassively as the slave's hand began to shake, the barrel of the weapon wavering slightly off target – and dangerously so, for anyone who now found themselves inadvertently in his line of fire.

I tucked my empty pistol into the belt of my under-tunic and switched hands with the second weapon. I cocked the hammer and checked that the priming charge was properly seated.

Blukka's pistol fired, and I think no one was more surprised than Blukka himself. The shot missed me by millimetres, the ball crashing into one of the pillars at the far end of the Hall.

I fired my second pistol, and finished the job started by the first. Blukka staggered backwards, slipped in his own blood, and fell heavily to the floor. His body went into its death spasm, the arms thrashing helplessly. It took a long time for them finally to grow still.

I walked slowly up to the motionless body. I nudged it with my foot. It didn't move: it was dead. Wordlessly, I dropped both pistols to the floor at its side. Of all the victories I'd ever won, I think this one – for all its necessity – was the one I felt least like celebrating.

I saw Tal Daqar staring at me from the dais, his gaze a mixture of disbelief and insatiable curiosity. Let him wonder: I doubted he would do so for long. Once he had worked out Zalmetta's involvement with me the rest would be easy. Blukka's mind had been too damaged by Daqar for her to save him as Celebe had saved her, but not so damaged that she couldn't twist it ever so slightly to her own will. She had tried to instil in the giant slave a sense of her own horror at the prospect of taking a life, but he had been too far gone for that. All she had been able to do was to plant a single suggestion, one that she sensed would prove useful in the future: Blukka could not harm David Shaw. It had been surprisingly easy, made more so by Daqar himself. Blukka had been told – more than once – to capture me alive. Zalmetta had simply extended that command into the indefinite future, then locked it off from any possibility of being rescinded. Had Daqar discovered the tampering he could no doubt have corrected it easily, but there had been no opportunity to discover it – until today. And now it was too late. And I felt like a murderer.

I turned away, facing Kandirak.

'I won,' I said. 'She's free.'

Kandirak smiled.

'Of course,' he said.

I said nothing.

'Do you doubt me, boy?' Kandirak asked.

'Perish the thought,' I muttered.

'She is free to choose,' Kandirak said, adding dryly, 'A luxury few of us enjoy in these troubled times.'

We all looked at him: me, Mrs Catlin, Luftetmek, Yarissi, all of us. There wasn't an ounce of real hope to share between us.

'She may choose to go with our ally, Tal Daqar,' Kandirak said, 'serving freely in whatever capacity he chooses, or she may choose to join the rest of you in the arena tomorrow.'

'I'll take the arena,' Mrs Catlin said, not even pausing for thought.

'Don't be an idiot,' I snapped.

Mrs Catlin turned to me and smiled.

I relented. 'I'm sorry,' I said. 'But really—'

'Apology accepted,' she said brusquely. She turned back to Kandirak. 'Now what?' she asked.

Kandirak laughed.

'I like you, woman,' he declared. 'I see now why Daqar is so keen to have you. To answer your question, you will be kept in the cells below this building until tomorrow morning. At that time, you and the army that tried to overthrow the rightful ruler of this country – me – will be led to our temporary arena and there, one and all, you will die.'

'Or not,' Mrs Catlin said.

'Oh, yes,' Kandirak assured her. 'You will die.'

She smiled at him. In his place, with only a whole country to back me up, I would have been worried.

'Remove them,' Kandirak told his guards. 'They no longer amuse me.'

We were manhandled from the Hall. As we went, I heard Yarissi call out, 'Kill a million free Resheki, and two million will rise up to crush you, Kandirak. You have betrayed our country, and you will pay for it.'

Kandirak's laughter rang through the building for a long time after that.

CHAPTER THIRTY-FOUR

New Endings, Old Beginnings

We were returned to the cell in which I had been confined after my audience with Mohred two days earlier. It had once been a wine cellar of some description, and was actually a warren of several chambers all interconnected. In it were upwards of a hundred men. And no wine.

'This is cosy,' Mrs Catlin said, giving me a frosty glance.

One of the men present, a lieutenant of the artillery, had been only recently captured. His name, as I learned then, was Ishbarah. Luftetmek confronted him as soon as the cell door was closed behind us.

'Five days ago,' he said without preamble, 'when the Librarian betrayed us: what happened?'

'Kandirak's filinta attacked us in the city,' Ishbarah said. 'We fought a rearguard action all the way back to what was left of the main gate. We lost nearly half of our men in the process. Once we reached the open plain they gave up the pursuit and we rejoined the rest of the army at the camp. The next morning, the flying machine arrived. It dropped exploding devices on the camp without ever coming into range of our weapons. Then it did the same to the troops we had left out on the field, guarding Kandirak's army. Once the guards had been killed, the filinta and their followers attacked the camp – what was left of it – and we were taken prisoner.'

'How many?' Luftetmek asked.

'Survivors?' Ishbarah asked. 'I do not know. Five thousand? It was impossible to tell.'

'Where are they being kept?' Luftetmek asked.

'I do not know, Captain,' Ishbarah said, clearly mortified at his lack of information. 'I was separated from them; so were the surviving nobles. They are being held in cells adjacent to these; I do not know which.'

Luftetmek looked at the rest of us.

'We will probably have one chance tomorrow,' he said. 'When it will come, and how big it will be, there is no way to predict. But it *will* come; and when it does, we must be ready.'

Yarissi said, 'Everyone in this room will follow you, Luftetmek. But you know what the others are like, the nobles and their ilk, and from what you have told me of your difficulties with them I cannot honestly believe we will be able to count on them.'

Mrs Catlin said, 'Perhaps someone would like to tell me what this is all about.'

Yarissi and Luftetmek looked at her, then at me.

'Yeah, sure,' I muttered.

'Take your time,' Luftetmek said to me. 'Yarissi and I will make what plans we can. You have earned a little time for this reunion.'

I nodded wordlessly and Mrs Catlin and I moved to a quiet corner of the cell.

'There's a revolution going on—' I began.

'I know all about it, Shaw,' she said in an intense whisper. 'What I don't know is why you're involved. Surely you don't approve of this debased society?'

I was startled by her ferocity, and by her familiarity with current events. The latter, I decided, was no doubt Tal Daqar's doing. I suspected his motives, and the validity of the information he had provided.

'This is a complex issue,' I told her. 'Don't judge anyone involved too quickly.'

'These people,' Mrs Catlin said, 'have a perfect opportunity to improve their lot. And what are they doing with it? They are reinstating a foul and outmoded way of life that no other nation on Shushuan has not abandoned.'

'All they want is a fair system—'

'Based upon universal slavery? I thought that you, of all people, would see the lie behind that philosophy.'

'At least they face the issues,' I snapped, irritated at the accuracy of that particular barb. 'They acknowledge the existence of slavery and try to make it a positive force in—'

'Oh, Shaw, for the Gods' sakes!' she said. 'Have you seen the reality that is the price they're paying for their grandiose dream? Have you studied the history of this country?'

'A little,' I said hesitantly. In truth, I had never had the opportunity to look at Resheki culture from an objective standpoint. 'They believe in starting everyone from the same basic level, and rewarding achievement and ability by social advancement. It's a kind of natural-selection mechanism—'

'It sounds laudable,' Mrs Catlin said, trying to keep the sarcasm out of her voice and almost succeeding. 'But in reality, it only works in places like Xacmet. Out in the country – and remember, Shaw, that Reshek is bigger than any three Vohung Kingdoms put together and most of it is rural, not urban – something like one per cent of all slaves ever achieve real freedom. The best that the rest can hope for is indentured servitude or, if they're really lucky, low-grade freedman status. This is the most class-orientated society on the planet, Shaw, and your friends are fighting to keep it that way.'

'Maybe you're right,' I said, not entirely convinced, 'but they're also fighting for the right to live by rule of law rather than by tyranny. They may not have got everything right, but at least in their own way they do believe in freedom, and I happen to think that that's worth fighting for.'

'I agree,' Mrs Catlin said.

I gave her a startled look.

'This is a bad society,' she said, 'but the one it's replacing – if Yarissi wins – is infinitely worse. I just wanted to be sure you weren't being used in all of this.'

'I'm not,' I told her.

'Good,' she said.

We looked at one another for several long and uncomfortable seconds.

'This isn't quite the reunion I'd been expecting,' she said.

'No,' I said. 'It . . .'

'If your feelings for me have changed, I think I'd rather you just said so.'

'It isn't that. It's just—'

'What?'

'This—' I waved my arms vaguely, helplessly. 'This is all I've wanted, all I've prayed for, to be here, on Shushuan, with . . . with *you* – Now that it's here, it's like I don't know what to do with it. Does . . . any of this make sense?'

She looked into my face, long and searchingly, then she slowly held out her hand to me.

'Come sit with me,' she said softly, 'and we'll talk.'

We sat down in the corner of the cell and we talked. We talked for the better part of two hours, about everything and nothing. I told her about the four years I had spent on Earth without her, and she told me about her time in Benza and later in Ragana-Se-Tor. We talked and talked and talked; sometimes saying nothing of any consequence, sometimes speaking words that seemed torn from our very hearts. And slowly, so very slowly, Mrs Catlin ceased to be the abstraction that my mind had made of her, and she became again a real flesh-and-blood woman; not immutable, not quite as I remembered her, but still the only woman I had ever known who had been able to capture my heart.

Presently she said softly, 'Your friends need you. Tomorrow will be . . . difficult.'

I laughed at the magnitude of the understatement.

'Tomorrow,' I said, 'may be our last.'

In formal Ladden she said, 'If so, then I am content.'

I held her in my arms, the touch of her body at once familiar and yet startlingly new and vibrant. And I knew that the words she had spoken were the truth. I knew, also, that the feeling they expressed was one I shared.

CHAPTER THIRTY-FIVE

Sacrifice

———◦◦◦◦———

The sky was grey and cheerless the following morning as we were herded through the streets of Xacmet. There was a chill in the air and a suggestion of rain, and the blood-red cobbles underfoot were slick with dew. All in all, it was not the sort of day you would like to have as your last.

Our plans of the night before had been long and convoluted. We had tried to allow for all possible variables – of which there was a seemingly endless multitude – and to take advantage of all those factors that might work in our favour – of which there seemed to be scant few. In the end, it came down to a recognition of what we had known from the start: improvisation would be the order of the day, that and an obstinate refusal to accept the hopelessness of our situation.

The streets were unusually quiet as we marched through them. It was early, to be sure, but not that early. We passed the high, arched entrances to cobbled market squares and yellow-lawned plazas, and all were deserted. Even given the current situation in the city, life, as they say, had to go on. Business needed to be conducted, people needed to eat. So where was everybody? The notion that the entire populace was waiting for us at Kandirak's 'arena' was too ludicrous for words: Xacmet's population numbered close to a hundred thousand.

'It looks like we were right about one thing,' Yarissi observed. 'We are being taken to the old market place, the Guild Square.'

We had speculated on this the night before. Both Yarissi and Luftetmek had agreed that this was the only place in the city that could be converted into a makeshift arena on short notice.

'A good omen,' said Ishbarah, striding along behind us.

Luftetmek glanced at me.

'We could certainly use one,' he muttered.

He and I, together with Yarissi, Ishbarah and Mrs Catlin, were in the forefront of the column of prisoners. We were all in manacles, and each man was chained by the throat to the man in front and behind. Any attempt at escape now would be disastrous, to say the least.

At the end of a downward-sloping alley we came to a massive stone gatehouse. Curtain walls, three storeys tall, spread out around it, and just inside the outer gate a narrow spiral stairwell ran upwards. Clearly, then, this was not a defensive fortification in the traditional sense, but rather, like much Vinh architecture, merely a cosmetic imitation of such a structure.

We were marched through the gatehouse and into a broad, four-sided enclosure. This, I needed no one to tell me, was the Guild Square, the ancient market place of Xacmet.

Its dimensions, at a guess, were perhaps a hundred and fifty feet by two hundred. There were lawns scattered about, and the typically Resheki cobbled walks between them, and in the centre of the enclosure a raised area, twenty feet or so to a side, that stood at about knee height. It looked a lot like a bandstand, though devoid now of all trappings.

What I had taken from the outside to be simple curtain walls now stood revealed as rather more. The ground floor on three sides of the structure consisted of a broad covered walk, or loggia, supported on massive stone pillars. The fourth side, that opposite the gatehouse, was two-thirds loggia but at its centre was a broad flight of steps, at the top of which was an open landing. From here, I assumed, the various guild masters of the city, at times when the square was doing business, would observe their various craftsmen plying their trades and, if necessary, give audiences to craft supplicants, or settle disputes between the multifarious traders in the city. Guild and craft law is, among the Vinh, secondary to House allegiance, but it is not without its importance in their culture, and the various masters within the guilds commanded a high degree of respect, even from members of Houses not their own. I suppose the ultimate expression of this lies in the office of Slave Master, in which is vested the power to declare any man or woman slave or free, regardless of their House or city or rank. Slave law is, consequently, the most closely governed and regulated on the entire continent. Offences against it are frequently punishable by death, or by lifetime servitude with no hope of parole.

The laws governing other professions are, mercifully, less draconian.

The open landing gave way on both sides to row upon row of small apartments, running right around the square to meet again at the gatehouse. A railed balcony fronted these rooms, which I assumed to be workshops for the various crafts and, possibly, administration offices for the craftmasters. (I learned later that these workshops were the most prized in the city. They were granted only to the very best exponents of each craft or profession.)

Above these workshops, the second floor consisted of an uninterrupted covered gallery, in which the city's nobles could view and, if they wished, purchase various goods without having to rub shoulders with the common people in the market square. The gallery had a profusion of windows so that, during the day, artificial lighting would never be necessary. And, I suspected, so that the common men and women in the courtyard below were never entirely out of sight of their lords and masters.

The architecture of the Guild Square was of a much older type than the rest of the city, far less fanciful and not nearly as decadent. It was functional but not unpleasing to the eye. I wondered if this square might not be the oldest man-made structure in Xacmet, perhaps in the whole of Reshek.

There were four smaller stairways leading up to the first-floor landing, one at each corner of the square. These had been boarded up. Recently.

In the square itself, lining the two shorter walls and crowded together so tightly that I wondered how they could breathe, were the men who had once been Luftetmek's victorious army. Ishbarah's estimate that five thousand had survived seemed reasonably accurate, though not all of those that I could see could be classed as either able bodied or fit for combat.

The men – fyrd, cavalry, nobles, Captains, all huddled together indiscriminately – were not bound, but they were being guarded by about a thousand pistol-wielding filinta. And on the balconies above them, other filinta stood, pistols and spears at the ready.

As soon as our column of prisoners was through the gatehouse, the huge gate was closed and, from pulleys slung at the top of the wall, a wooden beam was dropped into place to secure it. The beam must have weighed hundreds of pounds, and the slots in which it now rested were ten feet above the ground. The windlasses that would lift it and open the gate once more were located on the second floor, in the upper part of the gatehouse itself.

We were, it appeared, trapped.

I looked across the square at the open flight of steps leading to the first-floor balcony.

'That's our way out,' I told Luftetmek.

'I agree,' he said.

'So what's the catch?' I wondered.

'The landing can be sealed from the workshops on either side,' Yarissi told us. 'In times past, when guild law was more oppressive, there were riots here. The guild and craft masters, seated on the upper landing, were attacked and, in some cases, killed. After that it was made possible for them to escape into the workshops on either side. Steel gates can then be lowered to prevent their being followed. Similar gates are located at the top of each of the four corner stairwells, although I see other measures are in place today to keep us from using them.'

I nodded, wondering how strong those steel gates would be.

Guards moved among us then, releasing us from our chains. They worked slowly, separating each man from the group as soon as he was free and moving him into the mass of other prisoners that lined the walls. When the last of us had been released, the guards withdrew to the open stairs and marched up them, forming ranks down either side like human banister posts.

Onto the landing came Kandirak and Tal Daqar, followed by Zalmetta and Kziktzak and Mohred. I wondered if having Zalmetta here, obviously free and clad in the raiment of a Resheki woman, was a calculated insult by Kandirak to his 'ally' Tal Daqar. If so, it appeared to have had no effect. Daqar seemed entirely oblivious to Zalmetta's presence.

All around me, men were whispering to one another. Luftetmek and the others from our cell were trying to rally the rest of the army to our cause, to get them to fight as a unit and not merely to react unthinkingly to Kziktzak's attack once it came.

We were unlikely to be given weapons. It would be flesh and blood against Y'nys crystal. Even without his 'death ray', Kziktzak would have been a formidable opponent. I had felt the strength of his pincer-like hands, and knew from other experiences that few material weapons could affect Y'nys. What was needed here was the power of a Knight, or a Librarian.

I looked up at Mohred. He was lost in some private world of his own, unaware, it seemed, of what was happening all around him.

The upper gallery, I now saw, was filling up with people. The railed balcony on the first floor was also becoming crowded. Hundreds, thousands of spectators had turned out to witness our execution. For some reason, that saddened me.

The noise level in the Square was now increasing considerably, and those of us who were the centre of attention had ceased to whisper and were hurling orders and battle plans about with no regard for who might be listening. After all, what did it matter? The chances of our doing anything Kandirak had not allowed for were too remote for serious consideration. Our only chance, if indeed we had one, was that Tal Daqar had miscalculated the effectiveness and power of his minion.

From the balcony, Kandirak's voice boomed out.

'Today,' he announced, 'the last enemies of the new Reshek die!'

The filinta cheered. I looked up at the gallery; no one else appeared to share their enjoyment at the prospect.

Kandirak turned to Tal Daqar, seemingly unaware of the reception his words had received among the common populace.

'Release your creature,' he said.

Daqar beckoned Kziktzak forward.

Kandirak said, 'Clear the filinta from the Square.'

As one man, the thousand filinta backed away from their defenceless prisoners and moved towards the broad stairway. In minutes, they had ascended and passed through into the workshops on either side of the landing. The other filinta on the steps, those that had been our escort, followed them.

Daqar spoke to Kziktzak, his words not carrying to our position, and the giant construct stepped towards the top of the stairs.

In the Square, Luftetmek, Ishbarah and I began to arrange our men in groups. It was far from easy. We had had no time to rehearse, and not everyone was cooperating. But that we were meeting with any success at all was a boost to our spirits.

A group of our best men, a hundred in all, were making a living wall in front of Yarissi, much to the Kanaat's displeasure, and these would be the last line of defence should everyone else fall.

I took Mrs Catlin by the arm.

'Go with Yarissi,' I said.

'Like hell,' she shot back.

I was tempted to punch her in the mouth and let someone carry her to Yarissi.

'Please,' I said, 'you know I can't—'

'I know, I know!' she said, throwing up her hands. 'You can't fight if you have me to worry about.' She glared at me angrily, then said with considerable exasperation, 'You'd just better come back alive, that's all.'

She turned away and pushed through the press of bodies to Yarissi.

I looked up at the balcony. Kziktzak was descending the stairs. Kandirak and his entourage were filing onto the railed landing that abutted the open balcony and, at either side, the steel gates were being lowered.

'Don't wait,' I urged Luftetmek. 'Rush him.'

He nodded and turned to his nearest commanders.

'Biryn, Asagi, Ussun, attack!' he ordered.

I heard Yarissi's name burst from a thousand lips as the front ranks charged the advancing, stick-like figure of Kziktzak.

They were perhaps thirty feet from him when his head rotated on its seamless neck and the vertical red bar of his 'eye' came to bear on the men in the front of their line. The beam of red light, no thicker than a wire, flashed silently forth. It passed through the first man as though he had not been there, and dropped the man behind him to the earth, a cry of pain on his lips. Kziktzak's head turned, not particularly slowly, and the beam swept across the attacking soldiers. In seconds, dozens of men died. The beam was almost unstoppable. Whatever it was, coherent light or particle beam or something totally unknown to Earth science, it lost little if any of its energy in passing through a human body. Two, three, four men in a line would drop from a single contact, bodies sliced in two or arms and legs severed bloodlessly, the beam cauterizing the wounds as it went. Of the hundreds in that first wave, not a man was left standing.

'Scatter!' I barked at those around me. 'Come at him from all sides. He can't look everywhere at once!'

Frozen with all too understandable dread, the men were slow to respond.

Kziktzak looked across the Square at where I stood. The beam flicked out, and instinctively I threw my arms across my face, realizing instantly the futility of the act but unable to stop myself. The beam flashed past me, striking down men on either side yet, miraculously, leaving me unscathed. I didn't know what had happened, but I wasn't about to let the moment pass unexploited. Repeating my order to the men around me to split up, I began to circle around to try and outflank Kziktzak before he realized he had missed me.

I recalled Daqar saying that this would be an interesting test of Kziktzak's powers. What happened next, I could only assume, was a part of that 'test'.

As the creature moved deeper into the Square, and men began to swarm all around it – though at a respectful distance – the red bar of its eye changed. Its colour brightened, and when the beam lanced out again it was different. This time, it was a broad gash of red, almost a foot deep, and where it touched, men burst into flame. Cooler than the narrow beam, this new weapon could strike no deeper than a single man, but now the Square was thick with flame and smoke and the stench of burning flesh. A circle of fire now cut Kziktzak off from those who were as yet untouched, and in that circle men blundered about, living pyres that were too slow to die and for whom we could do nothing.

Kziktzak stepped through the circle of flame, and Luftetmek was suddenly there in front of him, screaming the war cry of Reshek and the name of Yarissi and anything else he could lay his tongue to. Behind him, scores of warriors followed his lead.

The Y'nys creature vanished under an avalanche of bodies, and for an instant it was impossible to tell what was happening. Then the pencil beam flickered out from amid the pile, and a grey-white arm smashed bodies aside with an impossible, effortless strength, and Kziktzak arose, Luftetmek held by the throat in one pincer and the dismembered arm of some unknown warrior held in the other; the creature's head turned slowly as it cut down what was left of the opposition.

Luftetmek kicked and punched like a wild man, but the creature seemed not even to notice him. Its head swivelled, it took in its surroundings and, pausing only to cut down those nearest to it, tossed Luftetmek aside and strode towards the centre of the square.

Half-choked by smoke, my eyes stinging from the flames, I tried to lead the men nearest to me around the worst of the carnage in the hope that we might succeed where Luftetmek had failed.

Kziktzak paused and scanned the Square once more. It

seemed to hesitate as it beheld the solid block of men whom we had assigned to defend Yarissi and Mrs Catlin, then its head continued to turn and the beam sprang forth yet again. The thing did not pause this time until it had completed a full circuit of the Square, men falling in their hundreds, and then it stepped lightly up onto the raised platform that I had noted earlier.

The wider beam flashed out, scorching across a whole group of men who had been, understandably, cowering at the far side of the Square, close to the gatehouse. It kept the beam on them until the whole assemblage was a mass of fire, the flames reaching thirty feet into the soot-laden air.

I looked wildly about me, searching for any option that might give us some chance to counter-attack, or at least escape. We had lost over a thousand men, and all in the space of perhaps two minutes.

On the balcony, half-obscured by smoke, I saw Mohred watching us, his face unreadable. At his side, Zalmetta stood leaning on the railing, her hands almost crushing the bar with the intensity of her grip. Mohred turned towards her, his lips moving, and then black smoke billowed across in front of them and I could see no more.

By the gatehouse, the blaze was lapping up the huge wooden gates. In an hour or so, it might burn through them. By which time we would all have been dead for over fifty minutes.

I caught sight of Luftetmek, picking himself up and shaking his head dazedly, and a mad plan came to me. He met my gaze and I gestured to him, signalling my intent. He simply nodded, and yelled to the men nearest him.

I cried out to those behind me.

'For Yarissi!' I yelled.

Terrified, facing certain death, a hundred voices yelled, 'Yarissi!' and we charged the podium at the centre of the Square.

Kziktzak turned towards us, and Luftetmek led his own charge – up the stairs at the back of the Square.

Others saw what he was doing, and rather than fol-low him to a possible escape route they gave voice to their passionate war cry and swarmed towards the centre of the Square.

Kziktzak picked us off effortlessly. His narrow beam chopped through a man directly in front of me and danced briefly over my own heart. I let out a cry in anticipation of the pain, but it didn't come. I was unharmed, the red cloth of my over-tunic unmarked. Through my confusion I heard pistol shots ring out, and turned to see Luftetmek and his men at the top of the stairs, throwing themselves at the iron gate that separated them from Kandirak and his followers. More gunfire erupted from unseen points on the walkway, and men in the square ran to replace those who had fallen.

A mountain of bodies now separated me from Kziktzak, the red beam flickering over men on all sides . . . The red beam that had been unable to penetrate my red tunic. Cursing myself for an idiot I tore the garment off and held it in front of me like a shield. Then I scrambled over the pile of dead and dying in front of me; all I wanted at that moment was one single chance to bring down the monster that was responsible for all this slaughter. It no longer mattered that the thing was only a machine, devoid of a will of its own, that Tal Daqar was the real enemy. The destruction of Kziktzak, in that moment, was all I could think of.

On the balcony, I heard the crash of the iron gate as it collapsed. Pistol fire erupted again, this time cut short, and I heard victory cries go up from a dozen places all along the first-floor walkway. That made no sense, but I had no time to look for an explanation. I was inches away from Kziktzak's Y'nys form, my fingers reaching for his 'throat'. His head flicked round, the red bar lined up with my face, and I threw the tunic over his head. I let out a wild and ecstatic yell, and the blunt end of his left pincer sent me sprawling.

It was seconds before my vision cleared and I was able to stagger to my feet, but a lot seemed to have happened. All along the balcony, common soldiers of Reshek were doing battle with the filinta, and most of them appeared to be too well armed for their arrival to have been entirely unplanned. Pistols and other weapons were being flung down into Kandirak's makeshift arena, and the whole of the Square seemed to have become a war zone. Out of all the chaos, I saw Ishbarah, two pistols shoved down his belt and two more in his hands, advancing across the Square towards Kziktzak.

He fired once, left-handed, and the heavy ball projectile clanged off Kziktzak's head.

The head swivelled, the red bar finding the Resheki lieutenant.

Ishbarah fired again, taking the creature squarely in its 'eye'. The Y'nys body rocked, crystal shards flying from its face, and for the first time the thing seemed actually to stagger.

Across the Square, I saw a black-and-white figure leap from the balcony and land lightly upon the grassy sward below.

Ishbarah cast aside the pistols and drew the others from his belt. He cocked one and took aim.

Zalmetta sprinted across the Square, rushing toward Kziktzak from behind.

Red light flickered in unfocused sparks from Kziktzak's eye, its head swivelling as though half-blind, seeking a target. It fixed on Zalmetta and the slender beam danced out to meet her. She dodged, Kziktzak's targeting system seeming to have lost some of its accuracy. Also, the beam no longer had its potency. It flickered across her body, leaving bloody lines where it touched, a zigzag pattern that would probably have stopped anyone else. Zalmetta ran on.

Ishbarah blasted Kziktzak with his third pistol, an incredible shot that hit the thing's eye-bar even though it was turned sideways on to him.

The head swivelled. It was impossible, I know, but I would swear I could read anger on that faceless face.

Ishbarah raised the last pistol, and the beam lashed out. The pistol fell away, the Lieutenant's hand amputated at the wrist, and he fell to his knees, his face contorted in agony.

Zalmetta leaped upon Kziktzak; her hands around his head, and jerked down with all her might. The head screeched, a gap appearing where its neck should have been. One of its pincers slammed into her face, and she lost her grip on its head. The head swivelled, noisily now, and the half-smashed red bar came to bear on her. The beam, a jagged, broken stutter of its former self, hit her in the chest. Smoke and flame erupted from her tunic, and she hurled herself onto the creature, clawing its head forward as the beam tore through her abdomen. There was a screech of tearing metal and the deadly beam flickered out, the creature's head now hanging from a ruptured metal rod. It struggled, its arms flailing helplessly, and Zalmetta pulled one final time. The head came away, metal and wire and seemingly fragile filaments of Y'nys crystal hanging out of its shattered neck.

Both Kziktzak and Zalmetta collapsed to the surface of the platform. Neither moved.

I shook myself, tried to focus on where I was and what was going on all around me.

The execution that Kandirak had planned had ceased to be the centre of anyone's attention. Now, and the sense of this washed over me like a tidal wave, the final stage of Yarissi's revolution was being played out. Kandirak's corruption had run its course. His filinta had had their day, and now the ordinary people of Reshek, who had never lost their belief in Yarissi or broken faith with his ideal, were asserting themselves. I felt a brief flash of pity for the filinta.

Just as the execution had been shunted from centre stage, so too had my role in events. Now, I was only another foot soldier, and at the moment an unarmed one. It was time for me to get back to my own mission in Reshek. What happened in Xacmet from now on was Luftetmek's business and, after that, Yarissi's.

I heard my name called out by a voice that was laced with pain. I looked around and saw Ishbarah trying to get to his feet, the stump of his right wrist a raw wound that he was nursing to his chest. Cursing the delay, but unable to ignore him, I rushed to his side.

'The creature—?' he gasped.

'Dead,' I said.

'The . . . the *other* creature,' he said, 'the female. I saw. Is she . . . ?'

'I don't know,' I said.

He leaned heavily against me, swaying in a wind that only he could feel.

'Go to your woman,' he said. 'I will attend to the . . . other woman.'

'Can you make it?' I asked.

'Only . . . one way to find out,' he said. He waved his good arm, almost falling over in the process. 'Go!' he barked. 'No one is safe in this madhouse.'

I nodded. At his feet were the pistols he had dropped. And his hand. I swallowed. Then I stooped and recovered the one pistol that was still loaded. I turned and headed for the group of men who guarded Yarissi and Mrs Catlin.

The men in the front rank regarded me warily, seeing the gun in my hand. No one's allegiance, I suspected, would be taken for granted today.

'I want my woman,' I told them. 'You have nothing to fear from me.'

The ranks parted as Mrs Catlin pushed her way through. The men closed up instantly, keeping Yarissi back regardless of what he might have wished.

'Come on,' I told her. 'It's time to get out of here.'

She followed me across the Square.

' "I want my woman"?' she echoed, her voice rich with disbelief.

We climbed up onto the central platform. Ishbarah was cradling Zalmetta's head in his good hand, her white hair trailing across him. Her body was a hellish criss-cross of wounds, any one of which should have been fatal. Her eyes, as bright and unreadable as ever, turned up to my face.

'I heard what you said in the Kanaat Hall,' she said to me, her voice little more than a whisper.

I fell to my knees at her side, unable to speak.

'You think I have no soul?' she said.

'You aren't like Blukka—' I said.

'Sometimes,' she said, 'I think you are a very foolish man, David Shaw.'

I glanced at Ishbarah, who seemed not to understand what was going on. I saw that he was inspecting her wounds and asked him, 'How is she?'

It was Zalmetta who answered.

'I am well enough to travel,' she said, her voice still weak but her tone determined.

Ishbarah looked up at me, his expression seeming to put the lie to her words.

'I'll get help,' I said.

I looked around, wondering just where I thought I was going to find anyone with the time or the inclination to assist any of us.

Walking across the battle-scarred square, heading directly towards us, was Mohred.

'Oh, hell,' I whispered.

I put myself between the approaching Librarian and the three people on the podium. I made sure the pistol was primed and the hammer in the full-cock position. I knew a bullet could no more stop a Librarian than a feather could stop a hurricane, but I intended to go down fighting.

Mohred climbed up onto the podium and stood glaring at me with undisguised hatred. With the oily black flames of burning bodies as a backdrop, he looked like the devil incarnate.

'I loathe you with all my soul,' he said. 'I have lived for your death for all the years since my son was taken from me.' I could see his fists, clenched white and bloodless below the sleeves of his robe. How would he strike? Lightning? Or would he beat me to death in an un-Librarianlike show of brute strength?

'I curse you with my every breath,' he said. He seemed to be on the verge of weeping. 'May the Thirteen grant you eternal damnation.'

Then, to my astonishment, he fell to his knees.

'I am powerless,' he said. 'My people have rendered me impotent because of what I have done. And . . .' He gritted his teeth, as though swallowing bile. 'And I must help you if I can.' He shot me a look like venom. 'What would you have me do,' he spat, 'now that, thanks to you, there is almost nothing I can do?'

For several seconds I was too stunned to speak. Then I said, furiously, 'I would have had you come down here ten minutes ago, you cold-hearted bastard. How could you watch this—?'

'I sent the charlaki woman!' he retorted. 'What more could you ask?'

'Nothing,' I replied bitterly. 'Nothing at all.'

I pointed the gun at his head.

Mrs Catlin put her hand on my arm.

'No, Shaw,' she said softly.

'He changes sides too easily,' I said. 'He'll betray us the first chance he gets.'

'No,' she said, 'he won't. Because we won't give him the opportunity.'

I lowered the weapon slowly. Would I have shot him, in cold blood? I like to think not, but in truth, at that moment, I think I might have.

'Fine,' I said, 'then let's get some use out of him.' I pointed at Zalmetta and said to Mohred, 'Pick her up. Then lead us out of here by the shortest route.'

He looked with distaste at the object of his instructions.

'It is half-dead,' he said. 'Why—?'

'I didn't ask for a debate,' I snapped. 'Now do it, or get out of my sight.'

Ishbarah looked doubtfully at the Librarian as he bent over Zalmetta's body. I heard the young lieutenant whisper, 'Go gently, Mugatih, or I will not be as merciful as Captain Shaw.'

Mohred picked Zalmetta up without comment. She moaned, but his touch was not rough. I think any movement would have been agony to her.

'The only way out is up the steps and along the landing to one of the corner stairwells,' the Librarian said. 'But there is fighting going on all through the workshops. Nowhere will be safe.'

'That's my problem,' I told him. 'Yours is just to show the way.'

'Very well,' he said.

We climbed down from the podium, Mrs Catlin helping Ishbarah who, miraculously, seemed not to be going into clinical shock, and crossed the Square toward the stairway. There was no longer any fighting going on in the Square itself, but we could see and hear a great deal in the first-floor workshops. This was going to be a hazardous trip. I took a tighter grip on the pistol and moved to the front of our pathetic little group.

At the top of the stairs we headed left, through the shattered remains of the gate Luftetmek and his men had breached. There was a score of bodies, filinta and rebels, in the rooms beyond. I bent over the nearest and took the sword from its lifeless fingers. As ridiculous as it sounds, no sooner did I feel the hilt of the weapon in my fist then my confidence increased a hundredfold.

I hesitated, disliking the idea of robbing the dead, then put my squeamishness aside to divest the body of its other armaments. They consisted of a hefty dagger, a shortsword – rare among the Vinh – and a powder horn and an ammunition pouch for a pistol. Of the pistol itself, there was no sign.

I gave Mrs Caltin the shortsword. To Ishbarah I said, 'Can you shoot left-handed?'

'I will manage,' he replied. 'Though I may need assistance to reload.'

Mrs Catlin said, 'I'll help you.'

He gave her a surprised glance, but mercifully refrained from voicing what was obviously going through his mind.

I pushed the pistol into his left hand.

The workshops that we moved through were a shambles. In some cases they had been so badly wrecked that it was impossible to tell for what they had once been used. Traversing them I had a sudden, and entirely inappropriate, sense of *déjà vu*. I knew what had prompted it; I was remembering the craft tents of the Ladden, from my first visit to Shushuan. The burst of nostalgia was brief but intense.

We were less than halfway along the landing when we came across the first of the fighting. Three filinta were beating two of Luftetmek's troops into a corner, one of the black-and-grey-clad soldiers using a spear to prevent either of the two from escaping.

I ran the spearman through, then engaged the closest of his

fellows. In seconds, all three were dead, and the two rebels cheerfully added themselves to our party. I was glad of the extra help, but didn't delude myself about how long their gratitude would last once we reached the street.

We came to the stairwell without encountering any opposition that we couldn't deal with, and I led the way down.

At the bottom a dozen bodies blocked the exit, mostly filinta, all hacked to pieces. I suspected they had been trying to keep someone out, which raised an interesting point. I had assumed that the fighting had erupted inside the building that formed the Square, a spontaneous reaction to the events taking place in the courtyard. Now it looked as though a premeditated attack had been organized to coincide with today's 'execution'. I wondered who had led such an attack, given that all of Yarissi's troops had been Kandirak's captives.

We emerged into a side alley, bordered on all sides by two– and three-storey buildings that closely resembled those of the Square. The street leading away from the back of the Square was steeply inclined, blocking our view of what lay beyond.

'Where now?' I asked Mohred.

'The nearest gate out of the city lies straight ahead,' he replied. 'But it takes us through an area where fighting is most likely to be concentrated.'

One of our two soldier companions said, 'That's the way for us!' and the two of them set off at a jog. In seconds, they had vanished from sight.

'What about the other exits?' I asked.

'Left is closest,' Mohred said, 'and probably quietest.'

I looked down the avenue he had indicated. It ran in an unbroken straight line for several hundred metres before curving out of sight. Side streets, narrow and dark-mouthed, let onto it in a dozen places. Anything could be concealed in those openings, anyone.

'Come on,' I said. 'And keep your eyes open.'

We hugged the left-hand side of the street, which had fewer openings. I had a creeping sensation between my shoulder-blades, an instinct I had long ago learned not to ignore.

'Ishbarah,' I said, 'watch our backs.'

'Right,' he said.

His voice was still thick with pain, but he was dealing with it.

'Catherine—' I said.

Mrs Catlin edged up alongside me.

'I really hate it when you call me that,' she said.

'Sorry,' I said. 'Linna—'

'Better,' she observed.

'Good, great,' I said, more edgy than the situation appeared to warrant. 'How much practice have you had with a sword lately?'

'Not enough,' she said, confirming my fears. 'But P'nad and his Marines have been teaching me that special form of unarmed combat of theirs.' She looked me up and down. 'I bet I could take you.'

I felt an entirely inappropriate arousal at the tone in her voice.

'We'll put that to the test,' I told her, 'when we're safely home again.'

'Home?'

'Benza.'

'Ah!'

We rounded the bend at the end of the road and stopped in our tracks. Ten yards away, the street ended in a cul-de-sac.

'Mohred!' I cried, furious.

'It's not my fault,' he retorted. 'I haven't been in this part of the city before. This way *does* lead to the nearest exit—'

'You idiot!' I snarled.

I cast about for an alley that might lead us out of this potential death trap.

Our heads all turned at the sound of conflict, not far off and rapidly getting closer.

'Down here!' I called, racing for the nearest alleyway.

The others were hard on my heels as we ran headlong into another dead end. The sounds of fighting were now very close, and from the volume I guessed it was not a minor skirmish. The occasional crackle of gunfire punctuated the continuous rattle of sword steel.

'Get behind us,' I barked at Mohred. 'Linna, on my left. Ishbarah, make that one shot count.'

We moved out of the alley at a slow trot, heading, inevitably, towards the battle. I peered up each alley that we passed, and found nothing but dead ends. Only on the other side of the street were there any viable exits, but those all led back to the Guild Square, and I had no plans to return there. The battle rounded a corner ahead of us and came whirling towards us.

I took in as many details as I could in one glance. The filinta outnumbered the rebels, though not by much. Most of the rebels were badly armed, which was their biggest problem. Their second biggest problem was that they were leaderless.

With a curse, I ran towards the conflict. Pushing through the retreating backs of the rebels, I yelled half a dozen orders to the men in the front rank, anticipating that most of them would be ignored. I put myself in the centre of the front line and kept shouting instructions, whilst at the same time engaging the enemy directly before me.

For a moment, the confusion that my appearance had caused – on both sides – brought the retreat to a standstill, and the advancing filinta ran forward onto a solid wall of sword steel and spears and assorted craft implements.

'Front rank, advance!' I yelled.

The filinta fell back, disorientated by the sudden turn of events.

'Second rank, advance to the right!' I cried, gesturing with my sword and in the process doing one of the filinta some serious damage.

In a straggly line, our second rank – if it could be dignified by such a title – swept around to the right, attempting to outflank the filinta.

'Forward!' I cried, pressing the attack more fiercely.

I saw some of our other men begin to swing around to the left, and gave a silent prayer of thanks that someone had had the wit to understand my plan and act upon it. In seconds, we had formed a pincer around the filinta, jamming them together and reducing the advantage of their greater numbers and superior weaponry by trapping two-thirds of their force behind the one-third that could get at us.

In this kind of battle, one of the biggest advantages an army can have is manoeuvrability. The rebels didn't understand this, but I was gambling that the filinta did, and that my blatant tactics would convince them that I was a dangerous opponent. In this kind of battle, the second-biggest advantage is to have your enemy terrified of you.

For several minutes, the battle raged on furiously. The filinta were professionals, but the rebels were better motivated. It was anybody's guess which factor would tip the balance.

I had been trying to identify the leader of the filinta, and eventually I managed to pick out the man with the highest rank designation on his uniform. As a leader, he was a pretty poor specimen, but he was all I had to work with. I closed with him and, over the din of the battle, I yelled, 'Tell your men to surrender!'

He looked startled. Then his face hardened.

'To you, slave-lover?' he said. 'Never!'

'You'll die to a man,' I promised.

'So be it!' he cried, and attacked me with renewed vigour.

I gave him a wound sufficient to put him out of action and resumed my place in our front line.

Behind us, I heard the sudden report of a pistol shot, the first I'd heard since entering the fighting. I risked a look back, and saw Ishbarah waving frantically, pointing down the street over our heads. I followed his gaze, and saw what looked like about a thousand filinta marching in our direction.

'Fall back!' I yelled.

The front rank of our foes, seeing our sudden retreat, pressed us harder then ever. In the distance, the reinforcements were now advancing at a jog. The only way out that didn't lead down a dead end was back towards the Square. I directed our flight in that direction, Ishbarah, Mrs Catlin, Mohred and Zalmetta preceding us.

The filinta gave us no chance to go into full retreat, forcing us to fight every inch of the way. And for every minute that we were delayed, we lost a dozen or more men. At this rate, we'd all be dead long before we reached the Square.

Even in the midst of this kind of conflict, I found a moment to wonder at the huge force of men that was bearing down on us. If so many could be spared for this kind of mopping-up detail, what did that say for the state of the fighting in other parts of the city?

We were down to barely thirty men when, inexplicably, we seemed to stop retreating. I cast a glance behind me, and saw a second group of filinta approaching from the opposite direction. Smaller than the first, this one seemed to consist of only a few hundred men.

Our immediate attackers eased off, many of them grinning with anticipation. We backed away from them, forming up in two lines, one facing each group. Mrs Catlin and the others were now sandwiched between the ranks, and I felt her push through to stand at my side.

I put my arm around her as the filinta slowly closed the distance between us. I wondered if they would give us the opportunity to surrender. From their expressions, it didn't seem likely.

'I wonder what happened to Yarissi,' I said, more to myself than anyone.

The filinta in front of us were almost within sword reach now.

'Get ready to charge,' I called to the men around me.

I caught one or two looks of startled disbelief, and watched as they turned to smiles of fatalistic satisfaction. If surrender was offered now, it would be thrown back with contempt.

'Ready—' I said, shifting my grip on my sword.

The filinta tensed, obviously only now taking the threat seriously.

'Ch—'

There was an almighty crash from above us, and tons upon tons of masonry came raining down into the street, burying the nearest ranks of the filinta. Stunned, but quick to take advantage of whatever it was that was happening, we all moved rapidly away from that side of the street, stumbling and half-blinded by the gouts of dust and debris that filled the air. A second crash sounded close to the first, and most of the buildings on that side of the street lost their upper storeys as though a giant hammer had struck them from behind.

I clutched Mrs Caltin to me, casting a glance in the direction of Mohred and Ishbarah. The Librarian was using his armoured body to shield Zalmetta, and the young lieutenant was crouching in the man's shadow.

I looked up, wondering what could possibly have caused so much destruction. There had been no explosion, nor any other kind of an audible warning. And to overturn so much stone so devastatingly would have required the muscle power of a thousand men. Through the cloud of dirt a vast silver shape thrust itself, floating effortlessly in the air above the street. For an instant I thought it was the ship of Tal Daqar, and then I felt my heart lurch, my body grow rigid with shock as I realized the truth. But how was it possible—?

The open spans of the vessel's two lower wings demolished more of the buildings as it descended to ground level, its whirling propellers catching the debris clouds and sending them whooshing off behind it.

I recognized every line of the craft's design, every plank and beam, every bit of repair work to damage sustained in battle over the city of Carmalt in the Vohung Kingdoms. Almost, ridiculously, I seemed to recognize parts that were brand-new, that I had never even seen before. As my senses reeled, one single thought kept hammering through my brain, one irrational, foolish, inescapable thought: she had come for me, my ship had come for me.

Over the stern castle bulwark two figures leaned and stared down at us. One, his smiling face as dark as ebony, waved as soon as he saw us, calling out the ancient Vinh greeting that was the same all over the planet.

'Tonoko da, Captain-jin,' he called.
I gave an almost hysterical laugh in reply.
'Da tono, P'nad-jin!' I cried.
Beside him, gleaming silver in the sunlight, was Celebe.

CHAPTER THIRTY-SIX

Beyond Freedom

———◇◆◇———

'Ropes away!' P'nad called to someone elsewhere on the deck of the *Mariner*.

I heard the cry echoed through the ship, and then her belly hatches flew open and scores of climbing ropes came tumbling down.

Only now did I stop to notice the one major difference in the ship. Gone were its trailing ballast weights, yet it was skirting the ground more closely than we had ever been able to manage before.

'Be swift, David,' Celebe called. 'Your enemies are closing in and we have no more troops aboard.'

I didn't waste time asking her to explain that last remark, but instead directed my battle-weary companions up the ropes to the *Mariner*'s hold.

Ishbarah had to be hauled aboard at the end of a noose, as did Mohred who could not climb whilst carrying Zalmetta, but the rest of us managed to make the thirty-five-metre ascent in record time.

As soon as we were on board I raced up to the outer deck. The interior of the ship was more refined than I remembered it, which was not surprising considering how basic it had been in those days. The upper decks, however, were just as I recalled them. I climbed to the sterncastle and clasped hands with P'nad.

'The ship is yours, Captain,' he said, 'just as she should be.'

'It's good to be back, old friend,' I told him. 'But for now, she's safe in your hands. I think I need to know what's going on – how in Gazig's name did you get here? And why?'

'I can answer that, David,' Celebe said.

I turned to her, smiling broadly.

'I am very pleased to see you, Celebe,' I said. 'I feared you surely killed.'

She smiled, the face of Ailette Legendre looking out from behind the mask of the Knight of the Thirteen.

'It was a close thing,' she confessed. 'But we can discuss such matters later. For now, by decree of the Thirteen, the rule of the tyrant Kandirak is to be brought to an end and the rule of Yarissi established. I trust you are happy with such a state of affairs.'

'For now,' I said. 'Though I don't see what business it is of the Thirteen.'

'This is their world,' Celebe said.

'No,' I said. I gestured to the men at the rowing stations on the lower deck. 'It is theirs.'

P'nad said, 'Captain, we cannot remain here—'

'You've got the ship, P'nad,' I said. 'Do what you have to.'

'Very well,' he said.

I stepped away from him, leaning on the guard rail. I looked around the ship, noting the differences. The capstans which once controlled the ballast weights had gone. The ship's wheel was unchanged, but slightly forward of it on the port side was a new station; it appeared to be a Library lectern, and a crewman stood at it as though awaiting orders.

'Observation height,' P'nad said to the crewman at the lectern.

'Aye, Cap— . . . uh, yes, sir,' the crewman replied, flustered. He gave me a nervous glance, then fixed his eyes firmly on the lectern.

I smiled. I had never seen the man before, and somehow his nervousness in my presence seemed slightly absurd.

'Been promoted, P'nad?' I asked innocently.

He gave me a sheepish glance.

'I was made a Captain last year,' he confessed, confirming what Celebe had told me so many months before.

'Well done,' I said.

He nodded, then called to the timekeeper on the rowing deck, 'Manoeuvring speed.'

I heard the answering cry, and the slow beat of the mallets on the great drum. The *Mariner* surged forward. I gripped the rail more tightly. I could feel the blood sing in my veins. I wanted, suddenly, desperately, to push P'nad aside and take command, to stand at the helm of my ship once again. I have said, often, and meant it, that I did not build the *Mariner* to provide myself with a career, nor with a powerful toy with which I might play. Yet somehow, in some way I would never quite understand, she and I were forever linked, one with another, till the end of time.

'Helm, come about to starboard,' P'nad said.

'Starboard, aye,' came the response.

The ship leaned almost imperceptibly into the turn. The boards creaked underfoot, the air moving more swiftly past.

Mrs Catlin climbed the steps leading to the sterncastle.

'Linna,' P'nad said by way of greeting.

'It's been too long, P'nad,' she chided him. 'You never came to visit.'

She was teasing, and I was surprised to see that P'nad knew it. It seemed they had become closer during my absence. I was glad, if a little jealous.

She greeted Celebe perfunctorily, and I had to smother a smile. They had never quite hit it off, somehow, and in some ridiculous fashion I think Mrs Catlin actually regarded Celebe as a rival for my affections.

She came and put her arms around me and together we watched as Xacmet rolled past below us.

We were cruising at an altitude of perhaps a hundred feet, and I asked Mrs Catlin how it was being achieved.

'You remember the chamber we found under the Uhrgratz village?' she said.

I nodded. It had been under the very airframe around which the *Mariner* had subsequently been built. There had been many Y'nys objects there, including lecterns and mutahiir. Some of the objects were so old they had degraded to carbon, or something like it.

'We worked out how to use one of the lecterns,' she said. 'It controls something in the metal plates that line the central part of the airframe. Seemingly, they were what was used for altitude control. It's not yet a perfect system, but better than the one we used to have to rely on.'

I nodded, not especially liking the idea of trusting Y'nys technology to such an extent, but trusting Mrs Catlin's own innate scepticism to have thoroughly field tested the device before installing it.

'Where are the rest of the crew?' I asked, recalling Celebe's comment of some minutes ago. I had noticed already that only half the rowing stations were manned.

'We put them off just outside the city,' P'nad said. 'They have been assisting the, uh, rebels.' He said the word with distaste. 'The crew of the *Freedom* were landed on the other side of the city at the same time.'

'The *Freedom* is also here?' I said with surprise.

'Both ships,' Celebe said, 'were packed with Vohung warriors, mostly Benzan. I told you, David, this is the will of the Thirteen. It is going to happen.'

Mrs Catlin said, 'The *Freedom* is now a galley, like the *Mariner*. And it too has a lectern to govern its altitude.'

'You've been busy,' I told her.

She looked serious, an unhappiness clouding her eyes that sent a knife through my heart.

'I had to,' she said quietly. 'Something to fill the days, and . . . the nights—'

I hugged her, so tight I thought I might crush her.

'I know,' I said, 'I know.'

'Fighting ahead!' a lookout suddenly called.

P'nad ran to the rail and looked over.

'Hard to port!' he yelled. 'Ground level!'

'Port, aye!'

'Ground level, aye!'

The ship went into a nosedive.

'All stop!' P'nad called.

'Rest oars!' came the call from the hortator.

I moved to the guard rail at P'nad's side. Below us, on a wide boulevard that ran through the centre of the city, hundreds of men were engaged in combat. Filinta on one side were pressing a fierce attack against an equal number of defending rebels. I couldn't work out, at first, what the rebels were defending. Then I saw, protected by a ring of men, two forms, one supine, the other kneeling and cradling the fallen man's head.

'I'm going down there,' I said.

'Shaw—?' Mrs Catlin said, not understanding.

'I, too,' Celebe said.

'P'nad, give us what cover you can,' I ordered.

'Aye, Captain,' he shot back. Turning to the timekeeper he called, 'Manoeuvring speed; port forward, starboard back.'

The timekeeper acknowledged and the ship began to rotate, its lower wings ploughing through the filinta. I heard pistol shots, and the sound of ricochets as they bounced off the *Mariner*'s frame.

I ran down to the nearest belly hatch, Celebe behind me, and went down the rope hand over hand.

We landed too close to the filinta for comfort, but the *Mariner*'s brute-force intervention had caused so much confusion in their ranks that none of them even noticed our arrival. I ran towards the rebel forces. Celebe charged the filinta.

No one barred my way as I pushed through to the two men they were protecting. Yarissi kneeled with Luftetmek's head in his lap. The Kanaat's champion had the broken shaft of a Resheki war spear buried in his chest.

I fell to my knees at his side. Yarissi was weeping helplessly. Luftetmek, incredibly, was smiling.

'Shaw—' he breathed, reaching out one bloody hand towards me.

I took his hand, not able to speak.

'I'm glad,' he said, 'you're here. Needed . . . a . . . witness . . .'

Yarissi was shaking his head, muttering 'no' over and over.

'Yes,' Luftetmek said.

He released my hand and, his fingers trembling, reached up and placed his own hand on Yarissi's forehead.

'Please, no,' Yarissi wept.

'By my hand,' Luftetmek said, his voice almost gone, 'freely and without reserve, I grant . . .'

'No . . .'

'. . . your freedom . . .'

'Master, no,' Yarissi sobbed.

Luftetmek's hand fell back.

'You earned it,' he said.

He smiled. His eyes closed.

Yarissi looked at me.

'I won't leave him here,' he said, that terrible, frightening look in his eyes.

'No,' I said, 'we won't leave him.'

Yarissi tried to lift the body, but he wasn't strong enough.

'I'll help,' I said.

'He was *my* master,' Yarissi snarled.

'He was my friend,' I said.

'I am so weak,' he cursed.

'No,' I said, 'you aren't. And he knew it.'

He looked at me.

'Please,' he said, 'I would appreciate your help.'

Together we lifted Luftetmek and carried him through the ranks of his men, away from the filinta, towards the waiting *Mariner*.

CHAPTER THIRTY-SEVEN

Last of the Bagalamak

————◦◦◦◦◦————

We took Luftetmek's body to the *Mariner* and, with Yarissi safely on board, the rebel troops on the ground withdrew from the filinta, whom we herded out of the boulevard in a not very gentle fashion. Celebe, on the ground, waved us away and stalked off into the city, employed in her own unknowable tasks for the Thirteen.

I returned to the sterncastle and stood once again with Mrs Catlin. Moments later, Yarissi joined us. He looked about the *Mariner* as he approached, obviously uneasy at being on board a flying machine and, effectively, at the mercy of her master.

'We must pursue Kandirak,' he said, not so overawed that he had forgotten his own mission.

'Where will he have gone?' I asked.

'When Usak attacked the Guild Square—'

'Usak?' I said, surprised.

'He had been preparing the attack for months,' Yarissi said. 'Did you not know?'

I shook my head, no. I remembered the former filinta from our first visit to Xacmet, when he had been so shaken by what Kandirak had done to the Bagalamak family that he had become an instant convert to Yarissi's cause.

'He will, I think,' said Yarissi, 'be my new Champion. A worthy successor to one who can never be replaced.'

Thinking of the Bagalamak reminded me of one other with whom I felt the need for a confrontation.

'When the attack began,' Yarissi went on, 'Kandirak fled with Tal Daqar. I would assume they made their way to Daqar's flying machine.'

I cast a glance at P'nad.

'We passed over the vessel as we approached Xacmet,' he informed us. 'On Celebe's instructions, we rendered it, uh, unsafe to use.'

I smiled. P'nad had been a slave of the Ladden, artisans and craftsmen all. Their respect for the work of other artists had rubbed off on him, leaving him with an inbuilt distaste for the destruction of property. Fortunately, his antipathy towards the Ladden as a race tended to compensate for this.

'In that case,' Yarissi mused, 'they would most likely have fled to Kandirak's family home, the ancestral seat of his House.'

'Where is that?' I asked.

'In the far north-west quarter of the city,' Yarissi said.

'P'nad—' I said.

'Come about,' he called to the helmsman. 'Manoeuvring speed only,' he called to the hortator.

The ship crept slowly above the city below, lookouts peering over every handrail for any sign of trouble. Mrs Catlin and I stood at the rear of the sterncastle, looking down past the trailing spike of the airframe at the carnage that the revolution had caused. We saw buildings burning, running gun battles between filinta and professional soldiery, massed conflicts between swordsmen and fyrd, and even some cavalry sweeping majestically through the wider streets, devastating everything in their path. The fighting, I guessed, would go on for days yet, but I now began to believe that the victory would inevitably go to Yarissi. It seemed as though every able-bodied person in the city was involved in the struggle, and few had chosen to side with the filinta.

Kandirak's abode was in one of the parts of the city that, so far, had been relatively untouched by the fighting. It was an impressive-looking building, unmistakably a palace in a region that was littered with palaces, and old. It was not, I thought, as old as the Guild Square, since it bore all the signs of encroaching decadence that seemed to typify much Resheki architecture from their more recent history.

The main part of the building stood in the centre of its own grounds, which consisted of sumptuous gardens and immaculately-kept lawns. There was even a stream running through the property, spanned by graceful foot bridges. I wondered how many slaves it took to maintain such a garden.

P'nad brought the *Mariner* down just inside the ornamental gatehouse at the front entrance.

'We have few men left on board,' he told me.

'They're Marines,' I replied. 'Keep enough for a skeleton crew; I'll take whatever you can spare.'

He nodded.

Minutes later Yarissi, Mrs Catlin, Ishbarah, twenty Marines and I were walking up the jewel-studded pathway that led to Kandirak's front door.

From a concealed side door two filinta sprang, pistols raised. A pair of javelins, the light throwing spears of Benza, flashed past my ear. The filinta, I think, never knew what hit them.

'Well done,' I told the two Marines responsible. I remembered them from the war against Droxus. 'Halke-jin,' I said to the one whose name I could remember, 'it's been a long time. How are you?'

'Well, Captain,' he said, beaming. 'And pleased you have returned to us.'

'As am I,' I assured him.

The main door was locked, but not barred. We threw our weight against it and, on the third try, it flew open, the lock clattering across the marble floor beyond.

Kandirak's palace was as impressive inside as out. White pillars supported a vaulted roof that was divided into huge, triangular windows, letting sunlight wash through no matter what the time of day. Balconies on three levels gave access to the upper floors in the wings of the building, and two broad, red-tiled stairways swept up from the mosaic floor to the first-storey landing. Black sardwood doors, inlaid with gold, silver and jewels, covered the walls on either side of us, hinting at the impressive number of rooms we were going to have to search through.

I glanced around, realizing that Ishbarah was no longer with us. He came through the front door a moment later, tucking a pistol down his belt whilst holding another in the crook of his right elbow. I smiled, relieved at not having to worry about him, something that had been bothering me since I saw him join this raiding party. I could, of course, as Captain of the *Mariner*, have had him kept on board, but I was not comfortable with the idea of dictating another man's actions. He was an adult, for all his youth, and an officer, and should have the right to choose his own path. Mrs Catlin was accompanying us as a result of the same line of reasoning, though in her case I might have made an exception – had I thought for one instant that anyone on board the *Mariner* would have dared attempt it.

'This way,' Yarissi said.

'Are you sure?' I asked.

'I have been in this place many times,' he replied, a hint of bitterness in his voice. 'When we planned the revolution, in the days when I counted Kandirak a friend. I know where he will be.'

We followed Yarissi through one of the doors; I gestured to two of the Marines to go ahead of him, just in case. The door opened onto a long passage, eight feet wide and, on one side, lined with ceiling-high windows. They overlooked an inner courtyard, a walled garden where, I assumed, family members could take the air without having to be exposed to public scrutiny.

The passage was richly carpeted and decorated with wall hangings, tapestries and such, and from the high ceiling hung a dozen crystal chandeliers.

We traversed the passage rapidly, and at its farther end passed through another door that led to a dining hall. Beyond that was an atrium, complete with indoor fountain and lush, semi-tropical vegetation, and beyond that an audience chamber. Nowhere in the entire palace had we yet seen a living soul.

'Yarissi,' I said, 'are you sure you know where we're going?'

He glanced at me. 'Oh, yes,' he said. 'I'm sure.'

We came to a part of the palace that was clearly the private dwelling space of the family: studies and lounges and bedrooms and such. In one, a terrified girl, little more than a child, watched us from behind a betasselled chaise longue as we passed. We did our best not to frighten her any further, and since Yarissi did not approach her neither did the rest of us. Yarissi led us to a narrow door hidden behind a drape. The door was open. Beyond it, twisting down into Stygian darkness, was a spiral staircase.

'Find torches,' I directed the Marines.

'There is a store through there,' Yarissi said, pointing, not taking his eyes from the darkness.

'He's down there?' I asked, peering past him and seeing nothing beyond the first four steps.

'Yes,' was all Yarissi said.

The torches arrived and we lit them. Yarissi followed the two Marines down into the cellars below Kandirak's House.

What we found was astonishing. Gold bars stacked twenty deep, chests full of jewels and jewellery, bolts of fabulously decorated cloth, richly woven carpets, fine pottery and porcelain, statues and sculpture, furniture that would not have looked out of place in an emperor's ceremonial chambers, and all of it piled or stacked carelessly with no semblance of organization or order. The contents of the several rooms that made up that cellar would have ransomed a small kingdom.

'Kandirak's plunder,' Yarissi said, his voice thick with anger and distaste. 'This was to have been used to feed and clothe our people. I always knew he had betrayed us, but I never suspected just how far his treachery went.'

From the darkness ahead, a voice said, 'You were ever a melodramatic fool, Yarissi.'

I heard weapons rattle all around me, and light flooded the cellar as dozens of lanterns were uncovered. We were surrounded by upwards of fifty warriors, not filinta, all of whom had that special look that only veteran fighters can achieve. Any of the men in that room, I thought, would have been a match for ten of Yarissi's fyrd.

Kandirak sat upon a chair at the far end of the cellar; others were piled up around it, haphazardly. He had a naked broadsword laid across his lap. Beside him, on the floor, kneeled Ylyrria Muti. She was watching him, her eyes wide. Of Tal Daqar, however, there was no sign.

'You will die today,' Yarissi told Kandirak.

The big man laughed. He stroked the braided queue that hung over his left shoulder, his right hand resting lightly on the hilt of his sword.

'I expect so,' he replied. 'But so will you.'

I was trying not to move, not to give any of the warriors that surrounded us the slightest hint of my intentions – not that I had any at that moment. I caught Ishbarah's eye and saw him shift his left hand slightly where it lay in the crook of his right elbow. I couldn't see the pistol that I knew he held, and neither, I assumed, could the enemy warriors.

'Yarissi, wait,' I said.

A dozen eyes followed me as I took a step forward. I hoped no one would be looking in Ishbarah's direction now, but it was a gamble.

'There's no need for slaughter,' I said, my tone reasonable. 'You've won the war, let's be magnanimous in victory.'

I saw Yarissi look at me as though I had gone mad, and even Kandirak appeared surprised.

'Perhaps exile would be possible,' I offered, moving Yarissi to one side as I stepped alongside him. 'The Thek continent is broad, and Reshek is only one small part of it.'

'Exile?' Kandirak said. 'You would exile me from my own land?'

'Better, surely, exile than death,' I said, stepping suddenly aside and yelling, 'Now!'

Ishbarah didn't let me down. The cellar reverberated with the pistol shot, and Kandirak went over backwards, blood splattering Ylyrria who let out a wild shriek of panic.

In a fraction of a second, the cellar was transformed to complete pandemonium. Benzan warriors are, it is said, the greatest fighting men on Shushuan. It is not an empty boast.

Outnumbered by more than two to one, they were in their element. Mrs Catlin, who has been known occasionally to yield to the demands of common sense, made no attempt at involving herself in the fighting. I made sure to keep her behind me as I took the attack to the nearest three warriors, my sword a flashing bolt of silver and scarlet in the flickering torchlight. It was Mrs Catlin herself who had first taught me how to fence; later, my friend Tor Taskus, at that time a Captain of Benza, had expanded upon my knowledge with tuition in the fearsome tactics of his people. But there is more to swordsmanship than knowledge and tactics and, even, experience. There is, I suppose, a willingness to risk all on the strength of your own abilities, to place yourself knowingly in the presence of death and to defy it with nothing more than your own mortal skills. The experience is, of course, horribly seductive, and not one that should actively be sought. I take no pride in the shadowy part of myself that seems to live for such moments, but neither do I reject it. Without it, without its strength and ferocity, the better part of myself would also, I think, not exist.

Warriors pressed me on all sides, and my blade drove them back to a man. I was conscious of cuts appearing on my arms and body, but they counted for nothing in the heat of the battle. My sword arm was bloody to the elbow, but my grip on the sword's hilt was firm, and the basket-guard was shielding my fingers and wrist from harm.

Not far away, I noticed Kandirak dragging himself to his feet. The bullet had missed his chest and struck him in the shoulder, a consequence, I assumed, of Ishbarah having had to use his left hand. Leaning on his sword-hilt, Kandirak surveyed the battle. He stared with a black malevolence at Yarissi, who was pinned at the centre of our warriors with Mrs Catlin and Ishbarah.

We were holding our own in the uneven contest, but I wondered how many we would have to lose in order to defeat Kandirak's forces. Already, both sides had lost better than a third of their number. I didn't doubt our victory for an instant, but the price . . .

From the entrance to the cellar there came a shattering war

cry; not that of Yarissi, but of Benza. Into the mêlée there suddenly charged the huge figure of P'nad, and with him a dozen Marines. Now Kandirak's troops were not merely outnumbered, but outflanked as well.

Kandirak took a step back, shaken. He looked about wildly, swaying, and then seemed suddenly to become aware of Ylyrria standing at his side. A feral snarl split his features and he caught her by the hair, yanking her up in front of him. The edge of his broadsword went under her chin and he glared at me with a fierce triumph.

'Call off your foreign scum,' he bellowed, 'or she loses her head!'

The two factions in the cellar edged warily back from one another. Kandirak's men were as rattled now as their leader, and had no way of knowing how much store we would set by the life of one child.

Ishbarah pushed past me, his second pistol aimed at arm's length for Kandirak's head.

'There are too many pawns in this game for a stalemate,' he said, the gun unwavering in his grip.

'Shoot,' Kandirak sneered, 'and in the time it takes for the charge to ignite I can slit her throat.'

He was right. The flintlock's design gave a split second's warning after the trigger was pulled, the breech flash preceding the bullet by just enough time for him to carry out his threat.

'Clear a way,' he ordered. 'I am leaving.' He looked at Yarissi. 'You have not seen the last of me, slave.'

He edged forward, his eyes flicking right and left. No one moved. P'nad looked at me. Others followed his example, including some of Kandirak's people. I didn't respond. This was no time for empty heroics. But there was no way we could let Kandirak go.

'Put down the pistol,' he ordered.

Ishbarah glared at him. Then, slowly, he did as instructed.

'Step away from it,' Kandirak said.

Clenching his teeth, Ishbarah obeyed.

Kandirak moved forward, Ylyrria lifted onto tiptoes by his

grip on her hair. The blade was pressed into the flesh of her neck, a thin red line appearing where it touched.

'If anyone moves—' Kandirak began, and the blast of a pistol shot cut him short, the ball ripping through the wrist of his sword arm, blood jetting from entry and exit wounds alike. Kneeling at my side, Mrs Catlin lowered her pistol: she had reloaded Ishbarah's first gun, unnoticed in the battle. And knowing her dislike for firearms, I considered that an especially fine shot.

Kandirak reeled, clutching his wrist to his chest. His men surged forward, and were checked in their tracks by P'nad's Marines. From nowhere that I could see, a second shot rang out, the ball taking Kandirak in the chest and laying him out. Ylyrria bent down and, calmly, picked up Kandirak's sword from where he had dropped it.

'I'll take that,' I told her. *Where had that shot come from?*

She didn't look at me. She lifted the weapon in both hands and turned to the supine figure of the erstwhile emperor of Reshek who, to my surprise, was still moving. She all but dropped the heavy blade onto his chest, then ever so delicately inched the point up to his throat. He stopped moving. In the silent cellar, his laboured breathing was suddenly the only sound.

Ylyrria said, her voice trembling but her hands very steady, 'Murderer of my family, I am freeborn and eldest survivor. I—' She hesitated; the words were very important, very ancient. She wouldn't want to get them wrong. 'I declare blood feud between our lines.'

'Ylyrria,' I said gently, 'that's enough.'

'Listen to him, child,' Kandirak gasped, not daring to move.

Behind me, a voice said, 'Do not interfere, David Shaw.'

Celebe stepped through the ranks of warriors. A smoking pistol hung from her right hand.

'She's a child,' I said urgently.

'She is Vinh,' Celebe said.

The words went through me like ice. For all my love of Shushuan, there were times when it horrified me. Was this, I wondered, why Ylyrria had always seemed so un-childlike to me, because I had been treating her like a human child?

'Do the right thing, Ylyrria Muti, last of the Bagalamak,' Celebe said.

I heard Kandirak's choked protestation, saw his hands flail helplessly, as Ylyrria put her full weight behind the hilt of the blade. There was a sickening crunch, and the point of the weapon emerged from the top of Kandirak's skull. I heard Mrs Catlin's sharp inhalation, and my own involuntary whispered oath.

Ylyrria sank down beside Kandirak's now-motionless body, beneath which a broad dark pool of blood was slowly forming. She glanced around, looking suddenly lost and very, very small.

'What have you done, child?' Celebe asked, her tone a study in neutrality.

Ylyrria looked up. 'I . . .' she began, then squared her shoulders and said firmly, 'I have avenged the House Bagalamak.'

'This was an act of justice?' Celebe asked.

'Yes,' said Ylyrria.

Celebe smiled. 'It was well done,' she said.

The words had an unexpected effect on the child. Whatever strength had brought her this far seemed suddenly to desert her, and her eyes began to fill with huge tears. She looked from Celebe to P'nad to Mrs Catlin to me. None of us seemed to offer her any comfort. From behind me, Yarissi stepped forward. He held his hand out to the child.

'It *was* well done,' he told her, smiling. 'Worthy of the ruler of a great House.'

She rushed into his arms, sobbing.

Yarissi glanced at me. 'You understand why she had to pretend to join Kandirak's House?'

I was beginning to.

'She couldn't risk being made a slave,' I said.

Ylyrria looked at me, wiping her eyes.

'I didn't *want* to betray you,' she said.

'There was nothing to betray,' I told her. 'I'm not Resheki. This war isn't mine. My reasons for being here have always been my own. You did what you had to.'

Slaves may neither declare blood feud nor uphold its rituals. Ylyrria's behaviour had never once been out of character – for a Vinh.

P'nad and his Marines marched the defeated warriors out of the cellar, and Mrs Catlin came to stand at my side, her hand finding mine.

'Can we go home now?' she asked.

I laughed.

'Yes,' I told her, 'we can go home.'

And at that moment I believed it to be true.

CHAPTER THIRTY-EIGHT

Decisions

I stepped out onto the sterncastle of the *Mariner* and into the first rays of the early dawn. Overhead and to the west the sky was a green-black dome sprinkled with stars. On the eastern horizon, it was layer upon layer of red and gold, the disc of the sun shredded by wisps of pale green cloud. There was a chill in the air, the first sign of encroaching autumn. I was conscious of Xacmet's proximity to the Plains of Ktikbat, and the kind of winters that that would imply.

This was the fifth consecutive dawn that had seen the *Mariner* moored over the Resheki capital. Her sister ship, the *Freedom*, was a thousand yards away to the south. Had I had my way, both ships would, by now, have been halfway to Benza, but other wills than mine prevailed in these matters, and I had no power to gainsay them.

One consideration that had kept me here was, at least, of my own choosing, and that was the fate of Zalmetta. For two days after her battle with Kziktzak she had lain at death's door, and few of her attending physicians had held out any real hope for her survival. On the third day she had been out of bed and helping to tend the other wounded. Her charlaki stamina and the mysterious energies contained in her Y'nys skeleton had not let her down. I think that more than one of her doctors had been disappointed at her recovery – I had heard the word 'dissection' whispered several times when they had thought me out of earshot. I was quite delighted that Zalmetta had been able to frustrate their scientific curiosity, and just as pleased to see her on the road to a full recovery.

'Good morning, Captain,' said the commander of the watch. He had been standing at the sternrail behind me and I hadn't seen him when I came on deck.

'Good morning, D'chak,' I said, willing my heart rate back down to normal. 'Quiet night?'

He snorted. 'Aren't they all?'

I laughed. Night fighting was not a Vinh preference.

On the forecastle I could see Mrs Catlin standing with her back to me. I was surprised to see Zalmetta at her side. They appeared to be deep in conversation. I hesitated, not wishing to intrude, but it had been Mrs Catlin's absence from our cabin that had brought me on deck this early. There was something I needed to discuss with her, and I had a feeling that this might be my last opportunity.

Zalmetta's recuperation aside, there were two other reasons for our remaining in Xacmet. One was of a military nature: it was by the will of the Thirteen that Joshima, Duke of Benza, had dispatched his forces to aid Yarissi in his revolution, and until the Kanaat was officially invested as the new ruler of Reshek neither the *Mariner* nor the *Freedom* would desert him. Celebe, as the instrument of the Thirteen, was on hand to ensure this, and not even my own status on the *Mariner* could give me the power to overrule her.

The second reason was more specific to myself, and was what I needed to talk to Mrs Catlin about.

As I watched them, Mrs Catlin and Zalmetta abruptly hugged one another and then the charlaki woman turned and descended to the main deck. I did likewise, and we met at the side of the starboard rowing station.

Zalmetta greeted me with a guarded smile; we had been jumpy around one another ever since that brief conversation in the Guild Square, neither of us really certain what the other was thinking or feeling.

'She is a good woman, your Mrs Catlin,' Zalmetta said to

me. 'And I think perhaps you are not such a fool yourself, despite your best efforts to teach me otherwise.'

I was totally lost for a reply, and watched in silence as she made her way aft. I wondered, briefly, what kind of a life Shushuan would offer her when this was all over, and found myself hoping that it would be better than the one I actually anticipated.

Forcing my mind back to the matter at hand I climbed up to the forecastle and a confrontation to which I was not much looking forward.

Mrs Catlin was leaning on the handrail at the front of the forecastle, staring up at the fading stars. She didn't look at me as I approached, but she wasn't ignoring me. I moved to her side and she came into my arms, her back to me, her body pressed to mine. We watched together as the light behind us slowly drove the last of the stars from the sky.

'Are you ready to tell me now?' she asked at length.

'Tell you—?' I said.

She laughed softly. 'Whatever it is you've had on your mind since last night.'

'Oh, that,' I said.

She said nothing, waiting.

'Celebe wants me to be at Yarissi's investiture today,' I said. 'I think I've worked out why.'

'Go on.'

'By Resheki law, I'm under sentence of death,' I said. 'And also, technically at least, a slave. There are factions in Reshek that still don't trust Yarissi—'

'The Lords of the old ruling Houses?'

'Yes. The people love him, but the nobility – some of it, at any rate – have yet to be convinced. Yarissi owes me a lot – not least because I was Luftetmek's friend – but he has to uphold the law. How he deals with me will be a kind of proving, as far as the old Lords are concerned. If he puts the law above personal consideration, they'll accept him – grudgingly, I expect, but they will accept him.'

'What if you're simply not here?' Mrs Catlin asked. 'I know the *Mariner* can't leave yet, but you and I—'

'There's more,' I said. 'Yarissi isn't the only one who's going to be tested today.'

She turned her face up to mine, a puzzled look in her eyes.

'If I reject Yarissi's judgement,' I said, 'it means I'm rejecting Vinh law, and the Vinh way of life. I'll be effectively telling the Thirteen that I can't accept Shushuan on its own terms, that I can't integrate. What do you think will happen to me then?'

'You'll be sent back to Earth again,' Mrs Catlin said quietly.

'And Celebe's here to witness it,' I said, 'and to enforce the Will of the Gods.'

Mrs Catlin turned in my arms and hugged me, her face pressed to my chest.

'It's not fair,' she said fiercely. 'After all you've done—'

'Yarissi will commute the death sentence,' I said, 'that much I'm sure of. But I doubt he can do anything about my slavery.'

'I'll come back to Earth with you,' she said abruptly. 'Better that than—'

'You won't get the choice,' I said. 'They want you here, that's already been decided. *I'm* the one who has to prove himself. And I've already made up my mind. Whatever the cost, I'm staying.'

'But as a slave you'll be giving up everything,' she protested. 'The *Mariner*, your rank, Benza – to say nothing of your actual freedom—'

'There's a price for everything,' I told her. 'Luftetmek taught me that. The most important thing to me – the *only* thing that's important to me – is you, and if the only way to keep you is to give up everything else, then that's a price I'm more than willing to pay.'

She looked up at me, eyes bright with passion and more than a hint of cold fury; Mrs Catlin had the same views that I did on the subject of slavery, and for mostly the same reasons.

'All right,' she said, 'then we'll face what's to come together.

Whatever happens, Shaw, you and I are not going to be parted again.'

'What are you going to do?' I asked warily.

'If Yarissi makes you a slave,' she said, 'than he makes me one too. He's not a monster, he'll find a way to keep us together—'

'That's a hell of a risk—'

'It's not a risk,' she said, 'it's a price.' She looked into my eyes, the fury mellowing somewhat but not the passion. 'It's a price *I'm* willing to pay.'

CHAPTER THIRTY-NINE

Final Reckoning

It was shortly after noon when Mrs Catlin and I finally left the *Mariner* and made our way through the bustling streets of Xacmet to the Kanaat Hall.

This was the first time I had seen the city and its occupants under normal conditions, and I found it as exciting and vibrant as the other Vinh cities that I had visited. Many of those abroad on the streets today were in a festive mood, and although merchants and vendors were hard at work rebuilding their various enterprises they too seemed more inclined to enjoy the day than to concentrate on maximizing their profits. Street parties were being held on almost every corner, and some of them were actually moving from one street to another as the crowds carried them along. Men of the city guard were everywhere, but their weapons were sheathed and their helmets doffed; their duties today did not appear to include anything more strenuous than the lifting of an occasional bottle. We were jostled by numerous bodies as we negotiated the main thoroughfare of the city, but this was only the natural boisterousness of the moment and not anything by which to feel threatened. We felt ourselves borne along by the mood of the people around us, our spirits buoyed up after our rather grim little talk of earlier that day. We were both laughing at everything and nothing by the time we reached the avenue on which stood the Kanaat Hall, and not remotely prepared for what happened next.

The crowd in front of us abruptly parted, a hush descending

from the farther end of the avenue, as a retinue of armed men marched majestically up to the front of the Hall.

I had never seen men – warriors – such as this before, not in any of the lands of Shushuan. They wore hooded scarlet cloaks that billowed around them as they walked, and each man wore a mask of gold that completely concealed his features. All of their accoutrements, from jewelled armbands to belt buckles and scabbards, were of gold, and each man wore a light crossbow at his belt. That, at least, told me that these were not Resheki. So who were they? And what was the significance of their presence in Xacmet at this time?

There were, I estimated, some fifty warriors in the party, all dressed identically, and in the centre of their procession was a single mounted figure. Like the rest of them he wore scarlet and gold, but he carried no arms and wore no mask. His face was tanned and clean-shaven, and his hair, beneath his hood, was jet-black, framing his face like a mane. The sense of power he radiated was awesome.

The party of warriors fanned out around the entrance to the Kanaat Hall and the mounted man reined in his gryllup at the foot of the steps. The guards on duty were visibly intimidated, but they appeared to have one advantage over me: they clearly recognized the man.

'Slave Master!' one of them cried. 'Welcome to our city!'

Slave Master! The words hit me like a hammer. If I had still entertained any hopes of escaping today's events with my freedom intact then the presence of this man saw them finally dashed. Any mercy Yarissi might have felt inclined to show me would now be snatched from us by the simple fact of this man's presence. Today, regardless of personal feelings, Yarissi could do no more – and certainly no less – than to treat me as Vinh law strictly dictated.

Behind me, a voice said, 'You were not informed of the Slave Master's impending arrival, Captain?'

I looked behind me; a small space had opened up in the hushed crowd, and in it, facing me, stood Celebe. I think the assembled Resheki were at a loss for an adequate reaction to what was happening; their country was rapidly filling up with terrifying personages.

In reply to Celebe's more-or-less rhetorical question I said, 'I was not. Should I have been?'

She gave a Gallic shrug but said nothing.

As the Slave Master was ushered into the Hall, a dozen of his warriors in attendance, I saw other faces approaching me through the crowd. One, I was less than delighted to note, was Mohred. The others, flanking him, were P'nad and the Captain of the *Freedom* and a pair of Marines. It seemed I was not the only one who didn't trust the Librarian.

I turned to Celebe.

'Coincidence?' I asked, indicating what remained of the Slave Master's retinue.

'Perhaps,' was all she would say.

Behind Mohred and his escort I noticed Zalmetta and Ylyrria Muti. Zalmetta was dressed now as a Resheki scribe, the formal black and white garb suiting her particularly well; its fastenings, I noted, were gold, where the tradition favoured silver. Ylyrria Muti, by contrast, wore the full court regalia of a noble woman, and looked every inch a princess. I bowed to the child as she approached.

'My Lady,' I said, not inappropriately.

She returned the gesture with a full-blown curtsy, then ruined the whole thing by grinning from ear to ear. It pleased me very much that whatever darkness had lurked in her soul seemed now to have been banished, and I just hoped that under Yarissi's rule the child could reclaim some kind of a normal life.

Turning away from her I confronted Mohred, and an issue that had been on my mind for many days now.

'In the camp of Luftetmek's army,' I said, no longer smiling, 'someone tried to kill me. Do you know anything about that?'

'I do not,' he replied flatly.

He seemed sincere, but I was not convinced. If Mohred had not been responsible for the arrow that had narrowly missed me that night, then who had been?

'When I was your prisoner,' I said, determined to get at least one answer out of him that I could believe, 'you were all set to torture me to death. Two days later, when Kandirak held his victory feast, you looked like a man who was on his way to the gallows. What happened?'

He clenched his teeth, and his fists; not so long ago, this confrontation would by now have been conducted to a backdrop of lightning and hurricane-force gales. Mohred's obvious frustration gave me a brief and ignoble sense of satisfaction.

'Librarians,' he said, 'are not able to communicate with one another through their armour, but during the time of which you speak I received a message in just such a fashion. It informed me that my actions against you had been observed and that, as a consequence, I was being stripped of all my powers. It also said that, very soon, the rule of Kandirak would end in blood and fire. And that I should, from that moment on, behave towards you more . . . appropriately.' He scowled even harder, the memory apparently as painful as any he had ever known. To lose the godlike powers of a Librarian . . . 'I assumed,' he muttered, 'that the message came from my people.'

'In fact,' Celebe interjected, 'it came from the Thirteen.'

Mohred blanched, but said nothing.

'Now that we are all here,' Celebe digressed, apparently deciding that enough had been said on that particular topic, 'I think perhaps we should attend the proceedings within.'

I felt Mrs Caltin take my hand in hers as we all followed Celebe into the Kanaat Hall.

It seemed, in the moment that we first saw it, that the Hall was jammed from wall to wall with people, Resheki men and women from all walks of life.

On the dais at the far end of the main aisle, Yarissi sat and conducted his affairs. He was dressed simply, in the garments of a common man. He bore no arms. Around him, grey-clad warriors kept a watchful eye on the assemblage that crowded the chamber. The entire space defined by the two rows of columns was packed with people; only directly in front of the dais, in a space scarcely ten feet deep, was the floor clear. Anyone wishing to address their new ruler was invited into this space, and as far as I could see the only way to get there was to join the hundreds-long queue. Then I realized that the Slave Master and his retinue were nowhere in sight, and looked over the numerous heads in front of me to try and work out what I had missed. Presently, I saw that the outer parts of the Hall, the two narrower aisles that lay behind the pillars, were less crowded than the centre aisle. Here, small knots of citizens and court officials were conducting business of their own, and one such group contained the aforementioned Slave Master. He was engaged in an apparently friendly discourse with several scribes and nobles, all of whom he seemed to know. It was all prosaic enough, and entirely failed to reassure me.

Within moments of our entering the Hall we were intercepted by no lesser a personage than Usak, Yarissi's new Champion.

'Captain,' he greeted me, offering his hand.

I took it, impressed by the gesture; even if my rank had been certain, his greeting would have implied a degree of equality that simply did not exist: Usak's new title was tantamount to that of Warlord. And he had offered his greeting to me rather than to Celebe or Ylyrria, either one of whom was senior to me in the Vinh social structure.

'You appear to have a full house,' I observed, wondering how long all of this was going to prolong my own personal misery.

'Kanaat Yarissi is the living law in Xacmet,' Usak replied. 'All men yield to his authority – some, over matters most trivial. But the Kanaat will delegate nothing, so . . .' He gestured, a little helplessly, at the packed Hall.

We both laughed, but there was an undercurrent of tension that I think we all sensed. The aftermath of Yarissi's revolution was not, I thought, going to be an immediate Golden Age, the festivities in the streets notwithstanding.

'You need not wait in the main aisle,' Usak continued, his words now directed at my entire party. 'When the Kanaat is ready, he will call you forward.'

I nodded, and we moved to the side of the Hall. I glanced briefly in the direction of the Slave Master and found him looking back at me. We held one another's gaze for an instant and then he looked away, speaking at length with one of the scribes. I suppressed a shudder; it had been like looking into the eyes of a viper.

'It would not be seemly for Yarissi to interrupt the business of his court for our convenience,' I heard Celebe saying to my companions. 'But by the same token the issues that we are here to settle are of considerable importance to the future of Reshek.'

She glanced briefly in my direction, but I said nothing. I had no intention of pre-empting my own role in today's proceedings. She gave me the ghost of a smile before continuing.

'Xacmet is now Yarissi's,' she said. 'His rule here is absolute. But Reshek is a big country, and Kandirak's filinta are everywhere. Many of the outlying Prefectures will now be armed camps, and not easily dismantled. There will be more blood spilled before this is over, and Yarissi has still to prove himself where certain factions are concerned.'

'The Lords of the old ruling Houses,' I said.

She nodded. 'If the rule of law, as laid down by the ancients, is to be truly what governs Reshek, then Yarissi must convince the old Lords that he truly represents that law. The people already believe this; the Lords are not so sure.'

'It *is* true,' I said vehemently, motivated by more than just a sense of self-preservation. 'I've seen him when he's quoting the law. It's almost a religion to him.'

Celebe laughed. 'I hope,' she said wryly, 'that the Thirteen do not hear you say that.'

I gave her a look. 'I hope they do,' I told her.

She scowled, but there was more than a touch of the old Ailette in her expression, and I suspected that, secretly, she shared my hope.

For better than an hour we stood and listened as Yarissi conducted his court. Usak had been right about the trivial nature of the petitions of some of the supplicants; in fact, some of them were so petty that I began to wonder at their authenticity. It seemed to me that some of those in the Hall were there for reasons other than obtaining justice; they were, I became convinced, stooges for what we had all started calling the 'old Lords', men and women who had been spoon-fed complaints simply to test

Yarissi's knowledge and his impartiality. If my suspicions were correct, then Yarissi passed every test with flying colours. His decisions were swift, decisive, and, above all, definitive. There is a fine line between the *word* of the law and the *spirit* of the law, and Yarissi walked that line like a circus aerialist. When matters were unclear, he erred on the side of blind justice; when malice or artifice was evident, he veered towards mercy for the victim. But never, ever, did he render a judgement that flew in the face of the law. It was a quietly awesome display, and not a little terrifying. If Yarissi was truly the law in Reshek, what would happen when he was no longer there?

Presently, Yarissi arose from his seat. The Hall fell silent. Every eye was upon him. To say that the atmosphere was electric would be to devalue the moment.

'I will hear you all,' he said quietly. 'But first, there are certain issues remaining from the recent times of trouble that must be resolved.'

I shuffled uneasily, and felt Mrs Catlin's hand tighten its grip in mine. Her nails bit into my skin, but her face showed no trace of fear.

'By the will of the people,' Yarissi said, 'and with the approval of the Lords of the ruling Houses of Xacmet, the House of the despot Kandirak, House Tchelnet, has been declared outlaw. Its people, from the highest to the lowest, are reduced to state slavery, as is the ancient custom. They will be granted an amnesty of one month, during which time they are at liberty to petition the other Houses for adoption. It is my wish that the other Houses should greet these petitions with the honest consideration they individually merit.' Yarissi paused, looking from face to face around the great Hall. 'My own House,' he said, 'was House Tchelnet. By this ruling, duly notarized, I am now no more than a slave of the state, and masterless.'

A murmur of concern went around the assemblage, the common men and women of Reshek greeting this news with evident distress. Following a slave during a time of rebellion had been one thing, but having one as the ruler of a nation would be unthinkable – and, from a practical standpoint, untenable.

Yarissi held up a hand for quiet and got it.

'Usak,' he called, 'of the House Adapazir.'

The Kanaat's Champion stepped forward.

'My Lord Usak,' Yarissi said, 'will you accept me as a military slave to your noble House?'

Usak said, 'I so accept you, I oid.'

There was some laughter at that, and I saw Yarissi smile. Like most of those in the Hall, I realized at that moment that this transaction had been very cleverly stage-managed. The laughter spread, and presently Yarissi called again for quiet. This time he didn't quite get it.

Usak said, 'I have studied your past record, slave, and find that you have had *some* military experience.' There was more laughter, now tinged with considerable relief. I saluted Yarissi's showmanship; this little display was earning him a new kind of respect. Facility with the law was one thing, but when it came to amassing a popular following few attributes could compare with a sense of humour.

'In light of your past record,' Usak intoned, 'I grant you immediate manumission, and a share of the spoils of war proportionate to your part in various campaigns. The sum in question comes to—' (He consulted a scribe who showed him a wax tablet on which numerous figures were written. Usak raised an eyebrow, then took the tablet without comment.) 'The sum in question,' he went on, 'comes to one hundred and fifty million crowns.'

Into the brief, and stunned, silence that followed these words, Yarissi said quietly, 'With your permission, Lord Usak, I shall use this sum to purchase my freedom. I ask that the monies in question be paid into the city treasury to pay for the rebuilding of —'

Whatever else he said was drowned by the roar of the crowd. When the cheers had died down, Usak said, 'I accept the payment, which I consider appropriate to the value of your service. Further, I promote you to the rank of Captain, and grant you an honourable discharge from my service. You are now a free man, citizen Yarissi.'

I glanced at Celebe as more cheering and laughter filled the

Hall. How much of this had she been privy to in advance? How much of it, I wondered, had she had an active part in?

'As a free citizen of Reshek,' Yarissi said, 'I now petition the elders of my city for permission to establish a new House.'

A ripple of anticipation swept through the Hall; even I found myself caught up in the feeling, for the founding of a new House was a truly momentous event. In Benza, no new Houses had been established in over three hundred years.

A scribe stepped forward from the back of the dais. I hadn't noticed until now but there were upwards of a dozen scribes seated behind the dais, all of whom appeared to be taking down every word that was being said. For all the levity of Yarissi's approach, I saw now that what he was doing here was deadly serious. Despite his powers in Reshek, Yarissi was not a Slave Master. Every act here today would have to be ratified if it was to be of any legal value.

'The city elders,' the scribe said, visibly discomforted at suddenly being the centre of attention, 'are pleased to accept your proposal, my Lord.'

He bowed quickly and hurried back to his place behind Yarissi.

'Will anyone contest with me,' Yarissi asked, 'for rule of this new House?'

No one spoke.

'Very well,' Yarissi said. 'By the laws of Reshek, I accept rule over the newest House in Xacmet. This House, henceforth, shall be known as House Luftetmek.'

The cheers came again, and this time the loudest rang out from my own lips. Yarissi waited for them to subside, his eyes bright with a pleasure that was tinged with sadness. It was, I knew, a finer monument to his old Champion than any he could have hoped for. His name would now be remembered for as long as Reshek endured.

When the uproar had died down, Yarissi said, 'Before I continue, I believe there is someone here who would address this assembly.' He glanced at Usak who called out, 'Celebe, Knight of the Thirteen, and those who stand with her: come forth.'

A pathway opened through the thronging Resheki and the eleven of us moved slowly and, in my case, warily forward.

'To these men and women,' Yarissi said, 'we owe much. Their sacrifices have been great, and yet none has asked for recompense.' He looked down at us. 'Celebe, Lady Knight, will you speak?'

'I will,' said Celebe.

She stepped up onto the dais and turned to face the Hall.

'The Thirteen Gods are pleased with the people of Reshek,' she announced.

A ripple of satisfaction went round the Hall at that; knowing that the Gods shared your continent with you tended to make their approval more than a formality.

'My mission here is now ended,' she went on, 'and I leave this great country in the best possible hands—' She gestured to the whole assembly. 'Your hands.'

A hush fell over the Kanaat Hall, as the men and women of the new Reshek faced a concept not often encountered on Shushuan, but one which, as a race, they had brought upon themselves. I wondered how many of them could fully appreciate the ramifications of their situation.

'Who will you have,' she asked, 'as your ruler?'

Yarissi's name shook the very pillars of the Hall, and Celebe turned to face him on the dais.

'If it is the will of all,' he said, 'then gladly do I accept.'

When the inevitable cheers had finally subsided, Celebe said, 'There are two here whom I would take with me when I leave.'

'Are they slave or free?' Yarissi asked.

'Free,' Celebe said.

'Then the choice will be theirs,' Yarissi said.

Celebe turned and called out, 'Lieutenant Ishbarah—'

The young Resheki warrior stepped forward, visibly startled at being addressed in this fashion. His tunic, I noted, had been adjusted to conceal the injury he had sustained in the Guild Square.

'The Thirteen have many tasks for those who are worthy,'

Celebe said to him. 'They consider you to be more than qualified. Will you accompany me to Asmina?'

I held up a hand, forestalling any answer. Celebe glanced at me, her face a patient mask.

'Speak, David Shaw,' she bade me.

'Are you proposing to make Ishbarah a Knight?' I asked. The young lieutenant could not possibly appreciate the cost of such a thing, but I could: I had seen it happen.

Celebe smiled.

'No, David,' said the voice of Ailette. 'Many – you, for instance – serve the Thirteen without making that sacrifice.'

I said nothing; I served no one, least of all the Thirteen. But I did not underestimate their power to use me, nor was I unmindful of the sacrifices they were capable of exacting from me.

'I am worthless as a warrior,' Ishbarah said bluntly. 'What use have gods for a cripple?'

'Such injuries,' Celebe said, 'are not beyond the power of the Thirteen to . . . remedy. Their help, however, always carries a price.'

Ishbarah gave a grim laugh, then said, 'If my Kanaat has no use for me—?'

Yarissi said, 'You will always have a place in my country, Lieutenant. But my greatest wish is that you live your life to its fullest. If the Gods can help you in this, then I gladly grant you an honourable discharge from our service.'

Ishbarah nodded, and said to Celebe, 'I will go with you.'

Yarissi said, 'Lady Knight, you said there were two you wished to have accompany you?'

'I did,' said Celebe. 'The second is Zalmetta.'

The charlaki woman stiffened at my side, then said dryly, 'A cripple and a monster. Your gods have poor taste.'

'My masters are wise in many things,' Celebe said, 'and you could learn much from them. You could learn much concerning yourself, and your people.'

Zalmetta looked at Celebe blankly for several seconds – the use of the word 'people' had not been lost on her – then slowly inclined her head. I gathered Celebe took this as an acceptance of her offer. She bowed briefly to Yarissi and stepped down from the dais.

Yarissi turned to P'nad and his fellow Captain. 'Your vessels and men,' he said, 'will always be welcome in our lands. But, for now, I think it best that you depart. You have our thanks, and our solemn pledge that should ever you need the people of Reshek, we shall be here for you.'

P'nad nodded.

'The man known as Tal Daqar,' Yarissi said, 'is still at large. Should you wish to pursue him, we will issue a warrant granting you the power to do so within our borders.'

'The *Mariner* will return to Benza,' P'nad said, 'but the *Freedom*, by your leave, will press the search for Daqar.'

Celebe said, 'It is the Will of the Thirteen that Daqar be confirmed slain.'

'So be it,' said P'nad.

'And now,' Yarissi said, suddenly smiling, 'to a most happy duty. My new House has, at present, a single member: myself. I would like to invite as its second member the Lady Ylyrria Muti.'

Yarissi's announcement was greeted by a round of intense whispers, none of which suggested that this particular suggestion had been anticipated. Ylyrria took a step forward; she looked totally overawed by her surroundings, but there was nothing timid in her reply.

'I am House Bagalamak,' she said.

It was, simply, the truth.

'There is no more House Bagalamak, child,' Yarissi said gently. 'The people will not permit it. And, in truth, I would not oppose their will even if I could. Your House committed terrible crimes against all Reshek, and though we hold you innocent of any wrongdoing, your House cannot be permitted to endure.'

As though she had known that this would be the answer, and had prepared for it in advance, she said simply, 'Then I accept exile.'

Yarissi seemed dismayed by her words. I myself was startled;

I had thought a place in the ruling House of Reshek was Ylyrria's greatest wish.

'Child,' Yarissi said, 'exile has not even been contemplated.'

'By your leave, Kanaat,' she said, 'I will go with the Lady Knight, if she will have me.'

I saw her lip tremble a little, and thought perhaps I had the first inkling of what was on her mind. As the last survivor of Reshek's former ruling House, Ylyrria would be forever a political pawn in Xacmet: the old guard would try to rally support to their cause by using her as a symbol, while Yarissi's more militant supporters would contemplate her assassination for precisely the same reason. Luftetmek had been right, all those months ago, when he had said that the child would never be safe in Reshek.

Yarissi was still looking down at her, his brow furrowed. I think he had been hoping to make some kind of political point himself by having the last survivor of House Bagalamak become the first addition to House Luftetmek. But also, in no small measure, he wanted to do what was right by Ylyrria. I wondered, briefly, which motivation weighed the greatest with him.

Eventually he smiled and said, 'So be it. Go with our blessings, Ylyrria Muti, Last of the Bagalamak. Not as exile, but as our ambassador to all the lands you will visit. I hope you will speak well of your people.'

Ylyrria had tears in her eyes as she said, 'I will, Kanaat, I will!'

She turned and walked over to Celebe, who said, to anyone who cared to hear, 'This pleases my masters.'

Yarissi said, 'Librarian Mohred, step forward.'

I had wondered what would be the fate of Mohred when Celebe had not spoken up for him earlier. Frankly, I didn't care much what happened to him, but I hoped Yarissi wasn't going to do anything too grotesque. (Although, I reminded myself, Mohred had betrayed the Resheki people when he sided with Kandirak, and that kind of crime wasn't taken lightly by the Vinh.)

Mohred stood alone before the dais, the rest of us giving him plenty of room.

'You have been a traitor to Reshek,' Yarissi said, 'and to your own people. You have no honour, and are completely untrustworthy. Is this an accurate assessment?'

After a moment's hesitation, Mohred said, 'It is.'

'Your own people have stripped you of your powers?' Yarissi asked.

Mohred held out his hands, a gesture of helplessness. His armour was now entirely inert, retaining only enough of its Y'nys nature to remain malleable.

'They have exiled you?' Yarissi asked.

'Yes,' said Mohred.

'You are friendless, homeless, craftless?' Yarissi said.

Mohred swallowed. 'Yes,' he said.

'You have blood feud with David Shaw and his, uh, wife,' Yarissi stated. 'Is it your intention to pursue this feud?'

'No,' Mohred said, the word almost choking him.

Yarissi nodded. 'Ex-Librarian Mohred,' he said, 'join House Luftetmek.'

Mohred seemed stunned. I myself was flabbergasted.

'You and I,' Yarissi said, 'have much in common. And Reshek needs men of knowledge. Join my House, and let us rebuild this land together.'

'I . . . I . . .' Mohred stammered. 'Yes, Kanaat! Thank you, thank—' He regained a little of his self-possession and said, 'I accept, Kanaat, gladly.'

Yarissi nodded, smiling.

'And now, finally,' he said, 'we come to the fate of Captain Shaw.'

Something odd happened to the mood in the Hall then. An edge crept into the proceedings, a sense of expectancy that was more akin to that of an operating room than a fairground. I felt that familiar itch between my shoulder-blades again.

'David Shaw,' Yarissi said, 'will you accept the verdict of this court?'

I looked around. Celebe was looking at me, her eyes invisible behind the lenses of her helm. Mrs Catlin, at my side, was glaring at her malevolently.

I looked back at Yarissi.

'Your justice is acceptable to me,' I said.

Yarissi seemed far from relieved by my answer. Oddly, I had the impression he would rather I had drawn my sword and fought my way from the room.

'By order of the former Emperor Kandirak,' Yarissi said, 'you stand under sentence of death.'

The Hall buzzed at that, but I remained impassive, saying nothing.

'By ancient tradition,' he went on, 'a new Emperor may commute all death sentences upon his accession to the throne. We have done away with emperors in Reshek, but by the will of the people I am now first among the rulers of the great Houses, and the power to grant pardons is mine. Willingly do I commute your sentence.'

I shifted uneasily; I had been a slave when Kandirak had handed out that sentence, and commuting it had one drawback: it publicly acknowledged the fact of my slavery, made it official, made it real. And, as if matters weren't already bad enough, it did so in the very presence of a Slave Master.

'You may, of course,' Yarissi said, 'dispute the ruling.'

I knew what he was suggesting. The *Mariner* was only five minutes away, and Yarissi would permit only a token resistance to my flight. By Vinh law I would be an outlaw on this side of the continent, and if word of my escape ever reached Benza I would be one there too.

Celebe was still looking at me; I wondered if she knew that I understood the purpose of that look, that I had already worked out what it was I was really deciding here today.

Yarissi was risking his own position to give me my freedom. The fact that it would be no freedom at all was irrelevant; he didn't know what was truly at stake. But even without Celebe's presence, I think my path would have been set. Luftetmek had died to put Yarissi here, the fate of his country, and his friend, meaning more to him than his own life.

I met Yarissi's gaze.

'I do not dispute the ruling,' I told him.

He seemed startled; after all, I owed nothing to Reshek. I had only been passing through, on my way to a more important destiny. Or so I had thought.

'The sentence, then,' he said heavily, 'is slavery.'

A great sigh seemed to go up all around. I sensed that, with those five words, Yarissi had secured a position for himself that was now unassailable.

'Have the slave removed until a place for him in my House can be established,' Yarissi said.

Mrs Catlin's arms went around me, clinging to me for dear life.

P'nad edged closer to me.

'Say the word, Captain,' he whispered, 'and this Hall will be swarming with Marines.'

I looked up into his dark face. His expression was fearsome, to say the least.

'P'nad, listen closely,' I said. 'Do nothing. Go back to Benza.'

He looked at me, torn between conflicting duties.

'This is my fight,' I said, 'and I can't win it at sword point.'

Usak's guards were closing in on me, a pair of slave bracelets in the hands of one of them.

Mrs Catlin looked up at Yarissi.

'Kanaat,' she said, 'I—'

'One moment.'

The voice was not especially loud, but it stilled every other voice in the Hall. Every head turned, and the owner of the voice approached the dais, followed by two of his scarlet-and-gold warriors.

'Kanaat Yarissi,' said the Slave Master, 'I would mediate in this transaction.'

Yarissi recovered his briefly shattered composure and said, 'Of course, Lord.'

The Slave Master turned and faced the men and women of Reshek. Not one of them failed to be cowed: like the Kanaat, this man was a living embodiment of the law, but unlike Yarissi he had no discretion in its application.

'Has this slave,' the Slave Master asked, indicating me, 'any known talents?'

Yarissi himself answered on my behalf, and he spoke now with all the authority of his office.

'He is a warrior,' he announced.

'His skill has been demonstrated to your satisfaction?'

'Many times.'

'And he has performed in this function whilst in a state of slavery?'

'It is a matter of record,' Yarissi said, 'that his slavery began during the reign of the tyrant Kandirak. Since then, the slave has fought many times for this country, and was instrumental in its liberation.'

The Slave Master nodded, and I wondered what exactly was going through his mind. Why had he suddenly taken an interest in me? Whatever the reason, I didn't see how it could be to my benefit.

'His manumission, then,' he went on, 'could be conferred at this time in recognition of these past deeds?'

'There is precedent for such a thing,' Yarissi said archly, glancing back at his own scribes.

'Duly notarized?' asked the Slave Master.

'Yes,' said Yarissi.

'In the presence of a Slave Master?' asked the Slave Master.

Yarissi raised one eyebrow.

'Yes,' he said dryly.

I actually heard someone laugh, though the sound was quickly smothered.

'It seems to me,' said the Slave Master, 'that to keep this man in servitude beyond this juncture would be to no one's benefit.'

'I concur,' Yarissi said.

The Slave Master nodded curtly.

'He is free,' he said.

A cheer went up, and in moments the Hall was ringing to the

sound of hundreds of voices shouting my name. I was stunned, bewildered. I hardly knew any of these people, yet they seemed as delighted by the Slave Master's words as I was.

The man who had been responsible for this tumult held up his hands, and the Hall fell silent once more.

'He will, of course,' he observed, 'be required to make the appropriate payments if he wishes to secure his new status.'

My elation faded as quickly as it had come. By Resheki tradition, manumission was inevitably followed by a period of indentured servitude while one's debt to one's master was repaid. And the period of servitude was seldom less than five years.

'What is the cost of one military slave to Reshek?' the Slave Master asked.

It was Usak who replied.

'Fifty crowns, Lord,' he said.

The Slave Master looked at me.

'Have you this sum?' he asked.

I opened my mouth to reply; all I had was the clothes I stood up in, and fifty crowns was better than a year's pay for a servant in the armed forces.

Something sailed through the air and landed tinkling at my feet. It was a silver coin, worth, if I recognized it correctly, a fiftieth of a crown. I glanced in the direction from which it had come and saw Ishbarah, the young lieutenant of the artillery, reach into his coin purse and pull out a second silver coin. In an instant, it had landed at my feet beside the first. And suddenly the air around me was filled with coins, some of silver, many only copper, but a few of gold. In seconds, there was upwards of a hundred crowns piled up all around me.

I looked at the men and women of Reshek who had, effectively, just purchased my freedom, and I was speechless.

'I think,' the Slave Master said quietly, 'you now have the sum in question.'

I couldn't reply, I could only stare open-mouthed as Yarissi and Usak both leaped down from the dais and clasped my hands in theirs, their faces beaming with pleasure and pride.

'What did you think, warrior,' Yarissi said softly, his voice not carrying beyond the three of us. 'That the people of Reshek would abandon one to whom they owed their victory?'

I glanced at the Slave Master; he gave me the briefest of cool smiles, and then turned away, his warriors following.

There was a surge of movement from the crowd, and then Yarissi and Usak and I were borne aloft on their shoulders, and everywhere men and women were cheering and singing. In the heat of the moment, Mrs Catlin had been torn from my side, but an instant later the huge figure of P'nad had ploughed his way through the crowd, Mrs Catlin on his shoulder, and she and I were embracing fiercely.

'*Now,*' I said, 'we can go home!'

EPILOGUE

The *Mariner* hung almost motionless over the desert butte, its forward belly hatch open and a rope ladder dangling from it. On the butte itself, the silvery spire of the Library seemed to shimmer in the blisteringly hot air, its surface a wash of rainbow colours in the early evening sun. Standing beside it, like some humanoid avatar, was Celebe.

I descended the ladder to stand at her side, Zalmetta and Ylyrria and Ishbarah close behind me. None of us wanted to be here any longer than was absolutely necessary, but there was one final matter I wanted to discuss with Celebe, and until now she had managed to avoid me every time I had tried to bring it up.

'Do not tarry here after we have gone, David,' Zalmetta said to me. 'The creatures we encountered here before do not make good climbers, and this butte is high, but you know the risk—'

'I do,' I said, 'and I thank you for your concern. I will . . . miss you, Zalmetta. You have been a good friend.'

A frown briefly crossed her face.

'The influence of Tal Daqar,' she said, 'has twisted both of our lives, and has made it difficult for either of us to trust the other. I hope that, if we should ever meet again, things will have changed.'

'I hope so too,' I told her.

I hesitated, then held out my hand to her. She took it, looked momentarily panic-stricken, and then pulled me into her arms.

373

I hugged her, and heard her whisper, 'If only you weren't so *ugly . . .*'

I let her go, laughing, and she gave me one of her rare smiles.

I turned to Ylyrria, who took a step back as though anticipating getting a hug of her own and not appreciating the prospect. Not wishing to upset her I simply gave her a courtly bow and said, 'I hope you find what you are looking for, Ylyrria Muti.'

She looked at me guardedly for a moment, then said, 'And I wish the same for you, Captain. We are both outlanders, now, and you have given me much to think about.'

I glanced at Ishbarah. 'You will look after her?' I asked.

'Insofar as the Thirteen will permit,' he said. 'Goodbye, Captain. Go with Gazig.'

'Go with Gazig, Lieutenant,' I said.

I turned to Celebe. What I had to say to her was for no one else's ears, so I switched to her native French and thereby excluded our companions from the conversation.

'You brought the Slave Master to Reshek,' I said.

She cocked her head on one side, not replying.

'You used me to secure Yarissi's position,' I said. 'He proved his impartiality to the old Lords, then you used the Slave Master's intervention to manipulate his decision into one that the common people could feel good about.'

'You are almost correct,' Celebe said.

'And for his part in things,' I continued, 'you gave the Slave Master Daqar's airship.'

'True,' she said, 'but it was not a bribe, if that is what you are suggesting. In the Slave Master's hands, the ship will never be used as a weapon of war. Had we left it in Xacmet, it would eventually have become one. The Thirteen are not yet ready to give Yarissi that much power.'

'You said I was "almost" correct,' I pressed her. 'What did I get wrong?'

'Do you recall,' she asked, 'the reason for Yarissi's visit to Zatuchep?'

'Is that relevant?' I asked.

She smiled. 'Indulge me, David.'

I frowned. 'He went to Zatuchep to get some kind of message from Daqar's Library.' I glanced at her. 'But he never got it, did he? You destroyed the Library.'

'The Thirteen sent Yarissi to Zatuchep,' Celebe said, 'to meet you.'

I must have appeared stunned. Certainly I was speechless.

'David,' Celebe said, 'do not underestimate your importance to the Thirteen. They very much wanted you to remain on Shushuan, but only if you would do so on Their terms. It pleases Them greatly that recent events have enabled this to come to pass.'

My expression must have been an accurate reflection of the depth of my confusion, because Celebe gave a very human laugh and said, 'You have all the answers, David. I think you just do not yet know the questions.'

I frowned at her. 'That's very . . . Zen,' I observed.

She turned to the Library and I sensed the passage of unspoken communication between her Y'nys and that of the Mugaraht.

'One last thing, Captain,' she said, now speaking the High Tongue once more. 'Tal Daqar yet lives. The *Freedom* will not find him. It is the Will of the Thirteen that you pursue him.'

'And what?' I demanded. 'Kill him?'

Celebe shrugged.

'And do whatever you think appropriate,' she said. 'It is thought that he now resides in the lost city of Thallusia, reputed to be the ancestral home of the ancient Thek. As long as he is at liberty, neither you – nor your woman – will be safe.'

'If he comes after me, I'll deal with him,' I said. 'But I am not a servant of the Thirteen. I won't do their dirty work for them.'

'As you wish,' Celebe said. 'But remember what I have said. Daqar is a dangerous man, both to you and to the peoples of this continent.'

'If he comes after me,' I repeated, 'I will deal with him. But I will not be used by whatever it is that lives in Asmina.'

'I think,' Celebe said, 'that They already know this.'

She beckoned to the others to follow her and stepped towards the Library.

'Go with Gazig, Captain,' she said to me.

'Bright Lady watch over you,' I replied.

Her laughter was like silver bells in the evening air, and I shivered in spite of the heat. A moment later, all four of them were gone.

I stood on top of the butte, alone with the Mugaraht, for some time, Celebe's words running through my mind over and over. I could make no sense of some of her insinuations, and what there was that did make sense was, frankly, horrifying.

Presently, I climbed the rope ladder back to the *Mariner*. On the sterncastle, Mrs Catlin and P'nad were waiting for me. I saw them exchange a puzzled glance at the expression on my face, but neither of them spoke as I moved to join them. I put one arm around Mrs Catlin, and she smiled up at me.

'Do we depart, Captain?' P'nad asked.

'Yes,' I said.

He called out orders, and the ship rose away from the butte, moving with increasing speed over the darkening desert below, the Library fading into the distance as the *Mariner* pursued Shushuan's sun into the west.

'P'nad—' I said.

'Yes, Captain?'

'What do you know about a place called Thallusia?'